The Wolf and the Sparrow

Laurie Sanford

RIVER LEAF PRESS

The Wolf and the Sparrow

Published by River Leaf Press

The Wolf and the Sparrow is a work of fiction. All incidents, dialogue, and characters are products of the author's imagination and are not to be construed as real. Any resemblance to actual persons, living or dead, events, or locales is entirely coincidental.

Cover Art by: Carpe Librum Book Design, carpelibrumbookdesign.com

Interior Art by: PangeaAzureArt

For more information, visit:

www.lauriesanfordbooks.com

www.linktr.ee/lauriesanfordbooks

To my bosom friend Shauna. Love you as long as the sun and moon shall endure.

One

THE COUNTY JAIL REEKED with a stench Faith couldn't quite put into words—like fruit left out too long on a hot summer's day, slowly decaying until it left an unrecognizable pile of waste behind. The concrete walls, no doubt once clean and whitewashed, harbored stains from age and neglect. Hallways stretching in every direction collected dust in the corners. Rodents scurried their way to mysterious alcoves hidden deep in the prison's walls.

Faith shivered, adjusting her lace gloves for what must have been the thousandth time and following the jailer's rapid footsteps as they pounded the hallway floor. She lifted a perfumed finger to her nose and drew in a whiff of lilac. A maid had taught her the trick long ago—dousing a finger in perfume before visiting any unpleasant place. Yet how long would her crystal bottle of imported perfume last her, with no money to replace it?

Throwing the idea off, she kept up time with the jailer and turned a corner. The days had flown when she could have whatever she wished at the snap of her fingers. Dinner parties, art lessons, ponies and leather saddles, a new dress for every occasion—all gone. She resisted the streak of dread threatening to wind through her. A lot of people got by with much less than her.

When they reached a bolted wooden door flanking the end of the hall, the jailer held out a hand to stop her. With expert precision, he unlatched each of the iron locks one at a time, then yanked the door open. Another form stepped through the open doorway—presumably a guard by his broad shoulders and bulging muscles. He moved aside for the jailer, who swept a hand toward the room beyond.

Faith straightened her shoulders, steeling herself for the task ahead. With every ounce of will she possessed, she forced her quaking legs through the door and into the scantily furnished room. The day she'd been putting off for months had arrived. She could escape reality no longer.

Her father sat in a chair behind a single wooden table, his elbows planted atop it and wrists secured by steel cuffs. His beady eyes tracked her every movement as she traversed the cement floor and dropped into the chair opposite him. Though not half a year had passed since she'd seen him last, she would guess he'd aged a decade if she knew no better. Deep creases lined his eyes, darkened circles beginning to form beneath them. His head, normally completely shaven, wore a ring of short hair around the edges.

"I'll be right outside if you need me." The jailer motioned to the brawny guard passing back through the door. "He'll stand by to make sure you're safe. You have fifteen minutes."

"Thank you." Faith meant to say more, but her throat collapsed in on itself.

"As if I am the one to fear between the two of us," her father ground out, his voice rougher and thicker than she remembered. "*I* didn't shoot *you* when we saw each other last."

Faith grasped her silk reticule, tucking it safely in her lap. "You know why I shot you, Father. It was necessary." Though remembering still showered her nerves in shards of ice. The feel of that cold, hard gun still singed her fingertips, as if she held it in her hands right now, determining whether to shoot the only family member she had left.

"Yes, you chose a harlot over me." His lip curled. "How could I forget?"

Harlot. Technically, yes—Cora had prostituted herself in Gold Strike for years, but Faith had never known a more loyal friend. Should she have chosen not to pull the trigger, that friend would now be buried in the local cemetery, a mere memory to a scattering of people.

"I chose to rescue an innocent." She tilted her chin up, drawing from a reserve of fortitude she was unsure existed within her. "I couldn't live with myself if I had let her die."

He let out a mocking snort. "You chose to protect the lowliest, most conniving of creatures over the father who loved and cared for you your whole life."

Against the sting of tears pushing behind her eyes, Faith flexed her jaw. "You were going to kill her. I didn't have a choice."

"And what if I had died, hmm?" His large fist thumped the table, rattling the legs. "How would you have felt then?"

She blinked rapidly. "For what it's worth, I'm glad you didn't."

Grunting, he shoved back in his chair and swung one foot to his knee. "I'm not so sure I believe that's true. That sheriff was willing to vouch for you. Had I died, you would have all my money to yourself."

And a lifetime of heartache. Didn't he understand he meant so much more to her than wealth? He was her *father.*

When she said nothing, his narrowed eyes perused her with suspicion. "That's why you're here, isn't it?"

She glanced up. "What?"

His stare hardened. "All this time, from my convalescence, to the trial, to my incarceration—this is the first time I've seen your face. You're running out of money, aren't you?"

Faith stiffened, her back hitting the hard frame of the chair. Of course he would bring this back to money. It was all that occupied his mind. How could she explain the myriad of sleepless nights she'd spent agonizing over that day in Gold Strike, wishing to have her father back, blaming herself? When he looked at her, he must have only seen a means to an end.

"I wouldn't know. I haven't been using any of your money." Save for the clothes on her back and the items she'd collected from her room at their house in Missoula.

Another disbelieving sound lit the air. "Haven't been using my money. That's rich. Do you expect me to believe you've been subsisting on your own at eighteen years of age, with no skills or life experience? Do be serious."

Faith shrunk inside herself at his tone. When had he come to hate her so? "On my own? No. I spent the winter with Cora and Ellis."

A curse flew off his lips. "That useless little saint of a sheriff and his strumpet? Why am I not surprised? They'll milk you for anything you've got—mark my words."

"They haven't asked me for a cent."

"Of course they haven't. Not yet." The corner of his mouth twitched. "What's she doing with him anyway? What about the brothel?"

Faith's hand scrunched her skirts. "Haven't you heard? The brothel is no more. It's been disbanded."

His lips parted. "I haven't gotten much news from Gold Strike, I'm afraid. When one's assets are unreachable, their employees tend to fall away. What happened to Madam Carey?"

"Why, she's in prison, like you." Faith shifted uncomfortably in her seat. "The sheriff found vast amounts of evidence against her proving she was making money selling girls."

"What they found in my office, you mean—when you gave them free rein to search it."

She sat straighter, shoulders squaring. "Yes."

His annoyed expression flicked with humor. "She tried to keep her name off the documents, but I made sure it was there in case she ever tried to double-cross me." His eyes found her in the dusky room. "You put a lot of women out of work with the stunt you pulled. What are they supposed to do now?"

Faith's stomach roiled. *Saved a lot of women from being sold, you mean.* "Those who wished to continue the profession were absorbed into the Wild Rose Saloon. The majority have gone elsewhere or found jobs around town. The building where Madam Carey's operated is now a school."

"A school?" One side of his nose snarled. "What kind of school?"

"The kind that teaches skills to those who need it." She knit her fingers together on the table. "They cook and they raise animals, garden. Cora teaches the girls to make beautiful clothes."

Another swear, laced with pure hatred. "I'm sure she does. That woman has many profitable skills." His head angled. "Has she taught them to you yet, with all this time you've spent together?"

Faith's cheeks heated. "She doesn't live that life anymore, Father. She's married. She's a respectable woman."

"A respectable woman doesn't need to open her bedroom door for money. If that sheriff weren't so obsessed with her, he'd see that for himself."

Pressing her lips together, Faith remained silent. He hadn't a care for what she said anyway. Speaking only seemed to aggravate him. From beneath his thick brows, he eyed her warily. How weak and pathetic he looked in his striped prison clothes after a lifetime of presenting himself in only crisp, tailored suits.

"What is it you want, then?" His voice was cold, hard. "Why did you come all this way to see me?"

Faith bit her lip, fighting the tremble aching to overcome it. *Because I wanted to see you. Because I missed you. Because my world was utterly shattered the minute I found out who you truly were.* But she couldn't speak those words—not to the hollow soul staring back at her now. If only she could reach beneath his layers and find the kind and loving father who'd reared her, but no. Her memories were false—of a man who didn't exist. A cleverly designed display of smoke and mirrors.

"I felt it was time to see you." She thrust back her emotion. "The winter snows have thawed, and the roads are safe for travel." Her shoulders lifted lightly. "It just felt like time."

"Time to come here and condemn me. To remind me what a terrible person I am for daring to try to give you a good life." He leaned back, observing her like a casual spectator with no dog in the fight. "You wanted to feel better about yourself for finally coming to see me."

"If that's what you prefer to believe, I'll not argue with you." Faith forced her back to straighten, her shoulders to remain rigid. "We spent a lifetime together before this happened. We had a happy life, a close bond. I'd prefer not to let that completely slip away." *No matter who you are.* "You're still my father."

His irritated gaze slipped to the corner. "The father you fed to the wolves. Seems like you threw out our relationship when you decided to shoot me."

Faith flattened her hands on the table. "I suppose this was all a waste of time. It's best that I go, then."

"What did they do to our house?" The question froze her before she could stand. She lifted her gaze back to her father. "After they arrested me and searched it, what did they do?"

She licked her lips, thrusting back the nostalgia that crept up just to imagine the beautiful Victorian mansion with its glistening windows and green fields stretching for miles. "I don't know. I went back once to gather a few necessary belongings and never returned. I suppose it's just abandoned now."

A low grumble emanated from his throat. "No doubt looted for all its fine possessions. I can only imagine vagrants camping inside. What of your horses? The rest of the animals?"

"They had to sell them, of course, with no one there to care for them." She looked down at her hands, still splayed atop the table. She wouldn't tell him they let her keep her best horse after Starlight neighed and bucked in protest so much the auctioneer freed the animal. "The proceeds went into your funds, of course—everything the bank is holding until you're no longer incarcerated—if they ever release you."

Something calculating passed through his eyes. "They told me I could release some of those funds, you know, in order to support you. A portion of the money is accessible because you're a dependent."

Her mouth dried. After months of living off other people's charity and trying to make money any way she could, that bit of bait felt like water to a wanderer dying of thirst. But what conditions came with it?

As if reading her thoughts, he returned both feet to the floor and leaned his elbows on his knees. "You're a smart girl. You know I'm a businessman. I couldn't have gotten this far without being shrewd."

Her teeth set. "What do you want?"

"I want to get out of here, of course." He glanced at the guard still stationed by the door. "I have an associate, Mr. Thaddeus Brown. He works on cases like these. He understands what to do, things these by-the-book lawyers just don't."

She swallowed. "You want me to use the money you free from your accounts to hire him?"

"Some of it. Most of it would go to you, of course, for your needs and—*wants*. I'm sure you still have them." His gaze skittered over her lace-trimmed gown, already wearing at the seams from overuse. "You're the daughter of a wealthy businessman, after all. Your proclivity for the finer things in life isn't going to disappear overnight."

Faith's nostrils flared, warmth tickling her eyes. How low of a person he took her for, to cheat the legal system so she could buy jewelry and new clothes. This Thaddeus Brown, whoever he was, couldn't be the legitimate sort—not if her father had failed to hire him in the first place. What type of evil would he cook up to free the chained man sitting before her?

Finding her footing, she rose to standing and pushed back her chair. "I appreciate the offer, Father, but I'm very well on my own. I don't need your ill-gotten money."

His stare slithered over her like that of a venomous snake. "What do you plan to do, then—live off the fleeting kindness of tender-hearted souls forever?" His head shook. "They have probably already grown tired of you—a young, useless girl sharing a roof with a newlywed couple. It can't be much longer until they throw you out."

Keeping a steel rod through her back, she lifted her chin. "I'll sort it through. I can do plenty."

"Yes, I'm sure the Wild Rose Saloon would love to have you." His malicious gaze shifted to the guard. "Take her out of my sight. She's no daughter of mine."

Faith kept her head high and the tears from her eyes until she'd walked through the prison and emerged into the sunlight. The life of comfort and ease she'd known so long was over. Her life as a daughter was over. Nothing awaited but an existence of solitude, with nothing and no one to pull her out of the mire her father had created.

She looked back at the dreary jail, her frame shaking with sobs. The only family she'd ever known had sworn her off for good. Alone in a wicked, bleak world, she had nobody but herself.

Two

THE NAME ATTRACTED GIDEON Valdez to the quiet town of Gold Strike long before his boots hit the dusty streets. When he'd first spied it among ads skirting a Billings newspaper, he'd imagined gold glittering off the mountains, or streets paved with it like the New Jerusalem. Even when he stepped off the stage to a single street lined in dirt-caked businesses and equally rough citizens, a smile lifted his lips. This town tucked in the Montana wilderness had potential.

Men in top hats and silver fob watches, drunks with stained clothing, and fine women sporting parasols all criss-crossed the crowded thoroughfare, going about their day's business. A good mix of money and desperation fit his purposes best. With the proud gait of a man who owned the keys to the city itself, he joined their mad rush.

Gideon slung his pack over his shoulder and strolled down the boardwalk past mercantile and tannery alike, soaking in the scents of leather and raw earth. All along the bustling street, people chatted and worked. Forested mountains rose beyond the huddle of buildings, their snow-capped peaks glistening beneath a full sun. This place was far more beautiful than Billings, and twice as exciting as the vast grasslands of Wyoming he'd just traversed.

A woman's giggle drew his attention. Gideon looked ahead to see an auburn-haired beauty with thick, glossy curls and a painted face make eyes at him and duck through a doorway. Her low-cut gown and accentuated bosom left no doubt as to her profession.

His gaze lifted to the signboard above the swinging double doors. The Wild Rose Saloon. Perhaps fate did have a sense of humor.

Following the scent of whiskey and cigar smoke, Gideon passed through the doors and into a familiar scene. A bar bordered one side of the smoky room, peppered with half-empty glasses of alcohol served to a line of inebriated patrons perched on barstools. Scantily clad women moved from table to table like songbirds hopping between branches.

His eyes focused on the center of it all, where men sat around circular tables, black and red cards in their hands spread out like bird feathers. Three separate games were scattered about the room, and it wasn't even noon. Yes, Gold Strike might prove the place that changed it all for him.

"Hey there, stranger." The redhead he'd spotted outside sidled up to him, her gaze openly perusing him from his boots to his muscular shoulders. "Did you follow me in for a drink—or something extra?" One eyebrow curved suggestively.

Gideon smirked back at her. "What kind of extra did you have in mind?"

"Whatever you want, sugar." She came nearer, emanating a strong floral perfume. Her fingers moseyed up his shirt before catching on his collar and pulling him close. "I do all kinds of tricks."

"I'll bet you do." He shook his head. He had no time for distractions. "Maybe later. Right now I'm just looking for a room."

Irritation flickered in her dark eyes. "That ain't my area of expertise, I'm afraid. You'll have to talk to Old Joe."

"Who's Old Joe?"

She flicked her head toward a man in his fifties or sixties with a paunch belly and a gray beard, enjoying the attention of three separate women.

"I see. Thank you for your—" Gideon looked around him, but the girl had already disappeared, off to flirt with some other eligible customer. So much for feeling adored.

Fashioning a path between the tables, Gideon passed through clouds of cigar smoke and stepped over puddles of spilled beer to reach the proprietor. Too immersed in the admiration of his doting employees, the man couldn't be bothered to look up at Gideon's approach.

Not until Gideon cleared his throat above the ruckus did the man lift a single begrudging brow. "Yes? Can I help you, son?"

"You Old Joe?"

"The one and only. Ain't that right, ladies?" The response provoked a chorus of giggles around him.

"Heard I might get a room here for the night. What's your going rate?"

Joe passed his tongue across his teeth. "Depends on what kind of room you want."

"I ain't proud." Gideon shrugged. "The cheapest room you've got will do."

"If you want the cheapest, you'll have better luck at the boarding house across the street." Old Joe slung a judicious glance at his tanned skin. "They don't mind Mexicans, neither."

Gideon's eyes shifted to the men playing cards. "No, I want to be where the action is."

"How's two dollars a night sound to you?"

"It sounds like extortion." Gideon calculated how much such a high hotel bill would cut into his profits. "What about a dollar-fifty a night if I promise to play here every night?"

Old Joe coughed. "Why do I care if you play here? Plenty of men play here who don't even stay in my establishment."

"With all due respect, you've never seen me play." Gideon pulled himself up, standing with confidence. "I'll give you a cut of the profits if you let me stay here at a discounted rate."

Old Joe's lips peeled back in a slow smile, revealing brown teeth. "If you're as good as you say you are, I might just waive your hotel bill altogether." Reaching into his back pocket, he produced a deck of cards. "We'll just have to see you play first."

"Are you sure you want to do this?" Worry lines emerged on Cora's forehead as she gazed up at the sunny home nesting among the elms. "Ellis and I are so happy to have you. You don't have to leave."

Faith pressed Cora's sleeve. "I've overstayed my welcome already. You two are newlyweds. You need privacy." She leaned closer with a sly smile. "At least until you welcome a baby."

"A baby." Cora waved her off. "I'm not ready for all that just yet. This town is just beginning to grow used to me as a homemaker. Add in mother and their heads might explode."

"It will happen for you." Seizing her carpetbag in one hand, Faith linked her arm with Cora's and started up the flagstone path. If she had faith in nothing else these days, she'd seen how life could change in an instant. "I only hope when you do, you'll let me dote on the poor child like the dear aunt I intend to be."

Cora smiled, her boots crunching wayward pebbles. "You'll always be a part of our lives." A sigh pressed from her as she eyed the Victorian two-story yet again. "I just want to ensure your safety. Are you sure about this place?"

"What, Abeline Baxter?" Faith laughed. "The woman is a doll. You've never met a kinder old lady."

The sweet aroma of Abeline's roses mingled with the evergreen forest beyond.

Cora hesitated. "Does she know anything about her husband's plans?"

"She still thinks her husband was a saint, and I'd like to keep it that way." Faith led them up the somewhat rickety stairs to a porch lined in potted geraniums. "She's old, and she deserves a better picture of her husband than the one we can give her. She isn't like me, with a lifetime of pondering her loved one's evil deeds ahead."

Her strident knock battered the woman's front door, disturbing the doves roosting in the eaves. If anything, she hoped to distract herself from the constant memories gnawing at her. An elderly woman in need of a companion might present the perfect opportunity.

In seconds, footfalls tapped across the floor beyond before the front door opened and the woman's twinkling smile greeted them. "Well, hello, dears. I had hoped you'd be by soon. I just put fresh gingersnaps in the oven."

"That sounds delightful, Mrs. Baxter. Thank you." Faith swept a gloved hand toward Cora. "You remember Mrs. McCraw, don't you?"

"The sheriff's wife. Of course." Not a hint of judgment laced her tone as she stood back to admit them. "Do come in, dears. I know it's early spring, but the air hasn't given up its bitter chill." She shivered at the mention of it.

The interior of the Baxter home reflected the woman Faith had come to cherish. Bright floral paintings adorned every wall above pristine forest-green furniture topped in lace doilies. Her carved end tables boasted glimmering glass vases filled with every flower available in the spring thaw.

Through the swirling scents of butter, sugar, and cinnamon, Abeline led them up a stairwell and down a hallway. "You have no idea how excited I am to share my home with someone again."

She clapped her wrinkled hands together, her skirts swaying as she walked.

"You're sure I'm not a burden?" Familiar fear lurched in Faith's chest. She'd never thought of herself as cumbersome before, but after her father's harsh message at the jail, she questioned even the most trivial of matters.

"Oh no, dear. You're not a burden in the slightest." Abeline stopped before a closed door at the end of the hallway with charming white paneling. "It's been ever so lonely here since Colton died. When I heard you needed a home, I practically begged Reverend Sommers to let me house you." Her eyes lovingly swept the sunlit hallway. "This house was our dream, but it's far too big for one person to be roaming around by herself."

With a playful wink, she turned the knob and opened the door. Inside waited a bedroom much like the one Faith had known in Missoula, except for the bare shelves and perhaps a few missing trimmings. Lace curtains bordered three tall windows facing the forest. A white dresser and matching vanity with roses etched into the wood lined one wall. On the other, a beautiful mahogany bed with a pink handmade quilt was nestled next to a bedside table holding a frosted kerosene lamp.

"This is my finest guest room." Abeline stood back proudly, running her hand over the immaculate headboard. "Designed for the daughter I never had."

"It's beautiful." Faith wandered into the space, her eyes catching on the corral fence outside the window. Starlight would have plenty of room to run here.

Cora joined her, looping an arm around her shoulders. "It truly is. You're going to be so much more comfortable here than you were in our little house." She inclined her mouth toward Faith's ear, her voice lowering. "And the minute you want to come back, you're welcome to."

A smile lifted Faith's lips. "This is almost too good to be true. Thank you for your willingness to help me, Mrs. Baxter. I don't know what I would have done without you."

Abeline's head tilted, her white hair catching glimmers of sunlight. "It's my pleasure. After everything you've been through, you deserve a proper home."

Proper home. Did she even know what that was? All her life, she'd had four pristine walls around her, the best food Montana could produce, the finest clothes, the nicest horses. Every possible opportunity. What did it all matter now? Her father had built it on nothing but lies, by stealing and cheating others with one falsehood after another. No, she'd never known a proper home.

Faith squared her shoulders. "I won't let this be just an act of charity. I've never worked hard in my life, but I plan to learn." She clutched the handle of her carpetbag tighter. "I'll help with the cooking and the farm if you tell me how. I'll get a job—"

"Hush now, child." Abeline's tongue clicked with her wagging head. "There's no need for all that. Colton left me with plenty. A woman your age shouldn't concern herself with finding work."

Faith drew herself up. "Nevertheless, I plan to. I will do what my father never dared. I will build an *honest* life for myself."

One corner of Abeline's mouth lifted sadly. "One thing at a time, dear. You don't have to build it all in one day." Her gaze dropped to the pathetic carpetbag in Faith's grasp. "Is that all you've brought?"

Faith glanced at it. "This is most of my world now. I have a few extra things in the wagon."

"I plan to help her make more clothes," Cora offered with a hand to Faith's shoulder. "She didn't want to take more than was necessary from her father's house."

"Understood." The knowing light in Abeline's eyes said she did. "Now then, let's go have a few cookies, shall we, girls? You can never have too many cookies."

Cora's laugh floated behind them as they descended the stairs once more. "What a delight you are after years of self-denial under Madam Carey."

Hours later, Faith sat at the edge of her new bed with a belly full of Abeline's baked chicken and more of her gingersnaps for dessert. Her hair, clean and braided, shed the soft odor of peony soap. Her cotton nightgown caressed her freshly washed skin in perfect softness. Despite her troubles, she had everything she could need or want. In this pleasant home with its equally delightful owner, she could breathe again—even if just for a moment.

Yet as her eyes drifted to the shivering trees outside her window, her father's words echoed across her mind. *She is not my daughter.* Tucking her legs beneath her quilts and pulling her covers high under her chin, she stared into the yawning darkness. She belonged to no one—like a piece of driftwood being tossed over tumultuous waves. Yet when the tide came in, would she wash up on the solid shore, or be pushed into the depths of the unknown? Shivering, she closed her eyes against the unwelcome thought and prayed for sleep.

Three

Morning beckoned Gideon with intrusive rays of white sunlight pouring through his window and the much-too-near crow of a rooster. "What kind of town keeps a rooster on Main Street?" he muttered, tossing his blanket over his head and tunneling deeper into the pathetic excuse for bedding in this place.

Old Joe had taken his request for cheap seriously, with a pillow akin to a pancake and sheets so rough, they scratched any time he moved. *Oh well.* With any luck, he'd be out of this place in a few weeks. No one ever let him stay long.

Another crow from that blasted devil and he jolted from the bed, throwing back his covers. After splashing a little water from a tin washbowl on his face, he pulled on his clothes from yesterday and shoved his feet into his boots. At least if he found himself up at this god-awful hour, he could get a bite to eat—if something so basic existed at the Wild Rose Saloon.

Without bothering to comb his disheveled hair, Gideon shoved a hat over it and stumbled into the hallway. He'd attached his room key to a chain last night. With a flick of his wrist, he locked the door and threw the chain over his head. No sense risking what little money he'd brought with him.

The saloon, crowded with drunken patrons last night, had descended into a ghost town in the morning's wee hours. Only Old Joe's prostitutes and a stray boarder or two sat around the tables eating what looked like pig slop. Old Joe himself was nowhere around, no doubt sleeping off the hideous amount of alcohol he'd poured down his gullet last night.

Gideon found an empty chair and kicked it back with his boot. Sliding into it, he reached for a bowl and the ladle sticking out of a pot unceremoniously set in the table's middle. Corn porridge slopped into his bowl. Gideon helped himself to two heaping ladlefuls and grabbed the dubious-looking spoon left on the table.

"You might find that's too much for you," said a brunette girl beside him.

He lifted a brow. "Why do you say that?"

One slim shoulder rose. "Try it and see."

With a wary look at the cereal in his spoon, Gideon passed it through his lips. Cold, flavorless goop squished between his tongue and the roof of his mouth. His once grumbling stomach churned at the thought of eating another bite.

"Well?" The girl looked at him expectantly. "What do you think?"

"Not the worst thing I've tried." Gideon shoved his spoon into his bowl and lifted another hefty mouthful. "It will serve to fill my belly, but your cook should be jailed."

She sighed listlessly, her pink lips puckering. "That's the problem. Anyone who knew anything about feeding a bunch of girls *was* arrested." Her spoon slipped through her fingers, clattering against her bowl. "Madam Carey was a mean old bird, but at least she fed us well."

Gideon cocked his head while shoving more slop into his mouth. "Madam Carey? Who's that?"

"Boy, you really aren't from around here, are you?" She gathered her shawl around her shoulders, concealing her low-cut nightgown. "She was the madam at the brothel down the street where I worked before here. She was arrested for kidnapping girls and selling them, so"—another airy sigh—"I suppose this is better than the alternative."

"What happened to the cook at the brothel? Maybe Old Joe should hire her."

"She stayed on at the brothel when they shut it down and turned it into a school. She said something about wanting to use her knowledge for good for a change." She drummed her fingertips on the table. "Whatever that means."

Gideon eyed her curiously. "You'd rather work here at the saloon?"

"Don't know as I have much choice in the matter. Don't really have many skills other than—" She trailed off, lending him a coy grin.

Gideon smirked before returning to his nauseating breakfast. He'd have to try someplace better tomorrow—perhaps the restaurant he'd spied on his way into town.

The legs of her chair squeaked across the floor as the girl sidled closer. "What about you, mister? Why are you here all alone, staying in a miserable room above a saloon?" Her leg brushed his, clearly intentional by the way she left it there.

"Just needed a place to stay is all." He glanced around at the barren saloon with an increasing number of vacated seats. "This town looked as good as any."

"This town is a poor man's trap and a rich man's goldmine." She draped both arms around one of his. "It's a good thing you found me. I can ease your troubles—whatever they are."

Gideon allowed his gaze to trace the graceful shape of her porcelain neck up to her flawless cheekbones and wide brown eyes. She gazed suggestively at him through thick, batting lashes. A young woman with such beauty could attract many a lonely man in these parts. Why would she waste her time working here?

"No, but thank you. I appreciate the offer."

She pressed closer, leaning into him. "Come on, now. Is it because I'm not all dolled up? Once I put my face on, you'll see. Then you won't be able to resist me."

Gideon scooted back, breaking the touch between them. "It's not that. You're beautiful." He took a swig of cold, bitter coffee.

"Already married?" She grinned slyly. "Can't say that stops many men in these parts from knocking on my door."

"No, I'm not married." He set his coffee tin back on the table. "If I were married, this is the last place I'd be."

"Ah, but you have a woman." She toyed with a lock of her hair. "Look at you with your strong jaw and your dark hair. Women are probably like putty in your hands."

Plucking his spoon from the remnants of his cereal, he stared out the window at the town just waking to the rising sun. Gideon knew the hardships of poverty all too well. He wouldn't condemn a woman for doing what she must to survive, though a prostitute's bed was the last place he'd care to be.

"I don't have time for women." He swung his gaze back on her. "The life of a gambler doesn't leave room for family."

Her eyes expanded. "You're the one I heard the girls talking about, aren't you? The one who took Old Joe for everything he had."

"If we had been playing for real money, I would have." Gideon finished the last of his cereal and let his spoon clang against the bowl. "Though I did pull in a hefty sum at the tables last night."

"My advice?" The girl stood and seized her bowl in one hand. "Hide your money. The first thing that's going to happen once people get wind of your skill is they'll try to rob you of your winnings." Her gaze flitted around her. "It's not even safe with the people here."

He nodded. "I know how to take care of myself, but thanks." After having his pockets emptied too many times, Gideon had developed a system involving the local bank and a well-placed pistol on his person.

"Well, sugar, I've got a job to do." She tossed her shawl over one shoulder and sashayed away, no doubt still attempting to entice him with every step.

Gideon laughed and rubbed a hand over his face. He often said he'd chosen a lonely life, but truth be told, it had chosen him. A combination of hardship and quick hands could do that.

With a stretch, he pushed up from his chair. He would need a proper shave and a bath before the gambling began, maybe something to eat other than tasteless mush. He turned toward the saloon's double doors, then froze.

Silhouetted by brash sunlight stood a girl of perhaps nineteen or twenty. She wore a fanciful lilac dress with ivory ribbons and matching gloves. Her blonde hair, pinned to the back of her head, hung down in a cascade of perfect curls. Luminous brown eyes scanned the saloon's interior as if searching for something before landing on him.

Gideon sucked in a quiet breath. Perhaps he had time for women after all.

Faith stood at the entrance to the Wild Rose Saloon, one hand on each of the double doors. The establishment, normally a beehive of activity in the evenings, looked more like the church at early services. No men sat around the numerous card tables, sloshing ale between them and gambling away their life's worth. In the fresh rays of morning, only a handful sat about eating their breakfast—a sad excuse for food by the looks of it.

Her eyes found a man standing by one of the tables, gaping at her. He had the rough look of a miner, with scruff on his face and disheveled clothing. He appeared as if he'd just rolled out of bed. Yet something in those eyes, dark and deep, stirred a feeling in her gut, like wood catching fire. She allowed herself one last perusal of his handsome features and swarthy skin before she detached her gaze and strode across the floor.

Though nobody stood behind the bar, the wood itself in this place bore the scent of liquor. She steeled herself, marching past the staring man and an empty table littered in used dishes, to a woman in a tight-fitting gown gathering pots from the tables. Faith cleared her throat. She would rather have come anywhere else, but the mercantile, restaurant, and every other respectable shop in town had already turned her away.

The woman tossed her a half-hearted glance. "Can I help you with something?"

Faith forced herself to stand tall. "I'm looking for Old Joe."

The trace of a smile lit the woman's face. "Old Joe doesn't get up before ten, but if you want to wait for him, you're welcome." A glint of misgiving brightened her eyes as they descended Faith. "Though I'm not sure I'd recommend a place like this for a woman like you."

A woman like you. She flattened her palms over her embellished skirts. She must look like an absolute snob in these clothes. The soiled doves in this sad excuse for a tavern probably had more money to their names than she did.

"I—I don't have much choice." She wrung her hands. "I need a job."

The woman's brow quirked, but she kept whatever thoughts she had locked in her pretty mouth. "Whatever you say. Old Joe will be ecstatic to hire you."

"I don't mean as a prostitute." The statement brought the woman's head up. "I'm not proud. I can do anything else, but I—" She gnawed on her lower lip. "I can't do that."

The woman pursed her lips. "You're a smart girl—*too* smart to be here. There must be someplace else you can go, a man who will keep you."

"Please." Faith took a tentative step forward. "My looks may deceive you, but I have nothing, and I'll not be beholden to another duplicitous man." Her jaw set, holding her emotions at bay.

After studying her a moment, the woman picked up another pot. "We'll have to see what Old Joe says when he wakes. There aren't many jobs around here for women, other than—"

"I understand. I'll do anything else." She exhaled. "It's just that I watched what Cora went through working for Madame Cary, and I can't—"

"Cora?" The woman came around the table, pot in hand. "You know Cora?"

"She's one of my dearest friends. I was living with her for a while, but I can't rely on her generosity anymore. I need to pay the woman I'm staying with."

"I'd do just about anything for a friend of Cora's." She smiled sadly. "She saved my life more times than I care to admit." She laid a hand on Faith's upper arm. "I don't care what Old Joe says. I'll hire you. I'll get him to see the wisdom of my decision, one way or another."

Faith blew out a relieved laugh. "Thank you. I promise you won't regret this."

"I'm sure I won't." She stuck out a friendly hand. "I'm Molly, by the way."

Faith slipped her hand into Molly's. "I'm Faith. Faith Carter."

"Oh, honey." Molly's head angled, pity crimping her brows. No doubt she'd heard of Faith's pathetic plight, just as everyone else in this town. "When can you start?"

Faith's gaze darted around to the discarded dishes strewn across the tables. "Right now if you'll let me." Scooping up several bowls, she stacked them atop one another.

"Good. I could use a helping hand." Molly flicked her head toward the table Faith had passed on the way in. "I'll collect everything off this one here. You get those and we'll bring them to the kitchen."

"Of course." After quickly pulling off her gloves, Faith laid them over the back of a chair and got to work.

The young man she'd spotted earlier still stood beside his chair, his gaze fixed to the floor but springing up Faith's way every so often. "Excuse me." She moved around him, collecting the rest of the dishes on the table. She paused at the ones before him. "Are you finished?"

"Yes, ma'am." His full mouth tugged up on one side as he tipped his hat to her.

Faith forced herself to lean over him, keeping as much distance as possible as she lifted his bowl onto the others.

"Thank you." His deep tone reached to her toes.

With a curt nod, she spun on her heel and gathered both stacks of dishes in her arms. She'd never carried a dish to the kitchen in her life, but one could always learn. Trailing behind Molly's rapid footsteps, she resisted the urge to glance back at the mysterious stranger, even as the feel of his eyes upon her never ceased.

"Who is that man out there?" Faith asked as they passed through a swinging door into a tiny kitchen. "The brooding one who wouldn't stop staring."

Molly crossed the crude plank floor, setting her soiled dishes next to a cast-iron sink. "I don't really know. He's some type of drifter. He stayed here last night, made a big splash at the poker table."

Faith fought the shiver that coursed through her. A man like that sounded dangerous, no matter the chiseled face God had given him. "Perhaps I'm too sheltered, but I found his stare unnerving."

Easing Faith's collection of dishes from her arms and lowering them to the counter, Molly laughed. "Can you blame him? You're a beautiful woman." She reached for the water pump over the sink.

"There are many lessons I need to teach you if you're going to work here. It's not just about cooking and cleaning."

"I admit, I don't have much experience with the opposite sex." Faith carted the last of the pots to the counter next to the sink. "My father kept me busy with tutors and horseback riding. I only interacted with males at the occasional ball."

Molly chuckled. "I'm afraid the men you'll encounter here are quite different from any you would meet at a fancy ball, especially now that Madam Carey's is shut down. Those looking for a woman's embrace have nowhere to go but here."

Heat crept across Faith's skin. She'd spent enough time around Cora to understand what went on in a brothel, but considering it still flushed her cheeks with heat. Perhaps she'd always imagined marrying a man who would shelter and care for her, and never have to ponder the type who lurked around places like this. She steadied herself on the wall. No respectful man would have her anymore.

Pumping water into the sink, Molly glanced up. "Oh dear, I don't mean to frighten you, but such realities must be discussed."

Faith blinked, nodding. "Tell me."

"First off, never stay here past ten o'clock. The men drink more and more, and become rowdier after the sun goes down." She heaved a stack of dishes into the sink and reached for a bar of soap. "They will try to proposition you. When you refuse, some might try to force you." Her eyes met Faith's over the soapy water. "You must be on your guard, and I recommend carrying a weapon."

Faith swallowed. "I have a gun. My father taught me to shoot." Though after she'd shot him, she'd vowed never to pick it up again.

"Good." Molly's hands worked at the bowl in her grip, scrubbing away the remnants of breakfast. "You should be fine if you stand your ground. Remind them there are other girls here for purchase, and go straight to Old Joe if they won't leave you alone."

"And Old Joe?" Faith had little experience with him, but from their brief encounters, she remembered him crawling with women. "Must I worry about him?"

Molly plunged her hands deep into the water repeatedly. "Not Old Joe. He'll try to convince you to become one of his personal entourage, but he'll not try to force you. He's a decent fellow underneath it all. He'll protect you."

"That's good to hear." The last thing she needed was yet another unsecure environment in which to spend her time.

A row of clean dishes sat upon a folded towel by the sink. Faith shook to life. "My, you've done all these, and I've just been standing here. I'm sorry." She rushed toward the sink and snapped up a towel.

"That's all right." Molly watched as Faith dried the freshly cleaned dishes and stored them in the cabinet. "You have a lot to learn, but I have every hope that you'll do just fine here, Faith Carter."

Four

Faith's back ached and shoulders stung by the time she stumbled out the double doors of the Wild Rose Saloon after a lunch of soggy beans and dry bread. Sunlight burned her weary eyes. The crowd rushing around her looked like an anthill teeming with busy insects, scurrying to and fro.

Since her arrival that morning, she'd helped Molly with the dishes, wiped all the saloon tables, swept the floors, and cleaned up the guest rooms. Every chore was new to her—dusting furniture, making beds, preparing the unappetizing meal she'd just endured. Yet something unusual swam through her veins—a sense of accomplishment like she'd never known. At least she would lay her head down tonight, tired, but alive in the knowledge that she'd done something for herself.

A smile slipped over her mouth as she gazed across the street and took in a familiar sight. Beneath an awning in front of the Mountainview Inn, Cora stood in her husband's embrace. The two stared at one another as only newlyweds could, speaking in quiet tones and sharing light touches.

As if sensing her eyes on them, Cora turned and squinted out the intrusive sunlight. "Faith?" The devotion on her face turned to joy. "That *is* you! Faith, come over here." She waved her on, propelling Faith's shoes across the dusty street.

"I was just wondering how you fared. I was ready to make a trip out to Widow Baxter's to check on you if I didn't see you in town."

Ellis hooked Cora to his side. "How was your first night with Mrs. Baxter, Faith?"

Faith pulled her gloves up higher, masking her hands, work-worn for the first time in her life. "She is delightful, and her home is quite comfortable." She forced a smile despite her fatigue. "I am indeed very lucky."

Cora's brows dove. "Was that the Wild Rose Saloon I just saw you coming out of?"

"Indeed." Diverting her gaze, Faith hugged an arm across her torso. "I got a job there. I was working all morning."

"Oh, Faith—"

"Settle down." Of course Cora couldn't resist her natural urge to mother. "I'm under Molly's tutelage. I shall do nothing but errands and chores. I have already learned to bake bread." What an eye-opening experience *that* was.

Cora's shoulders relaxed. "At least you have Molly to guide you. I can't help worrying about you in a place like that, though."

"You came from far worse, dear," Ellis said. "You survived, didn't you?"

"That is precisely what I'm worried about." She gave him a playful nudge. "I survived, but Faith deserves better than I had. She's a good girl."

Faith pointed her chin up. "I have attitude and a pistol. What more could I need?"

The pair laughed along with her. How wonderful to see Cora so happy after all she'd endured. Faith barely heard the footsteps running toward them before a boy appeared beside Ellis, red-faced and out of breath.

"Sheriff, you must come quickly. You're needed at the bank."

Ellis snapped to attention. "What is it?"

"I don't rightly know." The boy wagged his head. "Everyone there is in a panic. They said just to get you. I think it's a robbery of some sort."

"A robbery?" Ellis squeezed Cora's hand. "You wait here. I'll see what all the fuss is about." Dust clouded the air behind him as he ran with the child toward the Gold Strike bank.

Faith looked to Cora. "Are you really going to wait here?"

"And miss all the fun?" Mischief played on Cora's lips. "I'm only giving him a head start. Come on." Latching her arm around Faith's, she pulled her along like an impish schoolgirl sneaking where she didn't belong.

The breeze carried whiffs of the forested mountains, mingled with freshly sprouted wildflowers. The pair laughed as they scampered up the street, bypassing pedestrian and wagon alike. When they reached the bank, a crowd had already begun to form outside. Cora shouldered through it, dragging Faith along with her amid excited chatter and idle gossip. From the sound of it, everyone had a different theory in regard to Gold Strike's newest crime.

Clattering up the steps behind Cora, Faith entered a scene of disarray. Papers littered the floor, an inkwell shattered beside them and a puddle of black ink pooling nearby. Mrs. Ross, the kindly old woman who'd run the bank since Colton Baxter's death paced the floor, wringing her hands. Near the front counter, Ellis spoke with another employee, Mrs. Ross's son Bill.

"What happened here?"

At Cora's question, Ellis's head popped up and color flooded his cheeks. "I thought I told you to stay down the street."

"I'm sorry." She strode forward, a playful look flaring across her lovely features. "I forgot I was a child to be ordered around."

Ellis glared at her, but the hint of a smile teased his lips. "If this had been an actual robbery, you could very well be dead now, Mrs. McCraw."

Her shoulders raised in a casual shrug. "Then I suppose it's a good thing it wasn't."

"Sheriff, focus, please." Bill Ross shot Cora an irritated scowl. "We have to find the person who did this before that gold is gone for good."

Resting his hands on his belt, Ellis grunted. "We'll find them. If the amount you say is missing, that's an awful lot of gold to disappear all at once. The thieves won't be able to hide it for long—not with my deputies out scouring the countryside."

"Oh dear, oh dear." Mrs. Ross's chest heaved. Above her pink gingham gown, her white hair fell out of her coiled bun in messy wisps as her boots thumped the floor with increasing fervency.

Faith rushed to her side, looping an arm around her quivering shoulders. "Perhaps you should take a seat, Mrs. Ross. You're terribly upset, and I don't want you to faint."

"Thank you, dear." Mrs. Ross accepted the chair Cora held out to her, sinking into the seat with a huff.

Faith poured a glass of water from a pitcher on the counter and held it out to her.

"My, what helpful girls you are." The elderly woman's fingers trembled as she took the glass and held it to her lips.

"What gold are they talking about, Mrs. Ross?" Crouching low beside her chair, Faith rubbed the woman's back.

"It's everything. Far more than anybody here can pay back." Her eyes widened. "That money was supposed to go to the home branch in Helena."

Cora frowned from her other side. "You mean the money from the stagecoach robbery? What Colton Baxter was attempting to take to the train?"

Faith swallowed. *The money my father tried to steal.*

"Yes, all of it." Mrs. Ross inhaled an unsteady breath. "Thousands of dollars worth of gold gone in an instant. We have no way to pay it back." She choked on the words, retreating into a fit of sobs.

"Don't worry, Mrs. Ross." Cora leaned in, taking the water glass from her quaking fingers. "My husband is a fine lawman. He will bring that money back." Yet as her eyes rose to meet with Ellis's over the woman's head, doubt clouded them.

Ellis swung his gaze back to Bill. "Why was all that money still here anyway? It's been almost a year since the stagecoach robbery."

"After Mr. Baxter died, we didn't have anyone authorized to take it," Bill said. "The bank's headquarters in Helena handles the transport of money."

Mrs. Ross sniffed. "They were supposed to send a representative down months ago, but the man never came."

Her son nodded. "We've kept it locked in our safe ever since. We've checked it day and night."

"Every morning when I get here, I account for it all first thing," Mrs. Ross said. "And Bill does the same before we leave. I only noticed it today because—" She blinked, focusing on something behind Faith. "I'm so terribly sorry, sir. We were in the middle of a transaction, weren't we?"

"Think nothing of it, ma'am. It appears as if you have bigger fish to fry."

The deep, booming voice made every muscle in Faith's body constrict. From her spot on the floor, she swiveled back to meet with a pair of dusty boots and trousers. Her gaze climbed a solid frame and muscular arms knotted over a sturdy chest, before landing on a familiar face—the man she'd seen that morning at the Wild Rose.

He wore a confident expression as he addressed Mrs. Ross, but one side of his mouth quirked up when his gaze dropped to Faith. "Need a hand up, miss?"

"No, I—" She meant to say she planned to attend to Mrs. Ross more, but the woman had already vacated the seat behind her. Faith pushed herself off the floor in the most ladylike pose she could muster and rearranged her skirts. "I'm perfectly fine, thank you."

"You certainly appear to be."

Faith's eyes flashed to his dark, bold gaze. This man clearly had no regard for manners. She tried to unlatch her lips, but they felt glued together.

"Mr. Valdez, I hope this rather unfortunate incident hasn't soured your desire to do business with us." Mrs. Ross had returned to her station behind the counter, tears abated and all business after her display of emotion. "I can assure you this is a rare occurrence here in Gold Strike, and we won't let it happen again."

The man allowed his assured gaze to linger on Faith a moment longer before he turned back to the counter. "Not at all. I have every faith my deposit will be safe during my stay here." The two convened over a stack of bills and paperwork while Faith sidled up to Cora.

Ellis had already crossed the barrier between customer and employee, leading Bill down a wide hallway. "Let's have a look at this safe, shall we? You said this happened sometime since this morning? Who all has the combination to your vault?"

Bill scampered to keep up with him. "Just my mother and I. The only other person who knew it was Mr. Baxter. We don't even have it written down." Their voices faded as they disappeared around a corner.

Cora hooked an inquisitive brow. "Who is that man?"

Warmth invaded Faith's cheeks. "I don't know."

"He is handsome." Cora studied his profile as he concluded his business with Mrs. Ross. "He seems terribly interested in you."

"In me?" Faith tossed her a flustered look. "Where would you get such a notion?" Forget that those coffee-colored eyes had followed her everywhere around the saloon earlier.

"Just a hunch, I suppose." Cora's mouth tilted roguishly. "Oh, look at that. Someone I need to speak with outside." Before Faith could utter a word of protest, Cora had fled and left her standing there, vulnerable.

Tucking his wallet into his pack, the man turned her way. That smug, satisfied look hadn't left his face as he adjusted the bag on his shoulder. "Glad to see you're still here." His hand shot toward her. "I'm Gideon."

Palms suddenly sweaty, she swiped one across her skirt before shaking his offered hand. "I'm Faith." If she said the name Carter, would he automatically deem her unworthy?

"That's a nice name. *Faith.*" He tested it out, the full mouth beneath dark stubble lifting. "You work at the Wild Rose Saloon, don't you?"

"I suppose I do." She tucked her hands behind her back. "I'm not a—" Her cheeks darkened. *What was she saying?*

"That's good to hear." He must have finished the sentence for her, because a clever smirk pinched his lips. "I'm glad you're not a—" A muscle in his jaw twitched.

Faith touched a hand to her forehead. "I don't know why I said that. You're a stranger and I'm behaving perfectly untoward." Had her heart always stuttered beneath every man's scrutiny as it did with his fathomless eyes searching hers? Sweat emerged along her hairline at the thought.

"You're just a woman making her wishes clear. I respect that." His fingers raked through his thick shock of hair. "I'm sorry if I unsettled you earlier when you walked into the saloon. I just"—his chest expanded—"I didn't expect you, is all. I've been on the road a long time."

Relaxing, Faith allowed her gaze to wander across his sturdy shoulders to the pack slung on one side and down his arm, where a hat nested in his hand. He looked like a man who might have seen the world twice over, an ever-present restlessness in his tall frame. "I hear you are a gambler, Mr.—Valdez, was it?"

"Mr. Valdez was my pa. I prefer just Gideon." He looked down at his hat, turning it over in his hands. "Poker's my game, but I'll play just about anything people will let me. What about you?" His eyes found her again. "You play any cards?"

A laugh fizzled up her. "Me? Play poker?" She could just imagine the scandal she'd have brought on her tutors to have suggested the uncivilized game. "I've indulged in whist a time or two, but never poker."

"You're much too refined for poker, aren't you?" He perused the lace sleeves of her lilac gown.

Faith pressed a hand over her middle. "I'm not refined." If he only knew how truly degrading her existence was, with no money to her name and a father paying his just dues in prison.

The corner of his mouth jerked. "You could have fooled me."

Fighting the heat winding up her neck, Faith lifted her chin. Why did this man's opinion affect her at all? Why did she squirm more with each second his solemn gaze encompassed her? "I work in a saloon. There's nothing refined about me. Not anymore." How bitter those words tasted on her tongue.

Gideon considered them, running his fingertips down his square jaw. "In my experience, ma'am, it's not so much what a person does for work that defines them." His shoulders lifted. "Suppose I'm living proof of that."

Faith nodded. "Perhaps." Yet what else had defined her almost two decades of life, if not her father's profession? Edward Carter's daughter, heiress to a vast fortune, the most celebrated girl in all of Montana. Hadn't she worn these titles with pride, enjoying the way people looked at her, the admiration in their eyes? Who was she if that girl had vanished along with her father's money and reputation?

Footsteps pounded the hall again, followed by the mingling of masculine voices. "Don't disturb anything until I get back," Ellis said over his shoulder as he rounded the corner. "My deputies will take a look at all your doors. You should suspend all business until then." He stopped short next to Faith, his eyes sweeping the stranger.

"Ellis, this is Gideon Valdez." Faith rested a hand on the back of her neck. "Gideon, Sheriff Ellis McCraw."

Gideon nodded. "Sheriff McCraw. Pleased to meet you."

"Likewise." Yet Ellis made no move to meet the hand outstretched before him. His eyes narrowed on Gideon, an almost imperceptible movement, before he turned to Faith. "Do you need help getting home? I could have Wainwright drive you."

"No, but thank you." She fiddled with the strings of her reticule. "I'm expected back at the saloon in an hour. I'm only taking a break."

"All right." Ellis's troubled gaze darted briefly back to Gideon, heavy with quiet suspicion. Then he squeezed Faith's arm and headed for the door. "Just be careful. I'll send somebody by the saloon to pick you up after work."

It isn't necessary. I'll be fine on my own. But the words lodged in her throat beneath the hard lump that had formed there. Faith sheepishly looked back at Gideon, still regarding her with confident interest. When had she lost her ability to speak?

"Well, ma'am, I ought to be going too." Gideon screwed on his hat and tipped the brim to her. "Awful nice meeting you. I'll see you around the Wild Rose." With that, he sauntered out of the bank and into the sunny street, leaving Faith to stare after him.

Five

The sad ruffians who frequented the Wild Rose Saloon in the afternoons presented little challenge for Gideon's capable skills. Most could do little more than survive a few hands before he took everything on the table. He'd even found himself throwing a game or two just to sustain his interest.

Yet as night blanketed the town in darkness and the groan of bullfrogs from the neighboring stream, the tavern bloomed like a crocus in springtime. The Wild Rose, dingy and depressing by day, lit with hissing gaslight. Patrons poured through its doors—miners relieved of a hard day's work, merchants eager to put their feet up, rich men in expensive suits ready to lay down their cash for a bit of entertainment. Gideon grinned from his spot among the crowd. He would be happy to oblige them.

Several tables had already filled by the time he came strolling down the stairs from his room. Gideon, clad in a navy suit and knotted silk cravat, snaked his way through the crowd, examining each game. He'd slicked back his dark hair for the occasion, put on his finest gold cufflinks. With some of Gold Strike's choice citizens filing into the saloon, he couldn't be seen in a dirty pair of breeches and a soiled shirt. He would be viewed as an equal tonight, or they'd never dish out the mounds of money bursting beneath their tailored suits.

With eyes like the clever wolf he'd become, he stalked his prey, moving from one table to the next until he stopped at a group of older men engrossed in an intense poker game. Gideon watched the manner in which they each played—the cards they chose to keep and discard, how much they staked, how daring their choices.

At the end of several rounds, he stepped up to the lone, empty chair. Tinny notes from a piano filled the raucous space, making conversation difficult. Gideon's fingers curled around the back of the chair. "Gentlemen, might I join you?" he asked above the music and chatter, the clink of glasses bashing against one another.

The dealer paused, clutching the cards with one hand, his gaze scraping down Gideon slowly. His comrades did the same, exchanging wary looks with one another.

"The stakes are awfully high at this table," a man with a thin mustache and trimmed beard said. "Are you sure you can afford it?" His tone held a mocking quality as he lifted his glass and took a swig.

Gideon kept his composure beneath their inspection. "How much?"

The dealer plunked the cards on the table. "Ten dollars a round to buy in, but the price can get quite steep from there."

Gideon's mouth curled at the trifling amount meant to intimidate him. He pulled back his jacket to reveal a thick stack of banknotes peeping from within.

Swapping malicious grins, the men settled back in their chairs. A tall fellow with salt-and-pepper hair gestured toward the empty chair. "Sit down if you like—if you don't mind losing your money, that is."

The tasteless joke sparked a round of laughter among them. Gideon sank into the chair, inhaling the sweet scent of pipe tobacco curling around him. "I guess we'll see about that."

"That we will, boy. That we will." The cards feathered between his fingers like an accordion. "We're playing five-card draw. No limits." He expertly dispersed the cards one at a time, five for each man.

Gideon anted ten dollars, his other hand swiping the cards dealt to him. He didn't need to look at them to know his next move, but Gideon spread the cards to reveal a pair of twos, a four, an eight, and a jack. In a normal round, he could do wonders with a hand like this, but not for a first go around. He'd learned long ago when to hang back and when to charge on. An initial hand with a group like this demanded he relinquish control.

One by one, each player tossed in their ante.

"How many do you want?" growled the dealer to the thin man with the mustache.

With a purse of his lips, he surveyed his cards. "Give me one." The requested card slid across the table, its colorful, swirling design exposed before the man thwacked his palm over the top.

The dealer continued around the table until he came to Gideon. "What about you, son? Feel like playing with fire?" His mouth curled.

"I always do." Plunking three cards on the table, he hooked his finger. "Give me three."

"Got ourselves a proper gambler, I see." The dealer's eyes brightened as he shared a chuckle with his comrades. Three fresh cards pushed toward him. Gideon collected them and lined them up with his others, creating a perfect display of mismatched cards.

After a few beats thick with laughter and chortles from around the crowded saloon, the man to the left of the dealer leaned in. "Ten," he said, throwing an extra bill atop the disheveled pile in the middle.

"I'll see that and raise you ten more," the next man offered, tossing in a twenty.

"Come on, boys—let's show him how it's done here." The dark haired man next to Gideon spoke around a puffing cigar protruding from his mouth. "I've got a fifty. Who wants to match me?" His eyes fixed on Gideon as he threw the bill into the table's center.

Donning a smug expression came easy for Gideon. He reached into his jacket pocket and pulled out a crisp fifty-dollar bill. The bill fluttered from his hand, sailing over his pathetic assembly of cards onto the table.

The dealer whistled. "Sure hope you know what you're doing, boy." He put in his own fifty. "I call too."

The other two players followed suit, each producing the money required to stay in the round. When the man with the cigar plunked down a full house, the entire table groaned. Gideon hid his cards, as if too sheepish to reveal his folly.

"Better luck next time, boys." The man's words lisped around his cigar as he proudly raked in his winnings.

The next couple hands played out in a similar fashion, only Gideon folded somewhere along the way. His opponents needed to see him as anything but a threat. A nuisance, perhaps, but certainly not a threat.

When two pairs of high cards turned up in his hand, delighted tingles raced along his arms. Now was the time to put his skills on display. They would liken it to luck for several hands, not realizing his potential until too late. Then he would addict them to him—to finding a way to beat him, a way to break this bizarre streak of good fortune that had befallen the clueless newcomer. He could keep them coming back for more with this cycle in place for nights on end, playing coy until he'd drained them.

The triumphant elation of victory swept over him as he collected his bounty from the table. His rivals scratched their chins and glanced at one another, but nobody would admit he'd bested them. No, they would see their money returned in the next round.

A less ideal hand fell into his possession on the following deal, but Gideon could turn it into a winning bunch with a couple cards switched out. Just as he prepared to make that very request, movement caught the corner of his eye. He glanced sideways to find Faith bent over the next table, clearing it of empty glasses.

His mind went soft as his gaze slipped over her. Clad in a silvery blue gown that complimented her feminine form in a most distracting way, she collected glasses onto a tray. With a graceful rhythm, she continued on until the last glass clinked against the others, then leaned over to wipe the mess from the tabletop. Gideon held his breath as her gaze flitted up to his. Her dark lashes batted once before she glanced away and went on with her work.

"You still with us, son?"

Gideon shook himself to attention. "What? Oh, yes. Of course." Yet even as the words left his mouth, his eyes moved to find her again.

"How many do you want?"

"Umm…" He spotted her disappearing through the crowd with her tray hoisted on her hip. "One." *No, two.* He opened his mouth to correct himself, but the card was already deposited in front of him and the next man taking his pick. Gideon sacrificed his worst card and replaced it with the new one, his heart sinking. With two, he might have a winning hand. The sad display before him wouldn't stand up even in an amateur game. He'd have to pull a move he would rather not resort to.

His gaze lifted to the spot Faith had sashayed her way through the crowd. She could derail him from everything he'd come here to do. He must pull his head back in the game before Faith Carter ruined him for good.

The glasses on Faith's tray clinked together as she moved from one table to the next, collecting soiled tankards. The bitter scents of ale and whiskey assaulted her nearly as strongly as the choking cigar smoke. What a stark contrast from the familiar scents of home—maple syrup in the morning, roasted French coffee, lilac sprigs, and linens so clean they smelled like pure sunshine.

She glanced around her at the scruffy, inebriated faces. How quickly one could fall. Resting her tray on her hip, she turned and wound her way through the tables. Since Molly had put her on the floor to serve and clean up, she'd pocketed a couple dollars in tips—along with some unwanted suggestions. Faith already considered herself adept at dodging as she worked, what with the amount of men in this place with wandering hands.

She used her hip to push through the swinging door of the kitchen and plopped the full tray of glasses onto the counter.

Hands up to her elbows in soapy water, Molly beamed from before the sink. "You got a lot this time. Starting to get the hang of it?"

Faith winced, rolling her shoulder where an unfamiliar pain stung. "Starting to. I'm not sure how I'll keep on my feet all night, though."

"It's not so bad once you get used to it." Molly turned and began gathering glasses from the tray, dripping sudsy water on the floor as she plopped them into the sink. "Be glad you're not back here, turning your hands to prunes in this filthy water."

Tapping her fingers on the wooden counter, Faith leaned against it. "At least no one bothers you in here."

Molly shot her a questioning glance. "Who's bothering you, honey? Tell Old Joe and he'll put a stop to it."

Faith shook her head listlessly. "It's not so bad. I'm just not used to so much male—attention, that's all."

Molly's laugh carried in the little room. "You will get used to that, too. Just stand your ground and remind them you mean business if they ever try to get fresh." Her hands worked to hastily scrub food off a crusty plate. "Have you gotten any tips yet?"

"A few." Faith reached into her pocket, fingering the two bills and coins that jingled beneath her fingertips.

"If you learn to do it right, those will pay you more than Old Joe ever does." She dunked her plate into a basin of clean water, then set it on a towel to dry. "Look for the heavy players. There are a lot of them in here most nights, and they pay handsomely. You'll make what you need in no time."

Retrieving her tray, Faith tucked it under her arm and headed for the saloon. *Heavy players.* She'd intentionally avoided that group all night. Not only did the most affluent table contain Gideon Valdez, but the rest of the seats were occupied by friends of her father. What reaction would they have to seeing the great Edward Carter's daughter reduced to the role of a serving wench?

She blew back a pesky strand of her hair. One of them already had his hand up, beckoning for her attention. *I suppose they can't be avoided all night.* Though with every step across the crowded floor, she longed more for the quiet comfort of her room at Mrs. Baxter's house. At least she could hide from her mortification there.

"There you are, girl. We haven't seen you all night," the man who'd summoned Faith said. She would recognize that white hair and trimmed mustache anywhere. Mr. Coolidge often went hunting with her father in autumn, yet no recognition shone in his eyes as he looked to her from his fanned-out hand of cards.

"I apologize for neglecting you, sir. What might I bring you?"

"I'll have a gin straight."

"So will I," said a younger man beside him. *Henry Baker.* Her father had done business with him and invited him to dinner on several occasions.

The next man narrowed his eyes, studying her through wrinkled slits. "You look familiar, girl. Have you worked here long?"

I only played with your daughter every Sunday at church. She swallowed the thought, her fingers blanching on her tray. "No, I only just started, actually."

"That's funny. I wonder where I've seen you."

"You'll have to forgive him," the tall man beside him said. "He's not used to seeing women of such"—his licentious gaze flicked down her—"*refinement* in a place like this."

Faith's muscles tightened. He'd used the word refinement, but his eyes said something entirely different. They openly traced every curve of her figure, lingering places that painted Faith's skin in shameful heat.

"How much for a night? Once we're done with cards, of course."

Her teeth pushed together. "I am merely a server, sir. I am not for sale."

"Come now, every woman has her price." One brow hooked. "Don't you want to earn a little extra cash while enjoying yourself?"

"She said she's not for sale." The hard voice on his right snatched every eye at the table. Faith looked into Gideon's gaze—stern, unyielding, fixed solidly on her, but in such a different way than the man trying to negotiate a night of carnal pleasure from her.

Irritation sizzled in his eyes. "I believe I was asking the lady."

"And I believe she gave you an answer." Gideon slammed his cards into his palm. "Now, are we going to play or aren't we?"

The man passed his tongue across his teeth as if licking off an unpleasant flavor. "You're awfully bold for the newest man at our table. I hope you're prepared to lose whatever pittance you came in with." He swung his gaze, ripe with irritation, up to her face. "Brandy—for now." The words held a disguised promise, or perhaps a threat, as he took one last gander at her figure.

"And for you, sir?" Faith held her breath, forcing her gaze to drop to Gideon's reddened face.

He slowly dragged his eyes from his cards, his gaze hunting hers when they entwined. "I'll have a pint of ale—please."

Though she fought it, a smile twitched the corner of her mouth. Had anyone else at the table bothered to use the simple word of gratitude? Had anyone in the entire establishment? Her feet carried her with lighter steps as she sauntered off to the bar. It had been some time since a man stood up for her, especially among his peers. After her father's traitorous behavior, the memory of Gideon's clenched jaw and solid voice spread warmth across her body.

Inhaling the brash odor of liquor, Faith waited while the barkeep sloshed the men's orders into glasses and plunked them on her tray. Twice, she stole a glance over her shoulder at the recommenced game, color swamping her cheeks to find Gideon eyeing her over the top of his cards. Her heart fluttered, and she bit her lip. Perhaps she might enjoy working in this place after all.

With a tray full of spirits rattling in her hands, Faith returned to the table and began dispensing glasses before the players. She paused next to Gideon, tucking a strand of hair behind her ear as she laid the glass near his hand.

This close in the gaslit room, she could smell the lavender and citrus notes of his cologne, trace every vein beneath his amber skin. A chill skittered up her spine as his hand moved to take his glass, brushing hers on the way. Faith paused, her brows tapering. Beneath the cuff of his sleeve, something white barely peeped out. Before she could get a better look, he lifted the glass, thus concealing whatever lay within his sleeve.

He tossed her a tilted smile. "Thank you, Faith."

"Faith!" The old man who'd recognized her popped up from his chair. "That's it. You're Faith Carter. I knew I recognized you."

Faith's body went rigid as every eye at the table latched on her, awareness dawning. Their once-admiring gazes slipped down her form, still clutching her serving tray, judgment weighing every eye.

"You've fallen on dire times to be working in a place like this, haven't you?" Henry Baker said, shaking his head ruefully. "What a shame."

The man who'd propositioned her smirked. "My offer doesn't seem so bad now, does it?" He winked, the action cutting into Faith's core. "We'll talk later."

Faith said nothing, only clenched her jaw and straightened her back as she turned to the next table. She hadn't a friend in this place—not even Gideon. The first man she suspected of decency was nothing but a liar and a cheat. He would trounce on her heart, just as her father had, if she let him any closer.

Six

One side of Gideon's body had numbed by the time he finally threw the last of his cards on the table and pushed up from his chair. Most of the saloon patrons had left by now. Only a few drunken miners still peppered the tables of the Wild Rose—some of them drinking, others slumped over in their chairs and sleeping off their intoxication.

He glanced around at the stained tables and messy floor. A woman already pushed a mop across its surface, but he saw no sign of Faith. Since she'd delivered drinks to their table, he'd barely glimpsed her at all. Not that he had time to look. The men at his table had kept him on his toes with their quick moves and daring bets, but Gideon had managed to rake in a couple hundred dollars by the end of the night. Not enough for them to sniff him out, but enough to keep them wanting more. The art of gambling required a delicate dance, performed while keeping one's opponent thinking they called the shots.

Checking his inner breast pocket for his loot once more, Gideon screwed on his hat and made for the double doors. All night he'd drunk with the best of them, but denied himself the privilege of leaving the table and putting himself in a vulnerable position. Now the pressure inside him blared, an undeniable need.

Gideon shoved through the double doors and stomped across the boardwalk. Rounding the side of the building, he trekked toward the alley—a mere expanse of dirt and weeds beneath the half-moon's light. He found relief as he stared into the night sky, a brilliant smattering of stars against the milky coal beyond.

He felt small in this place—smaller still when he considered his position in the world—nothing but a lone drifter with no friends or family, only a few skills and the art of deception on his side. Faith's face flashed in his mind—the way her skin had glowed in the gaslight, the soft curve of her neck as she bent over him. She smelled like wildflowers, like a meadow after spring rain. He'd moved out of his way to touch her, the simple sweep of her delicate skin like the electrifying touch of fire. He sighed within himself. How was he to focus on work with a woman like that wandering around night after night?

"You're terribly bold to be lingering in the alley this time of night with all that money in your pocket."

Gideon jumped at the feminine voice behind him, not three feet back. Peering over his shoulder, he discerned Faith's form—a dark silhouette against the streetlamps' glow. Turning back, he quickly concealed himself. "What are you doing out here?"

Her shoes shuffled on the ground behind him. "Looking for you."

A disbelieving laugh fled him as he rearranged his shirt and trousers. "I'm flattered, but this isn't exactly the place for a meeting. I was—" A grin crawled over his lips as he turned back to her. "Well, I was indisposed."

If only he could see the beautiful blush of her skin in this light. Instead, he could only perceive that she crossed her arms over her chest. Her silence blared louder than the piano music streaming from the saloon at its busiest hour.

"I could say the same to you, Miss Carter—out here in the alley in the dark of night without a chaperone." He stepped toward her, his boots crunching pebbles. "You may not have much money to steal, but you certainly have other assets at your disposal that men will want to take from you."

"Men like the one who tried to buy me tonight?" She lifted her chin, a ribbon of moonlight glinting off her hair. "He might have persisted with me if you hadn't been there."

Gideon's jaw tensed. "I'd like to see him try."

A breath of wind swept over them, pulling strands of hair from her bun and whipping them around her face. He'd come close enough to see the emotion in her eyes, the way they glimmered with sadness as she stared through the darkness. Such beauty marred by so much pain. Who had put it there?

"I suppose I should thank you for what you said to that fiend." She hugged herself, buffing a hand up her arm. "He might think twice about doing it again when you're there."

"I'll not hesitate to defend you again if I must." He inhaled the pine that wafted through the crisp air. "Though a woman like you should find other means to support herself if necessary. You don't belong in a place like this."

Her eyes narrowed. "What is that supposed to mean?"

"It means you're elegant and sophisticated and beautiful." Slowly he eliminated the space between them, his hand reaching out to lightly tip her chin. "You can have any man you want at the snap of your fingers."

A tremor shook her lithe frame. Did she fear him even after the incident at the table? Reminding himself they had only just met, he let his fingers fall away. Why did it feel as if he'd known her so much longer, like when his thumb nested in the dent of her chin, it had come home to its natural place in the world?

"What if I don't want to summon a man with a snap of my fingers? What if I want to make it on my own? What then?"

His eyes traced every line of her determined face, admiring the soft femininity mingled with defiant strength. "It's very hard for a woman to thrive on her own, especially in these parts. Are you sure you don't want a man by your side?"

The fear in her eyes turned to hard stone. "Men have done nothing but disappoint me, promise to love and care for me, then turn out to be nothing but selfish scoundrels in the end."

His head angled. "What man?" Could some fool have the affection of someone like her and squander it so easily?

Faith cast her gaze away, deep into the night shadows. "It doesn't matter. It's already done."

"And there's nobody who can convince you otherwise?" His breath hastened to stand so close to her and imagine never touching her again.

She stepped away, drawing her arms in closer. "I shouldn't have told you that. I shouldn't have—" She touched the space between her eyes, skin that creased with worry. "What am I doing? I came out here to confront you, and I—"

"Confront me?" Gideon's brows dove. "About what? Stepping in when you needed help?"

"About cheating." She leveled her gaze with his, suddenly assured. "I saw you with cards up your sleeve. I watched carefully. I saw you slip two into one hand and one into another. You never would have won those last two games otherwise."

Nausea simmered up Gideon's throat, burning a path from his stomach. How careless had he become, to let anyone see him slip, even an onlooker? If she told someone, he was done for.

"You don't deny it?" Her gaze darted around his face.

"Of course I don't." Gideon swallowed. "I won't make you doubt your memory, what you saw. You're an intelligent woman."

Her lips parted, like she had words at the ready that didn't befit his response. "So you're not just a gambler. You're a cheat as well. You steal money from people."

"I prefer to think of it as taking advantage of the situation. Why bet on luck alone when I can assure myself a win?"

Faith's nostrils flared. "Justify it all you'd like, but it's dishonest. You are a thief."

His shoulders lifted. "Or simply a man dealt a bad hand in life who's found a way to beat a system of injustice and prejudice?"

"You're a fine piece of work." She disgustedly shook her head. "You tout yourself around town as an accomplished player, then you hide cards in your sleeves. You're no better than the man you played with tonight, the one who spent every second he wasn't looking at his cards trying to expose me with his gaze."

Jaw working, he stepped toward her. "Don't think that you know me after observing one fact about my life. There are a multitude of others you haven't seen—some that a woman like yourself couldn't even comprehend." A past so dark that at times, he couldn't bear to think about it.

"I know what I witnessed. I know right from wrong." She stuck her chin up, her stare unflinching. "No matter who you are or where you came from, you cannot stand there and tell me what you're doing is right. You make a pact with the men at your table when you sit down and play with them."

"Men like the one who would gladly rape you if given the chance?" His teeth clenched, ire foaming up his heated gullet. "Am I supposed to feel bad about taking money from rich men like that, who think they own whatever they see? I'm sorry to disappoint, but you'll *not* hear an apology from me."

Faith stared up at him, her breath hard, her face so close, he could have hooked a hand around her neck and pulled her plump lips to his. She blinked, her gaze tumbling briefly to his mouth before she moved backward. "Do what you like. You're just—" She bit her lip. "You're not the man I hoped, is all."

The statement pinched something in his chest. "Who did you hope I'd be?"

She shook her head once. "Never mind."

Gideon seized her shoulders. "What did you hope?" Did she harbor the same inexplicable feeling of belonging he had when he looked at her?

Her eyes ascended to his, raw and vulnerable beneath the moon's rays. "It's ridiculous. *Ridiculous.* And I'm even more ridiculous to think it." Emotion tinged her voice. "I suppose I was only trying to escape the reality I've come to loathe." A sad complacency settled over her, as if she'd battled a world of demons and lost.

Gideon fought the urge to brush back her hair, to wrap her in his arms and tell her whatever plagued her would vanish like the morning mist with time. But she'd already shut him out. She'd already decided who he was beneath his showy exterior, the flirtatious grins and looks that might once have attracted her.

"Are you going to tell Old Joe about me—about what you saw?"

She regarded him a quiet moment before her head wagged softly. "No, I have no loyalty to the men you cheated."

"I don't always cheat, you know." He squeezed one of her willowy arms before he let his hands drop away. "Most of the time, I win by merit. I am good enough to beat them, but this is a business. I need to be sure."

Her lips pursed in silent judgment, but she kept her opinion beneath them.

"Anyway, I'll be gone in a few weeks, so you won't have to endure my presence for long."

Her gaze flung up to his, questions alive in it, before she simply nodded. "Then you'll go on to terrorize the next town, I suppose."

"If terrorizing is what you want to call it." His mouth dimpled. "Now that I'm nothing but a common outlaw in your eyes."

"I didn't say that."

"No, but you said as much—and you're right. I am not the kind of man you should associate with, nor the kind you should converse with in darkened alleys. You're better than me, Faith Carter. You're better than me in every way."

She swallowed, a strange yearning in her eyes as they searched his. Her lips parted like she wanted to say more. She shifted ever so slightly toward him, then backed away again. What went on in that head of hers? If only he could reach beneath her surface and find out.

"You want to say more."

Her gaze bounced up, startled. "No, I don't."

"Yes, you do. It's written all over your face."

Faith touched a hand to her cheek. "You're standing much too close for me. Good night, sir." Whipping around, she stormed across the weedy ground and into the shadows between the buildings.

Gideon found himself jogging after her, passing through the narrow opening. Just as they reached the street, he caught her arm, preventing her from stepping onto the boardwalk.

She pinned an impatient look on his detaining hand. "You will kindly let go of me."

"Not until you say what you mean to." Gideon's fingers tensed as he stepped in front of her. "You have thoughts left unsaid, and I'd like to hear them." *I need* to hear them.

With a gentle huff, she passed a hand over her hair. "Oh, all right. Will you let go of me if I tell you?"

He nodded, waiting. Her gaze averted to the murky black before finding his again. Lanternlight from the rafters overhead gleamed in her doe-like eyes. "I just couldn't help but wonder when I saw those cards in your sleeve—"

"Yes?" Gideon lowered his chin, attempting to retain her flustered gaze.

"Well, you just came to this town, and I would never think this of a virtual stranger—"

"But you saw me cheating." His jaw tensed in preparation for what she'd say.

"I did see you cheating, just as I saw you at the bank this morning." She glanced at a couple passing by, barely managing a smile. "I've asked myself if that could have been a coincidence, but I don't have an answer."

Pressure struck Gideon's chest, bearing down on him. "You think I burglarized the bank?"

She shrugged. "I don't know what to believe. You waltz into town and suddenly that money's gone."

"They found out it was gone because I asked to have my money deposited." He gave her a disbelieving laugh. "Why would I draw attention to a crime if I had committed it?"

"A diversion, maybe? I don't know how criminals work." Her brow wrinkled. "The point is, I can't trust you, and I want to know." Her eyes beseeched him, radiant and devastatingly innocent. "Did you do it?"

Gideon took a breath that reached his very soul. How could he make her see the truth when she'd already peered into the worst side of him? It didn't matter what he said. She already saw him as an enemy of everything she stood for. "Of course I didn't do it. You can search my room. You can search my things—"

She held up a hand, quieting him. "I believe you if you say you didn't." Yet the doubt in her eyes told a different story. "I just don't want a part of whatever it is you're doing. I don't want to know about what happens in that saloon."

He stepped toward her. "It isn't as bad as you think. If you would only let me show you." But by her sunken shoulders and wary gaze, he knew she'd already shut that door.

"Faith." A male voice interrupted his thoughts. They both turned to see a portly man with a silver star affixed to his chest standing in front of the Wild Rose. Brimming with suspicion, his gaze swung from Faith's face to Gideon's, and down to his hand still clutching her arm. "I'm sorry I'm late. I meant to fetch you earlier, but I got stuck on a job."

Faith compelled her lips into a smile, but it didn't reach her eyes. "Deputy Wainwright, that's perfectly all right." She yanked her arm out of Gideon's hand. "I'm ready to go now, thank you."

Wainwright fixed his gaze on Gideon, taking him in from his proud shoulders to the suit he'd donned for playing cards with the affluent guests of Old Joe. Without ripping his glinting stare from Gideon, he paused. "Are you all right, Faith? You're not harmed?"

"No, I am quite unharmed and I'm ready to go." She slipped her arm through his and turned him away. "I've had quite the day, and I'm ready to be home again." Without bothering to cast another glance over her shoulder, she left Gideon in a ray of moonlight, watching her go.

Seven

EVEN AFTER A LONG day's work, Faith brushed and fed Starlight before stepping foot into Mrs. Baxter's kitchen. Her back roared in protest, the muscles in her legs cramped and stinging. It felt like the first day she'd learned to ride—all pain and stiffened muscles, with barely the will to lift her feet enough to trudge inside.

The kitchen of Mrs. Baxter's farmhouse glowed with the same radiant warmth as the woman herself. Presumably for Faith, she'd left a lit lantern suspended from a hook in the ceiling, shedding yellow light over the quaint furnishings.

A gleaming stove nested on one side of the room, beyond which stretched a wiped countertop with various porcelain canisters lining one wall. Her gaze drifted to the table, where a meal sat waiting for her—no doubt cold by now, but prepared by loving, motherly hands.

Faith shuffled across the kitchen floor and sank into an empty chair. She ran a weary hand over her face as her elbows plopped on the table. Just one day of work and she felt as if she'd carted the weight of the world on her shoulders. What lay in store for her tomorrow and the next day—a lifetime of working just to prove she didn't need her father's dirty money?

Gingerly she lifted the silver fork beside her plate and shoveled a glob of mashed potatoes into her mouth. They once, no doubt, would have melted on her tongue with the savory mingling of butter and herbs, but now they fell flat—more like dried porridge than potatoes. She held a crusty dinner roll up to the light, staring at it dismally and letting it fall to her plate like a hunk of rock.

"Oh, Faith, I thought I heard you come in."

The sudden breach in her thoughts made the fork slip through Faith's fingers, clanging against her plate. Mrs. Baxter appeared in the doorway, clad in a pink cotton nightgown and robe, her long white hair woven into a braid. "I'm sorry to have frightened you. I was worried something might have happened to you."

Faith pressed a hand over her galloping heart. "I'm terribly sorry, Mrs. Baxter. I didn't mean to worry you. I got a job in town and I had to work late."

"A job, you say?" She wandered into the kitchen in her stocking feet. "What type of job could keep you out until this late hour?"

Faith inwardly cringed to admit her new workplace to the proper old woman. "It's at the Wild Rose Saloon."

Mrs. Baxter's lips pursed playfully. "That is quite the place to find a job."

"I'm only serving tables and cleaning dishes." Faith simpered. "Nothing salacious, I promise."

"A pity." Abeline crossed to the stove and set a kettle on top. "A girl your age ought to have a little fun before she's strapped down with the responsibilities of life. I hope you at least enjoy it."

Faith shrugged. "As much as one can enjoy work, I suppose. It's all very new to me."

"I told you there's no need to find a job." Abeline ambled back to the table and eased herself into the chair opposite Faith. "I have plenty of money to support you until the right man comes along to sweep you off your feet."

The corner of Faith's mouth pulled up. *The right man.* Did such a thing exist? Even after her father had trounced upon her heart, left her open and bleeding, she'd nearly tricked herself into trusting another. Yet after witnessing his duplicitous nature, the truth blared so loudly, she couldn't ignore it. A man couldn't be trusted, no matter the lengths he traveled to appear different from the rest.

"I know you do, and I'm most greatly appreciative of you and your generosity, Mrs. Baxter." She folded her hands together on the table. "But I need to do this for myself. I need to know I can stand on my own two feet without my father's money. And besides"—she shook her head—"I'm not sure there's a man out there for me anyway. I might as well grow accustomed to the life of a maid."

A giggle burst from Mrs. Baxter's lips, dancing about the cheery kitchen. "Oh dear, don't resign yourself to a life of celibacy because of what your father did." Her eyes glimmered with mirth. "There's a world out there left for you to discover. Don't let him ruin it."

Faith took a drag of the cool air fluttering the lacy curtains, tinged in honeysuckle and cedar. "Perhaps you're right. There's a whole world out there I don't even know about." Yet reality dropped in her stomach like a metal weight. "I've learned of late that I am a trusting individual—one prone to believe what I want to about a person and ignore reality. I shared a roof with my father my entire life. I never had an inkling of who he truly was."

"You are afraid of it happening again—of being taken advantage of."

"Yes." The word barely squeezed from her throat. "I'm afraid I'll believe whatever I'm told again, and the man I thought was good and kind will prove something different in the end and break my heart."

Abeline pursed her lips thoughtfully a quiet moment. Behind her, the tea kettle rumbled with increasing force until a high-pitched whistle blasted from it and a pillar of steam shot into the air. Abeline pushed off the table and answered its call, removing the kettle from the stovetop and closing the dampers.

"You have a valid concern," she said as she picked up a tin on her counter. "You trusted somebody and they let you down. That takes time to heal." Stretching high, she reached into a cupboard and retrieved a porcelain teacup. "You must keep your eyes open and your mind aware, watching for things he won't tell you."

Tipping her kettle, she poured a generous helping of steaming water into her cup. "But I promise you there are good men out there who won't seek to deceive you. I am living proof of that. Colton and I were married for over forty years."

As Abeline spooned crushed tea leaves into her strainer, Faith retreated into silence. For all her sweet, well-meaning advice, she had no idea what kind of man she'd shared her life with. Faith had learned the truth from Cora that Colton Baxter had tried to steal all that gold for himself, and he would have killed Caleb if given the chance. Even a woman like this, smart with a solid head on her shoulders, had allowed a man to blind her. No, she couldn't become like her.

"Would you like some tea, dear?" Mrs. Baxter turned, giving her a craggy smile from within her cloud of ginger and chamomile. "It always helps ease my nerves."

"No, but thank you." Faith stood. "I should be getting to bed." She lifted her plate from the table.

"Please, dear, let me get that. You've had a long day."

Faith wanted to protest, but her aching shoulders agreed with Mrs. Baxter. "Thank you." She studied the woman gently mixing her brewing tea, a picture of serenity in the flickering light. "What about you, Mrs. Baxter? I'm sure it's far past your bedtime already. I'm sorry to have kept you up."

"Think nothing of it, child." She waved her off with a wrinkled hand. "My sleep is sporadic these days. The older I get, the less I can count on it. I would have been awake either way."

"Well, that's comforting to hear." Faith turned toward the door, anxious to climb the stairs beyond and fall into her bed. A noise halted her, and she leaned forward, waiting. It came again—a brash, thwacking sound barely lifting above the wind. "What is that banging? Do you hear it?"

Abeline paused, her spoon in midair, just as the thumping came again. "Ah, that." She shook her head, her spoon clinking against her saucer as she laid it down. "That's just the cellar doors. They sometimes clatter when the wind kicks up and make a terrible sound. I will have to secure them better when I find the time."

Faith ascended the stairs with the energy of a sloth and dressed for bed. The day's events kept running through her mind—finding a job at the Wild Rose, discovering the missing gold at the bank, her every interaction with the much-too-handsome and charming Gideon Valdez.

His dark eyes blazed in her memory, the way his ample lips crimped when he smiled. Why did he still occupy space in her mind after all she'd seen? She shook herself, casting off the memory like an unwanted scrap of trash.

With hair undone and garbed in a soft cotton nightgown from home, Faith stood at the window and gazed down at the corral situated by a shadowed barn. Under the white strands of moonlight, she could just make out Starlight's form, peacefully slumbering in the dirt. At least she had a safe and beautiful place to live where she could run as much as she wished.

Another series of bangs carried on the wind. Her gaze meandered to the cellar doors, not far from the corral fence. Faith's heart stopped. The banging came again—loud, insistent—but the cellar doors remained in place, untouched by the wind.

One taste of the food at Yvette's Kitchen was all Gideon needed to know he'd never eat that nauseating slop at the Wild Rose again. Sinking his teeth into a fine cut of well-done steak, he savored the blend of garlic and thyme bursting across his tongue. Scrambled eggs came next, buttery and fluffy, the perfect companion to the unmatched meat on his plate.

Groaning, Gideon wiped a linen napkin across his mouth and sat back. Would he even see any profit with this tempting restaurant only steps away from the saloon? He hated to imagine the bill he might rack up in this place.

Setting his fork aside, he lifted his cup to his lips and relished the scent of freshly roasted coffee before taking two sizable gulps. The nutty aroma satiated his every sense, warming him through. Gideon needed it after a night at the tables. He'd poured enough alcohol down his throat to fell a small elephant.

He never drank much on his own, but he found it important to match his competitors in every way—to put them at ease, if nothing else. This morning, he'd woken with a blaring headache and bags beneath his eyes.

Over the top of his coffee cup, he observed the street. People dashed to and fro, going about their morning routines. Farmers loaded crates from a wagon, carting them to the grocer. Children giggled, the sound floating behind them as they ran through the ruckus. Somewhere down the street, clanging had begun—perhaps the livery shooing horses.

Gideon smiled to himself. A hundred people with a hundred concerns, not one of them him.

His eyes clamped on a familiar figure as she bustled across the street and hurried down the boardwalk. Gideon self-consciously sat straighter, ironing the napkin on his lap. Trained hopelessly upon her, his eyes followed her rustling pink taffeta skirt and her form-fitting bodice until it disappeared down the way. A breath blew out his lips. Did she always need to look so beautiful? The rooster had barely risen.

Finishing off his coffee, he balled his napkin beside his plate and eyed the remnants of his food. Somehow the decadent display turned his stomach now that he'd spied her elegant frame skirting up the street. He cursed himself. Her words hit harder now that the alcohol had worn off and his mind cleared. *You're nothing but a pretender, Gideon. A worthless soul who came from nothing—and she knows it.*

Yet still he couldn't keep his legs from pushing him out of his chair, his hand from dropping his linen napkin over his half-eaten meal. *She'll be at the saloon all day, you fool. She works there.* Somehow, even his self-censures couldn't convince him to slow down as he dropped a few bills on the table and marched out the door.

The street had grown more crowded since he'd left the saloon for breakfast. Gideon elbowed through the crowd without heed for manners, sprinting down the boardwalk. His feet carried him to the Wild Rose within seconds, a ghost town compared to the jostling activity outside.

Nothing remained of the prostitutes who ate at sunup except a few discarded dishes and chairs out of place around tables. Just as Gideon pushed through the swinging doors, Faith emerged from the kitchen with a rag in one hand. She paused, her gaze descending him, before she snapped it away and strode regally toward the nearest table.

Gideon's breath caught as she bent over it and began scrubbing away the crusted food on the table's surface. Her hair, pinned high to the crown of her head, fell in wisps around her lovely face. Her plump lips pouted in concentration, a dewy pink to complement the maple hue of her eyes. Her skin shone in a band of sunlight, soft and golden-toned, begging for the touch of his hand.

Removing his hat, he held it at his waist as he advanced through the room, twisting a path between the tables to reach her. Faith didn't bother to look up when his boots slowed beside her. Instead, she set her jaw and worked harder, her tawny ringlets bouncing.

Gideon cleared his throat. "Faith." Somehow, the word felt improper on his tongue, yet he couldn't bring himself to say *Miss Carter*—not after the conversation they'd shared under the moon's rays. When she ignored him, he stepped forward. "About last night—"

She glanced up, artificial indifference in her eyes. "Nothing happened last night. I can remember nothing to speak of."

He licked his lips. "I do appreciate your silence in the matter, but the things we said—"

"I don't recall speaking with you at all, Mr. Valdez." Her sharp eyes invited no argument. "I took your drink order and that was all."

So this was how she wanted to play it—like that conversation never happened, like *he'd* never happened in her life. If only he could so easily cast *her* off.

"I think you've misjudged me. I'm not this miscreant you've imagined I am."

Faith continued wiping down the table without looking his way. "I assure you I haven't imagined a thing, Mr. Valdez. I hardly even know you."

"Blame it, woman." Gideon slammed his hat on the table, causing the wood to shudder beneath his hand.

Faith's gaze flew up. "I'm trying to do a job here, if you don't mind."

"And I'm trying to pour my heart out. It isn't easy."

A bit of color ripened in her cheeks. "You should have nothing to say to me where your heart is concerned, sir."

Her words planted an ache in his stomach. Why did they bother him so? She wanted nothing to do with him. He would pack up and leave in a couple weeks, never see her again. Yet he couldn't squelch the rush of panic in his chest at the thought.

"You know more of me than you let on. And I know more of you." Hadn't he glimpsed her vulnerability—the heart beneath her layers of concrete peering out as the moonlight played in her hair? Hadn't he felt connected to it by some inexplicable thread that reeled him to her now?

Her hands flattened over her skirts. "As I said, we hardly know each other."

"That well may be, but we know enough." His Adam's apple bobbed. "I know I'm not content with you pretending as if we've barely spoken, as if we don't already share secrets."

Her quiet stare searched his an agonizing moment before her lips set in a firm line. "I want to work without distractions."

Heat surged up his arms. "Fine." He seized his hat in one swift tug and jammed it on his head. "If that's the way you want it, that's what you get."

Her lilac scent trailed behind him even as he thundered away from her. Gideon cursed that woman with her alluring feminine presence, cursed her soft eyes and perfect skin. He had a job to do.

He stomped his way up the stairs and aimed himself toward his room. He'd taken only enough money to cover breakfast with him when he'd left this morning. Most of his winnings from the previous night would need safekeeping in the bank until he pulled it out again in preparation for tonight. He'd left hundreds of dollars stashed in a tin at the back of his dresser drawer. If enough people got wind of his earnings as the nights went on, some were bound to come sniffing around for a piece of it.

After thrusting his key in the lock, he banged into the room and let the door slam behind him. How had a woman gotten so far under his skin, he could barely control the raging pulse in his wrists? Gideon sank to the bed and combed both hands through his hair. He had to get out of this place sooner rather than later. Faith Carter would be the death of him.

Shaking off her memory, he stood and paced to the dresser. Better to get what he needed to over and done before the rest of his duties today. The sad layabouts with nothing else to do would trickle into the saloon soon. Gideon had a perfect opportunity to practice and spread word of his skill. Tonight he would unleash a little bit more, give those rich folks a taste of what he could do, but still not enough to make them run him out of town.

With a swift tug, he pulled the dresser drawer open and dug behind his shirts and trousers. His fingers closed around his tin box and yanked it out. A colorful label met his eye, the tin beneath once a storage container for his father's tobacco, now the vessel to carry his dreams. If only his father could see him now.

Gideon placed his thumbs beneath the lid and popped it open. His stomach somersaulted. "No." *No!* He glanced around at the floor in search of a fallen wad of bills, but nothing revealed itself. His gaze flung back to the tin, now just an empty silver tray glinting in the sunlight. He dove for the drawer, dug through mounds of clothes, heaping them on the floor.

When his drawer sat empty, he fell back on the floor with a thud. His breath rose in stolen gasps, pushing against his chest until he could barely breathe. All that money—gone. His head swam. It couldn't be true. He'd checked the tin just before he left for breakfast. Yet the open case splayed on the floor told a different story.

His gaze darted to the closed door before he clambered to his feet and crossed the room. Gideon fiddled with the handle, pushing the key in and turning it a few times with each pass. He couldn't blame a faulty lock for this occurrence. Somebody with a key had entered his room this morning and stolen his money. He gazed down the shadowed hallway, the wheels in his mind spinning. Everyone here was a suspect, even the beautiful Miss Faith Carter.

Eight

A SCATTERING OF PATRONS had come and gone by lunchtime—mainly a few habitual drunks, along with men with no jobs who couldn't keep their hands off the cards for more than an hour.

Faith's shoulders stung as she slumped onto a barstool and plunked down her plate. Thus far, she'd finished the morning dishes, wiped down the saloon, helped Molly with the guest rooms, and cleaned the privy out back. Every fiber of her soul had screamed out against scrubbing a toilet seat, yet Faith had clenched her teeth with determination and worked on. Forget her father and his money. She'd never go back.

Lifting the sandwich she'd made herself from what she could scrounge around the kitchen, Faith took a bite. The simple flavors of mustard and roast chicken on wheat bread might have under-whelmed her before. Today they made her taste buds dance, her shoulders easing with the realization that she'd earned it. The first meal she'd ever made on her own thrilled her every sense.

So full of life the evening before, the Wild Rose emanated the gloomy aura of a graveyard this time of day. Someone coughed in a far corner. An inebriated man fiddled with the piano keys. Rings of smoke rose from a single quiet game of poker, but one could almost forget this place existed during the day.

Footsteps creaked the stairwell before Old Joe entered her field of vision, sauntering down the stairs and wiping away his bleary vision. He adjusted his suspenders with a yawn and a stretch, his disheveled gray hair poking out in every direction. On sight of Faith, he yanked up his pants and settled them on his hips with a grin.

"Well, ain't it nice to see you're still here today. I feared we might have run you off last night—a gentle lady like yourself."

Faith finished her bite of sandwich and dabbed the corner of her mouth with a napkin. "I'm afraid it's going to take a lot more than a few drunken customers to scare me off."

"Glad to hear it." He lumbered up to the bar and leaned against it. "Molly says you earned your wages. As long as you work hard, I'll have a place for you. Although"—his gaze skittered over her face—"you could make a whole lot more money doing a different kind of job."

"A job I have no interest in." Faith's back straightened despite having no support from the barstool. "I'm perfectly happy cleaning up and waiting tables, thank you."

He scratched his balding head. "Well, suit yourself. The offer's always there if you change your mind. Pretty girls like you bring in lots of customers and lots of money all around."

"They'll have to settle for a smile and a gracious word from me."

"They should be paying me just for that." His mouth tilted in a wry grin. "A girl like you is one in a million. Your daddy's a darn fool."

The words cloaked her in an unexpected chill. Faith gripped the edge of her plate, watching her knuckles blanch. A fool he certainly was. So why did remnants of her heart still cling to him?

"Don't worry, young'un." Old Joe's voice brought her head up. "I won't mistreat you for what your pa did. He's lying in a bed of his own making. Didn't have nothing to do with you."

Her lips lifted sadly. "I thank you for that." She breathed out. "I know my father's a criminal. It came as a shock, but I've accepted it."

"Yeah, I always wondered."

Her brows gathered. "What do you mean?"

With a shake of his head, Old Joe tapped his fingertip on the bar. "He used to come in here, have secret meetings in the back. He and his associates would always come out looking like they'd hatched a plan to take over the whole world over a few whiskeys."

Faith's nerves tingled. How much did he know about her father's nefarious behavior? "Do you remember who any of those associates were?"

He thought a moment, stroking his chin. "Can't rightly say I do. I'm half drunk by that hour most of the time. I just figured they was probably up to no good, hiding in the back like they was."

"It was probably that scoundrel, Jeremiah Anderson. He certainly made deals with my father."

"No, it weren't him." Old Joe's lip pulled up in a disgusted expression. "I don't allow Andersons in my bar, especially that fool running the show."

"Doesn't that lose you business?"

"Hell if I care." Old Joe surveyed his saloon through slitted eyes. "This place might not look like much to the casual eye, but to me it's a sacred space. I don't need none of them dirty scoundrels darkening my doorstep. I don't need money that badly, especially after everything they've done in this town."

Faith gripped the cold glass she'd filled with water. "It sounds like you have a personal vendetta."

"If you want to call it that." Old Joe swiped his tongue over his teeth. "He's been a thorn in my brother's side many a year."

She frowned. "Your brother?"

"Ever heard of an outlaw named Red Fox?" When she nodded, he straightened up beside the bar. "He once was a little boy with fiery hair running around the countryside. My little brother." He sighed. "I couldn't stop him from going the wrong way, but I can at least turn away his enemies when they come calling."

Faith lifted her glass and took a drink, considering his words. She'd heard of the pair's long rivalry in passing. Jeremiah Anderson versus Red Fox, every person in town taking a side. News of the rivalry had erupted across the valley when the Red Fox Gang had surrounded Isaiah Anderson and gunned him down in the street.

She set her glass down on the bar, selecting her words carefully. "Is your brother—well, is he in these parts anymore? He seems awfully quiet."

He nodded slowly. "He has lain low ever since his son escaped the jail and certain execution." A mirthless laugh blew through his lips. "People like to think of my brother as nothing but a worthless outlaw, but he has a heart. He ain't like Anderson, stepping on whoever he can to get what he wants. The things he's done have destroyed my brother's life."

Faith angled her head. "You mean their rivalry as outlaws?"

"I mean kidnapping his woman, to begin with." At Faith's astonished look, he set his strong arms akimbo. "That's right. She was headed toward family in Billings and never showed up. Hasn't even sent word to her sons—something she would never do. Can't prove Anderson had a hand in it, of course, but who else would want to hurt my brother?"

His words still hung in the air as a familiar form swept through the swinging doors, dressed in a lovely silk gown. Cora brightened on sight of Faith, aiming straight for the bar. "I hoped I'd find you here."

Old Joe hooked his thumbs behind his suspenders. "Well, if it ain't the illustrious Miss Blackwell."

"Mrs. McCraw to you." She raised a playful eyebrow as she slid onto the stool next to Faith. "Don't forget I'm married to the law in this town."

"I ain't about to forget." He clicked his tongue with a shake of his head. "That scoundrel made off with a mighty fine prize the day he married you. I won't forget any time soon."

Cora's light laugh fluttered in the smoke-tinged room. "You look like you could use a stiff bracer, Joe—and quite possibly a bath."

"I reckon you're right." He sniffed an armpit. "Have to be in tip-top shape for the evening crowd. Excuse me, ladies." With a tip of his head, he disappeared through the doorway leading to the kitchen.

The smile hadn't left Cora's lips when she turned to Faith. "How is he treating you? With the utmost respect, I hope."

"Old Joe is a dear." Faith lifted the last portion of her sandwich. "He only floats the idea of me joining his girls about once a day now."

Cora flicked a wary gaze toward the smattering of prostitutes roaming about the saloon. "You hold strong. Nothing good can come from that life, I promise you."

"I know." Faith said nothing more, only tucked into her sandwich and finished it off in several bites. While a small part of her wondered at times if taking the job for a few years and stockpiling money wouldn't pay off, her good sense always won over. She'd witnessed the devastating consequences prostitution had wrought in Cora's life. She refused to become another cautionary tale.

With an empty plate before her, she sighed contentedly. "That's just what I needed after a morning on my feet. What have you been doing today?"

Cora straightened the lace sleeves of her high-collared gown. "Oh, not much. I taught a class this morning over at the old brothel. I showed the girls how to stitch a proper hem."

"Well, that's certainly not nothing. You're changing lives in that place, you know."

Cora looked at her, green eyes brimming with emotion. "I hope so. I hope what we're doing is making a difference." She plopped her elbows on the bar and leaned into it. "I still can't help staring longingly across the street when I'm there, just as I did when I worked there."

Faith covered her hand with gentle fingers. "Your dress boutique would be a smash across this entire region, I assure you."

Cora's mouth dimpled. "It's such a beautiful dream—to imagine the townspeople actually shopping there after knowing who I've been in my past life."

"It will happen." Faith squeezed her hand. "You were born to share your creations with the world."

"You're sweet." Cora gripped her hand and inhaled the clouded air. "Once I gather the courage, I'll have to find Sylvia in hopes of purchasing it from her. No one has seen the woman since last year."

"Yes, Old Joe was just telling me about that. He said Jeremiah Anderson took her."

"That well may be." Cora glanced furtively around. "Somebody had a hand in it. She was supposed to meet with family in Billings and she never arrived. Ellis has been investigating her disappearance, but so far he's come up empty."

Shivers crawled up Faith's spine. Enough crime had plagued this town for too long, from robberies to murders. Imagining yet another kidnapper on the loose made the hairs across her skin stand on end.

Cora caught her concerned expression and clamped a hand on her arm. "Not to worry. My husband's a mighty fine lawman. He'll get to the bottom of this, I'm sure of it."

Faith forced a nod, swallowing the lump in her throat. "What about the burglary at the bank? Has he found the money yet?"

Cora's lips compressed. "Not yet. Every lead has come up short thus far, I'm afraid."

Faith leaned inward. "What leads?"

Scooting closer, Cora threw one last look over her shoulder before angling in to whisper. "There were wagon tracks behind the bank that hadn't been there that morning. They led straight to Graves's mill."

"Adam Graves? The one who hired Caleb?"

Cora's head bobbed. "A witness said they saw a man with long hair loading something into a wagon bed, but when they searched the mill, there was nothing there."

Long hair? Flashes of her every encounter with Gold Strike's most hated outlaw flashed through her mind. "That could have just as easily been Jeremiah Anderson as Adam Graves. They both have long hair—the same color, too."

"I thought the very same thing. So did Ellis." Cora drummed her fingertips across the bar. "Graves was so obliging, too. He opened up the entire mill without question, let them search all his employees."

Faith chewed her lower lip. "Do you think Anderson created those tracks in order to frame someone at the mill?"

Cora's shoulders rose. "I wish I knew. Ellis took deputies out to search Anderson's ranch. He wasn't happy about it, but he complied. They found nothing suspicious out there. No gold. No newly disturbed dirt, either."

"But Anderson could have just as easily hidden his loot in the woods. Why would he take it home to be discovered?"

"Perhaps." Cora's brows worked, as if searching for an elusive answer. "Either way, they can't prove he did it—not without finding more clues."

"And Anderson is too smart to leave any evidence in plain sight."

"I'm afraid so. If he has the gold, he'll keep it well-hidden."

Faith's stomach turned to recall her conversation with Old Joe. "And Sylvia."

With a solemn expression, Cora nodded. "Her, too. There are only so many places he could hide her, but if I know my husband, he'll turn over every stone to find her, dead or alive."

Dead or alive. The expression launched a chill through Faith's frame. How many people had died for the unrelenting greed in this town, and how many more stood in the sniper's sights, just waiting to meet an early end because man wanted nothing but *more?* If only she had an ounce of power to stop it.

Movement caught the corner of Faith's eye. She turned to watch a muscular form descend the stairs, clad in a simple white cotton shirt and trousers, a hat fixed over his dark hair. The sight of him alone made her pulse quicken, before memories of the last few days sent it raging.

"The man from the bank. Who did he turn out to be?" Cora's question barely tickled her ear through her fog of unhindered thoughts.

Faith blinked, forcing her gaze to unlatch from him and settle on Cora. "Just a drifter who plays the tables. Nobody important."

"Your eyes say otherwise when you look at him." Laughter danced in Cora's expression, the low gaslight catching flecks of yellow beneath her lashes.

Straightening, Faith set her water glass on her plate. "My eyes should reveal nothing other than the truth—that I find him distasteful, and I'll be happy to watch him go when he finally leaves in a week or two. That's all."

"Mmmhmm." The seedlings of a grin couldn't escape Cora's lips as she looked from Faith to Gideon. "He hasn't a care for you either, I see."

Faith's gaze snapped to Gideon to find him frozen on the last step, his stare fastened upon her. Fire shot from his eyes—not the licentious spark of other scoundrels who frequented the bar, but an inferno so intense, she wondered what kindled beneath it. Did he hate her so easily for refusing to speak with him today, or did he see what her father did—nothing but a spoiled girl, too useless and unintelligent to stand on her own two feet?

Remembering the friend watching them in amused silence, Faith snatched her plate off the bar and stood. "Whatever you think you know, you don't. Now, I have work to do."

Without a glance back at Cora, nor the man still gaping from the foot of the stairs, Faith marched toward the kitchen with her head high and the last of her dignity firmly in her clenched hands.

Nine

GIDEON'S LEGS BOUNCED BENEATH the table. The cards in his hand seemed to blur into one—a jumble of black and red symbols with no meaning. He leaned back in his chair, coaxing his eyes to focus. He'd played a game like this a thousand times before. Why did he suddenly feel like a helpless child who didn't know how to swim, floundering in the depths of an ocean?

Seizing his drink, he threw back the remainder of whiskey in his short glass and set it back on the table. The liquor burned down his gullet, forging a path to his stomach, but providing his unsettled nerves no relief. He glanced up, every eye at the table expectantly fixed upon him. He had to make a decision—throw in another hundred dollars, or bow out? Did he actually have a choice at this point? He could barely see the cards in his grasp.

"I fold." He slapped his cards across the table, face down. The action elicited a raise of the brows here, a relaxing of the shoulders there. His gut twisted. He could have these fools if he could only get his head in the game.

Lifting his glass, Gideon held it over his head and waited for the pretty brunette in the busty bodice to refill his drink. She complied with a grin and a wink, letting her skirt brush Gideon's arm a little too closely. Her hips gave a dramatic sashay as she moved to the next table, no doubt for his benefit. Gideon gripped the glass, his fingers coating with spilled liquor. The scent of it would overwhelm him if he didn't need the distraction.

As they had at least twenty times tonight, his eyes strayed around the saloon, snagging on a particular figure moving through the crowd. Gideon didn't need to see through the acrid clouds of smoke that her blonde hair fell in beautiful, plump ringlets down her back, nor that her skin blazed in the gaslight, nor that her gown hugged her curves in an agonizingly perfect way. He didn't need to see her smile to feel it kindling inside him, stoking a heat that rushed through him. She had no obligation to keep her gaze decisively out of his path all night to show him he didn't deserve her—that she'd always be above him, and he'd never feel those plump lips against his.

Stubborn, pig-headed woman. She had decided who he truly was the minute she saw that extra card in his sleeve. She had dismissed him, accused him, purposely avoided his table all night. If only she weren't right about the man lurking within him, too jaded to care about morals.

"Take that and weep, boys," the pompous man in expensive tweed announced, tossing a fistful of cards on the table.

A chorus of groans rose around it. *Two pair, aces high.* At least Gideon had possessed the good sense to duck out before he lost more money. The little he had tucked into his pocket sneered at him. He had no room for error with his funds quickly diminishing.

"I expected more out of you, boy." The old man to Gideon's left clapped him on the back. "You played like a true champion last night once you got going. Where have you been this evening?"

Gideon shook himself, sitting taller. "Just biding my time." A half-grin slipped over his lips. "Just wait until I truly impress you."

Good-natured laughter rippled over them. With a quick swig of his drink, Gideon steeled himself for what came next. If he didn't want to be bankrupt by the end of the night, he would have to focus. No more eyes darting about, looking for potential suspects of his money theft. No more stewing about a woman who harbored so little care for him she had refused to meet his gaze all night.

"Gentlemen, if you don't mind"—the lout who had accosted Faith the night before pushed back from the table—"I need to stretch my legs."

"Here, here. I could use a break too." The older gentleman pushed up on his knuckles, then pointed one wagging finger at Gideon. "Don't try to sneak away, now. I have you right where I want you."

Despite his churning stomach, Gideon forced a laugh. "You *think* you have me at your mercy, but I still have a few tricks up my sleeve." If only he knew how many.

Remaining in his chair, Gideon watched the group scatter like a flock of birds on a wire. That's what they were, wasn't it? Vultures hunting for prey. His gaze flicked back to Faith. She was more akin to a sparrow—delicate, elegant, the kind of creature one handles with care. Not the type of woman who should ever get mixed up with the likes of him.

She stood now by the bar loading full glasses onto a tray. She swiped at a stray hair falling across her forehead, her every movement lithe and fluid. He'd heard whispers about her father, the scandalous cad who had cheated the entire town and cavorted with outlaws. They said this job was her just deserts after his multitude of sins, but he saw no sin in her—only the fearful heart of a woman wronged by a man she'd trusted.

She had just set the last of her drinks on the tray and bent to pick it up when a figure approached. Gideon bristled. He watched with increasing dread as his partner at the table wedged himself between her and the tray, forcing it back to the bar with one solid hand.

Faith stiffened like iron in the forge, stepping away from the man. With a look of amusement, he only came closer, speaking hushed words to her that flared color over her cheeks. Faith shook her head and tried to move away, but he caught her by the arm.

Pulse pounding, Gideon glanced down the bar at the bartender pouring drinks with his back turned to them. He swiveled around, scanning the saloon. Where was Old Joe—anybody who worked here who could help her? But her plight was hopelessly lost within a sea of drunken laughter, of hoots and hollers and careless revelry.

Faith tried to wrench away from the man, but his fingers held her arm fast, his body closing the gap between them. He whispered something in her ear, inciting a vehement wag of her head. She shivered, tears blossoming in her eyes and tunneling down her cheeks. Gideon sat forward with his splayed hands braced on the table. He could only take so much of this.

Then, with the force of a lion dragging away a helpless gazelle, the man yanked her out of the bar and into the night.

Faith trembled, her skin like fire where the man touched her. He pulled on her arm with such strength, she thought it might break off. They stumbled over the threshold and across the Wild Rose's porch, bypassing the sheen of lamplight for the darkened alley between the buildings.

The night air seared her lungs. Faith gasped it in, desperately trying to breathe between her whimpering cries, but her throat stung with every effort. Hot tears squeezed from her eyes, bathing her skin in moisture.

A moment ago, she'd been about her work, taking the latest drink order to the barman and waiting to deliver it. Then, like a wave that washes ashore without a single wind to predicate it, he'd grabbed her, whispered filth in her ear.

"Come on upstairs with me, honey. You'll change your mind once you've had a taste of me, I promise."

"No." She'd tried to pull away. "I told you I'm not a prostitute."

"It doesn't take a prostitute to enjoy a man like me."

"I said no."

He'd thrown himself over her, dug his fingers into her arm so roughly, her skin burned. "I'm trying to be nice and give you some money for it." His hot breath curled in her ear. "If you'd rather, I can take it for free out in the alley."

Faith's eyes had torn open, sore and brimming with tears. "You wouldn't. There are plenty of women here available for purchase."

A wicked sneer slid over his lips as his gaze dove to her pitching bosom. "I want *you*. If people don't give me what I want, I take it."

Now sweat sprang across Faith's skin as he tugged her out of view from the street and shoved her against the outer wall of the saloon. Her vision swirled, lantern light blurring into prismatic rays. She cried out—a frantic, choked sob. If only she could get the attention of those passing by on the street, but his hand clamped over her mouth, plastering her head to the wall. Faith tried to peel her lips back and sink her teeth into his flesh, but he pushed so hard against her, she couldn't move.

Fear tensed around her in throbbing bands as his other hand descended her bodice and began hunting her skirts. Faith kicked and writhed, sickening reality dawning. He was going to rape her. He was going to steal the last thing of value she had to her name. Her only hope for a respectable husband. He was going to strip her of any shred of dignity and leave her bare, forced to grapple with reality and blame herself for what he'd done.

The smell of bourbon and expensive cologne clouded her senses. His body flattened against hers, keeping her pinned to the wall while he struggled with her intricate gown. His malicious laugh skittered over her skin, ringing in her ears and drowning out the prayers for rescue she threw heavenward.

"This could have been so easy." His words pricked needles over her skin. "You could have *enjoyed* yourself and earned a little money to boot."

Enjoy his hands on her, his lecherous breath on her neck, his nausea-inducing advances? Never. Fire raged in her belly, the urge to fight back sparking down her limbs. Yet the harder she struggled, the stronger he held her, his hands and body an unyielding vice she'd never escape.

Faith gave in to racking sobs in the knowledge that part of her would be lost forever. She had no way to retain it, no say in the matter.

A violent force yanked at her. Faith shut her eyes to block out the inevitable, but with the movement, the weight upon her fled. The hands holding her against the saloon wall slackened. She could breathe again, her chest filling with fresh nocturnal air, reaching into her darkest places. A grunt of surprise filled her ears before her eyelids fluttered open.

In the vague light from the street, she deciphered two figures grappling with one another. A shadowed silhouette had her attacker by the collar, hauling him away from her. The scoundrel who'd pulled her into the alley fought with spirited might, his body writhing and arms thrashing. Her rescuer dodged the swinging limbs, flinging his body back like a ragdoll and tossing him on the ground.

Her attacker swore, lifting a hand to his scraped brow. Already the other man was upon him, straddling his body. His punches landed with deafening cracks that blasted through the still night. The man on the ground threw his hands up, aimed at the other man's throat, but his pursuer moved faster. Instead of succumbing to his blows, he ducked his head and rammed a solid punch to his gut that sent her attacker screaming in agony.

He lay back, clutching his ailing middle. "You won't—" He gasped, each rasping breath laced with pain. "You won't get away with this."

The man atop him leaned down, one hand on his throat. "I just did." Lifting the attacker's head, he bashed it against the ground with a single, powerful thrust. The man's head rolled back, his eyes closing and body limp.

Faith stood frozen in place for several seconds, her heart thrumming across her body. The man who'd come to her aid slowly stood, wiping an arm over his face.

"It's all right. You can come out from there now." That voice, so deep and familiar, lured her from the darkened alley.

Details of his face materialized as she moved into the light. Dirt smeared his face, sweat slicking his dark hair, but the same Gideon Valdez stared back at her, cold solemnity in his eyes. Her gaze faltered to the man lying unconscious on the ground, blood pooling from his nose and staining his fine shirt.

"You—" She swallowed. "You—"

"I had to." His tone, sure as the faithful sun, brought her eyes back to him. "He was going to hurt you. I couldn't let that happen."

A shiver coursed over her, and Faith hugged herself. Indeed, a minute longer and he could have—She shut her eyes. She couldn't bear to think of it.

"Are you all right?" His eyes swiftly scanned her trembling body. "He didn't hurt you?"

"No." Faith fought the chatter of her teeth. "At least not physically." Yet everything inside her screamed for a comfort so painfully far out of reach.

Gideon took a step toward her, his hand extended. "What can I do for you? What do you need?"

She pulled herself up, straightening her skirts and sniffing back her emotion. "Nothing. I'm fine. It'll just take a moment for me to collect myself."

"Collect yourself?" His gaze dipped down to the unconscious man and back to her. "Faith, you were just attacked. You can't just pick up and move on, act as if nothing happened. I'll get the sheriff—"

"No!" Panic raged through her to imagine Cora and Ellis finding out about this. "Just leave it be."

"Leave it be?" His dark eyes searched hers. "How can I leave it be? He should be punished."

"I don't want to make a big fuss about this. If people find out, they might—"

Understanding overwhelmed his features. "They might blame you."

"Exactly. Who would believe the daughter of the worst criminal in the region over somebody important like him?"

Gideon glanced at him in question.

"He's the son of a railroad man. His father controls the lines from here to Denver." Her lip pulled up as a quiet moan escaped the beaten man's lips. "He pretends not to know me from before, but he does. He's just as lewd and self-serving as he was in that life, only here he knows I don't have my father to protect me."

Gideon's head angled, his fists clenching at his sides. "You should have someone to protect you. You need someone."

"I'm perfectly fine on my own." Her hands plastered across her stomach, where echoes of her thundering heartbeat still pumped through her. "I will adapt. The only thing that trusting anyone else has ever gotten me is trouble."

He blew out a breath, his eyes mournful. "If that's how you wish to see the world. At least let me help you get home."

Faith shook her head, dashing away the last of her tears. "I haven't finished my shift. I've been gone long enough already." What if Old Joe fired her after he found out what happened? Where would she go then?

"You aren't stepping foot back in that bar. Not tonight." His assertion brought her eyes to his. "You're in no shape to work. I don't care how determined you are."

Her breath thickened. "But Old Joe—"

"He'll understand. I'll explain it to him." He held out his arm to her. "I'll take you home."

Her gaze slowly ascended his offered arm to his face. "But your poker game. I know it's important to you. You can't just leave in the middle."

"I can do as I please, and right now I wish to walk you home." His jaw set—determined, rigid. He would thwart her every effort to resist him.

At last, Faith nodded and slipped her arm through his, marveling at the instant warmth and reassurance that cascaded over her. "As long as you tell Molly I shall be back first thing in the morning."

Ten

THE LIGHTS AND MUSIC of Gold Strike faded as the pair traversed a quiet trail bordered in prairie grass. Out here, free of the town's noise and excitement, one could hear their every breath, feel their heartbeat keeping time to the cricket's chirp. Out here, one could nearly forget the cruelty humanity inflicted on one another—but he could no longer forget when he looked at her.

Gideon allowed himself a brief perusal of her profile as they walked together out of town and into the vast night. The darkness hid most of her features, but a strand of glowing moonlight illuminated enough to take his breath away. It traced the lines of her proud cheekbones, her straight nose, the lips that had tempted him since that very first day in the saloon. She was dignity and grace and beauty. She was perfection—a kind spirit and loving soul who'd succumbed to the horrors of a monster. Gideon swore he could pummel her father when he imagined how he'd hurt her.

She must have felt his eyes on her, but she kept hers straight ahead, leading them up a barren road toward the fragrant forest.

The wind picked up, tossing the branches about and filling the air with the invigorating scent of spruce. Owls called against the black night, hooting at one another until their sounds faded beneath the yelp of coyotes. This far from town, Gideon could almost imagine himself back in the wilds of his childhood—back in his mother's arms, where a peace he'd taken for granted had mantled his very existence.

"It's quiet out here." Just lifting his voice to say it ruptured the sacred stillness.

"I like it." Faith's eyes scanned the dense forest. "It reminds me of home."

"You didn't grow up in Gold Strike?"

Her head shook softly. "We always lived in Missoula. Not far from here, but a different kind of place. We had a ranch in the countryside, a beautiful home and pastures for miles."

The kind of place he could only imagine in dreams. "Do you miss it?"

"Very much." Her voice quieted, fading beneath the crunch of their shoes on the gravel-strewn pathway. "Sometimes I wish I were back there without a worry or care. Then I remember it was nothing but a lie, and the thought of it sickens me."

His arm tensed around hers. "It wasn't all a lie. You still had a childhood, an upbringing with much to be proud of, I'm sure."

A breath pressed from her, curling into the chilly air. "Perhaps. But it's all tainted now. It will never look the same to me as it once did."

The words stabbed at something deep in his gut. He might never have endured a criminal for a father or the wealth that came with it, but he understood the sentiment far too well. Just allowing a single vision of childhood to pass before his eyes was suffocating.

"You were brave to stay here." At her questioning glance, he shrugged. "A lesser person might have run when life got difficult, perhaps reinvented themselves." He should know. How long after the fires had died in the Rio Grande had he cut bait and vanished?

"I don't know that I really had a choice in the matter." Her voice quivered faintly. "I don't have any skills or experience with the world. The one friend I have is here."

"I'm sure you would make do just fine. A woman like you could walk into any city in the country and become whomever she wanted."

Her laugh eased the tension from the brutality of her attack. "Good manners and a proper education don't account for everything." Her hair brushed his arm with her wagging head. "I could barely find a menial position here because I begged. Imagine being in a place like Chicago or New York, lost in a sea of people all trying to realize their own ambitions. I'd be nothing to them, just as I am nothing here."

Gideon's heart swelled at her final, defeated words. "You only feel like that now because of what your father did. If people didn't know that, they would see you differently, I guarantee it."

Faith let the rhythm of their shoes fill the silence for a prolonged moment. "Is that what you're doing here? Reinventing yourself?"

Gideon met her gaze, the luminous eyes turned up to his in wonder. An unfamiliar sensation flickered over him—a temptation to tell her the tale that had led him to this point. His better sense crushed it. A good woman like her didn't need to burden herself with the woes of a friendless vagabond like him.

Detaching his gaze, he returned it to the shadowed road ahead. "There's not much to reinvent, I'm afraid. I'm a simple man."

"Simple. I doubt that." She paused, as if carefully selecting her words. "Where are you from, if you don't mind my asking?"

"Texas."

"Texas?"

"Yes, is that such a surprise?" He grinned despite the tug on his heart just to utter the word. "Do you have some preconceived notion about Texans that I should be aware of?"

She returned his smile, no small feat after her harrowing experience. "No. It's just far away, is all. It feels like the other side of the world."

"Two thousand miles. Not exactly the world, but it might as well be." The low thorny hills and river-bottom groves of home should have faded in his years of absence, yet they flared across his mind's eye as if he were still that little boy running across the wide-open plains, his sides aching with laughter.

"What brought you all the way from Texas?"

The innocent, inevitable question nearly stopped him dead. Gideon forced his feet to tread onward through a stretch where the forest thickened, nearly concealing the moon. He pulled her closer to avoid the tangled shrubs, inhaling the raw earth. How could he explain without tearing his heart open anew?

"The weather, mainly." He said it matter-of-factly, but he couldn't keep the edge of amusement out of his voice.

"You just had to go where it freezes over for months on end, where everyone is trapped inside their homes shivering from November to March?"

The corner of his mouth quirked. "Maybe I just like snow."

"Maybe you don't want to tell me why you came here."

He breathed out, the feeling cathartic, and watched it cloud in front of him. "Is it so bad to have a few secrets? A man needs them nowadays to survive in this world."

Faith was quiet for several seconds, the wind in the trees and the distant hooting owl speaking for her. When her voice emerged, it held a strained quality. "In my experience, men with secrets are dangerous. I don't like secrets anymore."

His fingers gently pressed through her sleeve, prompting her gaze to climb back to his. "It isn't that kind of secret." The hidden truth living within him belonged to the heart of a child, torn apart at the seams and forced to mature too quickly. It couldn't destroy anyone's life but his own.

Faith stilled, her eyes hunting his, the depths of her uncovered for the briefest of moments. Her lips parted, her hands clinging to his arm in a familiar rather than polite manner. As the wind picked up again and whipped strands of her golden hair around her face, she cast her gaze to the road.

"We're nearly there." She cleared her throat. "It's just over that ridge. I can manage from here."

"Nonsense." Gideon lifted her hand, relishing the soft sweep of her skin against his thumb, before setting it back on his arm. "I'll walk you the rest of the way. It's the least I can do after—"

She nodded, fear springing back to her eyes. How careless of him to bring it up again, as if she needed a reminder that without her father's protection, a man could steal from her body as he saw fit, and likely never face the consequences.

The pair strode the rest of the way in silence, the high moon casting glittering rays over the rutted dirt leading to a quaint farmhouse. Gideon paused in the drive, his appreciative gaze meandering over the charming home with gabled roofs and flower boxes in the windows.

"I don't know what your home looked like before, but this certainly isn't a bad place to rest one's head."

Faith took it in with a sigh. "No, it's lovely, and I'm grateful to Mrs. Baxter for her generosity, but"—her frame sank beneath her fine gown, now dirtied and ripped by that monster—"it isn't truly my home. Abeline may feel like a grandmother, but she isn't mine, and I can't live off her kind heart forever. This is only a resting place along the way."

He nodded, understanding. How many spots along his journey had become mere resting places? The concept of home felt elusive as snow in summer. "You'll find a place to belong, I have no doubt." A woman like her deserved a home.

She turned to him, as if preparing to say goodnight, and halted abruptly. A wrinkle creased her brow. "You have a scratch on your forehead."

"What?" Gideon let her go to tentatively touch his brow. He pulled back with a hiss at the sharp sting.

"You have wounds on your hands, too." Faith placed them in hers, examining them in the moonlight. "Look, there's dried blood all over."

Gideon retracted them, immediately regretting it when her warmth dissipated. "Nothing but a few simple cuts and scrapes. I'll fix them up when I get back to the saloon."

"I don't feel right about you fighting for me and then leaving you like this." Faith glanced back at the house. "If you come inside, I can see that they're properly cared for and dressed. I know Mrs. Baxter has ointments and bandages."

He stared up at the house again, a glowing beacon with warm light streaming from the windows amid a dark and unforgiving forest. Would this Mrs. Baxter accept him so easily—an unfamiliar man coming home with the unmarried, beautiful girl in her charge? The last thing he wanted was to compromise her standing in a household providing her shelter when no one else would.

Yet swinging his gaze back to her—those shining, sincere eyes, the innocent face that captured him more each passing moment, he found himself weak in the presence of her pull on his heart. Before he could even comprehend his own thoughts, he found himself nodding. "All right then, Miss Carter. Lead the way."

Faith felt as if walking through a dense fog as she climbed the steps to the farmhouse she called home and opened the front door. Holding it wide, she waited for Gideon to cross the threshold before shutting it behind him and pausing in the sitting room.

Her hands slicked on her skirts as she cast a look down the hall. Several lamps still blazed around the house. Abeline couldn't have gone to bed yet, but no sign of her surfaced throughout the quiet home. Perhaps she was reading in the library or making dough for morning. Best to find her before raising unnecessary scandal within her walls.

"Have a seat, will you?" She gestured to the set of plush green armchairs and matching settee with lace doilies adorning the back. "I'll just be a moment. I'd like to grab a few supplies and let Abeline know I'm home." *Gather my wits about me after nearly being raped and bringing a man home in the aftermath.*

As Gideon complied, Faith scampered off to find the old woman who would no doubt welcome Gideon's presence in her home. So why did her stomach constrict at the thought of telling her? Why did her heart sit high in her throat at the idea of him seated in the parlor waiting for her?

The kitchen rested in empty solitude when Faith charged through the door. *Odd,* she thought before moving back through the hallway. Abeline must have been in the middle of preparing something, for she'd left an open jar of leftover soup and bread-crumbs scattered across her kitchen counter. She never left messes like that behind, even for a short period of time.

The library and sunroom in the back produced similar re-sults—no Abeline and no sign of her, either. Lifting her skirts, Faith charged up the stairs toward the only spot left in the house to search. Every bedroom upstairs sat neatly as she always left them. No lamp burned on her bedside stand, so she hadn't yet climbed the stairs to prepare for bed. Faith set her hands on her hips. Where could the woman have gone? Certainly not to tend the farm at an hour like this.

Gathering a basket of supplies from the closet outside Abeline's bedroom, Faith hurried back down the stairs and into the parlor. Abeline had memories everywhere—trinkets on the shelves, pho-tographs on the walls. Gideon stood next to a black frame beside a bookcase, studying a photograph behind the glass.

As she burst into the room, he glanced at her sideways. "This is a lovely picture. Do you know who this is?"

Joining him, she gazed up at the image of a young boy in suspenders and short pants seated in a chair with an elegant woman standing behind him. The photograph was discolored at the edges and marred by water stains.

"The woman is Mrs. Baxter—from years ago, of course." Her eyes fell back on the lively-looking boy. "That must be her son."

He leaned closer. "I wonder how old this is."

"Thirty years, I'd say, at the least." She turned away and plopped down on the settee. "Now, come sit down so I can fix those hands." She patted the cushion next to her while she set her basket and bowl on the table.

He hesitated. "Isn't Mrs. Baxter joining us?"

Faith reached for the clean hand towel she'd brought in, avoiding his probing eyes. "No, I don't know where she is." She self-consciously rubbed the back of her neck. "It's just the two of us."

Silence pervaded the room a hair-raising minute before he finally sauntered across the hardwood floor and eased onto the settee beside her. "Are you comfortable with that? Just the two of us?"

Faith shot him an irritated glance. "Why shouldn't I be comfortable?" If he planned on hurting her, he'd enjoyed ample opportunity already.

A dimple surfaced beside his mouth, a disturbingly attractive feature. "This isn't exactly the type of situation a girl like you ever finds herself in. Didn't you always have a chaperone when you hosted male callers?"

"Stop making it sound so lewd." Faith shook out the towel in her hand. "I'm simply providing a service for a man who is injured. It isn't like you came here with the intention of courting me. Now wash your hands in that bowl there." She tipped her head toward the bowl she'd left beside her basket.

Gideon set his fingers in the water, sloshing them around. "Would your father have let you court someone like me—a wanderer who gambles for a living?"

"Of course not." She handed him a bar of soap. "He wanted me to court rich men, businessmen like him."

"Criminals?" His brow hooked playfully.

She gave him a pointed stare. "Be careful. He is still my father."

"I'm sorry." Gideon took the soap from her. "I meant it in jest, but I know it isn't funny." Rubbing the bar between his soiled hands, he worked until the once-clean water in her basin darkened with red and brown.

"The truth is, I never courted much of anybody—only those my father hand-selected, and I believe now those pairings were deliberate business prospects." How sharply her pride stung to admit it.

He studied her carefully. "In all your years of growing up in a world like that, nobody struck your fancy?"

Faith fought the heat inevitably creeping into her face. "Not really. Between my tutoring and horseback riding lessons, I didn't have much time to think about boys."

"But they thought about you, no doubt."

Faith's gaze bounced up from the towel in her hands, latching with his, then skittering away again. "I suppose I never considered it too much. Here, dry your hands with this." She handed him the towel without meeting his eyes again.

Gideon took it, his fingertips brushing her hand. "Nobody ever tried to court you, apart from your father's business prospects, of course?"

"A few." She twisted her idle hands in her lap. "The gentleman whose face had a rather unfortunate meeting with your fist tonight comes to mind."

He nearly choked. "That imbecile tried to court you?"

Faith nodded. "I don't even remember his name. I suppose it was the perfect revenge for him. I refused him, and he got to watch me fall. Then he tried to take what he thought was already his."

"He showed you once and for all how unworthy he is." Gideon bunched the towel in one hand. "He only reaffirmed your decision."

"I suppose that's true." Exhaling, Faith reached out. "Here, give me your hand."

Tingles peppered her skin as he laid his sizable palm on top of hers. He had swarthy, beautiful skin—not marred by deep calluses like working men, but not delicate either. Open wounds checkered his fingers, gashed and caked in blood along his knuckles—skin that had ruptured in defense of her honor. To protect her. The urge to slip her fingers between his and cling to his hand nearly overwhelmed her.

Briefly letting him go, she turned to Abeline's basket and retrieved a jar of ointment. After opening it, she dipped her fingers inside and covered the tips in a buttery salve. The scents of marigold and yarrow filled the room as she gingerly smeared it across each of his cuts. Gideon made not a sound, his eyes fixed upon her, his strong hands unmoving. She worked on until every inch of broken skin was covered in it.

"Does that feel all right?"

He nodded. "It feels just fine. Much better, in fact."

"Good." Her gaze briefly flitted up to his, butterflies winging inside at the dark, solemn eyes staring into her. "They should heal in a few days if you keep them clean. At least that was my experience volunteering at the local clinic." She reached for her roll of bandages and cut a long strip.

Gideon's warm hand rested over hers again as she gingerly wound the bandage over his veiny hand, the steady pulse in his wrist that made her breath hitch. Her mind grappled for something, *anything* to say to break the silent tension between them.

"I don't know what you'll tell your partners at the poker table when they see these wounds."

Gideon's lips compressed. "I doubt I'll have much more welcome at that table when they see what I did to their friend."

She glanced up at him. "But don't you need to play poker with the big spenders? This is your living, isn't it?"

Silence met her question for several seconds before his large shoulders lifted. "I'll have to find a new town. This isn't the gold mine I'd hoped for."

"Because I ruined it." Just as she'd ruined her father's life by choosing to save Cora and expose him. Just as she'd likely ruin anything she touched.

"Of course this isn't your fault. What blame can I possibly lay on a woman for being attacked?"

Faith didn't answer, merely stretched the last of the bandage and knotted it over his palm. Without warning, two enormous hands gripped her shoulders. She looked up into Gideon's sincere expression, his eyes searching hers.

"Don't you dare place blame on yourself for one moment. He chose to attack you, and I chose to defend you. You had no say in the matter—nothing to do with his decision or mine. Do you understand?"

Faith swallowed back the nauseating burn climbing her throat. "I understand. I just hate to be the source of you losing money. It isn't fair."

"I'll be just fine." He brushed a thumb over her arm before he let her go. "I needed to find a new town anyway. I'm losing more money than I'm making here."

Her brow wrinkled. "What do you mean?"

Gideon sighed. "I suppose I have no room to claim higher moral ground. You already know I'm a cheat." Shame smoldered in his somber eyes. "Somebody is stealing money out of my room. It's happened twice now—once before I suspected it, and again when I left some as a test."

Faith gasped. "Who would do such a thing? Did you lock your room?"

"Of course I did, but it doesn't seem to be stopping whoever is doing it." He absently fingered the bandage she'd wrapped around his hand. "It must be someone with access to my room. Somebody who works there."

"I can't imagine who." Faith's mind reeled. She knew little of the girls and not much more of Old Joe. None of them struck her as a thief, but then again, neither had the man she'd lived with and trusted for eighteen years of life. "How much have they taken from you?"

"Two hundred so far. I can't keep going much longer at this rate. I'll have nothing to my name."

Faith thought as she gathered her supplies and plopped them back into Abeline's basket. "Perhaps I can help you. We can find out who took your money and try to get it back." When he said nothing, she angled her head. "It's the least I can do after how you fought for me tonight. I owe you so very much."

"You owe me nothing." Reaching out, he slipped her hand into his, engulfing it in warmth and strength. "You are a beautiful person, within and without. You deserve so much more than what you've been given."

Faith managed the slightest of smiles despite her galloping heart at his touch. "So you'll let me help you?"

A light bit of mirth touched his lips. "If you see fit."

"I do." Her fingers relaxed within his. "I would like to be of help to you."

One of his thick brows hooked. "I thought I was nothing but a cheat."

"My feelings are conflicting. I have more than one about you." Faith latched her mouth closed before she could say more and utterly humiliate herself.

His hand hadn't left hers, its gentle throb pulsing through her. Gideon's intense gaze wandered from her eyes, past her nose, to her lips—lips that had never tingled as much as they did when his eyes rested upon them. If that miscreant in the bar could have produced half this reaction within her, she never would have refused him in the first place.

The front door clattered open, ripping their stares and hands apart. Abeline appeared at the threshold, red-cheeked and out of breath, her skirts dusted with soil.

"Mrs. Baxter!" Faith popped up from her seat and covered the distance between them. "Are you all right? You look like you've been out tramping through the woods."

Despite her disheveled appearance, Abeline chortled. "I'm quite fine, my dear. I was only seeing to the horses."

"Seeing to the horses?" Faith helped her brush off her frilly skirt. "It must be ten o'clock."

"The time does get away from me." She wiped her wrist across her brow with a contented sigh. "It matters little what time it is when there's work left to be done."

Work left to be done. The poor woman had trouble walking into town by herself, let alone working at this ungodly hour. "The next time you have chores to complete, please tell me and I will gladly do them."

Abeline waved her off with a laugh. "You have enough of your own troubles to handle, my dear. You needn't worry about me." She squinted at the cuckoo clock on the wall. "You're home earlier than I expected."

"Yes, well—" Faith's gaze darted nervously to Gideon, who'd risen from the sofa behind her. "I left early due to unforeseen circumstances. I do hope you don't mind that I brought a friend in. He had an injury that I wished to tend to."

"Not at all. My home is yours." The old woman beamed up at Gideon. "My, you're a strapping lad. Would you care for a cup of tea?" She laughed again. "Once I get myself cleaned up, of course."

"No, ma'am, but thank you. I was just on my way out." He flashed a meaningful look at Faith before moving past her toward the door Abeline had just appeared through. He tipped his head to them both. "Ladies, I hope you have a pleasant evening."

Faith watched him go, a whirlwind of emotions plaguing her. He would soon be gone, off to a different town to earn his money, as she faced the lion's den that Gold Strike could be on her own. Thieves lurked at the Wild Rose Saloon. Burglars haunted the bank. Outlaws roamed the streets.

She glanced at Abeline, who happily draped her knit shawl over the coat stand. Even she showed signs of her aging mind—leaving items haphazardly around the kitchen, waiting until the dead of night to feed the horses. Faith's stomach turned. How long until her luck ran out and she was truly alone to face a cruel and terrifying world?

Eleven

Gold Strike's lone mercantile buzzed with chatter in the midmorning hours. Women went about their shopping, collecting food items for their pantries and eyeing the neatly stacked silks and plaids on the store's far shelf. Gideon stuck to the front near the counter, avoiding their curious looks. The less attention he drew to himself in this place, the better.

Plucking a bar of shaving soap from a high shelf, he pretended to read the label. A smarter man would have already withdrawn his money from the bank and moved on, but his feet felt strangely rooted to this place, as if held down by unseen anchors—or perhaps he merely sensed the inescapable weight of a certain blonde with eyes the color of maple syrup.

Irritably scratching his scruffy face, Gideon tried to block out the picture clouding his mind of Faith sitting on that settee tending to his wounds, the lamplight flickering in her vulnerable gaze. Her leg had brushed his as she worked, her fingertips driving a sensation through him that surpassed even winning a game of poker by his own merit. She was life and breath and beauty, a gem such as he'd never imagined finding in his lifetime—and soon he would leave her behind.

After he'd walked her home the previous night, he'd approached the saloon with trepidation, half expecting to find the sheriff and his men examining the spot where he'd beaten the living tar out of that lecherous buffoon. On his way there, he'd concocted a script of sorts—what he would say to explain himself without divulging what Faith didn't want known.

Yet when he'd reached the Wild Rose, he'd found nobody milling about in front, only light and piano music streaming from the windows. In the alley, a pool of blood shone beneath the high moon, but Faith's attacker was gone. Gideon's fists clenched, his body on edge as he surveyed his quiet surroundings. If an attack came, he was prepared—yet none ever did.

When he went back to the game he'd abandoned, he found five empty chairs and cards thrown on the table in a heap. No sign of his partners remained—not even at the darkened tables in the corner where the wealthier customers enjoyed convening. Gideon had expected Old Joe to throw him out after what he'd done, but no censure ever arrived. He'd climbed the stairs to his room, locked the door, and slept with a pistol beneath his pillow. If not for Faith, he might have skipped town in the dead of night, but the thought of leaving her without explanation, of never seeing her face again, planted a queasy sensation within that warred with and won out over his better sense.

"You're staring terribly hard at that bar of shaving soap."

Gideon jumped, nearly dropping the bar. He turned to find Faith beaming up at him, a knowing smile denting her cheek. He couldn't help the responding grin that tugged at his lips. "I'm in need of a good shave." He passed a hand over his cheek, his bristled jaw scraping his palm.

"A little stubble on a man never hurt anyone." Her gaze dropped to the line of his jaw, which tensed under her appraisal. "I rather like it."

"Then, by all means"—Gideon twisted around and plopped the soap back on the shelf—"I shall leave it in place." Anything to see that admiring spark in her lovely gaze.

Faith laughed. "What are you even doing here this time of day? I thought you might be asleep or camped out in your room trying to catch a thief."

"That might be a wiser course of action for me." He gestured toward the produce lining the front of the store. "I came in for some food—maybe a bit of fresh fruit. There isn't much nutrition in what Old Joe serves at the saloon."

She wrinkled up her nose. "No, I wouldn't eat that if I were you. Molly is a nice person, but I'm afraid she makes a terrible cook. That's actually why I'm here."

"Oh, really?" His brows rose. "Were you hoping to improve on her recipes? If so, I might change my mind about eating at the Wild Rose."

Faith bit her lip, surveying the store as she spoke. "Maybe. I don't have a lot of experience, but I thought I could start with a pie or two. See if the patrons at the Wild Rose would enjoy it."

He smiled, crossing his ankles and leaning against the wall. "That sounds like a wonderful idea. See? You're already working to improve the place you were put."

She shielded her torso with one arm. "I'm trying to. I'm afraid I've never been much good at anything other than riding horses."

"Much like me with poker." He caught the sarcastic glare in her eyes and chuckled. "On a good day. I really am good at it, I promise."

"If you say so." She licked her lips, glancing at the cluster of ladies watching them from beside a candy display. How often did she have to contend with vicious gossips? Gideon would guess nearly every day. "Well, I'd best let you go. It appears as if you have what you came for." Her gaze landed on the basket in his grip, filled with a few apples and a fresh loaf of bread.

"I do, actually." He paused, unwilling to force his feet away from her. If only he could linger a moment longer, swimming in the depths of those eyes.

Faith pressed a hand over her bodice and looked self-consciously away. What had her father done to her? No wonder she couldn't look a man in the eye after the horrors he'd inflicted on her. If only he could be the person she needed, and not the liar and cheat who would only hurt her more.

"I'll be going, then." He tipped his hat to her. "Good day to you, Miss Carter."

Shouldering past the giggling bunch of hens convened near the door, Gideon paid and walked into the morning sunlight. The faster he got out of here, the better. Curse his feelings. He needed to leave—not only to save his own hide, but to give Faith the chance to find someone truly worthy of her.

"I'll take this bag of apples and this sugar, please." Faith flopped the sack across the counter, trying not to stare too hard out the window. Gideon's form was only visible a few more seconds before he disappeared down the street behind a woman in oversized flounces. It was for the best. She had no business harboring daydreams of a man who planned to walk away the first chance he got.

Fred, the man who ran the mercantile, rang up her items. She spied the group of women still huddled together, their judicious stares descending her. Hushed whispers lifted off them, followed by a snicker. She bristled as they covered their mouths to conceal whatever unkind words passed between them at her expense.

They would forever remember her for what her father did and the steep plunge from society she had endured. Nobody would ever again see her as Faith, the girl who loved horses and family, who gave of herself without being asked. Perhaps Gideon was right. She should open an atlas, point to a place, and go there. Create a new name for herself, a new life. She certainly wouldn't find much of one here.

Fred handed her the items with a smile and a friendly word, but the power of the eyes on her back simmered through her. Faith bit her lip. Her father had raised her never to retaliate, never to return an unkind word with impropriety. But what had her father taught her, really, other than his ability to steal and to kill?

Faith spun on her heel, her eyes narrowed. "Whatever it is you have to say, you can say it to my face. You needn't whisper it."

The women straightened, their hands resting over their bosoms as if she had offended their very existences by speaking the truth.

A young, thin woman with caramel locks fixed her with an imprudent look. "Why would you assume we were talking about you? We're only friends catching up."

Faith resisted the urge to roll her eyes. "Because you've been talking about me since I stepped foot in this store. You're clearly making a point of it." When they only simpered back, batting their judgmental eyes, she put her foot down. "I don't know what you've heard, but I had nothing to do with my father's indecency in this town. In fact, I helped put a stop to it."

The woman who'd spoken raised an accusatory brow. "We heard. A bullet isn't exactly a respectable way to solve such problems." Her lips puckered. "You were never respectable, though, were you?"

Faith's face heated at the chorus of sucked-in air and giggles around the girl. "I've never done anything indecent."

"Except for associate yourself with a harlot, walk around town like you own it." Her gaze flicked over Faith's gown as if it were nothing but a worthless rag. "And now you're one of Old Joe's girls at the saloon. That was always your ambition, wasn't it?"

Blood boiled beneath Faith's calm facade. She set her teeth. "Cora is my friend, and I will not apologize for that. I am not one of Old Joe's *girls.* I only serve and clean."

The woman tossed a self-important look at the others, her expression unconvinced. "Not according to the stories coming out of the Wild Rose." Her features quirked into a look of pride, as if she'd waited years to tear down the local rich girl from her gilded throne and would relish every second of it.

Stories? What stories? No doubt the disgusting pig who'd mauled her last night had a few tales to weave that didn't involve Gideon beating him half to death. No matter what she said, they wouldn't believe her—not with the heap of titillating gossip at their fingertips they'd been waiting for.

"This isn't worth my time." Standing tall, Faith spun toward the door, only to collide with a solid chest. Two hands coiled around her upper arms as her gaze ascended the flannel shirt and bushy chin before her.

Jeremiah Anderson's leering gaze dipped far below the respectable level. "Hello there, Miss Carter. I didn't expect to see you out and about this morning." He looked everywhere but her eyes.

Fighting the shudder that racked her body, Faith yanked her arm out of his grip. "I have no desire to converse with you."

A burst of giggles sounded behind her, the thin woman's sing-songy voice chirping, "I guess we know who she keeps company with now."

Struggling to break free of his other hand, Faith lurched toward the exit. Their derisive laughs followed her, clinging to her like the vines of a poisonous plant. They echoed across her mind, even as her feet hit the dirt street and began carrying her away.

Heavy footsteps tramped after her. "Where are you off to in such a rush?" Jeremiah Anderson's rasping voice wrapped its cold fingers around her bones.

Faith kept on, her chin high. "Haven't you heard? I'm one of Old Joe's girls now."

"Well, if that's the case, I'm coming to the Wild Rose right now."

She shot him a disgusted look. "Leave me be. I don't want anything to do with you." Dodging a wagon, she darted around the other side to avoid him. All too quickly, his long strides fell into step beside her.

"You may want nothing to do with me, girl, but I am a part of your life whether you like it or not. Your daddy made sure of it."

Faith's stomach constricted as she breathed in the pine-laced air. There was truth to his words—too much truth. Her father had immersed her in a world of danger for so long without her even knowing. "My father's sins are not mine. I refuse to bear his burden."

"I think you'll find the burden ain't so bad once you hear what I have to say."

She shook her head, her hair flying on the wind as she walked. "I don't want to hear it."

"But hear it, you will." His large hand jetted out again, snatching her arm before she could walk on.

Nostrils fuming, Faith looked at the spot he held her sleeve. "Unhand me at once before I scream." Surely someone would come to her aid against the most notorious outlaw in town, even after what her father did.

"I wouldn't suggest that, darlin'." He swept his jacket back to reveal the revolver holstered on his hip.

Faith's throat went dry. Would he shoot her here on the street with all these people around? This town was mad.

Grunting, he yanked her off the street and into a quiet alley between the buildings. Faith worked to keep her feet steady and her frame from jittering. Visions of the previous night shot through her—of her would-be rapist's hands on her, of his hot breath showering her neck. Yet once they'd achieved a bit of seclusion, his hand fell away from her.

Faith clenched her jaw and looked him square in the face. "What do you want, Anderson? I don't have anything."

"You have plenty." His eyes wandered her again. "I've got a comfortable ranch to my name that you could make a whole lot more comfortable."

She huffed, crossing her arms over her chest. "Did you really bring me back here to discuss domestication?"

Jeremiah spat in the dirt. "No." He gnawed on the tobacco rolling around in his mouth. "I pulled you back here to talk about your father."

Her brows gathered. "What about my father?"

"Fact is, he owes me a lot of money. I did jobs for him, dangerous things that nearly cost me my neck sometimes."

She tapped her foot on the dusty ground. "And?"

"And I expect to be compensated." Anderson rested his giant hands on his belt. "A man doesn't get that kind of work for free. He can't expect to reap the rewards for my services without payin' me what he owes me."

"I'd suggest you talk to him about it, then. He's at the state prison."

"I'm well aware of where he is." Anderson leaned against the building. "In fact, I've been to see him. Seems the state froze his assets once they convicted him of fraud."

Faith lifted her chin. "I don't see what any of this has to do with me. I don't have access to that money."

"Oh, but don't you?" His head cocked, his steady gaze drilling through her. "The way I hear it, your pa can extract enough money to care for you, to make sure you have plenty to live on if he sees fit."

She swallowed, her chest burning. "Clearly he doesn't see fit, with me working at the Wild Rose and living off charity. I haven't seen a dime of my father's money."

A moment passed, the air buzzing with the chatter of towns-people, as a sinking feeling pooled in her gut. Then Anderson pushed off the wall, stepping toward her.

"I've known that man for many years, and I've seen how he looks at you, how he wants to protect you." He stopped a breath in front of her, his gaze unflinching. "You have a lot more charm than you let on. You could have him eatin' out of the palm of your hand if you wanted."

Tears tingled at the back of her eyes. "No, I couldn't. He hates me."

"No, he just wants to be your protector again. He wants to know you need him."

She stiffened beneath his scrutinous gaze. "I can't do it." She wouldn't. She'd promised herself she'd never go back there, no matter her desperation. She'd never lower herself enough to beg from the man who'd ripped her entire world asunder.

Anderson reached out his rough fingers, hooking her chin and propelling it up. When Faith dared to meet his eyes, a promise lurked in their devious depths. "You're going to pay me one way or another." One more menacing step and he stood so near, his fetid breath skittered over her skin. "Either weasel that money out of your daddy's hands, or prepare to get to know *me* a whole lot better."

Twelve

THE LITTLE ROOM GIDEON occupied at the end of the upstairs hallway felt different with him in it. Faith silently observed the meager belongings he'd scattered about, the crumpled bedspread that must have smelled of earth and musk, like him. She had been here once before to launder the sheets, but never with him so near. Gideon was the only man—save for her father—she'd ever been alone with at all. The thought scattered apprehension across her arms and face as he paced the floor.

His solid form moved in a mesmerizing rhythm, his hands clasped over his mouth in thought. Bits of dark hair fell across his furrowed brow, lending a boyish charm to his masculinity. "If it's Old Joe, I can't stay here. If the proprietor of this place is willing to take my money, who knows what else he's willing to do?"

Faith bit her bottom lip. "I don't think it's Old Joe."

He paused his metrical walking to glance up at her. "Why not?"

Her shoulders lifted. "I don't know. He just doesn't seem like the type. He certainly isn't perfect, but he isn't dishonest."

"People will surprise you."

She blew out a breath. She knew that truth all too well. Perhaps Old Joe and her father *did* have something in common.

Gideon walked to the window, his boots thumping the floorboards. "Honestly, it could be anybody who works here or has access to the rooms."

"What about me?" Faith set her hand on her hip and playfully twirled a strand of her hair. "I work here. Am I among your suspects?"

He swiveled back, giving her a deliciously handsome grin before turning again to the window. "I have to admit I thought for the briefest of seconds when it first happened that it could be you."

"And? What made you change your mind?"

"You're too pure of heart." He shook his head and paced back her way. "Besides, you don't seem to care enough about money to bother to steal someone else's. You could have plenty if you cowed to your father's wishes."

Faith frowned. She told him too much. When had she allowed this outsider into her confidence? "I could be a thief if I wanted to be." She pointed her chin up. "You would never even suspect me."

He stopped short in front of her, the hint of a smile still on his lips. "Sounds like a lucrative career for you. Maybe we could be partners. A thief and a cheat."

She simpered playfully. "I'd like to think of myself as an opportunist."

"An opportunist it is, then." His hands settled on her shoulders, driving a bizarre thrill through her. "Are you sure you want to do this? You don't have to."

Faith took a drag of air, catching notes of his musky cologne. "I want to. It will be better for you to know who's stealing your money in the long run. Maybe you can get some of it back."

"I hope so." His hands fell from her arms. "I don't see how I'll last much longer here without it unless my poker partners hate that scoundrel as much as I do and decide to let me back in."

"That might just be the case." Faith glanced with trepidation toward the door. "You should go now before I'm missed. I'll let you know what happens."

Gideon nodded, hesitating a fleeting moment before turning for the door. "Scream if there's trouble. I'll be in town, but someone is bound to come if you call out. Molly, maybe Old Joe."

She swallowed. "I can't imagine much trouble up here. It isn't like the lion's den downstairs when everyone is drinking and gambling."

He paused, his hand on the doorknob, and gave her one last poignant look. "Just be careful."

The door shut behind him, his key scraping the lock from the other side before his footsteps retreated down the hall. Faith hugged herself, spinning in a circle, all alone in Gideon's bedroom. An inclination that rivaled her every lesson in etiquette whispered at her to paw through his things. She could find out a multitude of unsaid truths by exploring the man's belongings, but what kind of a person would that make her?

Her gaze ricocheted around the room, from his knapsack dangling off a hook over the bureau to his lightly rumpled bed. So few places presented themselves to hide. Perhaps if she ducked beneath the bed and positioned herself near the wall, Gideon's thief might not see her. Gathering her skirts, she dropped to her knees and inspected the space beyond the hem of his bedspread. It wasn't much, but it would serve her purpose.

Just as Faith set her palms on the floor and prepared to crawl beneath the bed, rapid footsteps pummeled the floor outside. Her heart jumped to her throat. She quickly surveyed her surroundings, but found no escape. She'd never be able to flatten herself and shimmy beneath the bed before that door swung open. Already a key jangled in the lock, its quick turn unbolting the door.

In a flash, Faith jumped to her feet beside the bed, attempting to slow the rapid surge of her chest. The face behind the door froze her in place. *Allison.* Of course it was Allison. The pretty dark-haired prostitute had made endless trouble for Cora at Madam Carey's.

She halted in the open doorway, her jaw slackening. Her red-rimmed lips formed an astonished "o" before she gathered herself again. "Faith! I didn't expect to find you here."

Faith smoothed down her skirts, her pulse still thundering rapidly in her wrists. "I came to change the bedding. It's been several days."

"But"—Allison's gaze tumbled to the doorknob where her hand still resided—"the door was locked. I had to use a key."

Obnoxious Allison and her attention to detail. Faith compelled an artificial smile to her face. "Was it? I must have accidentally locked it after I came in."

Allison's painted eyes narrowed, flitting to the bed, then back up at Faith. "You don't even have a change of sheets with you."

"I was going to get them once I pulled this one off." She patted the bed with as gentle a movement as possible.

Allison knotted her arms over her ample chest, her lips pursing coyly. "No wonder I can't get that man's attention, with you secretly up here amusing him."

Faith's cheeks filled with heat. "It isn't like that."

"Oh, isn't it?" One manicured brow hooked. "You're clearly not up here to make the bed. You're desperate for both money and a wholesome reputation. It's a brilliant plan, actually—entertain one man in secret—one making loads at the poker tables." Her lips pressed together in satisfaction. "I applaud you, Miss Carter. Well done."

Despite Allison's praise, Faith's nostrils ballooned and her heart beat harder. "I am not a prostitute. I am not entertaining him."

Allison assessed her once more before light dawned across her face. "For free, then? I've seen the way he looks at you. Are the two of you madly in love?" A giggle frothed just below her words, tinged with mockery.

"I am not sleeping with the man, for money or otherwise." Faith squared her shoulders. "Please don't spread rumors about me that have no roots in reality."

Allison grinned smugly. "Believe me, I understand the need to protect one's respectability. I had it once upon a time, too." Something wicked flickered in her eyes. "You can at least be honest with me. Come now, why else would you be in Mr. Valdez's room? I must admit I am jealous. He is a handsome catch of a man."

Faith set her teeth on edge. "And why are *you* in Mr. Valdez's room? Hmm? What reason could you possibly have? Were you hoping to entice him?"

Rolling her eyes, Allison sashayed into the room. "Oh, come now. I have better things to do with my time. Molly asked me to come in here and make sure everything was in order. She even gave me her key." She held up the glinting piece of brass.

"Molly."

"Yes, Molly."

As if Molly wouldn't have come in here herself to check the room. Faith could see straight through her, as if Allison were carved from glass. "Does Molly often send you to check the rooms? I didn't think you did much cleaning around here."

Allison shrugged. "I do my part when called upon. Don't insinuate I'm a lazy good-for-nothing. I have more than one skill, you know."

"Really? Because I've only ever seen you display one of them." A bizarre rage snaked over Faith, prodding her to fight back despite the warring voices in her head.

"This is ridiculous." Allison huffed and threw her hands down. "If you don't believe me, I'll prove it to you. Molly is right down the hall."

Prove she was nothing more than a conniving thief who had pilfered Gideon's money. Faith raised her chin. "Let's ask her."

"Gladly." Allison charged back the way she'd come, her heeled shoes clicking across the floor.

Faith thundered after her, forgetting all manner of decorum as they traversed the narrow hallway leading to the stairs. A door stood open at the end of it, revealing a silhouette of Molly against the morning sun as she swept a vacant bedroom. Both women clattered in, almost atop one another.

Molly's head snapped up. "What is all this?"

"Your new little *pet*, here, is trying to accuse me of lying." Allison lifted her head, her dark curls bobbing.

Faith thrust her hands on her hips indignantly. "There would be no accusation without cause. Besides, she accused me of plenty herself."

Molly straightened, her hands coiling around her broom handle as she looked between them incredulously. "Am I to understand two grown women are bickering over mere allegations?"

Allison stepped forward. "She is clearly nothing but a child. I told you not to hire her."

Molly released a shallow sigh. "And what has she done to warrant such claims?"

"I found her in Mr. Valdez's room." Allison jabbed a finger Faith's way. "She told me she was making his bed. *That* clearly was a lie. Then she insinuated I had unsavory reasons for being there."

Molly's shoulders pulled back in a barely perceptible motion. Her careful stare slid from Allison to Faith.

Faith's jaw tightened. "She tried to accuse me of sleeping with Mr. Valdez. She said that I was"—she choked on her emotion—"prostituting myself." After her experience in the alley last night, the word made her tremble with remembered terror.

Allison snarled at her. "You see? You see how she talks? Like she's so much better than the rest of us. I was only trying to pay her a compliment regarding Mr. Valdez."

"A compliment? You all but called me a strumpet."

"And you assume it's an insult. Look around you. Every other woman here is exactly what you're afraid of being called."

Faith's blood heated. "Yes, but I am not one."

"Why? Because you're a Carter? Because you're richer than the rest of us? Because your daddy in prison convinced you your name meant something?"

"Enough!" Molly's voice cut through their quarrel, solid and final. "Allison, please make use of yourself downstairs while I deal with this."

Allison tugged on her skirts and stood taller. "At least tell her you asked me to check on that room. She's bound to spread rumors among the other girls."

Sighing, Molly set her broom against the wall. "Please just go. We'll discuss it later when you both have calmed down."

"Unbelievable." Allison gave a sharp, clipped breath, swinging one last glare on Faith before she spun on her heeled shoes and click-clacked out the door. It slammed behind her, shuddering the wooden frame.

Molly's eyes shone with solemn disappointment when they latched on Faith. "Really? Fighting with Allison already, Faith? You've only been here a few days."

Faith's skin flushed as she tucked her chin down. "I know, and I'm sorry. She just came at me with all these accusations, and I couldn't suppress my anger as I wished to."

"Because she insinuated you could be a prostitute."

Faith's gaze bounced from the floor up to Molly, her hands spread over her skirts. "It riled me when I told her I wasn't and she wouldn't believe me."

Sunlight through the windows illuminated the slightest of divots between Molly's brows. "You do understand how she feels, don't you? You're using the term as if it's an insult, but for Allison it's the only way to survive." She swept her hand in a wide arc. "It's that way for all the girls here, just as it was for Cora. They didn't become prostitutes because they enjoy the work."

A hard, cold lump materialized in Faith's throat, spiraling downward until it reached her stomach. She plopped onto the bed, her knees suddenly weak and body fatigued. "I didn't mean it like that. I suppose I got used to thinking about it a certain way, talking about it flippantly in my old life."

Molly strode forward several steps, her shoes rattling the floorboards. "When you had your father's good name to elevate you and it was convenient to look down on women like us."

She blinked, her eyes unfocused and burning. "I didn't think I was looking down on you, but I suppose I was in a way. I didn't give every woman as much grace as I did Cora."

"And now, with your unique new perspective, you have the chance to right those wrongs." Molly sank to the bed beside Faith, her hand meeting with Faith's back. "It is a rare woman indeed who has seen both sides. You can learn compassion, teach it to others."

Hot tears bloomed in her eyes. Faith nodded and sniffed. "I'm beginning to understand it just a little after what happened last night."

The hand rubbing her back stilled. "What do you mean last night? When you went home early?"

Holding back her tears, Faith nodded again. "When one of the customers tried to take me by force in the alley."

"He *what?*" A whistle of wind sucked through Molly's lips. "What happened? Are you hurt?"

"No." Faith's body convulsed just remembering it. "Mr. Valdez saved me. He beat the man bloody."

"Good."

Faith took a shivering breath, unable to press it out again. "Perhaps I shouldn't be here. I was so scared. I thought—" But her words drowned beneath the sobs she tried so fervently to quell.

"Oh, Faith." Two arms came around her, Molly's soothing hand brushing back her hair as she held her against her shoulder. "I should have prepared you more for this place. It can be brutal for a woman, especially one who's never been on her own."

Faith swiped the balmy moisture from her cheeks. "I'm such a failure. I couldn't even last a week on my own. My father was right about me."

"No." Molly's firm voice sobered her. "Your father's wrong in every conceivable way about you. Do you understand?" She held her tighter. "You are a brave, strong, independent woman, but that won't stop the vilest of men among us. They think they can take without consequence. They see the strength in you and it only attracts them."

The notion spread shivers of anxiety over Faith's skin. What a cruel lesson to learn when she had nobody in the world to cling to.

"This ordeal will only make you stronger." Molly reached down to cup Faith's cheeks, lifting her face to the warm sunlight. "Use this experience to fuel you. Refuse to become what that monster thinks you are. Become who you want to be—a stronger person than he can ever hope to be."

Faith bit her lip to suppress her tears and wiped them with her skirt. "I hope that I can."

"You will." Molly tucked a strand of Faith's hair behind her ear. "It may take time, but you will. You have a reserve within you that you're only just beginning to tap."

A reserve of strength. Over the years, Faith had been schooled on her superiority, the dignity of her name and social standing. She'd never once considered the strength of character inside her that could accomplish impossible feats. If only she could believe in it as much as Molly apparently did.

"So Mr. Valdez rescued you, did he?" Molly's voice snatched her from her musings.

She looked up into Molly's thoughtful expression. "He didn't even hesitate. He just came at him and started swinging. It was magnificent to watch."

A smile inched up Molly's lips. "I'm sure it was. I'll have to tell Old Joe about what he did. He'll want to commend him."

Faith exhaled, her breath still uneven. "I'm not sure he's planning to stay much longer anyway, with the experience he's had here."

Molly frowned. "You mean what happened last night?"

Faith paused. How much would Gideon want her to say? Molly should know—to help her catch the thief, if nothing else. Beginning with the first morning Gideon discovered his lost money, Faith laid out everything he'd told her. Molly sat in quiet attentiveness until the room swallowed the last of her words.

"So you see," Faith said, bracing her hands on the floral bedspread, "I accused her only because I had cause. She had to have stolen that money. Why else would she have been there?"

At Molly's silence, Faith touched her wrist. "You didn't tell her to go into Gideon's room, did you?"

Molly's head shook softly, though something plagued her downcast eyes. "No, but I'm still not comfortable accusing her with so little information. I'll ask Old Joe what he wants to do about it, then I'll let you know." She managed a reassuring smile as she reached out to pat Faith's cheek. "Don't look so glum. We'll figure out a way to make this right."

Faith's shoulders fell. She would have to crawl back to Gideon with a potential suspect, but no solid evidence—and someone in Gold Strike would keep on stealing money from Gideon, from the bank, from anyone they could.

Thirteen

THE SPURS ON GIDEON'S boots jangled as he descended the stairs, every step more weighted and cumbersome than the last. The Wild Rose already burst with light and voices, notes from the piano floating away in the night. Normally Gideon's back would already ache from hours spent with the afternoon crowd, but today he'd kept to his room, wary of intruders and busy making plans in his head.

He scanned the milling crowd and peered through the smoke until he found his thief, clad as always in something beautiful, her hair pinned up and falling in tiny ringlets to the nape of her neck. *Allison*, Faith had told him—the girl he'd met that first morning at breakfast, the one with sad eyes and a complacent expression. He should have known it would be someone like her, with little morals and nothing to lose.

Self-consciously he patted his jacket pocket, where a hard rectangular lump sat beneath the fabric. He'd withdrawn everything from the Gold Strike bank this afternoon—all he'd need for the tables and his entire life savings. It would be no safer there—with criminals breaking in and stealing massive amounts of gold—than it would be on his person. At least here he could defend his money with his fists, or gun, if need be.

The curling smoke drifted enough for him to see through its veil. The wealthy men he normally played with ringed the table already—all but Faith's assailant, of course. One had a deck of cards in his hand, thwacking them against his fingers, but no one made a move to play.

Chills perked his skin. They were waiting for him. They had as much of a plan as he did.

Willing confidence into his every stride, Gideon punched his way across the floor and slipped into his usual chair. Every eye at the table revolved on him—stone serious, deadly, the kind of look reserved for a man one might call to duel in the streets.

The oldest of his partners leaned forward on his elbows. "We have a thing or two to talk about since last night."

Gideon lifted his brows in feigned naivety. "Last night? Why so?"

Cold steel passed through the man's gaze. "Don't be coy with me, boy. I have a lot of clout around here for a reason. You know what you did, and we demand an explanation."

Gideon popped his knuckles, stretching his legs in a relaxed pose. "You take issue with me defending a woman's honor?"

"We take issue with you nearly killing a respected man in our community," a low voice growled from his right.

The older man nodded. "Doc says Ben could have died with much more blood loss. Might have if we hadn't found him in time."

Gideon sniffed. "Seems like he would have deserved it."

A foot stomped, the player to his left lurching forward. "Careful what you say. You are the outsider, not him."

Without flinching, Gideon met his stern gaze. "I never had a thing against your friend. I wouldn't have touched him if he'd kept his hands to himself."

The man chuckled humorlessly. "If he wouldn't have propositioned a harlot, you mean?"

"She isn't a harlot." Gideon's cold stare slid into each of theirs. "She told him that time and again. He refused to listen."

"Every woman in this place is a harlot if you pay them enough."

The muscles in Gideon's jaw twitched. How familiar was the oft-cited sentiment that one's social status corresponded with their moral code. He had no hope of swaying them. The most he could do was defend himself in this moment.

"I was there. I saw what happened. It wasn't a mere proposition. He had her pinned against the wall and she was screaming. She was telling him to stop, but his hands were all over her."

The men at the table exchanged guarded glances before the oldest spoke up again, flicking ashes from the tip of his cigar into a tray. "Why should we believe you? You could have just as easily been jealous over that woman's affections and decided to take out the man she was with."

Gideon arched one brow. "We can ask her if you'd like, find out where her affections lie."

The man's lips pinched in dissatisfaction as he searched for Faith among the swarm of girls by the bar. "I've known Edward Carter a long time. He had a lot of people fooled, but he's nothing but a liar and a cheat. Stands to reason his daughter won't be any better."

Gideon's teeth set. How disgustingly unfair to judge her over something out of her control. "I suppose we're at an impasse. No matter what I say, you're determined not to believe me, truth or no." He swallowed. "Are you going to hand me over to the sheriff?"

Another flurry of meaningful looks zipped across the table before the older man reached for his whiskey. "McCraw doesn't seem to know about it, and we'd like to keep it that way."

"Because you know your friend is guilty."

"Because we like to deal with matters ourselves out here." He fixed Gideon with a warning look. "You'd do best to understand that now, before something unfortunate happens to you."

Gideon's eyes narrowed into slits. "Are you threatening me?"

"Just telling it like it is." The man took a swig of his drink and set it down again, letting the amber liquid slosh around. "If you haven't realized it yet, a lot of power resides at this table—power to promote or to bring harm, depending on how we see fit." His head angled. "What should we do with you?"

"Seems as if I don't have much say either way." Gideon's lip pulled back. "Why don't you just tell me what you want?" He'd met enough men like this in his life. They always had an agenda.

A pert look of satisfaction overwhelmed the man's face. "A man who gets straight to the point. I appreciate that. I'll not mince words, then." He took a drag of his cigar and blew out several elegant rings of smoke. "We've discussed this and come to a conclusion. If you do not comply, we will have no choice but to turn you in to the sheriff, and I promise you, things will not go well for you."

Gideon bristled. "And your friend? He will agree not to turn me over to the authorities?"

"He's doubtlessly happy to avoid public notice in his position. He stands to gain more than anyone else from your compliance."

Feet shuffling beneath the table, Gideon sat forward and cleared his throat. "Which is? What type of compliance do you expect from me?"

The man to his left, who'd largely remained silent, spoke up. "We stand to lose more than anyone else with that money missing from the bank. We all had shares in it. Some of us are partial owners of the home office."

Gideon scoffed. "You want me to find out where it is? Any fool can tell you Jeremiah Anderson has it."

"Perhaps." The older man tented his wrinkled fingers. "He may well indeed, but no one has been able to locate it—not even the sheriff and his men. We need you not only to find it, but to retrieve it."

"Me and my formidable army?" Gideon's head swung left and right. "I don't exactly have a lot of manpower on my side."

"You'll figure out a way." His partner slapped the cards against the tabletop. "You've already proven yourself resourceful."

In other words, we don't care how you do it, just get the job done. Men like the ones leering at him now thought little of who they stepped on to attain their wishes. Looking around the table, Gideon assessed each of the faces staring back, gauging their apprehensiveness, their resolve. Which one of them would crack first under pressure?

"What's to stop me from taking my horse and leaving this place?" He spread his hands on the liquor-splotched table. "You know nothing about me. I could be gone in an instant, and you would have no one to do your bidding."

The man with white hair looked sternly down his prominent nose. "We know enough about you. You've already shown us what makes you tick." He turned his scowl on the cards in his hands, shuffling them back and forth. "You came in here pretending to be one of us—a ruthless gambler, a wolf in sheep's clothing. But you didn't account for her, did you?"

A sickening ache sprouted in Gideon's core. If not for her, he would have picked up and left a long time ago. Almost without his consent, his eyes drifted to where she stood collecting drinks by the bar. With a quick swivel of her head, she noticed him staring, first casting a worried glance over his companions, then letting her gaze entwine with his. Her cheeks heightened to a beautiful color before she blinked and looked away again. For all his loathsome traits, the man was right. She'd ruined him the minute he set eyes upon her.

"She is a lovely girl, isn't she?" The letch's voice made his skin crawl. "I always thought so. She was beyond my reach, though—a married man with children her age."

Gideon snarled as he pivoted back. "She's still beyond your reach."

The man's bushy brows rose. "Do you plan to beat me too, then? I wouldn't suggest it."

Gideon's stare hardened to stone. "Do you plan to hurt her? Then I just might." His fingers flexed, burning from knuckle to nail. "I'll do what I must to protect her."

The man tossed an amused glance at his friends. "She really does have you at her mercy, doesn't she? You'll make this easier than I anticipated."

Gideon sat back, knitting his fingers together on the table. "So it's blackmail, then. Her safety rests upon my ability to meet your demands."

"If you wish to see it that way." The man fanned the cards out on the table. "I prefer to look at it as an opportunity. We keep you out of jail for assaulting the son of one of the wealthiest, most respected men in the region, and you do Gold Strike a favor by catching a crook. Miss Carter needn't even be involved, unless you rope her into it—or fail, of course."

Cold sweat layered Gideon's skin as he once again let his gaze rest on the beautiful blonde, now hoisting a tray of spirits. She'd already endured enough, with her father's betrayal and a town lining up to condemn her. The thought of her in peril drove lightning bolts through his body. She deserved so much better than this place, these people. He would do anything he could to protect her.

"What do you say, son?" The raspy words sank into him like the heat of standing too close to fire. "You think you're up for the challenge?"

Gideon set his shoulders and looked his opponent dead in the face. "You'll have your gold before the week is out. Now enough of this. Deal the cards."

Never stay after ten o'clock. Molly's advice pealed through her mind as Faith allowed herself to slump into a barstool at last. The arches of her feet ached. Her back smarted and cracked. She'd meant to go home hours ago, yet something always needed doing—tables tended to, messes cleaned up, dishes washed. Each time she even thought of leaving, a new voice sprang up, begging for her attention.

She covered a yawn with her hand. How late was it anyway? Midnight? The sky outside appeared black as slate, with hardly a star to punctuate its enormous canvas. The Wild Rose looked nearly as desolate, with only a few drunks slumped over in chairs, and most of the patrons gone or shuffling out the door.

Her stomach lurched, reminding her she'd forgotten to eat dinner in her mad rush around the bar. *Perhaps Wainwright will come for me.* Perhaps not, after she'd let Gideon take her home early last night. He probably thought she no longer needed him.

She gazed listlessly out the double doors, still swinging as bootfalls faded down the boardwalk. After last night, the idea of walking the forest trails alone launched shivers down her arms. But what choice did she have? She couldn't exactly bed down here.

"You look worn out." A deep voice made her jump, hand over her racing heart.

Faith turned to find Gideon slipping onto the barstool next to her. "You frightened me."

"I'm sorry. I didn't intend to."

Her body eased as he settled into the space beside her, his arm brushing her sleeve. "That's not a compliment, you know"—she released a short laugh—"calling someone worn out."

His brow wrinkled with concern as his eyes meandered over her. "I only meant to say you look tired from the way you're sitting. It wasn't an insult to your appearance. You're always—" He looked away, fixing his gaze on the line of overturned shot glasses behind the bar.

Faith bit her lip as warmth spread across her face. How had he meant to finish that sentence? If only she could pull back his layers enough to see the core of the man sitting next to her.

"How much did you win?" She snatched his gaze from the bar. "It looks like you were successful from what I saw."

A low groan rumbled in his throat. "I made enough. It will at least cut some of my losses."

"But you wished to make a profit here."

He laughed mirthlessly. "I thought this town might be my proverbial gold mine. That will teach me a lesson or two about counting chickens."

Faith breathed in the whiskey-laced air. "Things may turn around for you. You can never be sure until it happens." She'd learned that the unfortunate way. Sometimes they turned for the worse.

Silence settled over them a few uncomfortable seconds before he shifted next to her. "I know I said I was leaving real soon, but I think I'll stick around a while."

Her traitorous heart picked up speed. "You will? For how long?"

"Don't know." He fiddled with his shirt cuffs. "Not forever, but I have some things to do."

Faith fought the smile trying to weasel its way across her lips. If only she could keep her bodily instincts under control at his news. The man should mean nothing, yet she couldn't deny the thud of her pulse as his eyes searched hers.

"I thought you might be interested in helping me—when you have the time, of course. I don't know many people here."

"Help?" She tossed him a quizzical look. "What kind of help do you need?" Her imagination wouldn't stretch far enough to picture her pathetic skills actually aiding somebody like Gideon.

"I'm afraid it's a long story, but I'm willing to tell it if you're willing to listen."

Her brow cocked. "Sounds intriguing. Does this mission of yours involve danger?"

Rather than the playful reaction she expected, he softly pressed his lips together. "I'm afraid it may. The last thing I want to do is put you in harm's way." He stared into his open palms. "I'm unsure who else to turn to. You're the only one I—the only one I trust."

The word sprinkled warmth over her like drops of balmy rain beneath the sun. Faith let her gaze trail the bold veins running down his muscular arms, to his hands lying open on the bar. Hands like these could fell a tree or plow a field, commanding them with sheer size and strength. But right now his hands sat empty.

Stealing a breath of courage, Faith brushed her palm against his and let her fingers coil around it. She didn't flinch when his gaze shot to hers in question. Instead she held his hand tighter. "I will do whatever I can to help you. Tell me what you need and I'll do it."

Fourteen

"You will have to show me how you ride like that." Gideon released a self-deprecating laugh as he glanced down at his own relaxed posture atop Phantom. He'd purchased the black stallion only last year, but thus far he'd proven a dependable horse.

Faith eyed him with a clever smirk, her back never leaving its elegant, rigid position. "It stems from many years of equestrian lessons. Though I doubt you'd enjoy riding like this anyway. It isn't exactly comfortable."

"Then why do you do it?" Gideon urged his horse on with a gentle nudge of his heels. "Nobody here is judging the way you ride."

"That well may be, but I have lessons and reprimands drilled into me." She shook her head with a chuckle. "I can almost hear my teacher yell at me when I slip even slightly out of position."

"Well"—he glanced at her sideways—"I promise not to yell at you, even if you commit such an egregious mistake."

The beautiful laughter in her eyes could have drowned out a symphony. Gideon fought to keep his eyes on the trail ahead rather than her. Sunlight dripped through the canopy of evergreens, sparkling across her hair like gemstones. *Keep steady, my friend. Remember why you're here.* He reached out to stroke Phantom's mane and thrust his inclinations once again beneath the steady rhythm of his hooves.

The forest basked in the twitter of birds and gentle rush of spring wind. The foliage had thickened with the warming weather, fresh shoots budding from bushes and flowers blossoming in spectacular arrays of red and yellow. Pine branches swayed in the breeze, mingling their spicy scent with the nectar-bearing blooms. In the entrancing fold of its wild forests, Gideon could almost forget he would leave this place shortly.

"Molly didn't mind you taking a day off?" he asked, his gaze fixed to the winding trail.

"Are you joking? She practically begged me. She told me seven days is too much, especially in a place like that."

"She's right; you're working yourself half to death." He led Phantom over a fallen log. "You should take some time to rest." Which she might be if he hadn't dragged her out here.

"I did enough resting my first eighteen years of life. I'm ready now to work." Her voice held a determination he wouldn't argue with.

"That doesn't mean you don't need rest. You're only one human being." A human being with much to prove, he guessed.

She glared at him from the corner of her eye, though a hint of mirth lurked behind it. "I'm perfectly capable of determining my own limits, thank you—but you'll be the first person I contact when I require a man's opinion."

Gideon hid his smirk as he flicked his reins over the horse's neck. "I'll keep it at the ready, then—for the day you request it."

"I can hardly contain my excitement." She led them up a crest in the mountainside and down a sloping trail flanked in white-barked birches fluttering with fresh green leaves.

"I don't know how you expect to get around without me anyway," Faith said. "You don't know this countryside at all."

Precisely why he'd pulled her into this harebrained plan at the detestable risk to her safety. He needed her for her navigation skills—if not her aim—if the stories of her father's capture were true. Never mind the enjoyment of her company.

"I am indeed grateful to you. These trails are like an indecipherable maze to me."

She laughed, the pleasant sound warming him. "It's not so bad once you have lived here a while. Everything centers around these mountains." She flicked her head toward the mammoth giants now hidden through the veil of trees.

"How much farther to the Anderson Ranch do you think it is?" They'd already ridden close to an hour.

Faith squinted through the trees. "Not much. I can't say I've been there before myself, but I certainly know the way. The Anderson Gang's whereabouts are the worst kept secret in the whole county."

From everything Gideon had learned of him, the gang's ringleader seemed like a sloppy excuse for an outlaw—botching robberies, his relatives getting shot in the street. A man like that could be easily outmaneuvered, but his unpredictability made him dangerous. What would he do if he caught them?

"Do you have any idea where he could be hiding the gold on his ranch?"

Faith pondered his question silently, then shook her head. "Cora says he has a ranch house and barn and several outbuildings on the property. We can search those, but if he's smart, he'll have already buried the money in the woods." Woods too expansive to hunt, if their journey proved any indication.

"Perhaps we should start there. Look for any place with newly disturbed dirt."

"Maybe." She shrugged. "I'm not sure Jeremiah Anderson has any real reasoning behind the things he does. I think he behaves according to his whims most of the time."

"Why does the town fear him so much, then?"

She looked at him incredulously. "He's a menace who will stop at nothing to get what he wants. He's nearly killed a few of my friends. He threatened me."

A lance of alarm shot up Gideon's back. "What do you mean he threatened you?"

She turned her eyes to the trail. "You needn't worry. I don't think he'll act on it. He merely thrives on intimidation." She sighed. "Apparently my father owes him money for work he did. He's demanding payment."

Gideon scoffed. "Which he has no use for if all that gold is buried somewhere on his property."

"Exactly." She fell into silence a few moments while the animals trod the uneven trail. "I don't know if that's a clue or not, though. He might terrorize a debtor whether he needs the funds or not. That's how he keeps power in this place."

He gripped the reins tighter. "Well, he'd best not terrorize you again if he doesn't want to end up like that fool in the alley outside the Wild Rose."

Even in the shifting sunlight, the blush in Faith's cheeks shone clear. Her eyes met his in silent assessment before they swept demurely away again. "You're a dangerous sort of man, are you? Prone to violent fits of rage."

Gideon adjusted the brim of his hat. "If you're asking if I can fight, the answer's yes—but I don't like to. That man gave me every reason to beat the living daylights out of him. I would do it a thousand times more if necessary." His jaw worked, the rage coursing through him that night working its way up his ruddy throat.

Faith leaned over her horse's neck and pet her mane in loving strokes, stealing the occasional glance at him. Uncertainty dwelt in her eyes, coupled with intrigue. Could she see he would never hurt her, only defend her with his life if necessary? Could she feel how much his soul ached to protect her? He'd nearly determined to open his lips and tell her just that when she slowed her horse with a gentle tug and gazed into the forest before them.

"I think that's it. Straight ahead."

Gideon trailed her gaze down a dirt path beset by branches to a cluster of buildings skirting a meadow. He ducked low enough to peer beneath the branches, discerning the crude outline of the farmhouse and barn beside it. Nobody stirred outside the dwellings except a couple horses pent up in a corral. He scanned the yard again, then honed in on the house. Not a hint of movement or sound revealed a person on the place.

"Do you think he's here?" he asked in a hushed tone.

Faith's brow wrinkled, her focused stare still pinned on the ranch. "I suppose we can't be certain, but I don't see anyone. Perhaps we should wait and see if anybody comes out."

Gideon nodded. "Not a bad idea." In one quick motion, he swung his leg over Phantom's back and landed on the ground. Bending low, he selected a rock from a smattering of pebbles on the ground.

"What are you doing?"

Gideon strolled forward, just beyond the cover of branches. "Testing your theory." Advancing into range of Anderson's house, he swung his arm back and launched the rock straight at its shabby siding. The object collided with the house an instant later, smacking the wall near a filthy window. Gideon retreated into the brush, waiting. The chickens in a nearby pen squawked and fluttered their wings, but not a soul stirred.

Gideon surveyed the house once more. "I don't think anyone is here—at least not a live person."

From atop her horse, Faith shot him a wary look. "Don't talk about death. It's the last thing I need to think about right now." Her voice tremored, yet she set her shoulders straight.

"Come on." He motioned with his head through the trees. "It won't be so bad if nobody's here."

"No, but what if they come back?" Yet in the very same breath, she kicked Starlight into motion and trailed Gideon as he traversed the rest of the trees on foot, leading Phantom by the reins.

A pent-up horse whinnied on sight of them, kicking at the corral fence. Free-roaming geese honked and scurried out of their way as they carefully crossed the dusty yard. The air held a strange quality, like even the invigorating forests and mountains couldn't improve on the Andersons' body odor and tobacco habits.

"Let's tie them up over there." Gideon pointed toward a hitching post poking up from the ground.

Wordlessly, Faith slipped from her mare's back and led her to the post. After slipping her reins over the wood, she brushed a hand over her creamy coat. "We'll be back shortly, Starlight. Don't worry. You let us know if there's trouble." She nuzzled her face against the horse's snout and gave her a quick embrace.

Gideon sidled up to her, endeavoring to keep his gaze anywhere but that shimmering hair and flawless skin. "Where do you think we should look first?"

Her brow furrowed, concentration overtaking her lovely features. "Let's start with the barn. He hid Julia Broderick in the barn before, and Jim Sawyer. Who knows what we might find there."

"The barn it is, then." Treading the dirt beside her, Gideon flexed his hands, stiff and pained after the long ride.

A tattered-looking barn rose before them, all weathered wood and peeling paint. Weeds sprinkled the exterior, forcing them to trudge through the unkempt barbs. Darkness shrouded the inside, only a few shafts of light leaking through the dubious roof. Doves stirred and cooed in the rafters, but no other sounds of life disturbed the tranquil quiet.

Faith's forlorn gaze ascended the stacked bales of hay. "I can't imagine what it must have been like for Julia to be kept in here." She shivered. "Just the thought of someone like Anderson having control over me makes me sick to my stomach."

"He never will." He couldn't quite be sure where his certainty sprouted from, but Gideon's voice held a steel resolve, inviting no argument.

Faith's gaze wandered into his, searching for a brief moment, before she nodded. "If you say so. I'm certain of nothing anymore."

"Well, I'm certain." His chest burned the longer her eyes hunted his. "I'll be certain enough for us both. Anderson will never hurt you, I promise. Neither will that cad who attacked you at the bar." As long as she let him occupy the space beside her, he would protect her with his very last breath.

She gave a shivering sigh, then looked back at the empty barn. "Come on, let's have a look."

One by one, they searched the stalls, finding nothing but sprinkled hay and occasional piles of manure. The back of the barn yielded nothing but a closet containing old, rusted tools.

"There are some more outbuildings back here," Faith said as they stepped into the sunlight.

Gideon surveyed the dirt as they made their way across it. Nothing appeared disturbed; only bootprints marred its surface. He paused as a glimmer winked at him from among the trees. It appeared too low to the ground to be someone holding a weapon. Was that scoundrel so sure of himself he'd leave gold lying out in the open?

A gasp snatched his attention to Faith, who stood before an open shed. Gideon's feet carried him swiftly to her side. "What is it? What did you find?"

She backed away, hand over her mouth. Gideon, stepping around her and setting his hands on the doorframe, let his eyes adjust to the meager light. Items materialized one at a time—a pair of saddles, a rake, a stack of lumber—before coming to rest on an axe leaning against the wall.

She gulped loudly. "There's blood on that axe."

Hunkering down, Gideon reached out to pull it closer. The blade, rusted and worn with age, did, indeed, carry traces of dried, crusty blood, but it also had something else sticking to its sharp edge. "These are feathers." He plucked one downy white feather from the blade's edge and held it up to her. "They use this axe to kill the chickens."

"Chickens?" Her befuddled gaze dipped to the weapon and back at him. "How would you use an axe to kill a chicken?"

Gideon held in the laugh sizzling in his throat, his mouth creasing. "How, exactly, do you think chickens are killed?"

"I don't know, but I never imagined an axe." She hugged herself against an involuntary tremor. "I suppose I never thought about the steps necessary to put them on my table. I never imagined something so brutal."

"It's the quickest way for them to go." He rose and set the axe against the wall. "Either way, it proves nothing about Jeremiah Anderson."

Faith listlessly turned in a circle. "I don't see any gold here either. I suppose it was foolish to imagine we'd walk in and solve the case with a snap of our fingers."

Gideon dusted his dirty hands on his pants. "There's still plenty to check around here."

She sighed. "I suppose you're right. We haven't even looked in the house yet. I just keep thinking of Anderson coming back while we're looking—how he'll react."

Did it bring back memories of what her father had done? He reached out to touch her shoulder. "If this is too much, I'll take you home. I never want to frighten you."

"No." Faith lifted her chin, burying any inkling of her fear. "I will help you. I made a promise, and I have no intention of breaking it." Her resolve never faltered as she marched out of the shed, her skirts brushing the narrow doorframe.

Gideon followed behind, content to watch her purposeful walk a moment longer. This woman would fight a hurricane if the opportunity called. What an incomprehensible thing to find himself lured by, but snagged and yanked away like a helpless fish, he was.

Her eyes flashed with curiosity when she turned his way. "Did I miss something?"

His brows rose. "What?"

"You're staring. I thought perhaps you had an idea I hadn't yet imagined."

His lips puckered in a smirk. "No, I was swept away in my own thoughts."

"Oh." She straightened her stature, glancing at the house. "Are you ready to search inside? It would stand to reason Anderson might hide his most valued possessions in the place he protects most."

Gideon nodded slowly. "It does. It's worth a look, anyway." He threw a glance over his shoulder at the treeline, where something still winked from amid the dense foliage. "There's something I'd like to take a look at first."

Faith trailed him for several steps. "What is it?"

Gideon squinted. "I'm not sure. It's probably nothing. Why don't you wait here while I investigate? It should only take a minute."

"Wait here?" Faith implored him with the eyes of an injured puppy. "What if they come back?"

He glanced down at the reticule hanging from her wrist, which he knew concealed a pistol. "You can handle yourself with a gun. You've already proven that."

She drew the bag against herself. "I suppose so. Just hurry, please. This place makes me feel so uneasy."

Gideon touched the brim of his hat. "I'll be back in two shakes of a lamb's tail, just you watch." With that, he left her to wait beside that old threadbare house, staring after him as he jogged across the field and into the woods.

Faith suppressed every jolt threatening to course through her as Gideon scampered away and disappeared into the thick pines. She drew a breath through her nose, all dust and animal excrement. She had shot her father when the pressure rose. She had found herself a job. She hadn't run when danger found her at the saloon. So why did her heart pound so wildly now? Why did her chest feel like it might explode? *Stop being so frightened. Pull yourself together.* Yet no amount of self-censure could quiet the taunting voices inside her head.

Shaking herself, Faith twisted around to survey the property once more. A pair of horses inside the corral had taken to the shade of the barn. Starlight stood calmly beside Phantom, drinking water from a tin trough. Her gaze swept over the messy yard, coming to rest on the house. What kinds of things would they find in Jeremiah Anderson's personal lair? What type of secrets could a man so blatantly immoral possibly harbor? She shivered at the thought.

With a quick glance around, she tiptoed across the dirt and peered into one of the unwashed windows. She could see nothing through the layer of filth clinging to the glass. Cupping both hands around her eyes, Faith strained to see in. Only a table and a stove revealed itself, a set of empty chairs and dishes on every surface. No surprise that Anderson lived like a pig. He behaved like nothing less in town.

Curiosity niggled within her. With a breath of courage, Faith stepped to the front door and tried the handle. *Unlocked.* What kind of fool left his ranch unattended and his door unlocked for anyone to come waltzing in, as if he wanted to be caught?

Faith twisted the knob and pushed the door inward. The hinges screeched upon her intrusion. She forced her rickety legs to climb the front steps past the threshold. She didn't need Gideon. Separately, they could do twice the work before any of the Andersons got home. If she could just squelch the palpable fear thrumming across her body. *It's only fear. It isn't real.*

Propelling her reluctant legs forward, she wandered into what looked like a kitchen disguised as a pigsty. Dishes peppered the table and even the floor. A pot of something like mush sat on the soiled stovetop attracting flies. Faith steeled herself against the noxious assault of body odor leaking from every surface. How a person could live like this, she couldn't begin to understand.

A few more careful steps led her to a sitting area of sorts with stained lounge chairs and more dishes sprinkled about. A flannel shirt was thrown over the back of one, sweat-stained and caked in dry mud. Faith lifted it gingerly in two fingers to search the pockets. Once satisfied, she moved about the little room, checking beneath furniture and in cupboards. Nothing but more mess.

She sighed, standing back to assess her surroundings. Only a hallway with what appeared to be bedrooms remained. She glanced out the window. Perhaps she should wait for Gideon before exploring any further. He said he'd only be a moment. She gazed back down the hallway, weighing her options. If she found something on her own, she might actually impress him, convince him she wasn't just the helpless daughter of a wealthy businessman. The vision of admiration shimmering in Gideon's eyes compelled her onward.

The floorboards groaned beneath her shoes as Faith crossed the kitchen toward an open bedroom door. The unpleasant odors in this house intensified the farther she ventured, forcing her to cover her nose with the back of her perfumed hand.

She paused at the doorway and lightly pushed the door farther inward to reveal the entire room. Her blood froze as she made out first a foot, then a leg, then an entire form asleep on the bed.

Faith's breath hitched, her heartbeat thundering in her veins as she stiffened up like a corpse in the doorway.

His head was turned—long tendrils of tangled hair covering part of his scruffy face—but she had no doubt based on the hair itself and his muscular form. She'd inadvertently crept into Jeremiah Anderson's bedroom as he napped.

Faith stepped back, the floorboard behind her protesting with a sharp squeal beneath her weight. The next step proved no quieter. Her heart stopped as Anderson stirred and blinked in confusion. Faith took another shaky step, but it would do no good. His eyes had already found her in the shadowed hallway, brimming with perplexity, before a sinister sheen slid into its place.

Fifteen

Icicles pricked Faith's entire body as she stood in the threshold of Jeremiah Anderson's bedroom, staring into his eyes. Her heart galloped, smashing against her ribcage until she thought it might cease working altogether. Her legs threatened to give way.

Perhaps she should reach into her reticule and pull out her gun. As her gaze drifted across his bed, she thought better of it. Atop the tangled sheets sat a rifle, no doubt loaded and ready to combat an intruder such as herself. She could do nothing but stare, her mind racing to procure an explanation that might save her and Gideon both in this moment.

Anderson pushed himself to a sitting position, rubbing sleep from one eye. "For a minute there, I thought I was having a very, *very* good dream." His bold stare skittered down her. "You're the last person I'd expect to come knocking at my door, honey." The words planted a satisfied grin on his whiskered lips.

She bristled under his brazen stare. "This is the last place I expected to be, as well." The last place on earth she would have wandered of her own accord had she known he slumbered within.

"Did you come to discuss my terms?" His brow hooked suggestively. "This is a forward way of negotiating, especially for a girl like you."

Faith swiped at the obnoxious flyaways crowding her sticky forehead. What could she possibly say to explain her presence here that wouldn't invite unwanted advances? A man with an ego like Anderson would no doubt gladly accept she'd come here out of sheer desire, but if she played that card, she would have to deliver on her promises.

She forced her voice from wavering. "I think I can get my father to pay."

His shoulders relaxed. "Well, that's a little disappointing."

"You don't want my father's money?"

"*My* money. And of course I do." A flick of irritation lit his eyes. "I just thought with you showing up here like this, you might have made a different choice."

Her throat went dry. Her father had always painted Anderson as a cruel, ruthless killer—someone whose conscience had been uprooted in the name of petty greed. Yet sitting here before her was a lonely, pathetic soul asking for a companion. Suddenly a light dawned in the distance, illuminating a path out of this place.

"I'm just a girl, Mr. Anderson." She feigned a bashful look. "I know little of what you speak."

His face softened at her confession, his bristly jaw slackening, his eyes sparking with humor. "Believe me, I ain't looking at no girl—but I think I understand. Your daddy kept you in a comfortable cage, locked away from men like me."

"Exactly. It's—frightening." She managed a sheepish smile. "This world is all very new to me."

Anderson inched forward on the bed, throwing a blanket off himself. "Yet you came anyway. You came all by yourself."

She set her hands behind her back and nodded. How long until Gideon realized where she'd gone and followed her? He would destroy her ruse in a valiant attempt to rescue her.

"I see the benefits of our combined effort. You wish to be paid for your work, and I don't want to spend the rest of my life in a saloon. The way I see it, we can help each other."

Anderson wore a guarded yet curious expression. "Help each other, you say? How so?"

Against her every instinct, Faith trod forward and sat on the edge of his mattress. With a silent prayer, she lifted her face and looked directly into his scrutinous gaze. "You seem to have every confidence that I can affect his sensibilities simply by being his daughter, but I am less certain." Her eyes drifted to the rifle flung across the bed. "I'd like to have more muscle at the ready if I need it. A certain degree of leverage."

A satisfied grin pulled up one corner of his mouth. "Oh, darlin', I certainly have the muscle, but what could a man in prison stand to fear from me? He's already had everything he knows stripped away from him."

"Not everything." She bit her lip, then plunged ahead before her mind could stop her. "I wonder how he would feel about his only daughter living with the most notorious outlaw in Montana's wilds, under the very roof of his beloved mansion." Even while the idea turned her stomach into a tumultuous sea, Faith kept her stare even with his. This had to sound believable or she didn't stand a chance.

"You're a clever little minx, aren't you?" His wicked eyes searched her face. "You could destroy a man with a single glance of your eyes."

"I only wish to take back what he stole from me."

He quietly assessed her before clicking his tongue. "You have more of your father in there than you realize. I can work with a girl like this."

Faith compelled her lips up, though his sentiment launched icy pricks of dread through her entire frame. Did she really have her father in her—the conniving, backstabbing criminal who would rather murder the innocent than face his own misdeeds? God help her if that was true.

Anderson stood up from the bed and extended his large hand. "Come on, let's discuss this more out in the kitchen. A respectable girl like you shouldn't be in here."

Faith slipped her hand into his, willing her fingers not to shake. Did her discomfort show so blatantly? If she kept this discussion short, she might leave this place with her life intact.

She stole a glance at the windows as they passed into the crowded kitchen. No sign of Gideon revealed itself through the dirty glass—only Starlight and Phantom peacefully drinking water side by side.

"I'm rightly sorry about the mess." Anderson bent to collect dishes off the floor and stacked them atop one another. "Haven't had a woman out here in some time."

Julia Broderick, perhaps? Or Sylvia Hammond? Faith didn't wish to guess what happened to women out here. "I don't care about the mess, only about business." Faith slipped into a chair facing the windows. Perhaps if she could get him to turn his back to the outside, she could warn Gideon before he betrayed them.

"I'm beginning to like you more and more, Miss Carter." Anderson set the soiled dishes in a cupboard in the corner and turned her way. "You want some coffee or something?"

"No. Thank you." She folded her hands on the table. "I don't plan to stay long."

"I'm right sorry to hear that." He rounded the table, his boots jangling with every heavy step.

The hair on Faith's skin rose. *Just another foot more. Just sit in that chair and I can relax.*

Anderson laid his hand on the chairback, pausing. "You must have ridden a long way. You sure you don't want something to eat?"

The smell of breakfast still festering on the stove shot an arrow of nausea through her. "No, I've had plenty. Thank you."

"What about your horse? I've got hay in the barn." Before she could distract him, his gaze swung to the window. Anderson froze, looking out at the horses for several seconds, as if trying to comprehend what he saw. When his eyes found her again, they'd hardened. "Why are there two mounts out there?"

"Two mounts?" She released an airy laugh. "I'm not sure I understand."

"You're not stupid. You've already shown me that much." Anderson's hand tightened on the chair. "Now, I asked you a direct question, and I expect a direct answer."

Faith's breath came harder, her lungs burning. She could say nothing without incriminating Gideon, if he still had a chance to get away.

"Miss Carter, I suggest you tell me where that second horse came from before I walk out there and shoot them both."

Gideon stood beneath an aromatic canopy of pines, frowning at the forest floor. Another wild goose chase. He'd run back here, hopeful the glimmer he saw at a distance could lead them to the sought-after gold. Now he stood over a wheelbarrow, his hopes dashed. He kicked at the disappointing contraption, sending it tumbling into the dirt. What a waste of time. He could have been helping Faith look for that money.

Emerging from the trees, he covered his eyes to block out the sun as he gazed across the field at Anderson's ranch. No sign of Faith remained where he'd left her, just a barren patch of land and grazing chickens. Had she gone to hide out in the barn until his return? He cursed himself as he ambled across the pasture toward the house. He never should have left her alone because of her fear, if nothing else. She needed to know he would be by her side.

Gideon poked around the barn and outbuildings, but Faith was nowhere to be found. He stood with his hands on both hips, scanning the yard. Phantom and Starlight remained where they'd tethered them, seemingly undisturbed by the missing woman. The trees around Anderson's ranch rustled and swayed, their branches the only sound other than the horses' tongues lapping water.

He turned to the house, perusing the sloppy paint job and weathered wood. Could she have gone inside without him? Surely not after the bright fear alive in her voice. He advanced forward, then halted as a figure passed by the window.

Gideon's blood surged. That was a masculine form—powerful, well-built. Jeremiah Anderson's signature hair swept through his view before he disappeared out of sight. Gideon's heart plummeted. There in the space left vacant by Anderson's powerful form sat Faith. Silent words passed through her lips, her eyes flicking up to the man inside.

His hand moved to cover the pistol on his hip. Should he charge in and rescue her? Sweat moistened his browline. His hasty intervention might put Faith in even more peril. Yet how could he watch her, stuck inside with that loathsome lout?

Anderson's hulking form passed behind her and made for the door. Pulse thumping wildly, Gideon scurried across the dirt to the shadows of the barn. He ducked low and hunkered down just as the front door to the house swung open and boots battered the rickety steps.

"Woman, you can't tell me you ain't got no accomplice," Anderson's growl of a voice thundered over the property, eliciting a whinny from one of the horses.

"Just because somebody accompanied me here doesn't mean I have an accomplice." Faith's voice rang strong and true despite his accusations. "That is a hard and frightening ride for a woman to take by herself."

"All right, then. Where is this protector of yours?"

"I told him to take a walk. I wanted to speak with you alone."

"Wanted to seduce me with your feminine wiles is more like it." More stomping and boots dragging through the dirt. "I don't believe you came here for what you say."

"Why else would I have come here? I stand to gain nothing by snooping around your ranch."

"I don't know, but I plan to find out."

Panting, Gideon moved forward and peered around the side of the barn. Anderson stood apart from Faith, a gleaming revolver in one hand and Faith's reticule in the other. Gideon gingerly retrieved his own weapon, holding it at his pumping chest. If he could get a clear shot at the outlaw, perhaps he could take him down with one bullet.

His tongue spurted out to wet his lips as he took aim at the broad form. Should he miss, Anderson would surely gun him down, perhaps hurting Faith in the process. He couldn't let that happen.

His gun leveled on Anderson's chest. His finger hooked the trigger, his pulse throbbing against the cold steel. Gideon leaned in and closed one eye. Pulling back the hammer, he took another breath. Now or never.

As if sensing his presence, Anderson spun away. He peered through the dusty air, his narrowed eyes searching. Gideon pulled his pistol back and plastered himself to the wall. How had Anderson known? *Blast.* He should have taken the shot when he had it. For the second time in his life, hesitation could cost him everything.

"I know you're out there," Anderson's authoritative voice bellowed. "I have your girl, and if you care even a horse's rear end about her, you'd better show yourself now."

Gideon pressed to the wall, leaning forward just enough to spy Anderson with a handful of Faith's beautiful hair, his gun jabbing beneath her chin. Faith whimpered lightly, but even when he yanked on her hair, she barely let a sound pass through her tremulous lips. Cold resolve washed over him. He wouldn't let Anderson hurt her, even if it meant sacrificing himself.

"Did you hear me, boy? I don't like waitin'. Come out now if you don't want to be takin' a body home with ya. You have to the count of five."

"You don't have to count. I'm here." Gideon scooted out of the barn and gained his feet, both hands held up beside him.

"Well, who do we have here?" Anderson lifted his head triumphantly. "Put your gun on the ground, boy. Kick it over to me."

A look passed between Gideon and Faith as he complied, his gun tumbling into a cloud of dust as it careened over the earth. Did he see relief in those eyes? Hope? Did Faith think they stood a chance against this maniacal mountain of a man?

"That's right." Anderson stooped just enough to pluck the weapon off the ground and shove it in his belt. "Protect the pretty girl at your own expense. Oldest tale in the book."

Gideon's jaw clenched. "So is that of the man willing to hurt a woman for his own advantage."

"Hurt a woman?" Anderson snorted. "I wasn't about to hurt no woman, especially one who can help me get what I want from old Carter. I just knew you was too weak to challenge me." His head angled, his stringy hair lifting on the wind. "Ain't you that poker player I heard rode into Gold Strike not too long ago? Shouldn't you know the difference between a bluff and the real thing?"

Gideon's teeth gritted. "I refuse to play games with this woman's safety."

A derisive laugh lit the air, Anderson glancing playfully between them. "Caught you in her snares already, did she?" He studied Faith's profile from the side. "I've got to admit, she is real pretty."

"Lay a finger on her and I'll kill you."

Anderson's nostrils flared with his wicked grin. "And how, exactly, do you plan on doin' that when I've got your gun?"

Gideon's fists clenched at his sides. "I'll kill you with my bare hands."

The outlaw's scornful eyes descended him. "Boy, I would like to see you try. Any day you want to fight, just let me know." He pulled on Faith's hair again, his bristly cheek coming alongside hers. "You should have heard the perverse things she was sayin' to me while you waited out here like a coward. Seems to me she's in the market for a real man, not one scared of his own shadow."

Blood raged through Gideon's veins. He pumped his hands again, his nostrils fuming and lips tight. Every inch of his body begged him to unleash his fury on the poor excuse for a man now taunting him. But Anderson still had a pistol in his hand. He could still harm Faith no matter what he said.

"Nothing to say?" Anderson's look turned smug. "I didn't think so. Now, I want to know what the two of you were doing poking around my property."

Faith stood straighter. "I told you. I came to speak with you." Through the dust and gauzy sunlight, her eyes silently warned Gideon to play along. "I need your help to get my father's money."

"Yet you lied to me when I spotted your horses outside." His low laugh rattled Gideon's nerves. "I'm not buying what you're selling, girl. You better tell me the truth before the rest of my gang rides in and you have a lot more men to contend with than just me."

Gideon's heart thudded. If that happened, they would have no way out of this place. They might keep her for her usefulness, but he doubted they would leave her unharmed. And without anything to offer them, he was as good as dead.

A defeated look had entered Faith's eyes. Her lips parted, her expression imploring him. Gideon softly shook his head, but she had already made up her mind. "We came to look for the missing gold," she said matter-of-factly. "Maybe for Sylvia Hammond too."

Anderson blinked, as if processing the information one word at a time. Then a bold laugh burst from his lips. His hand released Faith's hair, his gun diving into his holster. He laughed again, harder this time, holding his side in his glee. "You came here looking for gold?" His hand brushed down his whiskers. "And for Sylvia Hammond? Am I hearing this right?"

Faith pulled away from him, his jesting met with a glare. "You act as if it's such a far stretch of the imagination. You are every bit capable of stealing money that doesn't belong to you, of kidnapping women. You've done both before."

"I won't deny that." He gave one last stilted chuckle. "Heck, I wish I'd been the one to take that gold out from under the banker's nose. I tried to steal it once and failed. Money's probably cursed anyway."

Faith studied him with a keen, unconvinced eye. "Why should we believe you? You've been a cancer on this town ever since you set foot in it."

"I don't care if you believe me, sweetie." His forehead wrinkled. "The sheriff already searched this place high and low and came back empty-handed. You won't find nothing he didn't."

Her arms crossed over her chest. "And Sylvia Hammond?"

"What about Sylvia Hammond?"

"She's been missing for months now. You can't tell me you didn't have something to do with that."

Anderson strode toward her, his threatening body looming close as Gideon fought with everything he had to stay rooted in place. "Not that I owe you an explanation, Miss Carter, but I ain't seen Sylvia Hammond since she took off on that train. I don't know where she went, nor do I care."

"From the mouth of the man who's made an enemy out of her husband." Faith's fingertips tapped along her arm. "You're the very first person who would wish to harm her."

He snarled. "I don't give a fig what happens to Sylvia Hammond."

"You hate Red Fox."

"With everything in my God-fearing soul."

"His gang killed your brother, and his son walked away from a murder conviction."

Anderson growled. "I don't need a reminder."

Despite his intimidating presence, she propped up her chin and looked him squarely in the eye. "They took your brother. Why wouldn't you, in turn, take Adrian Fox's mother?"

A death-like silence enshrouded the farm. Gideon waited, his pulse pounding, as Anderson stared into Faith's unflinching eyes.

Gideon held his breath, his enamored stare focused only on her. Anderson stood at least a foot above her, all muscle and brawn, pure intimidation. Yet Faith stood her ground with a clear head and unshakable bravery. Gideon had never wanted her more than in that moment.

When Anderson spoke again, his low voice ground out, mournful and strained. "Sylvia Hammond deserves to die. They all do. But I ain't never raised my hand against a woman, and I don't plan to start now—unless you give me a reason."

His broad chest swelled, his jaw like callous stone. He would entertain no more talk of his involvement in these schemes. The angered stare of a provoked hornet swung from Faith to Gideon.

The young gambler understood the reality of their situation. They had boxed themselves in on every side, placed themselves at his mercy. If they wanted to be free of this place, they would either have to out-maneuver him or overpower him, and he would make either option close to impossible.

Sixteen

Dust stung Faith's eyes, forcing her to blink away the gritty sensation. Fury blasted through her, hot and loud, building every second she stood staring at the loathsome outlaw. Her skin still flamed where he'd held her, as if his rough fingers had left an imprint.

She considered their situation once more. Anderson had holstered his pistol, but he could snatch it back in a wink. Neither she nor Gideon had anything to defend themselves with, and if they waited much longer, his posse would surround them. If they hoped to get off this ranch unharmed, they had to move quickly.

Gideon met her gaze through the sunlit air. Did he have a plan to rescue them? The uncertainty in his dark eyes gave her little hope. Faith dragged in a breath of milkweed and pine, an idea taking shape. If he didn't take action, she would.

"What do you plan to do with us?" Gideon asked.

Anderson's satisfied smirk revolved from her to him. "That all depends on what you can give me. Do you have anything to offer?"

She squeezed her teeth together. Of course they had nothing to offer. After a failed and humiliating mission, they sat like two flightless pigeons on a rail, waiting to be picked off.

"What do you want?" Gideon's voice remained steady, though his fidgety steps gave him away.

"A man like me can always use more money." Anderson set his enormous hands on his hips, his fingers far too close to his pistol.

"We don't have any money." Her words pressed out with the edge of irritation. He must have known they had nothing. An orphaned woman working in a saloon and a drifting gambler? He just wanted to play with them like a child dangling a spider from its web.

"Well, that does put you in quite the spot, doesn't it?" The outlaw's lips pursed impishly as his leering gaze descended her once more. "Of course, there are other forms of currency in this world, aren't there?"

Gideon stepped forward without hesitation. "Her virtue is not a form of currency, Anderson. You'd best get any idea to the contrary out of your head now."

Anderson glared back from the corner of his eye. "You don't have much of a leg to stand on, Valdez. Bargaining may be your only hope."

"I will *not* bargain with *her*."

Anderson snorted. "Once enough men get out here, I might not have a say in what happens to her."

"You always have a say." Gideon's arms rippled from his clenched hands to his elbows. "You're in charge out here. You make the rules."

"And you were both dim enough to come out here of your own accord. No one forced you to play with fire."

A sensation of dread dropped inside Faith. They had nothing to sway him with. Even if she could use her unique position with her father, he had no reason to keep Gideon alive. The longer they stayed here, the better chance her innocence, so fearlessly guarded by her companion, would be slaughtered.

Their heated words became an incoherent buzz in her whirling mind. Her gaze narrowed on Starlight, now looking her way from her spot beside Phantom. She had always proved such an intelligent, obedient horse. One ear twitched as her eyes locked on Faith. She knew trouble stirred. Her senses alerted her to danger.

Faith allowed her chin to dip and rise again in a barely perceptible motion. The animal straightened up, awaiting another signal. Faith nodded once more, tapping her fingers against her skirts. Starlight released a loud huff and backed away from the post Faith had only loosely looped her reins around. She stuck out her palm, halting the beast. *Not too quick, Starlight. Don't attract his attention.*

Casting a furtive glance at the arguing men, she ensured Anderson was too involved in defying Gideon to notice her horse unhitched, standing apart from the other. Faith slowly revolved her palm toward herself and inched the animal closer with her fingers. Each time Starlight began to neigh or excitedly come too fast, she stopped her. Obediently, her mount traversed the ground in ginger steps until she stood half a foot from Anderson, her snout close enough to blow down his shirt if she wanted.

Somewhere along the way, Gideon had taken notice of the advancing horse and intensified his quarrel with Anderson. The outlaw's flesh had reddened, his voice booming over the yard as Gideon tested his last nerve.

"The two of you came trespassing on my land. I don't owe you a gosh darn—" He scowled, swiping at his neck. "I don't owe you a thing. In fact, you both should be begging for my mercy. Nobody comes out here and leaves without—" At another brush of the horse's breath against his hair, he reeled enough to finally notice Starlight standing near. "What in blazes?"

"Stand up, Starlight." Faith's command launched the horse's front hooves into the air.

"Blast." Anderson dove for his gun, but the horse's majestic frame already towered over him.

"Forward, Starlight. Kick." One swift shove of her hoof collided with Anderson's shoulder and sent him sprawling on the ground. A string of curses lifted off his lips as he held his shoulder and his gun skittered across the dirt.

"All fours, Starlight." Faith covered the earth between them in a few quick strides and jumped on the horse's back. "Come on." She whirled toward Gideon. "We need to go."

Gideon glanced toward Phantom.

Faith held the excited animal in place. "We don't have time." Her breath hardened as Anderson began to roll on his side. His gun lay in the dirt, but he had both of theirs, too. "We don't have time to get him."

With one last wayward glance toward Phantom, Gideon snatched Anderson's gun, jogged to catch up, and swung up behind her in the saddle. His strong arms came around her, anchoring at her waist.

Ignoring the pleasantly dizzying effect his touch had on her, she flicked the reins over Starlight's neck and kicked her sides. "Yaw!"

The horse burst off like a firework, blasting over the weed-dappled ground and into the cover of trees in a few powerful strides. Faith gripped the saddle in her clenched thighs as Starlight climbed the mountainsides, fashioning a winding path through the dense foliage. With every hoof beat, she led them farther from Anderson's clutches and into the heart of the deep woods.

Faith had traversed these trails a thousand times, yet they'd never beckoned her like today. Never had the air felt so crisp and clean. Never had the sweeping branches seemed to reach down so lovingly and welcome her in. The stench of Anderson still clung to her, his unwashed bedsheets and dirty dishes, his liquor-tinged breath. Faith shook him off her as she rode on, relishing the sturdy torso of the man now warming her back.

His large hands squeezed her sides. "I think we're far enough away now if you'd like to rest, perhaps collect ourselves." His breath danced along her neck in a delightful way.

Faith glanced back the way they'd come. "What if he follows us?"

Gideon emitted a low chuckle. "With the path you cut through the woods, I doubt the best tracker in the world could find us. Besides"—he patted Starlight's side—"thanks to this beauty, he's injured. I don't see him riding out after us anytime soon."

"No, but his gang very well could." She sighed. "I suppose you're right. Starlight deserves a break, if nothing else, after what she did for us. There's a lake not far from here. I'm sure she wouldn't mind the drink."

The slanting shadows of early afternoon fell across the forest as the pair journeyed through the dense woodlands to the shimmering blue body of water nestled in the foothills. Faith hadn't noticed her hunger until that moment, but the sight of the freshwater lake launched pangs in her stomach. Before her father's disgrace, afternoons at the lake had meant evenings of fried fish.

She slowed Starlight near a sandy bank and waited for Gideon to jump down first before accepting his hand and slipping off. His fingers grasped hers a moment too long, flushing her cheeks in color. Faith twisted toward the lake, forcing him to relinquish her hand. Fate had pushed them physically together too much of late. She had to remedy that if she wanted to think with a clear head.

"What's this place called?" Gideon ambled forward, taking in the sparkling blue array tucked quietly into a corner of the shadowed forest. Mountains capped in snow stood behind it, their rolling foothills reaching around to cradle the serene waters.

"Mirror Lake," she said, savoring the mountain breeze as it swept her face and tossed back loose tendrils of her hair. "I spent many good days here in childhood." Before reality tainted those memories and robbed them of their joy.

"I've been many places, but I—" Gideon squinted against the glimmering rays of sunlight. "I'm not sure I've seen anything this beautiful." He turned just enough to watch her from the corner of his eye. "But perhaps it's the company I'm with that makes it so."

Faith tried desperately to suppress the smile pinching her lips. "You're trouble, aren't you, Mr. Valdez? You know just what to say to make a girl blush." Sweeping her skirts aside, she strode to the edge of the lake where the water met the sand in a soft, silty shore.

"I'm not trying to make you blush. I'm trying to pay you a compliment." His deep voice drew closer behind her. "I apologize if receiving a compliment is embarrassing."

Without glancing back, Faith bent to unlace her boots and kick them into the sand. Her stockings came next, a considerable feat in the art of modesty with Gideon right beside her. She beamed up at him as she wiggled her bare toes in the sand. "A lake like this just isn't the same with shoes on."

Gideon laughed, tossing off his own shoes as Faith lifted her skirts a little higher and ventured into the shallow water. Ice prickled her feet and ankles, a rejuvenating kind of cold that evoked memories of days long gone. The embrace of nature could almost wash away the sting of her father's horrible deeds. If only it could erase them from her memory, wipe out the day she'd stood there with a choice and a revolver—and picked integrity over the man who'd reared her.

Faith ventured along the shoreline until she came to a series of large rocks bordering the lake's edge. She slipped onto one, watching with amusement as Gideon navigated his way barefoot to where she sat. He had the look of a child, with trousers rolled up mid-calf and a boyish grin etched across his face. He'd left his hat behind with Starlight, letting the full sun illuminate his black hair and the wind toss it about.

Faith set her feet on the rock and tucked her knees beneath her chin. Had she ever dared sit in a man's presence like this, no shoes and relaxed, without the worry of appearing improper or making her father look good? She pulled in a long breath and let the breeze beat her skirts. Her forced venture into the real world had never felt so much like freedom before.

"This water is freezing," Gideon said as he splashed through it toward her. "Do you actually swim in this?"

Faith's shoulders lifted. "Sometimes. When I'm in the mood for a brisk swim. It warms up a little in summer."

"It's criminal." Yet he was still chuckling when he came to a hefty log and plopped down beside her.

"I take it the water's warmer where you're from?"

Gideon found a dry place for his feet on a sandbar. "Much warmer. In fact, you can swim all year long in some lakes in Texas."

Her brow arched. "You're a long way from home."

Silence settled over them for a few beats. Gideon let his eyes wander the colorful wildflowers painting the verdant foothills. "I'm not sure I would call it home anymore. It's where I was born, but I haven't been back for many years." His voice faltered, rasping the final word.

Did just thinking of it really awaken such pain? At the risk of provoking more, she indulged her curiosity. "Well, why did you leave it, if you don't mind my asking?"

Gideon's head shook. "I don't mind, but"—he stooped to pluck a rock from the ground and smooth his thumb over its surface—"it isn't a pleasant tale. I'm not sure you'll want to hear it."

Her arms fastened around her folded legs. "Of course I do, if you don't mind me knowing. I mean, I thought we were..." She stopped before her words betrayed her.

His eyes flashed into hers, dark and meaningful. "You thought we were what?"

Faith let her gaze entwine with his. "Friends, maybe? I know we've had a rocky go of it so far, but after you saved me—" *I would do anything for you.*

His full lips lifted poignantly. "See, I said you would like me once you got to know me."

Faith rolled her eyes. "Yes, be very proud of yourself, Mr. Valdez. I do like you." So much, her heart squeezed just to say it.

"I like you too, Faith Carter." He sighed, leaning back and releasing his rock into the air. They both watched it careen in an upward arc, then fall and plunk into the water. "I suppose if I know your scars, you ought to know mine."

Only the twitter of birds and rush of wind in the trees disturbed the tranquil quiet as he set his arms on his knees and hung his head. "I don't even go back there in my memories much after what happened." His voice was raw, laden with grief. "It's too painful to think about."

His feet shifted, disturbing the rocky soil. "I came from a family who lived in the Lower Rio Grande region since well before it was annexed. Texas was home long before the rangers rode in to claim it."

Sorrow haunted his gaze as he stared listlessly out at the lake. "Every year they moved in farther, claimed more of our land, said we owed them due for living on American soil."

Faith frowned. "Why would you owe them anything? This country is free. It doesn't cost to make a home here."

"Not for some people." He picked up another rock, turning it over in his hand. "It's different for Mexicans, though. The rangers would push us around because they knew they could. The government would allow them to."

The sentiment pinched something in her gut. Faith turned the words over and again in her mind. She knew so little of Texas or southern states, of the nation that lay beyond the border. "Is that why you left? Because they were encroaching on your land?"

He stared at the stone in his hand a prolonged moment. "In a way it is." His voice choked and his fingers clenched around the stone. "I was only a boy. They kept coming back, demanding more. No matter what my parents and grandparents gave them, they were never satisfied."

He turned dark, burdened eyes to her, his soul looking out through their coffee-hued depths. "They came one night and threatened to kill us unless we gave them more." His shoulders fell. "We had nothing more to give."

Faith looked on in silence as he hurled another stone into the lake, rippling the water around it. "They burned our houses—every last one in the village. They shot everyone who tried to escape."

A harsh breath whisked down Faith's throat, her hand flying to her mouth. The gruesome picture splashed across her mind's eye brewed nausea deep in her core. How could humanity perform such cruel acts upon one another? How could anyone be so ruthless?

When the shock dissipated, her hands slowly fell from her face. "How did you survive that?"

Gideon stared at a distant spot on the horizon, his gaze hollow. "My father had given me a gun for protection. I shot at two of the rangers, and I ran for my life. I never looked back."

Her jaw hardened. "Good."

His eyes met hers again, his grief palpable in their somber depths. "I could have saved my mother if I'd taken the shot sooner, but I was scared and I hesitated." His chest swelled. "She died because I was a coward."

"No." Faith leaned forward, grasping his shoulder. "Don't do that to yourself."

He sniffed back his emotion. "It's the truth. I saved myself, didn't I? I could have saved her." His strong jaw worked, his breath pressing hard through his nostrils.

Faith's heart lurched at the sorrow in his eyes, the myriad of regrets that would never find absolution. "You can't blame yourself. I know, for I *did* pull the trigger and have wondered if it was the right choice since that moment." Her fingers constricted on his shoulder. "No choice is the right one when it comes to life and death." If only she could convince herself of her own words.

Gideon's eyes, dark as onyx gleaming beneath the sun, searched hers. He kept his steady gaze latched with hers an achingly tense string of moments before he lifted her hand off his shoulder and placed it between his. Their warmth tunneled through her entire body, reaching the ends of her fingers and toes. One side of his mouth pulled up before he bent low and gently brushed those lips across the top of her hand.

"If more people like you existed, Miss Carter, I would have a whole lot more faith in the world we live in."

Seventeen

FAITH'S WILLOWY HAND FELT like the petals of a rose beneath Gideon's fingertips. He held it firmly in his grasp several more seconds, savoring the quickening pace of her pulse. Did her heart rush when she looked at him the way his did for her? Did being in his presence feel like the first real home she'd ever known?

He swallowed back his thoughts and let her hand slip away as he gazed across the sparkling lake. He barely knew her. To empty the contents of his heart so boldly might very well scare her away. Besides, he had nothing to offer a girl like her. She'd been reared on luxury, fine clothing and gourmet food, a home that would no doubt make his wildest dreams look like mere rubbish. As soon as he located this stolen gold, he would pack up and move on with his life. He would forget her, allow her to find a man worthy of her character and beauty, of the unblemished heart peering out through her eyes every time she looked at him.

Plucking the last of the stones he'd collected from the log beside him, Gideon turned it around in his fingers. "I've done enough thinking for today, enough dwelling on the past." Strategically angling back his arm, he tossed a flat rock across the top of the water and watched it skip along the surface.

"No more dwelling on the past, then." Faith set her elbows on her knees and rested her chin on her hands. "What do you suggest we do? Fight more outlaws? Put our lives on the line looking for more gold?" The barest of smirks dented her beautiful skin.

Gideon pursed his lips, studying her profile brimmed in sunlight, letting his gaze wander the lustrous blonde hair partially hanging around her shoulders after Jeremiah Anderson's assault. "I have a few ideas, though I don't think a girl like you would agree to them."

Curiosity edged out the shyness in her bright eyes. "And what ideas are those, Mr. Valdez?"

Finding his footing, he pushed off the log and stood to his full height. "If we were in Texas, you wouldn't even need to ask. There's only one thing we would be doing." His hand lifted to the buttons on his shirt, slowly descending as they unclasped one by one.

Faith flushed and glanced away. "I'm sure I don't understand."

He finished with the last of his buttons and pulled his shirt over his head. "We would swim, of course—with the kind of temperatures we had in Texas. If you saw a lake, you got in it."

Her eyes swung back to him, cautiously avoiding his bare chest. "You really want to swim in this climate? That water is freezing, I promise you."

With a laugh, Gideon bent low and splashed his fingers through the gentle waves. "It isn't so bad. I've certainly swam in worse. Besides"—he couldn't keep his admiring gaze from playfully skittering over her—"I can't remember the last time I had a swim partner as beautiful as the lake itself."

Faith rolled her eyes in good humor. "You, sir, are a genuine flirt."

He gave her a satisfied grin. "Just making an observation."

Her arms wrapped self-consciously around her knees. "Well, I don't want to get in there. It's too cold. You'll see. As soon as you jump in, you'll change your mind."

Gideon cocked one brow. "Care to wager on that?"

She eyed him suspiciously. "What do you mean?"

His head flicked toward the lake. "If I can stay in there longer than two minutes, you join me. If not, I'll admit my defeat and never ask you again."

Her eyes narrowed. "And have me soaking wet the entire ride home?"

He shrugged. "Won't that be worth it? To lord your victory over me?"

"Fine." Faith looked at him self-importantly. "But you'd best dry off in the sun afterward. And don't complain to me when your teeth are chattering and your whole body is shaking. I've tried to warn you."

Gideon faced the lake as if challenging an old foe. His torso warmed beneath the feel of her eyes on his back, burning into him. His muscles tensed as he approached the lapping water's edge. It took only a dip of his toe for the cold to slice through his frame.

Gideon stepped gingerly over the colorful rocks, ignoring each new jolt of ice as it shot up his body. With water up to his knees, he turned back to waggle his eyebrows at Faith. He would walk through the Arctic itself if it meant getting her in this water.

Once the chill hit his waist, he had no choice but to charge ahead and dive beneath the waves headfirst. The bitter temperature cascaded over him, numbing his skin in icy prickles. Gideon employed his muscles, propelling himself through the water and warming his extremities despite the brutal cold nipping at him. His head shot out of the lake with gusto, droplets of cold water flying off his hair.

Treading water, he peered through his bleary vision at Faith seated on the shoreline.

She shook her head. "Cold enough for you?"

"It's perfect." His legs worked harder, keeping him afloat and staving off the biting cold.

A laugh burst from her full lips. "You're a liar. That water is nothing short of torturous." Mirth danced in her eyes, the water reflecting off their warm depths.

"You say torturous; I say invigorating." He made a show of diving beneath the water and springing up again, frolicking about as if enjoying a bath in the heat of summer. The more he made her giggle, the more his heart strained to hear more.

After several blissful moments, the shock had worn off his skin. "I do believe that's well beyond two minutes, Miss Carter."

She recoiled. "It can't be."

"Ah, but it is." He swam closer to shore until his bare feet squished the muddy lake floor. "It's time for you to hold up your end of the bargain."

Faith glared at him. "You're not really going to make me get in there, are you? Just because you're crazy enough to brave those waters doesn't mean I am."

"The way I see it, my word is my bond." He tried to keep the smugness off his face, but still it inched onto his lips. "You're not the type to go back on a deal, are you?"

Pinning him with a defiant look, she determinedly pushed to her feet and set her hands on her hips. "Well, turn around then."

Gideon scoffed. "What?"

"If I'm to get in that water, I'll drown in all this. Let me shed some of these layers."

He could only stare for several more seconds before he nodded and turned away. His heartbeat accelerated at the rustle of her clothing behind him. Suddenly the wisdom of this idea eluded him. She was a respectable girl from a wealthy family. He could ruin her reputation and her life if he didn't tread carefully. Yet before his tongue could utter the ideas raging through his mind, the sound of her splashing feet hit the shallow water behind him.

Faith shrieked, her cries of shock punctuated only by delightful strands of laughter. Gideon turned to find her waist-deep in the water, clad in a corset and petticoats. Her dress and bustle lay discarded over the rocks, along with the ribbon that had bound the last of her hair. It fell freely over her shoulders now, catching the sun's rays in golden glimmers. Gideon's heart stuttered as she looked at him above the water, her lovely face illuminated by moving reflections.

"I hope you're happy, Mr. Valdez. It will take hours to dry out these petticoats." She shivered against the cold, but kept on through the water until it covered her shoulders.

"I *am* happy." In fact, a happier time he couldn't remember as he studied her, a perfect vision of light and beauty, silhouetted by aromatic pines and swaying wildflowers. When he stumbled out of Texas as a lonely child, he never could have pictured such wonder even existing.

Faith licked her lips and stared across the water. "Now that you dragged me all the way out here, you aren't even going to speak with me?"

Gideon shook himself to life. "I'm sorry, I'm just—" *So lost when I look at you, I can't find words.* "Distracted."

"Ah, yes. Distracted. No doubt you wore your mind out attempting to lure me into this ice vortex."

He grinned back at her. "That was my plan all along."

Her arms swished through the water with captivating grace. "So the hardened stranger is more than just a gambler, I see. He traps unsuspecting women in the wild and freezes them to death."

Gideon's head fell to the side. "I hate to deliver dull information, but the man you see before you is indeed only a worthless gambler, and not a good one at that." After the fiasco he'd created in Gold Strike, he might very well consider a new profession.

"You were good enough to beat Old Joe and those other men when you wanted to"—she simpered at him knowingly—"despite having a few extra cards up your sleeve."

He returned her smile. "I fear you know too much about me."

Whether intentionally or not, she moved closer through the water. "That can't be true. I hardly know a thing about you."

"You know where I'm from, what happened to my family." Gideon's toes dug into the malleable earth. "You even know my faults and the parts of me that are not exactly genuine."

A thoughtful look entered her eyes. "Yet I still don't truly know you."

His feet pushed harder into the soil. "What more is there possibly to know?" And how much could he reveal before he shattered in front of her?

"Why you're a gambler, perhaps?"

Gideon's broad shoulders lifted. "After I left Texas, I didn't have much of a choice. I crossed paths with a traveling poker player willing to take me in. He told me I had a gift."

"You never thought of doing anything else, even after you grew up?"

His chest ached. "It's what I know how to do. Trying something else would feel like—"

"Starting over?"

He nodded. "Like trying to learn how to swim when I already know how to fly."

Her lips pressed softly together, deliberation warring in her eyes. "But a life like that must be, well—it must be lonely, isn't it? Never staying in one place. Never putting down roots."

A familiar ache stirred in his belly, the same sad resolution settling over him. "A man like me doesn't have roots—not after they were torn away so long ago."

The skin between her eyes dented. "You deserve more than that, Gideon. More than flitting from town to town until the locals run you out of it. You deserve to have a life and a family of your own."

"No." His voice came out gruffer than he'd meant it. "No," he said, softer this time. "I don't want a family." Not more people to worry over. Not more people to love and lose at the hands of greedy men. He wouldn't go through it again. He wouldn't put a woman through it.

Disillusionment clouded her eyes as she sank deeper into the water until it touched her chin. "You won't ever get married? Not even if you meet a person you truly love?"

Gideon heaved the mountain air, normally a refreshing tonic. Today it filled his lungs with pressure, searing through him until he thought he would never draw another breath. How callous he must appear to her, this unblemished angel. How seriously he wished he could cast aside promises to himself and sweep her up in his arms. No woman had ever made his choices seem so impossible before.

"I'm a lone wolf. I was always meant to be." To imagine otherwise invited too much pain, too much risk.

Dipping her head back, she doused the rest of her hair and stared up at the blue sky. When she finally leveled her gaze back with his, tiny drops of water peppered her temples. Dark lashes framed her solemn eyes. They had no need for words. Her mournful gaze said everything—far more than his heart could take.

His eyes dropped to her chattering teeth. "You're freezing."

"That's because you insisted I get in this ice bath disguised as a lake."

He reached out, brushing the matted strands of hair from her face. "I just wanted to see you have a little fun."

"Fun? Is freezing to death your idea of fun?" Her eyes swept away from the fingers gently pushing back her hair. "Or proclaiming your deep need to spend your life alone—is that how you add enjoyment to your days?"

Gideon moved his fingers through the water, as if working through the questions in his soul. "You shouldn't waste a single worry on me. My life has been like this a long time. It isn't something you can change."

Her eyes met his over the water, vulnerable and empathetic. "You tell me not to care. How can I not after what we've been through together already?" Her full lips pouted with emotion. "How do I stop myself from caring?"

Gideon's breath hardened, his body like an immobile stone in the midst of the lake. Every wave attempted to pull him closer to her. He dug his heels in the pliable earth. No matter how strongly the currents tugged, he couldn't give in. She deserved so much better than him, a life so much grander than the one he could offer her. Each moment they spent gazing at one another with their hearts open lured them ever closer to falling over a cliff.

Gideon tipped his head to the side, converting his melancholy to playfulness. "I know just the way to make you forget about your concerns."

She frowned. "You do?"

"I do." Before she could ask another question, he swiftly smacked his hand against the surface of the water, dousing her in its spray.

Faith's mouth fell open. Her blonde hair plastered to the sides of her face. Freezing droplets clung to her skin, rolling down her neck. Swiping back her unruly hair, she fastened him with a hard glare. "You, Mr. Valdez, will pay for what you've done."

With a sudden blast of her arm, she launched a wall of water at him. Gideon yelped and spun away, only to be caught beneath her attack.

He turned back, his hair thoroughly soaked and a feeling of glee coursing through him. "You're in for it now, Miss Carter." As he chased after her through the icy waves, Gideon had to remind himself this was all just a beautiful dream that would soon come to an end.

Eighteen

THE SCALLOPED GABLES OF Abeline Baxter's home rose through the treetops just as the pink sparkling bands of dusk lit the sky. Faith relaxed against Gideon's solid chest, lulled nearly to sleep by Starlight's steady gait beneath them. He clicked his tongue, encouraging the weary animal up the last slope leading to Abeline's cheerful flower garden and cobbled walkway.

Though the lake's moisture still soaked through her clothes and made her itch beneath the arms, Faith had never felt so pacified as she did leaning into Gideon's warmth. She savored his closeness, the feel of his strong arms cradling her. She could pretend for the briefest, most glorious of moments that his nearness translated to love, that his presence would prove abiding in her life rather than a mere flash in time.

Evening shadows stretched over the lawn, the first crickets emerging and singing a nocturnal medley. Gideon slowed Starlight near a sprawling oak tree and sat a moment in stillness. Faith smiled, nestling the side of her face against the soft bristle of his neck. Did he want to hold on to this moment as much as she did, maybe the last excuse they would have to shelter in each other's arms?

All too soon, he eased her forward and dismounted. Faith's spirit sank as she took his offered hand and landed in the dirt beside him. No more rides together atop Starlight's back. No more swims with only the two of them and not a soul to condemn their lack of propriety. Reality hit her hard in the face after she'd penned Starlight in for the night and turned to look up at him.

The barest of smiles crinkled his eyes—eyes full of admiration. "It's been quite the day."

"Indeed." Faith fought the blush inevitably creeping up her neck whenever his gaze wandered her face so fully. "I know we could have died, but it was still the best day I've had in a very long time."

He reached out, cupping her jaw in his warm fingers. "Me too."

Faith managed a shivering breath, ripe with spring evergreens and Abeline's roses. "We haven't eaten for hours. You should come inside."

Doubt clouded his eyes as they shifted across the forest and into the shadows. "I don't know how safe it is for me to be here. I don't want to bring more trouble on you."

She scoffed. "If anything, I feel safer with you here. Anderson is no doubt looking for us both."

His concerned gaze turned back to hers. "Does he know you're here?"

Her head shook. "I don't think anybody does, except for Ellis and Cora. We'll both be in greater danger the minute we set foot in town."

His jaw set. "We can't let that happen. We can't let Jeremiah Anderson ruin your life, dictate where you go."

"What other choice do we have?" She waited, breath stuck in her throat, as deliberation knit his brow. *Ask me to come with you—to leave this place.* Her heart had already surrendered.

Instead, he took her hand, stared quietly at her fingers. His simple touch launched wondrous shivers over her body. "I don't know, but I'll think of something. I can't leave you at his mercy."

Her chest stung, her breath barely escaping. He still planned to leave her after everything that had transpired between them, after their hearts had opened to one another. *I am a lone wolf.* The words pealed through her mind again, devastating as the first time he'd uttered them. Gideon wished for a life of solitude, and her presence only threatened that.

"You should—" Her voice choked, and she tried again. "You should at least get something to eat before you go."

His eyes met hers—solemn, understanding. He finally nodded. "All right."

As if the most natural thing in the world, Faith turned her hand over and laced her fingers with his, leading him into the house. She would continue to play this role as long as he let her, to conveniently forget he wouldn't always be there.

The farmhouse sat in quiet tranquility as they stepped inside. Kerosene lamplight glowed from frosted glass lamps in the windows, but not a sound stirred from within.

"Abeline!" Faith called. She led Gideon toward the stairs. "Abeline!" No one answered back from there, either.

Her brow wrinkled. "I wonder where she could be."

"For an old woman, she seems gone quite a bit."

Faith continued on down the hallway. "She's very active. She has her cooking and gardening, and still tends to the animals by herself. I know she has activities in town that keep her busy, like quilt circle."

Indeed, the kitchen smelled of sugared blueberries and butter upon entering. A fresh pie sat on the table with one piece cut out of it.

"That looks amazing." Gideon moved toward it, but didn't relinquish her hand.

"I'm sure she wouldn't mind us having some since it's already cut into." Faith at last let him go to pull out a chair and plop into it.

Slipping into the chair next to her, he pulled the pie closer. "It's not rude of me to show up unannounced and then begin digging into her baked goods?"

Faith laughed. "I'm sure she'd be more insulted if you *didn't* eat her pie. You saw how she welcomed you last time. She doesn't care that you're here."

His dark eyes twinkled. "Then perhaps I've found a new home. The grandmother I never knew I needed." Standing, he crossed to the cupboard and retrieved two plates from inside.

Faith simpered as she watched him dole out two sloppy pieces with a pie server. "You don't want to have a proper dinner first?"

"A proper dinner? Where's the fun in that?" Gideon licked a finger as he slid a plate in front of her and handed her a fork.

Her fingers closed around the utensil, brushing his. "Ah, adulthood—when you're finally free enough to act like a child if you wish."

"Grand, isn't it?" He sank the tines of his fork into his dessert, two dimples emerging when he tasted the first bite.

The pair enjoyed the fruity treat in companionable silence, only the clink of their forks disturbing the gentle gusts of air flowing through the window and ruffling the curtains. A romanticized picture of her future snuck up—a portrait of the two of them seated side by side, needing nothing but the other's presence to find contentment. Despite her most concerted censures, she couldn't squelch the girlish hopes growing inside her when she looked his way.

When nothing but crumbles remained on their plates, Gideon collected their dishes and washed them in the bin beneath the window. Drying his hands on a dish towel, he reluctantly looked her way. "I should probably go."

Faith's back stiffened. "Go where? To the Wild Rose?"

He shrugged. "Not sure where else I could go."

"I don't think it's safe for you. What if Jeremiah Anderson comes looking for you?"

Gideon tossed the towel over the edge of the wash basin. "I can't avoid him forever. I'll have to go back sometime. So will you."

The prospect knotted her stomach. She toyed with a wooden fruit bowl placed at the table's center. "I would feel better if we went back together—if we at least had each other to rely on."

Another breeze blew in, the smell thick with dirt and sap. Gideon's intense stare locked on her. "Are you afraid to be alone? Is that it?"

She fought the tremors coursing through her. "It seems silly after all that's happened, but—"

"You're allowed to feel afraid. You're allowed to have human emotion."

His words settled into her, touching the places she kept buried beneath her brave surface. Had anyone ever told her that before—that she had permission to feel? That she could voice her own needs without sounding like a selfish, spoiled child?

She propped her chin up. "I think you should stay here with me."

His dark eyes kept steady with hers. "If that's what you feel you need, then of course I'll stay. But, Faith—" His head shook. "What about Mrs. Baxter? I'm sure she doesn't want a strange man sleeping under her—"

"She doesn't have to know." Boldness encompassed her, a fiery, determined flood coursing through her veins. "If you sleep in my room and sneak out early with me when I leave for work, she'll never know the difference."

He swallowed, color brewing from beneath his shirt collar. "You're sure you want to risk it? You could lose the only place you have to live."

Disregarding every warning voice in her head, Faith pushed to her feet, her chair scraping the floor behind her. "I'm sure." She held out her hand. "Come on, let's go before she comes back from whatever it is she's doing."

His strong hand slipped into hers, every bone and vein pressing back against her skin. The stairs creaked beneath their feet, the world fading farther away the higher they climbed. Faith steeled herself against the inner chidings of her father. *Never go anywhere with a man and no proper chaperone. Don't place yourself in a dishonorable position.* She held tighter to Gideon's hand. Her father had lost his right to instruct her the minute he chose money over integrity.

Slipping soundlessly through the door, she waited for Gideon to pass through before easing it shut. Her fingers lingered upon the door as it gently clicked, a quiet breath pulling inward. What was she doing, bringing a man into her bedroom, at night no less—a man who could flatten her with a mere glance of his eyes? Faith lit a lamp with the flick of her wrist rather than let herself think.

"Your room is very nice." Gideon glanced around at the polished furnishings and lace curtains in the windows, avoiding her form near the door.

"I am very blessed to be here." Faith compelled her feet forward, though they protested as if captured in ice. "Please make yourself comfortable. You must be comfortable if you are to sleep here."

He hesitated, rubbing his hands together before inching toward the bed and sitting down. He set his hands on either side of him, perching them on the edge of her mattress. "Are you sure about this? If anyone finds out—"

She halted him with a hand to his chin. Gideon turned his deep, expressive eyes up to hers.

"I told you I'm sure. We both need protection against Jeremiah Anderson, and the best way to get that is to stick together." Her thumb swept gently over the cleft in his chin. "My reputation was ruined a long time ago when my father decided to hurt people for money. One night alone with a man won't change anything."

Throat bobbing, he nodded. "I'm glad you trust me enough to let me stay here."

A smile pinched the side of her mouth as she let her hand drop away from him. "Should I have any reason not to trust you? You've defended my honor, been blackmailed because of it. You've been alone with me many times and never—" She bit her lip, heat rising in her cheeks.

Gideon stared up at her, his swarthy skin glowing in the lamplight. Strands of dark hair fell into his eyes. "You can always trust me, Faith." His voice was low and raw. "But I'm not always sure I can trust myself."

When she merely angled her head and frowned, he took another breath. "You are probably the most beautiful creature I've ever laid eyes on. It's not an easy thing for me to spend all this time with you and not—" He caught himself, his nostrils ballooning as his gaze fell to the floor.

"Because of your desire to be alone?" Her voice barely sounded in the quiet room.

He nodded, keeping his eyes fastened to the floor. "I don't want to start something I can't finish, but spending time with you weakens my resolve every single day."

A dam burst forth within her, emotions spilling out. Faith flattened her hands over her abdomen. Not because he didn't want her. Not because who she was disgusted him, but because he had to move on. Alternate explanations had plagued her for days, but this she could bear. As long as he saw her as something beautiful and not the worthless burden her father had proclaimed her to be.

Backing slowly away, she moved toward the bureau. "I might as well start getting ready." She reached into a drawer for her folded nightgown. "If you don't mind turning away, I'll dress for bed."

Gideon blinked forlornly up at her a brief moment before he respectfully swiveled away, maneuvering his body in the opposing direction. Faith's fingers shook as she unfurled her soft cotton nightgown and laid it atop the bureau. Layers of clothing came one after the other, freeing her until she stood almost nude in the chilly air. Every few seconds, she glanced at Gideon, but not a single muscle flinched. He kept his head still, his gaze fixed to the wall.

Soon she was dressed again and gathering her discarded clothes. "You can look now. I'm decent." Yet as she went about bundling up her used clothing and stuffing it in her hamper, she felt anything but. Gideon's words echoed across her heart, a mirror of her own desire. Could she stay as strong as him, knowing he intended to leave her?

He set his hands in his lap, swinging his gaze to the window, where the sky had darkened and stars begun to speckle the night. "It's so peaceful here."

She smiled contentedly, pacing to the window. "It is that. I love looking out at this view, especially at night."

The trees danced in the wind, the moon painting a luminescent ribbon across their jagged curtain. Starlight rested with two other horses in the corral below, her every huff throwing clouds of vapor into the air. At this vantage point, one could easily forget the war raging beyond the tranquil fields and fragrant forests. Faith followed them to the edge of oblivion, where distant fog shrouded their lush beauty.

Letting her hand fall from the lace curtain, she pivoted to Gideon. His eyes had fastened on her now, the look in them threatening to drain all the strength from her legs. She crossed her arms over her chest, cuffing her hands around the bare skin beneath her cap sleeves. Her hair hung freely around her shoulders now, hopefully concealing anything too salacious the thin fabric of her nightgown might reveal.

Slowly he stood, as if rising before a holy relic. His gaze swept her lamplit face, her neck and collarbone, before he looked away with a gulp. "I shouldn't be here."

"You should."

His head wagged, more of his scruffy hair falling over his eyes. "You will be safe enough out here by yourself if Anderson doesn't know where you are."

Growing bolder, she uncrossed her arms and clenched them at her sides. "I think we both know that's not the only reason you're here."

He blinked, his eyes climbing to hers. "It isn't?"

Faith stepped forward, delicious chills peppering her skin at the earnestness in his gaze. "Not unless you don't feel about me the way I feel about you." A weight freed from her chest to admit it. Even if he utterly rejected her, she'd spoken the truth of her heart.

His fingers lifted, sweeping soft tendrils of hair from her face. "Whatever feelings you have for me, you should forget them." Yet the tenderness in his touch defied his callous words.

"You said I was the most beautiful creature you'd ever beheld."

"You are, without a doubt."

"But you care nothing for me." How could that be?

"Oh, *preciosa*. I do care. I care too much. In fact"—his thumb traced her cheekbone to her jawline—"I care enough to know that you deserve far better than me."

Faith took another defiant step forward. "I want *you*."

His eyes darkened at her words, plummeting to her lips and lingering there before he took in a breath and moved back. "You don't want me. I'm a liar and a cheat. I move from place to place because they all eventually catch me or run me out."

Faith set a hand on his chest, where the thud of his heart reverberated back. "You are good and kind. You rescued me when nobody else cared. You were there for me, and you have been ever since."

"You grew up with wealth and power. There's still a chance you could get it back."

"I don't want that." Her hand scrunched his shirt. "I've had wealth and status. It brought me nothing but heartache. I just want you."

Gideon released a shaky breath. "You make it hard to say no."

"Then say yes." She pulled him closer, her heart in her throat. "Say yes, Gideon."

Fire erupted in his eyes, burning through the sizzling air until it scattered her skin in a thousand wondrous sparks. His heartbeat hammered beneath her palm, his breath quickening a second before his lips crashed into hers—warm, commanding, washing her in euphoric bliss. Gideon's strong hands cradled her head, his lips moving against hers like a man deprived of water and drinking for the very first time.

Faith melted against him, her hands finding the shifting muscles of his back, her entire body surrendering to the thrill of his affection. His palms slid down until they reached the valley of her lower back, squeezing as if to keep her here, shielded from the outside world. Faith shivered as his kisses deepened, one hand rising to weave with her loose hair. She could stand here forever, lost in the feel of him, sheltered within his embrace. She could die in these arms.

Just as she'd snaked her arms around his neck and allowed her fingertips to twirl with the ends of his hair, a scream tore through the farm and wrenched them apart.

Nineteen

Gideon breathed heavily, raking a hand through his thick hair. He gazed through the lamplight at Faith, his hands still fixed to her lower back. "What was that?"

Seconds ago he'd dwelt in the utter perfection of her presence, his lips locked with hers, his body alive in the ecstasy of kissing her for the very first time. Then, an earth-shattering scream had torn him away from her. His hand clenched her dress. Whatever it was, he couldn't fail to protect her.

She retracted both hands from around his neck and laid them against his chest. "I don't know. It sounded like a woman. Abeline could be in trouble. We need to help her."

Without hesitation, he led her toward the closed door and yanked it open. The hall and stairwell sat in silence as they descended to the sitting room below. Nothing appeared out of place from before—the pie still half-eaten on the kitchen table, the open window emitting a pleasant breeze.

Breathless, Gideon spun in a circle. "Do you think somebody came in through the window and attacked her?"

Faith stepped toward the window, her look dubious. "It doesn't appear as if anyone's touched it—or anything else in here." She gazed out at the black night. "I think I heard the scream come from outside."

His head bobbed as he reached for the pistol holstered at his waist and checked the bullets. "I'll go out and check. You wait here."

Faith stepped forward, her chin propped up. "I'll do nothing of the sort. I'm coming with you."

"It's too dangerous. You should wait here."

"If it's too dangerous, I want to be with you." Her lips pressed determinedly together. "Please, Gideon. I don't want you to face down whatever it is alone, and I don't want to be here by myself, either." She hugged her body against an involuntary shiver.

He sighed. "All right, if you insist. Stay close to me, whatever you do. I don't want whatever happened to Abeline to happen to you too."

A look of dismay shadowed her face. "Do you think Jeremiah Anderson found us? Do you think he hurt her?"

"I don't know what to think." He slammed the gun back in its holster and seized her hand. "Let's go find her."

The night air had dipped several degrees lower, nipping at his skin as Gideon pulled Faith alongside him. A strong wind howled down the mountains and tossed the trees about. Except for the cluck of chickens in the coop and an occasional snort from the horses, not a sound rose over the rush of blood in his ears.

Gideon stood tall, surveying the property, searching for anything that could have produced such a sound. Had the poor old woman fallen down a hill—perhaps cut herself on one of the rusty gates sprinkled throughout the property? Could she be lying alone somewhere—bleeding, afraid, too weak to find help?

A murmur rose, garbled speaking, someone talking loudly and quickly. Faith pressed closer to Gideon's side as he tentatively stepped toward the barn, closer to the source of the noise. Gideon eased back one of the creaking doors, but only darkness and the aroma of hay greeted him.

"It was coming from over here, wasn't it?" He looked questioningly at Faith.

She nodded. "Somewhere over here. I heard it too."

Gideon let the barn door slip shut again, standing back as it crashed against the splintered wood. He turned and immediately jumped, the hairs on his neck rising. There in the muddled shadows of the corral stood a hunched form, only the outline of her visible beneath a thin stream of moonlight.

Faith gasped. "Abeline?" She let go of his hand and rushed toward the old woman. "Abeline, are you all right? We heard you scream."

Mrs. Baxter fixed them with broad eyes and parted lips, shock engulfing every inch of her wrinkled face. "Faith. Gideon. I didn't know the two of you were here." She glanced behind her and back again, as if in search of something unseen.

Faith set a gentle hand on her shoulder. "We came back not too long ago. We were looking for you. Are you hurt?"

Abeline blinked and smoothed out her wrinkled skirts. "No, I'm not hurt. I just—" The words fell dead, like she couldn't find them in the recesses of her mind.

"Are you sure?" Faith looked her over for any signs of injury. "We heard you screaming."

"Screaming?" Mrs. Baxter's face screwed up in a befuddled expression.

Gideon supported her by the elbow. "We heard a voice, too. Who were you talking to out here?" Did the poor elderly woman even remember?

She concentrated, looking around herself. "There's nobody out here but me. I was only tending to the horses."

"Out here again at night tending to the horses?" Faith shook her head. "It isn't right. You should let me do that from now on."

A laugh lifted off Abeline's creased lips. "I'm not dead, dear. I am perfectly capable of taking care of my own horses."

Faith pointed Mrs. Baxter toward the farmhouse. "Yet you're out here alone in the dead of night, yelling for help. There must be a better solution."

Abeline lifted herself up in a defiant pose, her chest puffing. "As I said, I'm perfectly capable, and I'll not have you young whippersnappers try to tell me otherwise." Her determined expression slipped just enough to reveal the confusion beneath. "I don't know why I screamed. I must have thought one of the horses was liable to kick me. They do that sometimes, you know."

Gideon slipped her crepey hand into his. "Here, Mrs. Baxter. Let us help you get inside."

With a swift tug of her wrist, she freed her hand and glared at him from the corner of her eye before marching toward the house. "I can walk just fine, thank you." The moonlight defined her stoic profile as she bustled off toward the front door with dogged force.

Faith released a breath as she turned toward Gideon. "She's a sweet old woman, but she doesn't like feeling helpless. I can understand her in that way."

Gideon couldn't help smoothing the hair back from her face. "Neither of you are helpless, but it does seem like she needs more assistance than she's willing to admit."

"Yes, it seems she does." Faith brushed a hand up and down her arm. "I should be here for her more often, perhaps help her in ways she may not notice. I didn't realize her mind was slipping."

Grunting an affirmative, Gideon glanced around the quiet farm. "I've only met her once before, but she had me fooled too." His head flicked toward the barn. "I suppose we should finish whatever she didn't, so she doesn't try to come out here again in the middle of the night."

"That's a good idea." Faith linked her arm around his back as they crossed the yard and opened the barn.

Alfalfa and hay captured his senses as Gideon pulled the door back for Faith and stepped in behind her. "Is there any kind of light in here? I didn't see her with a lantern."

"She keeps one on a shelf over here, along with a box of matches."

Footsteps padded through the hay before a match scraped a striker pad and a flame erupted in Faith's hand. She touched it to the wick, sending the shadows fleeing as the barn lit with wavering orange light.

"There's plenty of hay here." Faith held the lantern high as beams of light cascaded over the stacked bales. "I don't know how she keeps it so well stocked at her age, but I've never seen it empty."

After whipping a knife from his pocket, Gideon sliced through the string holding the bale in place and let it spill out. He glanced out the window at the horses convened by the corral fence. "It doesn't look like she gave them any."

"That's not a surprise." Faith set her lantern on the floor and swept aside her hair, bending low to gather a bunch of hay in her arms. "She probably came out here to feed them and completely forgot. Poor woman."

Gideon followed suit, shoveling as much hay as he could with his arms and trailing her out the barn door. The horses appreciatively snorted and whinnied as the couple dumped their loot into several troughs fixed to the fence.

"That should appease them for a while." Faith patted Starlight's neck before walking beside Gideon back to the barn.

The structure glowed in radiant serenity when they returned, gentle waves of lantern light flickering across the walls. Crickets chirped around them, a far-off owl calling across the forest. Pigeons stirred in the eaves, their wings softly brushing the rafters as they settled in together.

Gideon watched the gentle sway of Faith's hips as she sashayed across the barn. Did she have any idea how captivating she was, from her elegant movements to the heart wishing for nothing but to help her fellow man? A voice inside chided him, a persistent reminder that he couldn't let his heart entangle with another's. Yet somehow its magnetic pull refused to listen to the mind attempting to protect him.

With ginger footsteps, he crept behind her until he stood only inches away. Then his arm shot out, hooking her around the waist and pulling her to him. Faith released a breath of surprise before it dissolved into a giggle. She turned in his arms, hay clinging to her nightgown.

Her skin glowed an amber hue in the lamplight, her eyes like crystals. Her blonde hair framed her face, thick and glossy around her shoulders. Her eyes hunted his face, lingering on each feature before they returned to his.

"Have you no sense of propriety, Mr. Valdez?" Her mouth dimpled with a contented grin.

"None at all."

Gideon had no hesitation this time. His head dipped swiftly, his lips finding hers. The arm still clasped around her waist held her tighter.

Faith responded to his every kiss, her fingertips sweeping the side of his face, her lips smiling against his. How could life be so spectacular, even for just a moment? Gideon found himself wishing he could hold her forever, her soft hair beneath his fingertips, her warm lips pressed to his. He could live off her presence for the rest of his life.

But all too soon, she broke the kiss, her eyes fluttering open. "You're going to have to sneak past Abeline since we ruined our cover."

His hand scrunched the back of her nightdress. "Do you still want me to stay?" How difficult would it be to sleep near her and remain a gentleman after all this?

Her eyes, thoughtful in the dim light, matched his. "I do, Gideon. I want you to stay."

A hard breath pressed from his chest. "Very well." He would honor her, even if it meant sleeping across the room. He would not fail her—not this precious creature who had inexplicably walked into his miserable life.

The squeal of a hinge reached them just before the sound of a door slapping against a frame. The pair drifted apart, their eyes focused on the entrance to the barn, but only darkness clouded the space they'd come through.

"What do you suppose that was?" Gideon asked, his hand protectively pulling her closer.

She shook her head. "Abeline could be coming out again. We should stop her before she hurts herself."

Taking her hand, Gideon followed her to the barn doors and stepped up, pushing one back a fraction to peer around it. His body froze, tingles journeying up his spine at the sight before him. His hand constricted around Faith's.

"What is it?" Her voice barely touched him, full of trepidation. "What's out there?"

Releasing her hand, Gideon set a finger over his lips to indicate silence. With a hand to her shoulder, he positioned her before the crack in the door and propelled it open the slightest bit more. Faith gasped.

Instead of an old woman as expected, a broad-shouldered man stood only feet away. He stared up at the house and surveyed the quiet yard around him, his telltale long hair lifting on the breeze. The swollen muscles beneath his rolled-up shirt sleeves expanded, his raspy breath throwing visible clouds of vapor into the air.

Moving stealthily, Gideon silently eased the door back until it settled once again. He turned fearful eyes to Faith. "It appears that he's found us," he said, barely a whisper in her ear.

She pulled back, searching his face. "How? And where are the rest of his men?"

His shoulders lifted, an explanation so elusive it pained him. "I don't know."

She bit her lip. "What do we do now? We can't let him hurt Abeline."

"No, but I can't let him hurt you either." His hand found hers again, squeezing with a reassurance he didn't feel.

Boots crunched ominously through the dirt, the sound nearing.

"He's coming this way," Gideon said. "Quick, extinguish the lantern."

His nerves rattled as she quickly complied, blowing out the flame. Wordlessly, he tugged her back across the hay-sprinkled floor until they came to the stacked bales along the wall.

Faith slipped behind them, tucking her legs in tight and leaving Gideon enough space to sandwich himself between the stacked hay and the wall. He took one last gander through the dark at the barn doors, where heavy footsteps approached. Faith's hand blasted through the quiet and pulled him down just before the door groaned inward.

Footsteps creaked across the floor, each one quickening Gideon's heart. He leaned close to Faith, settling his arm around her, gleaning comfort from her warmth. If the worst came, he would kill for her. He had to.

Onward the footsteps crept, careful and deliberate. Darkness enshrouded the barn, now silent as a tomb. Dry hay crunched beneath Anderson's boots, his scent—mingled sweat and sawdust—clouding the air the closer he came. Gideon stiffened when a head rose into view, then husky shoulders and a broad frame. Anderson's silhouette moved past them, his eyes undoubtedly sweeping fruitlessly through the dark.

A hand reached for Gideon, soft fingers lacing with his. Gideon clasped Faith's hand tightly, noting the rapid thump of her pulse. She put on a brave face for everyone else, but she'd chosen to be vulnerable with him.

Anderson kept up his ominous walk until his fingertips scraped the wall. He turned, feeling along one side. *Funny, I've never heard him so quiet,* Gideon thought, wishing he could voice the peculiarity to Faith. Every time he'd crossed paths with Anderson before, he'd endured nothing but hollow self-praise. Somehow the criminal was far more terrifying when he didn't boast about his vast accomplishments.

Seemingly finished with one wall, he crossed their way—feeling, hunting, sniffing the air for them. Gideon's arm coiled tighter around Faith as the footsteps slowed mere inches away. *Stop where you are. Turn around and go back.* But his hopes vanished to dust the moment a hand swept the air near his ear.

Without thought, Gideon lunged for his gun, whipping it out and training it on the blackened figure. Anderson sucked in a quick breath, no doubt reaching for his own weapon. Hastily aiming, Gideon readied his gun and fired toward the sound of metal swiping leather.

A loud grunt, followed by a string of curse words. Metal clattered to the floor, presumably Anderson's gun tumbling from his hands. Gideon volleyed another shot into the expanse of black, but the form had already retreated, boots thrashing the floor in a mad dash to escape.

Holstering his pistol, Gideon sprang up from his crouched position and launched himself toward the outline of Anderson's hulking shape. Just before he could reach the door, Gideon hurled himself through the air and plastered himself over the outlaw's back. Anderson struggled, but Gideon tensed his arms around him, his muscles swelling. Gritting his teeth, he wrestled him to the ground.

A succession of thumps and scrapes filled the barn as the two grappled for several minutes. Sweat poured from Gideon's hairline, cold and salty on his lips. Anderson tried relentlessly to wiggle out of his hold, but Gideon's hands clenched on his shirt, pinning him in place.

A fist flew through the air, landing on his jaw. He fell back a dizzying second, one hand covering the throbbing spot. The reprieve gave Anderson just enough time to writhe out of his grip and begin to crawl away.

Breath heavy, Gideon lurched for him again, managing to catch only a fistful of his shirt. He would not go free this time. He would not continue to harass Faith and bring misery into her life. He had to stop him.

With a roar, Anderson broke free of his grip. Desperate, Gideon grabbed at anything he could discern in the dark. His hands clamped around a wrist. Moisture leaked over his fingers as they constricted around the flailing arm, his nostrils detecting a metallic odor. Anderson howled, attempting to twist away from him. *His hand.* Gideon must have hit his hand when he shot blindly into the barn.

One enormous foot hammered down upon his, flinging pain up his leg and throughout his entire body. Anderson shoved him backward, simultaneously ripping his arm away and knocking Gideon to the floor. Gideon scrambled up again, only to find the barn door tossed open and slapping on its hinges.

He clambered across the floor and into the dirt beyond, finding his footing. The moon had risen higher, shedding white light all the way to the forest and highlighting Anderson's fleeing form. Gideon's legs pumped after him, following the trail of blood sprinkled across the ground.

Anderson's thick mane flew behind him as he ran, his colossal form unmistakable. Just as he hit the woods, Gideon ground to a halt. He watched helplessly as Anderson swung atop his horse and galloped into the dense foliage.

Gideon stared after him, flattening a hand over his side where pain had bloomed with his exertion. Whatever happened next, he couldn't leave Faith's side—not for a moment. Anderson knew their location. He sensed their vulnerability. He would not leave Faith alone until someone stood up to extinguish his threats.

Turning away, Gideon trudged through the night. He would have to be that man or lose her forever.

Twenty

ANXIETY PROVED FAITH'S CONSTANT companion as she went about her duties at the Wild Rose, cleaning up glasses and wiping down tables. A game to her right exploded in shouts and cheers, making her jump. Faith held a hand over her heart, the thump below it slowing. Every sound startled her after their escapade with Jeremiah Anderson the day before. Every interaction put her on edge.

As she bent to place pints of ale on a table, her gaze wandered across the crowded saloon to Gideon. He had a fistful of cards in one hand, but his protective stare never left her for long. His dark eyes tracked her every movement, warm yet watchful. He glanced at the door more often than she did, no doubt expecting Jeremiah Anderson to walk in any second.

Collecting a tray of dirty dishes, Faith hoisted it high and wound her way through the spirited games and drunken conversations until she reached the kitchen. The quiet solitude offered there eased her nerves after a day spent on her feet, serving the local patrons and watching for Jeremiah Anderson. She wished she could hide out in this cozy space, away from the boisterous sounds beyond.

With a sigh, Faith diligently got to work, setting soiled dishes and glasses in the sink. The door swung open, revealing a cheerful face. Molly had her own collection of dirty dishes stacked neatly atop one another.

"Hard at work, I see—like always." She tossed Faith an appreciative grin. "Honestly, I don't know what I'd do without you. We got the best gift when you walked through our doors."

"That's a kind thing to say." Faith took the tray from her and set it on the counter. "In fact, I can't remember ever receiving a better compliment." After all that had transpired with her father, most days she felt worthless and a burden to anyone she came near.

"It's the truth." Molly dried her hands on an apron cinched around her waist. "You may have been raised on riches, but you're a hard worker and you've proven yourself. It's selfish of me, but I hope you never leave."

Faith laughed blithely. "Someday I will, unless I want to be washing dishes for the rest of my life."

"I know. It's not a fate fit for a girl like you, but I'll hold on to you as long as I can." Molly sidled up to her before the sink, edging Faith's peripheral vision. "You seem distracted today."

Faith's brows rose, her gaze never leaving the task at hand. "Hmm?"

"Ever since you came in this morning, you've appeared on edge. Didn't you enjoy your day off?"

Faith's hand froze on the water pump. How much could she say without endangering Molly? The need for a friend to confide in bit at the better sense warning her to keep quiet. "I'm fine, it's just"—she set the last of the dishes in the sink and began filling it—"it's just this business with my father."

"Hmm." Molly's arms crossed over her chest, her look knowing. "That will always be a problem. What happened yesterday to afflict you so?"

Faith swished her fingertips in the water, deliberating on her choice of words. "Jeremiah Anderson happened, unfortunately."

"Anderson?" Molly stood straighter. "What does he have to do with all this?"

"Gideon and I decided to go looking for the lost gold yesterday."

Molly's hand flew to her elbow. "You *what?*"

Faith turned just enough to meet her worried gaze. "I know it sounds ridiculous, but so much depends on this. We thought we might as well look."

Molly's fingers slipped from her arm, her mouth round. "What happened? Did he hurt you?"

"Almost." Just remembering peppered Faith's skin in goose-flesh. Remembering the stern touch of Jeremiah Anderson's hand as he held her sent shivers coursing through her. "We had two run-ins with him, actually, and both times we prevailed. He's been kicked by a horse and shot, but he never backs down."

A long breath blew out Molly's lips. "No, that he doesn't. The man's been shot more times than a practice target, and unfortunately he never dies. He's what my mother would call a cockroach."

"Yes, well, if this particular cockroach comes after me, I don't know how much chance I'll stand at evading him a third time. He seems terribly determined to get what he wants."

"He won't come here. Old Joe hates that lout. He knows he's as good as dead if he tries."

Faith pumped more water into the sink, lending her a dubious expression. "I know their history goes back a long time, but is it enough to compel Old Joe to defend me, someone he barely knows?"

Molly's sputtering laugh filled the room. "Any excuse to make an Anderson pay is enough for Old Joe. If he is foolish enough to show his face here, Joe will put a stop to him. You're safe here."

Staring into the sudsy water, Faith scrubbed at the crusty dishes. Such lovely promises, and yet doubt remained. Was she really safe anywhere?

"Hey." A gentle hand touched her shoulder, prompting her to look into Molly's eyes, bright with sincerity. "I've known Old Joe for a long time. He will protect you. He won't let Anderson hurt you." She bumped Faith aside with a swing of her hips. "Now get on out there and serve. I'll take care of these."

An ominous premonition trailed Faith as she snatched up her serving tray and passed back into the saloon. It had only grown rowdier, with a group of men huddled around some dice on the floor, casting them and erupting in shouts every few seconds. The prostitutes had emerged in full force, crowding an already congested barroom.

Her eyes met with Gideon's across the smoky air. In his solemn stare, she found security, affection, devotion. She silently reminded herself again she needn't go alone on this wild journey. He held out his hand, if she could only extend her trust enough to take it.

The double doors swung open, turning Faith's blood to ice. Her hands clenched around her serving tray at the figure standing there, surveying the crowd. She inched backward. If she moved carefully enough, perhaps she could escape into the kitchen, come up with a plan with Molly, but as Jeremiah Anderson's sinister gaze found her across the room, her hopes diminished.

Faith's desperate stare darted around—first to Gideon, then hunting for Old Joe. Within the mass of reveling men, Gideon threw down his cards and pushed up from his chair, aiming himself straight for the outlaw.

With egotistical confidence, Anderson strode in, several of his posse at his back. Of course he brought reinforcements—the coward. Why he'd faced them alone in Abeline's barn, she still couldn't piece together.

The powerful urge to run shot through Faith's body, but she resisted. Instead, she held her head high, her knuckles blanching on the tray in her grasp, as Anderson thundered across the crowded space. He fixed her with a determined stare, eyes that promised violence, lips curling over his browning teeth. Anyone who stood in his path quickly removed themselves on sight of him, providing an open path in which to walk.

Though he walked with a noticeable limp, Anderson closed the distance between them, now only steps away. Faith's pulse thumped in her throat, her breath hastening. In seconds, he would reach her, could do anything he wished to the woman who had boldly trespassed on his property and lied to his face.

A moment before he descended on her, Gideon blocked his hasty march. He stood tall and strong before her, facing the enemy down, his arm muscles straining.

Anderson's sneering gaze descended him. "I suggest you stand back. I'll deal with you in a minute. For now, I've got my sights set on the woman."

Gideon didn't flinch. "You'll not go near her. Do you understand? Never. You never get to bother her again so long as I draw breath."

Anderson released a worthless snort of a laugh. "That's easy enough to fix, now isn't it, boys?" The outlaws behind him all reached for their holstered pistols.

Panic raged in Faith's quivering form. They were going to start a gunfight in here. There could be so much senseless bloodshed, so many lives lost—Gideon's first. The man showed no fear as his foes threatened to remove him with a single blast of their guns.

"I think we both know you're in for much more opposition if you start shooting in this place," Gideon said, his voice a growl.

For the first time, Anderson glanced around before looking back at Gideon, his nostrils ballooning. "Seems to me I've got a fight on my hands either way. I might as well start it by watching you fall."

"Why? So you can prove a point?" Gideon shook his head. "Is your pathetic pursuance of Faith Carter worth dying over?"

Anderson's lip pulled back. "No one comes on my land, into my home, and doesn't answer for it."

"And what about Abeline Baxter's home? Does an old woman deserve no consideration? Is her property not as sacred as yours?"

A question shone in Anderson's eyes, his forehead rumpling. "Boy, I don't know what you're talking about. What does old Baxter's widow have to do with anything?"

Faith's fearful gaze landed on the hands gripping his belt. Neither appeared injured or bandaged. Hadn't Gideon said his hand was shot in the fight?

"Feign ignorance all you like," Gideon said, "but I know you were there. You've been tormenting the people of this town for far too long, and I'm here to put a stop to it."

Snickering, Anderson tossed his unruly hair back. "You and that meddlesome sheriff. I've heard this tune before. You're all gonna stop me. Yet here I am, just as before, taking what I like and doing what I want."

"You will not take what you want from *her*." Gideon's teeth clenched as he moved closer, his stance unyielding. "You will not do what you want to *her*."

Anderson met his challenge, unblinking, every bit as defiant as Gideon. "That ain't up to you, boy. I'm five seconds away from having one of my men put a bullet in you."

"Do it and I'll put a bullet in *you*."

Every eye snapped toward the source of the newcomer's voice. Old Joe stood not five feet away, his rifle trained on Anderson.

The outlaw scoffed. "It's been some time since I've seen you, Joe. Still as charming as ever, I see."

With stone-cold solemnity, Old Joe stared down the barrel of his rifle. "You should have stayed on the other side of town—far away from this establishment. You ain't welcome here. You know that."

"I go where I please." Anderson sneered, disdain dripping from his twisted scowl. "Anybody who takes issue with it should take it up with me."

"That's just what I'm doing." Old Joe's head flicked toward the doors. "Go on and git before my patience wears out. Ain't no Anderson welcome in here. I told your brother the same last time he come in here lookin' to get drunk."

Anderson's jaw worked. "Say another word about my brother and I'll put you on the floor."

Faith shifted from foot to foot, her hands slick on her skirts. Isaiah Anderson had succumbed to wounds inflicted by bullets from a member of the Red Fox Gang. The murderous rivalry had existed between the two families for generations. Even in her genteel home and family, she hadn't escaped the folklore surrounding them.

"Your brother was a menace, and he deserved what he got," Old Joe said, his expression merciless.

Fire raged in Anderson's eyes, his hand tightening around the hilt of his pistol. "I'm gonna kill you, Fox—just like I'm gonna kill your brother, and anyone else who disrespects the Anderson name."

Old Joe tightened his grip on his rifle. "Go on and try it. I bet I get three of you before you can even touch me."

Faith's stomach ached as she glanced frantically between the pair. The last thing she wanted was to draw attention to herself, but— "If you start a gunfight in here, innocent people will die."

Old Joe breathed heavily, his concentrated eyes refusing to leave Anderson's rigid form. "They're bound to die anyway, with this louse infecting the town."

Her feet carried her forward several steps, her arms spread wide. "Think about the girls. Think about Molly."

Old Joe blinked, his Adam's apple bobbing. He held his malicious stare on Anderson a tense moment before his shoulders relaxed. "Out in the street, then. Away from my customers." His hands clenched white around his gun. "Your demise is long overdue, Anderson. I'll deliver it swiftly and gladly."

Anderson's lips curled in a spine-tingling smile. "I'll be happy to face you, Fox. Even happier to watch you die."

A collective breath released over them as Anderson lifted his hand and began walking backward through his gawking crowd of devotees.

Old Joe lowered his gun, handing it to Gideon. "Here. I won't need this one out there."

"You shouldn't have to fight for us," Faith said.

"This ain't just about you." Old Joe summoned men from around the room with a simple nod to each. They pushed back their chairs, readying their weapons and sauntering toward the doors after the Andersons. "This war has been brewin' for a long time. Any Anderson that's breathin' is a threat to a Fox. It's time to settle this once and for all."

Her heart galloped at the brutality in his eyes. "This can't be the only solution. There has to be a better way than killing people."

The light of compassion slipped into his gaze as it briefly met hers. "There is no other way, darlin'. What you've known thus far was a sheltered existence. That don't exist for the rest of us. Out here is a dog-eat-dog world, and I'll be darned if I let an Anderson run it."

His boots pounded the floor as he trailed the crowd of people spilling out the double doors. The streets, tranquil only minutes before beneath dazzling strands of lantern light, now swarmed with people, their excited chatter bouncing off the storefronts. Faith tossed Gideon an uneasy look as they approached the furious melee. This wouldn't just be a fight between two men. The supporters on each side primed their guns and waited at the ready. This could become a battle.

"Come on, girls—everyone upstairs." Molly ushered the prostitutes with a sweep of her arm. "Lock your doors. Grab anything you can use as a weapon." Her eyes brimmed with terror as she looked out on the street, conveying heart-stopping reality. If the Andersons prevailed, every person in this place had their own lives to protect.

Gideon's arms came around her as Faith gripped the doors. She leaned into his gentle touch, peering out at the two groups forming in the street. They faced each other down, bodies posed, teeth bared, waiting for the signal to begin.

"This is going to get ugly," Gideon said. "We should leave before the shooting starts."

Faith turned hesitant eyes up to him. "What about Molly? What about the rest of the girls?"

"You can't do anything to protect us," a feminine voice said before Molly appeared beside them, a revolver in one hand. "He's right; you should go. I can't stand the thought of something happening to you."

Emotion clogged Faith's throat. She looked from Molly back to the dozens of spectators lining the boardwalk, seemingly unconcerned about catching a stray bullet. People across the way huddled inside the mercantile, peeking out from a display window. Gold Strike, as wild and turbulent as it had proven before, had never felt more like the midst of a battlefield. Death loomed so near, she could taste it.

"Come on." Gideon's strong hand on her back urged her forward, just as a gunshot split the air. Another blast reverberated down the street, and then another, until the world became nothing but a barrage of gunfire and smoke. Screams poisoned the night, cries of agony and wrath overwhelming it.

Faith choked on caustic air. A hand yanked her backward from the clouds of smoke and into the saloon. Pulling her beneath a table, Gideon draped his arms around her and shielded her from the onslaught outside.

"Someone must have shot from within the crowd." His voice hummed in her ear, the only comforting sound amidst the horror outside. "I was looking straight at Anderson when the shooting started. He seemed as surprised as everyone else."

She shuddered. "It wasn't Old Joe, either." Her heart squeezed, the words dying on her tongue. It didn't matter now. Likely everyone on the front lines of this fight was shot. Faith thought of Old Joe, how he'd taken her in without question, how he'd treated her kindly after what her father did. He deserved better than this.

Yet the shots came, over and over, a seemingly endless assault. Despite her fear, a cold realization sank into her—the sickening knowledge that death thrived only feet away from their huddled position. When the shooting slowed, voices rose beyond the double doors—ordered shouts, boots pummeling the dirt.

"What's happening?" Her voice trembled, her body shivering.

Gideon held her tighter. "It sounds like some of the ones who are left may be retreating, and others are chasing them." He lifted his head just high enough to get a partial view of the scene. "It looks like the fight is leaving."

With Gideon's assistance, Faith crawled out from beneath the table on her hands and knees. Nearby, Molly did the same, still clutching a revolver to her chest.

The scene outside turned Faith's stomach inside out. Men lay scattered across the street—moaning, rolling, most of them bent and motionless.

Gideon's hand slipped into hers and hauled her back as she pushed her way out the doors. "It still might not be safe. They're armed men."

She looked into his worried eyes and tugged him along. "I have to, Gideon. I have to."

After a moment's hesitation, he nodded and allowed her to lead him onto the boardwalk. Gunsmoke still hung in the air, a powdery haze that smothered all breath and drove one's hopes into the dirt. Faith coughed against it, plastering a hand over her mouth. The gloom of death and destruction had already seized this once-beloved street, snatching it in vicious claws coated with blood.

Beside her, Molly let out a whimper, her hand flying up to block the choked screams buried deep in her throat. Faith followed her gaze to a body splayed across the ground, fresh blood shimmering beneath the lanterns. Old Joe's eyes lay open, his vacant stare gazing at nothing.

"No!" Molly dropped to her knees beside him, her dress crumpling around her. She shielded her face in two open hands, tears raging down her cheeks.

Faith buried her face in Gideon's chest, sobs wracking her own body. He held her close, smoothing back her hair, his hand rubbing circles over her back.

A moan at her feet snagged Faith's attention, driving her gaze to a shadowed figure lying across the ground. She jumped back, the familiar tangled mane sprinkling icicles over her skin. Yet as her gaze drifted down him, her rigid form relaxed. Jeremiah Anderson could do nothing to her now, with the bloom of dark blood spreading across his chest.

Letting go of Gideon's hand, Faith knelt beside him. Leaning close, she met his gaze, stunned but still coherent. Pity swelled in her heart. A more terrible man she'd never met, but the lonely person inside peered out as he stared into her face.

"You weren't at Abeline Baxter's house last night, were you?" Her chest rose in desperation.

A pained growl radiated through him. "I don't know what you're talkin' about, woman."

Her lips compressed determinedly. "This is no time for games, Anderson. You're as good as dead. Don't lie to me."

A pathetic wisp of a laugh escaped him, followed by a liquidy cough. "I didn't leave my ranch last night. I stayed up until the sun rose, lickin' my wounds and thinkin' how I was gonna get the two of you back." He blinked, confusion clouding his eyes. "Doesn't appear I did a very good job of it."

Faith shook her head. What a waste of a life. "You're a fool, Anderson."

His mouth crimped in the corner. "Yeah." Then, as if falling into a pleasant dream, his eyes slipped shut and his body re-laxed.

Releasing him, Faith sat back on her heels and swiped an arm across her face. The dark presence of death around her pressed close, cloaking her in its sinister chill, a cruel reminder that if she didn't do something fast, it might very well come for her next.

Anderson looked so peaceful now, so free of the malicious games that had typified his life. *I don't know what you're talkin' about, woman.* He hadn't. Why lie when he teetered on the brink of death and knew it?

She looked up at Gideon's face, gazing back in sad reflection. The man who'd attacked them in Abeline's barn still ran freely around Gold Strike and would surely strike again if they didn't find him first.

Twenty One

THE DRUNKEN REVELRY AT the Wild Rose had converted to sullen quiet as Faith dragged her way back in beside Gideon. Empty tables sat around the saloon, littered with cards and half-consumed whiskeys and ales. Chairs had been toppled in haste, canes and scarves discarded on chairs, glasses shattered as men scrambled out the door to observe the gunfight. Now, only hollowness remained.

Several injured men were hauled inside, groaning and clutching bleeding wounds. Their comrades sat over them, pouring alcohol from the bottle into their mouths and offering weak reassurances. The establishment's soiled doves began descending the staircase with hands over their mouths and eyes bespeaking the living horror they'd all just witnessed. No matter how hard the West could make a person, it didn't prepare one for a ghastly scene like that.

Molly marched past them all with her back straight and bloodied skirts rustling. Her stoic walk betrayed nothing of the sorrow no doubt swathing her, but her eyes couldn't hide it—reddened and still ripe with tears, heartache looking out from deep within her soul.

Faith squeezed Gideon's hand before letting her fingers slip from his. "I'm going to check on her. She might need something after—"

He nodded, stepping away without further explanation.

Faith swallowed, gathering her skirts as she trailed Molly up the stairs. What could she possibly say to a woman who'd just watched her dear friend fall? In all her years of tutelage, she'd never been taught the proper words.

If Molly noticed her standing in the open doorway to her room, she didn't acknowledge it. Instead, she flew around, opening dresser drawers and chests, stuffing her clothes in a valise on the bed. Every time a sob quaked her frame, she pulled herself up, dashed away her tears, and kept on working.

Faith gingerly stepped into the room, wincing when a floorboard creaked beneath her shoes. Molly stopped for only a second to acknowledge her, then folded the blanket in her hand and piled it in among her dresses.

"What are you planning to do?" Faith's hands twisted in front of her. "Where are you going?"

"I don't know, but I can't stay here." Molly didn't miss a beat as she spoke, turning toward a vanity for her cosmetics and perfumes. "Old Joe gave me a comfortable life here, but whoever takes up the reins in his place won't be so generous. I'll have to go back to—" She shuddered. "No, I won't. I'll find something else, somewhere else. I don't care where I have to go."

Faith glanced at the open door, where girls still filed past down the stairwell. "What about them? What will happen to everyone else?"

"I don't know, and I can't care at the moment." Molly assumed a determined air as she rifled through her vanity drawer. "I've looked after these girls long enough. They'll find their way on their own if they're smart. If they're not, I suppose they'll find the next horrible madam to dictate their lives for them."

"You don't have to be so brave, you know. You can take a moment to grieve what just happened out there."

A pained laugh lit the air. Molly bent over her valise and buttoned it shut. "I don't have time for grief. I've lived this scenario already. Without a man to protect this place, vultures will immediately descend, stealing possessions and taking what they can from us for free." Her head shook emphatically. "Except this time I won't be here for it, and neither should you. Grab that boy and get out of here while there's still a chance."

Before Faith could answer, Molly shoved a bundle wrapped in a velvet pouch into her hand.

"What's this?" She carefully pulled back the fabric to reveal a significant stack of money.

"It's Gideon's winnings—what disappeared from his room."

Faith's fingers curled around the loot. "You found it? You found out who took it?"

"I took it." Molly reached for her bag and clutched it nervously in her hands.

"You what?" Suddenly, it felt as if she'd dropped a weight in Faith's stomach.

"Joe and I saw him cheating right away. I told him he should run him out, but Joe saw it as an opportunity to make extra cash off someone else's dishonesty. I didn't feel right about it, but those fools down at the poker tables don't exactly deserve honest treatment."

"But you—" Faith stepped back, struggling beneath the burden of her revelation. "You were the one who took it? You knew I was trying to help him catch that person."

"Yes, and I sincerely regret that now." Molly reached out to lightly touch her arm. "I manipulated you by sending Allison in when I did, and I lied to you when you both came in here. I thought I was simply stealing from a thief, but I determined to make things right when you told me what he did for you and how good he'd been to you. I was wrong."

Her fingers gently constricted on Faith's arm. "Listen to me, Faith. You have so few options left, with Old Joe dead and your father in prison. If he makes you happy, if he treats you right, you should go with him. I've wasted too much of my life running away from love and vulnerability. I can't stand to think of you like I am now, with nowhere left to go and a mountain of regret."

Faith stared back, her body tensing. The beauty and warmth of her kiss with Gideon radiated through her, but trust him with her heart enough to run away together? She shivered. She could end up disappointed, abandoned, *betrayed*.

"You're so sure this place is going to go up in smoke. What if it doesn't? What if life only gets better?"

"Oh, darling." Molly's head fell to the side, pity wrinkling her brow. "If you'd seen what I've seen, you would know. You wouldn't doubt the words I'm about to tell you." Her hand clamped Faith's wrist, the solemnity in her eyes heart-stopping. "Get out now, or you'll never get out at all."

Chaos reigned supreme in the tavern, not long ago chock full of inebriated clientele, gambling away their money and getting drunker by the second. The air, once filled with laughter and buoyant piano music, now suffered in heavy silence and anguished cries.

"Here, take this." Gideon uncorked the bottle the men at his table had ordered and handed it to a mountaineer kneeling over his friend.

"Much obliged." The untidy man accepted the bottle and held it to his companion's lips, a cursory attempt to keep him comfortable. With a wound like the one seeping from his abdomen across the floor, little hope remained.

Sweeping his hands over his sweat-slicked hair, Gideon caught sight of Faith descending the stairs. At least she was unharmed, safe from the rampant destruction around them for the moment.

He met her at the base of the stairs. "Is she all right? Does she need anything?"

Her head wagged softly. "She's leaving. She thinks there are just more problems to come here."

"I can't fault her for that." He glanced around at the blood-splattered floor crowding with injured men. "This place has become a hospital. We should leave too. I found Phantom in the chaos outside. Anderson must have brought him."

Something solid landed in Gideon's hands. He blinked at the mysterious bundle. "What's this?"

"It's your money. She took it." As his gaze shot up to hers, she sighed. "I suppose you never really know a person, do you? Not the whole person—only the parts they want you to see." The disillusionment on her face could have stilled a crowd.

He seized her hand, pulling her down the last step. "Come on, let's get going. It isn't safe here."

"It isn't safe out there, either." Her fingers squeezed his. "Not with the man who attacked us last night still on the loose. We have to find him."

"Yes, but where? If not Jeremiah Anderson, he could be anyone."

Faith's brows narrowed in concentration, her teeth clamping down on the tip of her thumb. "Do you remember that first day we spoke, when the bank had just been burglarized?"

He nodded. How could he forget her in that lavender gown, her blonde hair pinned up and falling around her neck in wispy tendrils? She had taken his breath away.

"Cora told me witnesses saw a man behind the bank with long hair—that wagon tracks led to the mill, but they found nothing there."

Gideon frowned, attempting to follow her train of thought. "That's when they searched Jeremiah Anderson's place based on both the description and his reputation, I'd wager."

"Yes, but he isn't the only man in town who looks like that." A light dawned in her eyes when they met his. "Adam Graves has the same dirty blond hair as Anderson's, and a similar build. They said he was cooperative and let them into every building at the mill, but what if he'd taken it elsewhere already, or hidden it well?"

Gideon's heartbeat accelerated. The smell of sawdust on his attacker burned in his memory. "Why would this Adam Graves want to steal from the bank? Isn't he a business owner in Gold Strike?"

She shrugged. "I thought my father was an upstanding citizen only months ago. What reason does any man have to steal a vast amount of wealth other than wanting money he didn't rightfully earn? He may not be obvious like Jeremiah Anderson, but he has as much reason as anybody else."

Gideon glanced out the door, where more and more people trickled into the street. "There's chaos out there. It would be the perfect time to go snooping around the mill."

"I agree." She tugged on his hand, leading him through the double doors. "Everyone is too distracted right now to notice us."

Her words burrowed into him, evoking a strange sense of fear. Nobody would notice them, yes, but would anyone know if they walked straight into a trap and buried themselves alive?

The air outside still hung thick with gunsmoke, the agonized cries of dying men giving way to loved ones wailing in grief. Shouted voices directed his attention to several lawmen riding up on horseback, the sheriff at their head.

"Faith!" A woman's voice broke through the confusion. "Oh, Faith!" In seconds, Cora emerged from the crowd. The two embraced with ardent affection, clinging to one another.

"I was so afraid you'd gotten caught up in it." Cora pulled back, wiping tears from her cheeks.

"I'm fine. I'm perfectly fine." Faith's eyes flicked meaningfully toward him. "Gideon was with me the whole time."

"Oh, bless you. Bless you." Cora squeezed his arm. "I don't know what I would have done had anything happened to you. I tried to get here as soon as I heard the shots, but you know Ellis. He's so protective."

As if on cue, the sheriff swung from his horse's back and trod toward them. "It's so good to see you, Faith. I trust you're unharmed?"

She nodded, offering a reassuring smile. "Not a scratch on me."

"Good." He carefully scanned the ground littered with dead men. "Did you see what started this? I noticed Anderson over there."

"It was Anderson and Old Joe." Faith hugged herself at the memory. "They challenged each other. Old Joe wanted to defend his brother."

Ellis nodded, his look thoughtful. "I figured as much. Foxes and Andersons can't seem to coexist peacefully for too long. What I can't figure is why Anderson would even come near this place, unless Old Joe provoked him."

Exchanging glances with Gideon, Faith forced her voice to speak. "Old Joe didn't provoke him. I did."

Gideon stepped in. "*We* did."

One of Ellis's brows arched. "Care to explain?"

"Yesterday, we went looking for the missing gold"—she shifted from foot to foot—"at Jeremiah Anderson's ranch."

"You what?" Ellis's jaw tensed. "What could possibly have possessed you to do something so foolish?"

Faith held out a placating hand. "I know it was foolish and it angered Anderson, but we think we found something out that could be important."

"We thought Anderson followed us back to Abeline's ranch last night and attacked us," Gideon said. "But it wasn't him. We think it was Adam Graves."

Ellis glanced between them. "What does he have to do with any of this?"

"Darling, didn't you say you were looking into Mr. Graves?" Cora offered, only to be swiftly silenced by his stern look.

"My wife means, of course, that he is a part of our investigation." He cleared his throat. "Yet I fail to see how you've linked Adam Graves to what happened at the bank."

"Didn't you check the sawmill first when that gold was stolen?" Faith asked.

"Yes, but our search yielded nothing. Adam Graves has cooperated with us every step of the way. He isn't a suspect."

"Well, perhaps he should be." Faith lifted her chin. "It was dark last night, but the man who attacked us bore a striking similarity to Jeremiah Anderson. As far as I know, nobody else in Gold Strike can declare a similar claim."

Ellis carefully considered her words. "And what was he doing at Abeline Baxter's farm, exactly?"

She sighed. "That, I don't know. Not yet."

"Unless he's using her place to hide the gold," Gideon said. "The poor woman is losing her memory. It would be the perfect place to go unnoticed—especially if he didn't know Faith was there."

"Sheriff, we need you!" one of the deputies called from the saloon door. "In here!"

Ellis raked a hand through his hair. "These are all important points to consider, but I don't have time for them at the moment." He squinted over his shoulder at the activity building outside the Wild Rose. "I'll be back as soon as I can to discuss these matters, but please, in the meantime"—he looked from Gideon to Faith, a grave warning in his eyes—"don't go snooping around any more ranches. Don't tell anyone what you know, and *please*, stay here until I get back. I have enough to deal with already."

His boots carried him away, every determined step throwing dust in the air. Despite his censure, the spark of rebellion brightened Faith's eyes as Sheriff McCraw vanished into the saloon.

"You're not going to listen to him, are you?" Cora asked.

Faith glanced her way before her head finally shook. "I have this awful premonition—like we don't have much time." Her eyebrows raised in supplication. "If we wait too long, it could prove detrimental to me and to Gideon—perhaps even Abeline, more people in this town."

Cora squeezed her hand. "You don't need to explain to me. Just please, *please* be careful, and come back before my husband notices you're gone." She turned her protective gaze up to Gideon. "Promise me you'll take care of her."

His brow wrinkled. "You aren't going to admonish us for going against your husband's wishes?"

Cora's lips puckered into a knowing smirk. "My husband is incredibly good at his job, but he does have one flaw. He can't admit when he needs extra help." Her hand swept the air, indicating the mass of fallen bodies. "Today he needs nothing *but* help. I harbor no doubts regarding his abilities, but he is only one man."

Gideon narrowed his gaze. "He already knew about Graves, didn't he?"

"You did not hear that confirmation from me." Cora leaned slightly closer, her voice lowering. "All I can say is please use caution when you snoop around that man's affairs. Don't venture too far without the help of Ellis and his deputies. All right?"

Faith bit her lip, hesitating briefly. "We'll just poke around the mill and come straight back. We won't confront him."

With a reassuring pat to Faith's shoulder, Cora surveyed the bloodied street again. "There can't be much more of this, or everyone in Gold Strike will simply cease to exist."

"We won't let that happen." Gideon hooked an arm around Faith's shoulders. "We will find answers."

Twenty Two

THE RAISED VOICES AND pandemonium surrounding the saloon shootout trickled down the street as Faith and Gideon slipped through the shadows. Citizens rushed madly toward the scene they'd just vacated, frantically searching for loved ones or wanting a look at the aftermath. Faith ducked out of their path, clinging tightly to Gideon's hand. If Adam Graves indeed had something to do with the missing gold, they had no time to spare.

Graves's mill sat in a current of moonlight, in silent contrast to the spectacle outside the Wild Rose. The buzzing of saws had died hours ago, the building that swarmed with activity by day now dark and abandoned. A creek trickled past, the soft lap of its currents rushing over the rocks beyond the mill.

Faith glanced over her shoulder at the gathering group in the street. "Let's get this over with before the novelty of the gunfight wears off. People will soon want to go home and talk about what they saw."

Gideon pressed close, his hand on her back a constant comfort. "Have you been here before? Do you have any idea where we should look?"

Approaching the structure, she touched her fingertips to the splintery siding. "I don't have the first clue. I would see the men working when I came into town from time to time, but I know nothing about what lies inside."

Creeping through the darkness, they rounded a corner past saw blades and loads of lumber, a wheel that spun with creek water by day. The scent of sawdust tinged her nostrils as they stepped into an alcove and began inspecting the equipment. Nothing appeared amiss. Everything had its proper place, neatly stowed on tabletops or within the cabinetry.

Gideon stooped and pulled on several doors, examining the interiors. "Unless Graves has some type of hidden compartment in here, I don't think it's in these cupboards."

"It would be foolish of him to hide it where his workers could easily get to it. Surely Ellis would have found it if he'd hidden it in here."

His feet shuffled beside her. "Why don't we look for an office? Maybe a storage shed."

"That's a good idea." Faith felt along the wall until she came to a door. Her fingers skimmed the rough wood, hunting for the handle and turning. *Locked.* Her shoulders fell. "Whatever's in here is important enough to keep away from just anyone."

"There might be another way in. Come on." His hand found hers in the black, their fingers entwining.

The pair traversed the maze of tables and saws until they emerged back into the night. Gideon pulled her toward the creek, a sparkling cascade beneath the moon.

"There's a door over here too." He pointed toward the back side of the building, equipped with a door and adjacent window. "It's worth a try." Yet a jiggle of the handle ground their hopes to dust.

Faith cupped her hands around her eyes, peering in through the glass. "That looks like an office, all right. It must be where Graves keeps his records."

Gideon's jaw worked. "We need to get inside. He could be hiding a host of things in there."

"How do you suppose we do it?"

Bending, Gideon plucked a sizable rock from the earth and held it up.

Faith let out a startled breath. "Don't you think someone will hear us?"

"They're all too worried about the gunfight. They won't hear us with everything going on down the street."

Gulping back her anxiety, she nodded. "Do it, then—quick, before someone passes by."

Licking his lips, Gideon hinged his arm back and released the rock. It sailed past them, colliding with the window. Gingerly, he reached through the splintered hole and unlocked the knob from the inside. The door squealed open, slow and ominous.

Neither bothered to close it behind them as they scampered inside. Faith flew to the desk, eager to search the drawers. "If only we'd brought a lantern." She glanced around, but her search proved futile. "How are we supposed to see anything in this light?"

In haste, she pulled each of the drawers open and rifled through them while Gideon searched the rest of the office. Her body sagged more with each fruitless minute spent pawing through papers she couldn't read anyway. A stash of pipes met her fingertips, the odor of tobacco greeting her. Then, a box of pens and various knick-knacks.

"There's nothing of interest in this desk. Have you found any-thing?"

"Nothing." Gideon's voice muffled as he stuck his head in a large cabinet. "Just a lot of scraps of wood and tins of shellac."

Faith joined him at the cabinet, squinting through the muddled light to watch as he scoured each of the shelves inside. "I'm sure

Ellis looked through all of this. He's nothing if not thorough." Another door to her left caught her attention—presumably the one they'd found locked in the main part of the mill.

"Wait a minute." Gideon dropped to his knees, leaning far into the cabinet. His knuckles rapped against the back. "This sounds hollow."

He removed several stacks of wood and glass bottles and set them on the floor. After crawling across the space he'd just cleared, Gideon knocked on the wood again and pressed his ear to the panel. "This is definitely hollow. Either the wall is paper-thin here, or he's hiding something."

Faith leaned back to scrutinize the wall behind the cabinet. "It appears normal—like it leads into the worker's floor."

Straining, Gideon tugged on the panel in question until the wood loosened and broke free. A hoot followed his discovery, then a series of scuffling sounds.

"What is it?" Faith hunkered down, peering into the cabinet at a darkened cavern. Gideon had disappeared into the mysterious space, now just an unseen source of chuckles and scrapes.

"This is unbelievable." Several bangs resounded through the wood, presumably Gideon bashing his hands against the sides. "There's a whole space in here designed for concealing something—likely a closet he converted into a hiding spot."

Excitement thrummed through her body. "Is there anything inside it?" A priceless stash of gold, perhaps?

Several seconds passed by as he searched. "I wish I had a light, but I don't think so. It feels empty. Whatever he had in here, he already removed."

She leaned against the inside of the cabinet. "It's suspicious, though—that he has a secret hideout, that he fits the description people saw, and that the wagon tracks led here."

Gideon's face emerged from the compartment beyond, a wide grin capturing his features. "It's more than suspicious. I do believe we have our man."

Outside, a horse whinnied, followed by the clomp of hooves. Faith froze as footsteps approached, crunching leaves in their path.

"Someone's coming." Gideon's voice barely registered in her swimming head. "Quick, we have to hide—and not in here. We're easy targets. If we climb in this cabinet, he's bound to find us."

A cloud of vapor flew past the window, shadows shifting until a form on horseback made a black silhouette against the moonlight.

Shaking herself, Faith came alive with the pull of Gideon's hand. "That door," she said breathlessly, lurching toward the handle. "It's right here beside the cabinet."

The thud of a man alighting from his horse shook the building, menacing footsteps nearing as Gideon yanked the door open and pushed Faith through. With a single glance over her shoulder, she beheld a solid form stopping outside the office and bending to inspect the broken pane of glass. Then the door behind them clicked quietly shut, blocking her view.

She clung to Gideon's jacket. "We could run. This part of the mill is open to the outside."

His arm curled around her as he surveyed the vast space beyond. "He's bound to be here in seconds. The moonlight will give us away."

"What, then?" Terror gripped her as shoes smashed through the discarded shards of glass on the floor. "He's almost here." Against her will, her voice tremored.

"This way." Gideon stealthily led her between the tables. "Under there." He indicated a spot where two walls met and a table jutted out to create a covered space beneath.

Faith scooted in and made room for Gideon just as the door they'd passed through screeched open. The seconds ticked by, brutally long, as Gideon huddled close and anchored one arm around her. Boots scuffed the floor, drawing ever closer to their hiding spot. The fragrance of sawdust swirled through her.

Faith's heart rammed to her throat, moisture rising across her skin. She reached for Gideon's hand and sank against him as his fingers enclosed around hers. He laid a gentle kiss on her forehead, its sweet warmth remaining. If this proved their last moment, at least they had each other.

The footsteps slowed near the saws, the outline of the man's boots pointing their way. Something cold brushed Faith's cheek. She reached out, her fingers meeting with the jagged edge of a saw blade. With sickening clarity, the fact awakened inside that they'd unwittingly positioned themselves by a table saw. If Graves decided to employ it, only gruesome death awaited.

The man must not have possessed a lantern himself, because he slowly traversed the interior of the mill with no light to guide him. When he reached the outer tables and looked out across the moonlit street, Faith held in a gasp. The hefty form from last night stood beneath the glowing moon, a revolver primed in one hand. With the scrutiny of a hawk, he surveyed the quiet night until finally satisfied. Boots tramped past their concealed position, aimed toward his office.

"We have to get out of here," Gideon said, his breath hot and weighted with concern.

"Wait, no. Gideon!" Faith's hand tensed on his arm. "He knows someone broke in here. He knows he's suspected, and the gold isn't here."

Only the hurried cadence of his breath met her words. "Are you saying we should follow him?"

"He's spooked. There's a good chance he could take us straight to the gold."

His heavy sigh blew back the wisps of her hair. "We just nearly got caught. I don't want to put you straight back in harm's way."

Her temperature rose at his resistance. "If we don't go now, he'll be gone with the gold." Already the creak of Graves mounting his saddle filtered back. "It isn't just about the money. It's about helping Ellis and keeping the men at the saloon from harming you." Her fingers coiled tighter around his, urging him. "This may be the only chance we get. We can't hesitate."

Horse hooves clopped past, Graves and his mount rushing by in a flurry.

Gideon stood, his eyes fixed to them. "Is Starlight nearby?"

Faith crawled into the open and joined him at his side. "She's just outside the corner cafe. Thank God I didn't tether her near the saloon."

He grunted an affirmative, his eyes still trailing the fleeing rider. "Get her, then, and I'll watch where he goes." His head shook. "I can't believe I'm about to chase after the man we just evaded."

In minutes, Faith had retrieved Starlight and returned for Gideon atop the mare's graceful back.

Gideon climbed up behind her, his solid chest at her back as he pointed through the forest at the ridge. "Up there. He just went between those trees."

"Yaw!" With a kick to Starlight's sides, Faith launched her into action. The pair had spent many hours together, perfecting the art of their communication, honing the animal's skills. She knew exactly where to go when Faith steered her reins toward a rocky path that would circumvent the main trail and carry them into the woods in half the time.

Faith held tight to Starlight with her thighs as they began their ambitious ascent. Gideon fiercely hugged Faith, his muscular arms encircling her. After a bumpy ride over rocky outcroppings and uncultivated terrain, the soft blanket of forest enveloped them.

"Where is he? Did you see where he went?" Gideon leaned close, his cheek brushing the hair around her ear.

She gazed into the darkness. "This trail only goes one way—unless he cut through the woods. He must be traveling north."

The needle-strewn trail twisted among the evergreens, swept by the cool spring breeze. Shadows lurked from every side, treetops stretching to a cloud-brushed sky, branches creaking and swaying. The wind howled as they blasted through it, Starlight's majestic body conveying them across the wild landscape.

They rode on for what felt like hours, chasing a phantom. Graves could have long ago ventured off the path, but Faith kept on flicking the reins across Starlight's back and urging her over the hilly terrain. Despite the heavy darkness, patches of moonlight peeped through, revealing fresh hoofprints marking the road ahead. Faith inhaled the aromatic breeze, determination fueling her. They would find Adam Graves and bring back the gold he'd deviously stolen.

The pair traveled on in good faith, hoping to catch a glimpse of Graves's retreating form, until they came to a dilapidated fence running alongside a well-worn road. At the top of the hill, Adam Graves urged his horse over the last bend and disappeared from sight.

Anticipation whispered through Faith's frame, her heels compelling Starlight into a faster pace. They were nearly there—so close she could almost feel the gold bars sliding beneath her fingertips. Never mind the tremor of fear that bolted through her to recognize they'd fled miles from protection.

When they crested the hill, a farmhouse rose into view—once undoubtedly charming, but now a vestige of days long gone. Details emerged as they carefully traversed the shadows—gabled roofs, scalloped siding, a broken stained-glass window. Graves had already tethered his mount to a tree and disappeared, presumably within the decaying walls of the once beautiful Victorian.

A weathered sign, half fallen off the fence, caught Faith's eye. *Hammond.* The name hit hard, reality dawning. "I know this place."

Gideon's grip on her tightened. "You've been here before?"

"No." She thought back to the conversations she'd shared with Cora and all she'd told her about Caleb and Julia Broderick. "I've heard of this place. It belonged to the Hammond family. It's been abandoned for years with no one to tend it."

"Hmm. Sounds like the perfect place to stash a loot." Gideon pointed toward a rough-looking barn about a hundred yards from the house. "Why don't we hide Starlight behind there? Close enough to reach if we need her—"

"But concealed enough to keep our presence hidden."

"Yes."

Directing Starlight to the shadows of the barn, Faith slowed her by a hitching post. Eerie quiet enveloped them as they slid off the horse's back and surveyed the abandoned farm. Bat wings rustled and brushed one another in the eaves, punctuated by high-pitched squeaking. Faith shivered as the sound of scurrying lifted from the barn. The long-neglected structure undoubtedly housed a plethora of rats, their miniature feet padding the ground and tails sweeping the floor as they ran.

"Did you make sure the gun is loaded?" Anything to distract her from the spine-chilling turn of her thoughts.

Gideon pulled his pistol from its holster and checked the chamber. "It is." He tucked it back in and reached for her hand. "Come on. If we're going to do this, we should go now. We can't let him get away with the gold. We're the only ones who know he's here."

She nodded, slipping her hand into his. With every step, her confidence wavered. Perhaps they should have listened to Ellis when he warned them to stay put. Instead, they had willfully wandered into yet another perilous situation.

With the reassuring warmth of Gideon's hand in hers, she propelled her feet onward. The two of them cast long shadows over the wild grass as they advanced toward the decaying home. The wind whipped over them, pulling at Faith's gathered hair and shaking the trees. Their trunks groaned and bent, the whole earth shuddering amid the bluster.

The crunch of their shoes over the uneven drive resounded in her ears. Surely with every step they took, they announced themselves to the man inside. Yet nothing stirred as they approached the sagging front porch and climbed the unsturdy stairs.

The door pushed back on rusty hinges, announcing their arrival with an eerie squeal. Faith grimaced, carefully stepping around broken shards of glass. An empty foyer greeted them, the once doubtlessly beautiful entrance now coated with dust and cobwebs. Faith clung tight to Gideon's arm as he speared a finger toward the shadowed floor.

"That looks like bootprints," he said in her ear, his breath sweeping her skin.

Nodding, her fearful gaze ascended the switchback staircase, where, even in the dim light, the dust appeared unsettled. "What do we do? Do we just"—her fingers closed around his bicep—"follow him up? He's bound to kill us if he gets the chance."

He brushed a hand over her hair. "It isn't too late to run. I'd rather keep you safe than find that gold." The deep timbre of his voice rumbled through her.

Faith met his gaze, tempted with every fiber of her being to take the escape he offered. But why come all this way and turn at the first threat of danger? How could she face herself in the mirror if she cowered now?

"I have to do this, Gideon." Her hands gripped his. "My father started this when he chose to target Colton Baxter. He was willing to kill a man to get what he wanted. He was willing to hurt people." Her breath hitched, shivering with emotion. "I have to prove I am not him to this town. I have to right his wrongs."

"To the devil with this town."

"Gideon, please." She squeezed his hands. "I must do this."

After an agonizing few seconds, he finally released a breath. "If this is what you need to do, then I'm right here beside you. I'll do whatever I can." He leaned in, his breath warm across her knuckles, before he kissed her hand. "I'm with you in this fight until the end, Faith Carter."

Twenty Three

THE SMELL OF DUST and rotting wood permeated the air as Gideon clutched the banister. He paused, surveying the quiet house once again—the worn-down furnishings and aged walls barely visible in the soft strands of white moonlight. This place had once housed a family, hopes, dreams, an optimistic future. Now only a shell remained—ghosts of scattered ambitions haunting the deteriorating walls. His fingers clamped on the banister. The once beautiful abode could now become a site of sheer horror.

Gripping Faith's hand, he climbed higher. The stairs groaned beneath their weight, threatening to give way. With every creak of the floorboards, his heart rate accelerated faster. To face his own demise didn't scare him. Nobody would care if he died, but the woman at his side—she was a brilliant light, and the world would darken without her.

They paused at the top of the stairs, straining to hear, yet no sound came other than branches being tossed by the wind outside. A narrow hallway stretched before them with doors flanking either side, but in the near black, a person could barely discern one from the other.

Faith's breath rasped beside him. "I can't see anything. Can you?"

"No." He nearly whispered the word, but it bounded down the hallway and back again. "I wish we had a lantern." Yet a lantern would reveal their exact position to their enemy. Gideon shook himself with the reminder that a dangerous man likely crept within these walls. How foolish of them to venture in here with little protection and no plan.

"Come on." Before he could voice his concerns, her hand tugged him onward. "Let's find him."

Their feet shuffled soundlessly down the corridor. Cold soaked into Gideon's bones, enhanced by the eerie shivers racing over his skin. As they walked, his eyes adjusted to the meager light, and their surroundings sharpened. A door at the end of the hall stood open, a shaft of moonlight just pooling outside the threshold.

"There." Faith's murmur drove beneath his skin. "He must be in there." Her breath quickened, the hand she'd placed inside his tensing.

Gideon drew out his gun and held it close as they walked. His heart throbbed, every hair on his skin standing on end with each inch they moved forward. When they finally reached the open door, Faith inhaled and pulled him onward, as if staring her fear in the face and declaring victory.

A few seconds lingered as they stood at the room's threshold and scanned the inside. The floor was illuminated by moonlight flooding in one window, yet nothing disturbed the silence.

Faith gasped, drawing his attention to the floor, where a heap glimmered beneath the moon. "It's there." She dropped his hand, stumbling forward. "All the gold—it's there."

Numbly, Gideon let his gaze wander the collection. Something didn't feel right. It couldn't be this easy to wander in and find such immense wealth. Tingles pricked his skin as Faith knelt in front of the gold bars and began lifting them in her palms. "Faith, get back. This feels like a—"

Before the words had fled his mouth, a figure lurched out of the dark and pounced on Faith. She yelped a panicked cry that swung Gideon into action. He trained his pistol on the hulking form, but he couldn't distinguish Faith's body from her attacker's in the scant light. Holstering the weapon, he dove for the struggling pair.

"Get off of her, Graves." He seized the man by the back of his shirt, yanking to no avail.

Graves had one arm around Faith's neck, the other secured at her waist. She desperately writhed within his hold, but his superior strength overpowered her.

"I said, 'let her go!'" Gideon's hands seized each of Graves's broad shoulders. Gritting his teeth, he pulled at him with every ounce of strength he possessed.

Graves panted amid his exertion. "If you want me to let her go, you'd best get out of here. Leave me to my business."

"Leave the two of you alone? Never." He wedged his knee into Graves's back, eliciting an anguished cry. "We both know why you're here. You're not going to get away with this."

Graves grunted, fury seething from his clenched teeth. "If you want to keep your girl alive, you will. I won't give you long." His arm constricted around her neck, an ominous threat even in the dark.

Gideon dug his knee in harder. "We know who you are and what you've done. We won't let your crimes go unpunished."

Despite the arm coiled around her throat, Faith pushed her chin up. "We know you attacked us at Abeline Baxter's farm last night, too." Her eyes flashed as they met with Gideon's. "He was covered in your blood."

Graves's blood. How could he have forgotten? Gideon had imagined he'd shot Jeremiah Anderson, but Adam Graves's hand undoubtedly bore the wound. Thank heavens for Faith's quick thinking. She twisted to expose Graves's injured hand, just as Gideon swung down hard on it with his elbow.

Graves howled, releasing Faith in one staggering movement. Before he could grab hold of her again, Gideon slammed his boot into the bandaged hand, conjuring a string of curses and guttural moans from Graves's lips.

Faith rushed into Gideon's arms, her hasty breath warming his skin. Gideon cradled her against his solid chest, his arm hooking protectively around her. His keen stare fixed to Graves's form now sprawled across the floor.

"You're a fool, Graves." Gideon breathed heavily, his pulse thumping. "You had a good life here. Why would you go and ruin it by stealing from the bank?"

From his spot on the floor, Graves glared back. "You don't know a thing about my life."

"I know you run a successful mill, that you have dozens of employees."

"And mounting bills, increasing responsibilities, a life I never asked for."

Gideon scoffed. "What did you expect—for the world to bow at your feet, hand you money on a silver platter?"

His teeth gritted. "We didn't all have fathers who gave us whatever we wanted."

Faith shivered within Gideon's hold. "I'd rather have been reared by an honest man than all the riches I once knew."

"An honest man would have been nice too." A mirthless chuckle lifted from Graves's lips before he groaned again. "Some of us didn't have either. Some of us made something of ourselves, no matter the hand we'd been dealt, no matter the atrocities visited upon us as children." A haunted pain shone out through his eyes. "Some of us had to stand on our own two feet long before we had much ground to stand on."

Gideon's muscles tensed. "So what if you did? I had all those things happen to me, and I didn't feel the need to steal from a bank."

"No, but it didn't stop you from cheating people." In the hushed silence that followed, Graves shook his head. "You're just as much a crook as I am, only you do it at a poker table."

"How do you know what I do at the poker table?" Gideon pulled Faith closer against him.

"You must know word gets around in a place like this. I know all about you, Mr. Valdez—how the men with deep pockets at the Wild Rose are blackmailing you." His gaze slid to Faith. "I know about you too, Miss Carter. Those misers can't wait to get their hands on you, daughter of the most notorious thief this town has ever seen."

"Faith had nothing to do with her father's crimes." Gideon stepped between them. "If anybody wants to hurt her, they're going to have to get through me first."

The corner of Graves's mouth ticked up. "A challenge I'm sure many will gladly take. Anything to repay Edward Carter for the damage he's caused in Gold Strike."

Faith released a tremulous breath. "My father doesn't care what you do to me. I am the least of his concerns."

His eyes met hers, deeply held sadness echoing back. "That's something we have in common then, Miss Carter. Thankfully our fathers only define our lives as far as we let them."

Gideon's nose snarled. "You talk of this camaraderie, yet still you want to hurt her."

Annoyance clouded Graves's eyes as they found him again in the dim light. "I don't want to hurt anybody. I just want to leave this place with enough money to survive without having to look back. Enough money to support my ma."

Gideon's mind reeled, collecting everything he'd heard of the stagecoach robbery on Miner's Trail and the incidents that had followed. "You were part of this all along, weren't you? You employed

Caleb Broderick at the mill. You planned to frame Caleb for the robbery and get away with the gold yourself, didn't you?"

A grainy laugh sputtered from Graves's throat. "Sure looks that way, don't it? But no"—his long hair shook with his head—"Caleb and I had an honest relationship. He was a good employee and a better man. I had nothing to do with the robbery. Jeremiah Anderson and Edward Carter took care of that on their own. I saw my opportunity to strike when the gold sat there day after day with no one coming to claim it."

Faith frowned. "That doesn't explain how you got access to it. I heard the bank employees say nobody knew the code to the vault—not even some of them."

A sly grin slipped over his thin lips. "Now that is something I can't tell you without hurting the people I love most."

Letting go of Gideon, Faith stood firm before Graves and stared him down. "You're a threat to the people I love most, too. Why were you at Abeline Baxter's last night? Were you planning to hide your money there? Hurt a poor innocent woman who's too old to defend herself?"

A curious look overtook his features before Graves pursed his lips. "Miss Carter, I'm not the enemy you imagine. I just planned to steal some gold and be on my way. I never meant to hurt anybody."

Her fists clenched at her sides. "Yet you attacked us in Abeline's barn. You were there for a reason. I know you were." She bent closer, fire in her eyes. "What did you plan to do to my friend? Why were you on her farm?"

The momentary friendliness in his eyes converted to ice. "There is much you don't know, and that's exactly how it's going to stay." With that, he relaxed against the floor, finality written across his strong face. He would offer them nothing more.

"You won't be so tight-lipped when we get the sheriff in here," Gideon said, seizing Faith gently by the wrist. "I'm sure he'll be happy to retrieve all this gold and hand it back to its rightful owners."

Graves laughed coldly. "I already have the sheriff convinced I'm nothing short of a saint. He won't believe you. I'm the one who's been shot through the hand, after all." He held up the injured body part, where a dark stain had seeped through the bandage.

"He'll believe me," Faith said. "He married my best friend. He knows I would never lie to him."

"Ah, but what does he know of this one?" Graves's disheveled head nodded toward Gideon. "He's new in town. Nobody knows much about him." One shoulder lifted. "He's already mixed up in all sorts of trouble, and he's been seen cheating at the local saloon. Sounds like the ideal person to blame—the sort who could easily trick you into unwittingly helping him get a whole lot of cash."

Faith's lip curled. "You wouldn't dare."

"Oh, I would, if it helps me save my own hide." Graves rapped his uninjured hand on the floorboards. "If it means saving my hide, I'll say anything I have to—but I still don't want to."

Gideon held in the incredulous comment threatening to escape him. "And what is it you want?"

"You know what I want." Graves's stare tumbled reverently over the gold. "We can even split it up if it suits you. There's far more than I'll ever need. I just want out of this place."

The suggestion stilled Gideon, his eyes locked on the gold—mounds of perfect bars gleaming in the moonlight. With just a portion of this, he would never have to work another day in his life, never have to play poker again, never have to cheat anyone. Settle down in an ideal place, a home without the threat of being run out. Visions of an idyllic future danced before his mind's eye, tempting as bait to a hungry fish.

Then his gaze focused back on Faith, and the fleeting dream disappeared. She looked on him with such belief. So much grace. He couldn't disappoint her now.

"I loved a girl like that once." Graves's gravelly voice pulled him back to the present. "When I was young. I saw nothing but stars, attainable dreams when I looked at her. She was so darn pretty, I almost couldn't believe she was real."

Gideon looked at him in pity. "You should have stuck with her. Maybe you'd be a better man today."

"No." He heaved a weighted sigh, his gaze drifting across the room as if he'd gone to dwell in the faraway space of his memories. "I never got the chance. My father took that from me too."

"Your father forbade you from marrying?" Faith asked, her voice sincere.

"We would have made a fine pair. We were both from upstanding, respected families." His gaze cast into the shadows, burdened with unrealized dreams. "When I made my intentions known to my pa, he laughed at me. He said I could never get a girl like that without any real skills or ambition. He said she would scorn me before I even stepped in the door."

Faith drifted farther from Gideon, clearly enthralled with his story. "You could have married her without his permission, couldn't you? He couldn't have stopped you."

Graves's lips pressed together, past sorrows masking the animosity beneath. "By then my confidence was shaken. I decided to seek schooling first, before I got up the nerve to tell her how I felt. But it was too late by then. She'd already run off with a local deviant. Started having babies before I had even finished my studies."

"That's awful." Face stepped toward him, her fingers falling out of Gideon's hold. "You did all that for her and she just married someone else?"

"She didn't know how I felt about her. I was a coward back then." He sighed. "At least I got some learning out of the deal. Taught me how to run a business, how to oversee employees."

"How to steal when necessary," Gideon put in, cynicism edging his tone.

Graves shot him an unapologetic look. "You know all about that. Don't pretend you don't. Don't hoist yourself on a pedestal and look down at me. At least I own who I am."

Gideon sneered. "To us, maybe—after we caught you. Not to the rest of the world."

"They'll all soon know it too, won't they? When I'm gone without a trace, and they never recover their gold."

A dark, foreboding sensation churned in Gideon's stomach. This man would do anything to claim the life he felt denied in his youth. Would he resort to hurting Faith, choosing riches over human life?

"What do you say, Valdez?" His intrusive voice plagued Gideon's wayward thoughts. "This could be good for us both. I get money and security far away from this rotten town, and you get a new life, maybe with this beauty right here."

Shifting from one foot to another, Gideon met Faith's innocent stare. She was worth far more than all the gold piled on the floor. For the first time, a new realization sprouted. His integrity was worth it too. No amount of money could buy her love, or his soul.

Reaching out, he recaptured her hand. "We aren't playing your game, Graves. Faith Carter deserves more than a life on the run, and I plan to be part of that life as far as she lets me." His fingers tightened around hers at the gentle smile on her face. "Come on, Faith. Let's figure out a way to round up all this gold and give it back to the bank where it belongs."

Graves rose up on his elbow, panic brewing on his face. "I would advise against that, Mr. Valdez. You won't ever get this chance again. You'll regret walking away from it."

"The only thing I'll regret is not choosing this path sooner." He angled toward the hallway, searching in the shadows for anything they could use to collect the gold. Yet before Gideon could discern much of anything, a shot blasted through the dark. He clutched his shoulder, where pain blossomed outward. His hand came back, covered in crimson. Suddenly dizzy, Gideon collapsed on the floor.

Twenty Four

Faith shuddered as Gideon crumpled to the floor beside her. Gunsmoke clouded the air, the sound of the shot reverberating through her. She turned toward Adam Graves, still prone on his back on the floor, her limbs quaking. His pistol glinted beside him, his expression both ominous and triumphant.

"How dare you." She took an unsteady step forward, the world swaying around her. "How dare you!" It was all that would pass through her clenched teeth.

Graves lifted one unaffected brow. "I'll do what I must to protect what's mine. Stand in my way and I'll shoot you too." Climbing to his feet, he holstered his pistol and began stacking the gold into neat piles.

A desperate breath rasped from the floor. "Don't do it, Faith. It isn't worth your life."

"Gideon." She scrambled across the floor to reach his side, dropping to her knees. "Oh Gideon, what has he done to you?"

A dark spot spread at his shoulder, staining his clothes. "It's just—" He winced, his face contorting in pain and his breathing heavy. "It's just a flesh wound. Luckily he isn't a very good shot."

Breathless, Faith unbuttoned his shirt and pulled back the material to reveal the injury. "Flesh wound or no, we need to stop this bleeding." Fingers trembling, she tore off a sizable chunk of her underskirt and pressed it to the wound.

Gideon released an agonized cry that drove to her bones.

Working quickly, Faith seized a long strip of her dress and tied it securely beneath his armpit and around the makeshift bandage. "That will have to do for now. We'll need a surgeon to remove the bullet."

Gideon lifted his head just enough to warily eye his bandaged shoulder. "Where did you learn to do that?"

"I volunteer with a doctor in town." She sat back on her heels, swiping a wrist across her perspiring brow. "I've assisted him on many medical procedures. I've watched him dress wounds before."

He breathed out. "You're remarkable."

The space beyond them filled with scrapes and pounding boots. Faith turned to watch Graves produce a burlap sack from his belongings and begin lifting gold bars into it.

"All the money in the world won't buy you happiness," she said. "You know that, don't you? Look what my father did. Look how miserable he is now."

Without affording her a glance, he continued shoving the gold into his pack. "Sure can't buy happiness, but it will provide security for my family. I'm willing to take the chance." He reached for the last of the gold and tossed it in among the other bars.

"You would risk a man's life for the chance at money you didn't earn." Faith glanced sadly back at Gideon, still clutching his arm and writhing in pain.

"No blood needed to be spilled." Graves stood and slung his pack over his shoulder. "If he would have listened to me in the first place, I wouldn't have had to shoot him. I'm not a violent man."

Two steps from the doorway, he paused, inclining his ear toward the window admitting the light of the moon. "What was that?"

Faith listened closely, catching the clomp of horse hooves outside. Her heart lifted. Could she hope for rescue, or someone to finish the job they'd come here to do? The tangle of men's voices drifted up from the yard, accompanied by horses neighing and blowing out night air.

Graves stomped to the window and swore under his breath. "It's the sheriff and his men. He must have followed the two of you here."

Faith gripped Gideon's hand, her heartbeat accelerating. Ellis could put a stop to this man once and for all. He could get Gideon to a doctor before he bled through the pathetic mounds of fabric pressed over his wound.

Washing a hand over his unruly hair, Graves scanned the yard with precision. No doubt, he wouldn't take being cornered by Ellis's men without a plan forming in his mind.

"What are you going to do?" her timid voice filled the quiet room.

Graves flicked a glance of annoyance her way. "There isn't much left to do. There's a whole group of them out there. There's no use in hiding, hoping they won't find me." Securing his pack to his shoulder, he nodded at Faith. "Come on, now."

Her blood froze. "What do you mean 'come on'?"

"I mean on your feet." In one mighty tug, he yanked her off the floor and ripped her hand out of Gideon's. "If the only way is out, I'm going to need some cover."

Faith's breath quickened as he shoved his pistol into her side. Icicles peppered her skin, heat flaming in her core. He wanted to use her as a human shield.

Gideon pushed up on his arms. "You leave her be, Graves. If you have an ounce of honor left, you let her go."

With a snort of derision, Graves jammed his pistol harder against her. "I'll give her back when I'm done. They won't risk shooting her to capture me."

Yet her hopes sank deeper with every step he pushed her toward the door. Faith met Gideon's eyes as he struggled to sit up from the floor. Her head shook. *No, don't hurt yourself. It isn't worth it. Don't anger him.* Yet Gideon's protests trailed them as they moved down the hall to the stairwell.

Outside, the air nipped Faith's skin. The breeze carried notes of balsam and honeysuckle, a soothing balm despite the turmoil waging inside her. She held her head high and followed Graves's every directive until they'd traversed the porch.

Fingers coiled around her ribcage, Graves's raspy breath hot on her hair. Faith's feet moved over the uneven ground, steady despite her hammering heart. She would face this moment if it meant getting Gideon the help he needed. She would do anything for him.

When they got within sight of Ellis and his deputies, Graves seized a firm handful of her gown and positioned his gun at her neck. Ellis stood near his horse, swinging to attention as Graves tramped boldly into view. Not a muscle flinched, every eye fixed upon them.

"Adam Graves." Ellis shook his head. "I knew you were part of this."

Graves's sinister laughter ruffled her hair. "It's a good thing these two dunderheads followed me here then, or else you might have caught me."

Ellis's careful gaze shifted to Faith and back again. "Did you know we caught on to you?"

"I had an inkling, Sheriff. That's why I never came out here again after I hid the loot."

"The gunfight in town gave you the perfect opportunity to ride out undetected."

Graves's body shifted. "I admit I didn't expect you to pursue me with the chaos in town today."

Ellis set his legs wide, his hands on his hips. "Luckily my wife insisted I follow these two. Somehow she knew they would lead me straight to you and the proof I needed to bring you in."

With a strong tug, Graves drew Faith closer. "Did she account for this? Seems like a mighty fine risk to take, unless she doesn't care about the Carter girl here."

"Oh, she cares a great deal for her." Ellis's jaw flexed. "But my wife trusts me. She knows I won't do anything to harm Faith."

Her heart echoed back the sentiment. She had shot her own father to protect her dear friend. Now Cora had sent Ellis to her side.

"That's right, Sheriff." Graves's breath quickened. "All I want to do is get on my horse and ride out of here. Let me get far enough away and I'll let her go."

Deliberation knit the sheriff's brow before he pressed his palms outward. "I won't sacrifice this young woman's life for money, but what you possess is extremely valuable. It could destroy many people's lives if it doesn't find its way back to the bank."

A haughty laugh filled the air. "Are you asking me to reconsider?" Graves clicked his tongue. "I put a lot of work into this, Sheriff. I put my life on the line. I intend to see this through."

Ellis shifted, studying Graves's position. Was he hatching a plan? "From what I can tell, you waltzed into the back of the bank without the employees noticing you. You took the gold back to the sawmill and transported it out here. There's not much work involved in all that."

"Can I help it if you made it easier for me to steal a fortune? I put in the necessary effort."

Ellis glared in return. "You're working for that teller from the bank, aren't you? Bill Ross, I think his name is. He helped you."

"I've never met him before in my life, but you're welcome to blame him if you want to. Sure beats telling the whole town you failed to catch anybody."

Ellis cocked his head. "If you didn't have help, how could you have possibly known how to get into the vault? I know that old woman at the bank didn't help you. She was beside herself with guilt over what you'd done."

Graves's snicker chilled Faith's skin. "Asking a magician to reveal his secrets, are we? You'd have better luck poking around town than trying to pull that fact out of me."

Ellis's gaze slipped barely perceptibly into the shadows before finding them again. "Who is it you're trying to protect, Graves? Who are you doing this for?" He took a single step forward. "I've researched your background. No one knows where you came from or who your family is. You just showed up in Gold Strike one day and built a business from nothing. No roots, no family. Nothing but what you've worked hard to accomplish here. Now you're going to throw that all away so you can live a life on the run?"

The gun at Faith's neck began to shake. Graves repositioned the hand grasping her dress. "I don't need it anymore. It means nothing to me. I've proven my point and now I can move on."

"Proven your point to whom?" Ellis took another slow, hardly noticeable step.

"That's none of your business, Sheriff. My life is none of your business."

"Yet clearly this is personal." Ellis glanced again behind the pair. "Help me to understand."

"You don't need to understand." His voice came harder, nearly a shout. "All you need is to let me pass and I'll be done with this town for good. You'll have your answers and you won't ever have to hear from me again."

Ellis frowned. "Have my answers? So you *do* have connections to this town. We just haven't put the pieces together."

Graves gripped Faith's gown harder. "Quit poking around where you don't belong, Sheriff. My patience is running out. If you don't let me by, I'll shoot her."

"Shoot her and you'll have nothing to bargain with. My men will gun you down on the spot."

Breath hissing in her ear, Graves released a desperate growl. "I need this. I need to show her that her belief in me is valid. I need to give her a good life—the life that's been taken from her."

Ellis's fingers stilled in the space before him. "Show who, Graves? Who are you doing all this for?"

"No." Graves's head shook desperately. "We've been through too much—suffered too much. I won't let you drag her into this too."

"Whoever you speak of, she isn't in trouble." Ellis's voice remained steady and calm, the only beacon of hope in Faith's whirling mind. "I only want to help."

"I don't want your help, Sheriff. I just want to leave." Graves pressed his gun firmly into Faith's neck, his fingers trembling.

Her breath hitched. Every second, his movements became more erratic, his breathing faster. Much more of this and he might pull the trigger whether he meant to or not.

"We'll let you go, Graves. We'll let you go." Ellis managed one more entreating step. "Lower your gun, and I'll order my men to clear a path." He snapped his fingers above his head. "Wainwright, the rest of you, move back. Give him space."

His deputies obeyed, easing their horses back. Relief and fear spun through Faith, twisting together as Graves's gun left her skin. Would he keep his word not to harm her if they let him ride off into the dark forest with her atop his horse's back? Doubt weighed heavy on her soul.

Faith closed her eyes, lifting a silent prayer before opening them to a path ahead illuminated by white moonlight. She squared her shoulders, her mind racing back to that day in the jail when her father had disowned her for choosing her integrity over him. The guilt she'd experienced that day dissolved. She would walk on, punished for following the path of good, perhaps, but firm in her beliefs.

Just as Graves prodded her forward, another motion yanked her swiftly down. Faith gasped. Graves's hold on her pulled her back, then released altogether. Off balance, she teetered with arms windmilling until falling to the dust with a hard thump.

A struggle ensued above her, grunts and shouts, men locked in heated combat. Footfalls pummeled the earth around her, Ellis and his men swarming in like a cloud of yellowjackets. Through the fog of confusion, she vaguely noticed Graves's gun discarded in the dirt beside her.

Faith peered through the dark to find a mass of writhing forms struggling as if one unified beast. At last, the scuffle died down as Ellis bent over Graves's form lying prone on the ground, digging a knee into his back. Breathless, he cuffed Graves's hands behind him.

Faith pressed a hand to the side of her face where it had met the coarse ground. A breath hissed through her teeth at the sudden sting, her fingers coming back bloody. She breathed easier as she watched the lawmen drag Graves to his feet. One of them must have snuck up behind him during their conversation. No wonder Ellis had kept glancing at the shadows. Reality seized her as she discerned a form lying on the ground, clutching his shoulder. *Gideon.*

Ferociously, Faith scrambled over the ground, collecting dirt on her hands and dress. She leaned over Gideon's body, squinting in the dim light. The struggle had dislodged her bandages, fresh blood staining his shirt. He groaned through every labored breath, cringing against the pain.

"Gideon, you fool." She clutched the lapels of his shirt, her tears meeting his skin as she bent near to kiss his cheek. "You ridiculous fool. I love you."

His grimace converted to a cheeky smirk as she turned toward the sheriff. "Ellis, he needs help. Graves shot him prior to your arrival. He has a bullet in his shoulder and he's still bleeding."

Ellis dashed to their side, looking down in concern before whistling with his teeth. "Wainwright, come here. You have medical training, don't you?"

"Yes, sir. My father was a surgeon in the Civil War." He raced toward them, dusting his hands on his trousers.

"I need you to look at this man. He's taken a bullet to the shoulder."

"Of course." Wainwright crouched briefly beside Gideon, pulling back his shirt enough to reveal the ghastly wound beneath. "This needs immediate attention." He glanced up at the other deputies. "There's a wagon over there. Help me lift him into it. Be careful."

Moments later, Wainwright knelt beside Gideon in the bed of an old wagon, cleaning his wound with alcohol and fishing out the bullet with a pair of pliers from his emergency medical kit. Faith sat on Gideon's other side, cradling his head in her lap and running her fingers through his hair. Through it all, Gideon kept his teeth clenched and his eyes shut, the only sign of his pain the tears squeezing out from beneath his lids.

After an agonizing amount of time, Wainwright had stitched his punctured skin together and sat back with a relieved sigh. "He should recover nicely. I don't believe his blood loss was too great, thanks to your quick thinking, Faith."

She offered him a weak smile. "I wish I could have done more—never insisted he come out here in the first place."

"Then we wouldn't have caught our man." Wainwright gazed down at Gideon, who had fallen unconscious somewhere during the procedure. "You both did a brave thing. You should be proud."

The night had grown bitterly cold. Faith shivered against the chilling winds as Wainwright left them alone in the wagon. She stroked Gideon's hair, watching as they compelled Adam Graves onto the back of a horse and rode off toward town.

Ellis retrieved the bag of gold discarded on the ground and peered into it. His head shook softly. "So much money. So much destruction in the name of wealth."

"It was more than wealth for him," Faith said from her spot inside the wagon bed. "He had other motives."

Ellis's thoughtful gaze swung up to her. "I do believe you're right, though I don't know how I'll possibly force him to reveal them. He seems as tight-lipped as they come."

"It would help if we could find this person he's protecting—perhaps speak with them." Faith thought back to that dreadful encounter in the upstairs room. "He mentioned something about wanting to take care of his mother."

"His mother?" Ellis's brows knit. "I've been investigating him for a while. I never found anything about a family."

Faith shrugged, her gaze falling back on Gideon's sleeping form. "Perhaps I misunderstood. Perhaps he has family somewhere else. Either way, he can't hurt us anymore. The gold is safe and he'll be behind bars."

"I'll do everything in my power to keep it that way." In a few easy strides, Ellis crossed to the wagon and set his arms atop the side. "I don't expect the court to go easy on him, especially after he stole the gold associated with the Baxter murder. The town still sees their departed banker as a venerable saint."

Faith shivered. "After everything I've heard of him, I'm glad he's gone. I can't imagine sharing a roof with him. Abeline is such a kindly soul. No wonder she didn't see through his deceptions."

"At least she can live a life of peace now." Ellis thumped the side of the wagon. "I'll get you hitched up and home. Do you think Mrs. Baxter will allow him to spend the night, since he needs convalescing? We can't take him back to the saloon in its present condition."

"No, we certainly can't." Faith traced Gideon's hairline. "Abeline will be happy to have him. She'll probably insist on nursing him back to health."

"If she gives her blessing, I'll go back to the saloon and collect his things. He's going to need a lot of care."

As Ellis set to work hitching the wagon, Faith could only stare wistfully at Gideon's slumbering face, swallowing back the intense fear lifting inside her. Words of affection had flown from her lips earlier that night, but their sentiment hadn't changed. He could destroy her if he wished to, and no matter how much she tried to convince herself not to trust, she couldn't help putting her every hope into Gideon Valdez.

Twenty Five

FATIGUE WEIGHED HEAVY ON Faith as the wagon bumped over the earth, nearing Abeline Baxter's serene home tucked in the woodlands. An unseen weight tugged on her eyelids, her skin peppered with gooseflesh despite the blanket Ellis had found for her. She gripped the side of the wagon, watching as the picturesque Victorian rose into view through the quaking evergreens. Would Abeline even be awake at this hour? She detested the idea of ripping the old woman from her much-needed rest.

As the wagon ground to a stop near the front door, Ellis hopped down, along with the deputy he'd brought with him. The two gingerly lifted Gideon and carried him up to the house as Faith scooted out of the wagon. The wind rushed over the trees and grasses, chilling her skin. At least she could relax again with Graves behind bars. No more surprise attacks in the barn, nothing to disturb Abeline's peaceful life here.

Mrs. Baxter appeared at the door, clad in a white nightgown, with her long silvery hair braided down her back. "Oh my, what's happened?" Both wrinkled hands plastered over her cheeks as she stepped aside to let Ellis and his deputy pass through.

"I'm very sorry to disturb you, ma'am." Ellis grunted as he heaved Gideon through the front door, both hands looped around the sleeping man's armpits. "We had an incident earlier tonight involving your ward, Faith Carter."

"Faith?" Abeline's hands gripped the door as she stretched on her toes to see past the men.

"I'm all right, Abeline. You needn't worry." Once the men had carted Gideon inside, Faith pressed herself into Abeline's comforting embrace.

"Thank God you're unharmed, dear." She brushed her hands over Faith's hair. "What happened to your friend?" She turned to the group in the sitting room. "Don't worry about my sofa. You can set him down there."

The men did as directed, easing Gideon onto the cushioned furniture.

"Poor man took a bullet to the shoulder," Ellis said, straightening and stretching his back. "We apprehended a burglar earlier tonight, and the suspect shot Mr. Valdez in an attempt to flee."

"Oh, my." Abeline shut the door, blocking out the whirling winds. "A burglar, you say?"

Faith crossed the room and sank into the chair beside the sofa. "The man who stole all that gold from the bank. Gideon and I followed him out to the old Hammond place."

Abeline's mouth opened slightly, a rush of air bursting through it. "The man who burglarized the bank? How dreadful." Her fingers covered her gaping mouth. "You must have been so frightened."

"Yes, well, it's over now," Ellis said. "The criminal has been apprehended. He'll face trial for his misdeeds."

"That's a relief, I suppose." Abeline took a step forward, her feet unsteady. "And the man you caught? He's unharmed as well?"

Ellis nodded. "Quite. Just a few scrapes from the scuffle of being arrested." His head shook woefully. "He put up quite the fight. He even tried to take Faith here hostage."

"Oh, how wretched." Her lips crimped in pity. "My dear, you must inform me of anything I can do to help you. I can't imagine such an ordeal."

Faith set her hand on Gideon's arm. "I'm fine, but he needs a place to stay while he recovers. He has nowhere else to go."

"Of course. He's welcome here as long as he likes." Abeline's gaze already cast about the house. "We'll have to get him to a proper bed when he can manage it. He'll need blankets, a good pillow—"

"All in due time." Ellis patted Abeline's shoulder. "You're a good woman, Mrs. Baxter. Gold Strike needs more like you, especially after the events of tonight."

She frowned. "More events than those you've just divulged? I admit I'm isolated out here, but—"

"There was a gunfight tonight on Main Street," Faith said from her spot on the chair. "Many are dead or injured. It took Old Joe and Jeremiah Anderson."

Ellis heaved a weighty sigh. "I'll have to be getting back into town. There are many people looking for answers, and even more fearful of what's to come after this."

Abeline offered him a half-hearted smile. "You certainly have your work cut out for you, Sheriff—but if there's anyone up for the job, it's you."

"I appreciate that, Mrs. Baxter." Ellis flicked his head toward his waiting deputy. "Let's get going. Give these people time to rest. I'll be back with his things in a little while."

"Thank you, Ellis." Faith stroked the soft hair on Gideon's arm. "We owe you our lives."

When the squeak of the porch steps receded into silence, Abeline hugged her frail frame and visibly shuddered. How ghastly events like those that had transpired tonight no doubt affected a woman in her elder years. She must have felt even more helpless out here, alone and vulnerable.

"It's over, Abeline. Most of the people causing trouble in this town are either dead or locked up."

Abeline's gaze met hers, a haunted sadness clouding her normally bright eyes. "I'm glad of that. There were too many ruthless killers walking our streets. But still I—" She looked out the window at the black night. "I can't help thinking about all those people mourning their loved ones tonight, no matter the trouble they'd gotten themselves into."

Faith gripped Gideon's flaccid hand, drawing in the scents of clementine and cinnamon that characterized Abeline's home. "It's a tragedy. I'm just glad it doesn't have to touch us, this home."

Abeline's mouth lifted sadly. "Indeed." As if remembering herself, she stood straighter. "My, I haven't let such melancholy overtake me since Colton died. I'd best get to work helping this boy. Do you think he'll rouse soon? What about you? Are you hungry? You've been through so much. I have meatloaf and potatoes in the icebox, and I was going to make a custard pie."

Faith smiled gratefully. Leave it to Abeline to fill their bellies in a time of crisis. "Thank you, Abeline. Perhaps I'll be hungry shortly. Right now my stomach is still twisted in knots."

"Of course." She clasped her hands together. "You've been through a great deal today. Let me care for you as much as I can." With that, she set off toward the kitchen, ready to solve the world's problems with her whisk.

Slipping to the floor, Faith propped herself on her knees beside the sofa, clasping Gideon's hand in both of hers. He had such a peaceful look to him, even after all he'd endured. His dark hair fell over his forehead in feathery wisps, his eyelashes thick and soft atop his cheeks. Faith's gaze traced the strong lines of his face—his jaw and cheekbone, the handsome curve of his nose. How had she not fallen under his spell the very first moment she'd seen him in the saloon?

The memory struck her—how he'd bothered her at first, how angered his cheating had made her. If she could only have those moments back to relive them, to appreciate him from the very beginning.

Her heart squeezed. Love was a dangerous thing. Hadn't her father taught her that well enough? Love meant giving someone the ability to trample one's heart, to rip them from the inside out. Faith sighed. He'd already told her he wanted solitude. He had no room for her in his life. What hope could she harbor, loving a vagabond who would never settle down, never want to raise a respectable family?

As if reading her thoughts, his eyes began to slowly drift open, his lashes batting away his fatigue.

Faith gasped, clutching his hand as she leaned closer. "Gideon. Can you hear me?"

He winced, though one side of his mouth pulled up. "Of course I can hear you. He didn't shoot my ears."

"You rogue." She laughed, settling closer beside him. "I was so worried after what you did—how you came to my rescue after you'd already been shot. I thought you would bleed to death."

He took a hard breath, his wrinkled brow revealing his pain. "It didn't matter much to me in that moment what happened to me. I only wanted to make sure you were safe." His fingers lifted just enough to brush hers. "I love you, Faith. There was no way I could deny it as I lay up there in that room all alone. I couldn't let him threaten your life. I would give mine if necessary."

His words lifted her heart, joy spilling out across her extremities. "I love you too, Gideon. I don't know what I would have done if you'd died."

His gaze bent weakly toward his shoulder. "What happened? I can barely remember anything."

"Deputy Wainwright stitched you up. He said you should make a full recovery."

"A deputy knew all this?" His eyes glinted with amused sarcasm.

"Apparently he's more than just a deputy. He's one of many guardian angels." She held his hand to her chest. "Just like Mrs. Baxter. She says you can stay here for as long as you need. She only wants to see you get better."

His brow hooked playfully. "She isn't afraid I'll entice you with my charm and good looks?" He tried to laugh, which died to sputtering and a regretful moan.

"She knows you aren't strong enough to walk up the stairs yet, let alone seduce me with your charms."

His lips puckered smugly. "It won't be long until I am. Just you wait, Faith Carter. I'm coming for you."

She leaned on his solid shoulder. "I'll be waiting." Her fingers laced with his. "I'll always be waiting."

Silence pervaded the room, tranquil and happy—the kind of quiet that filled one's soul to the brim. Faith thought Gideon must have fallen asleep until his fingers squeezed hers. Her head lifted, her gaze meeting the dark solemn eyes staring back.

"What is it? Can I get you anything for your pain?"

"It's not that." His voice caught, his eyes searching hers. "The things we said to each other tonight, the words we shared—"

"You mean about being in love?"

He nodded. "I meant every word I said, but Faith—"

A warm feeling trickled over her, understanding along with it. "You're afraid."

He paused, his expression sober. "More than I've ever been in my whole life. Suddenly there's something to lose, and the thought of losing *you*—"

Faith pushed a reassuring hand through his thick shock of hair. "You won't lose me; I promise."

Tortured pain filled his eyes. "You can't promise that, Faith. My mother and father—they promised me that too, and then they were taken by evil, greedy men. They had no say in the matter. No matter how much we loved each other, it wasn't enough."

His words sank into her, soaking through her skin and touching her deepest parts. The horror of watching his family die at such an early age would stick with him forever, a constant reality for them both. Yet if he let his fear rip them asunder, those treacherous rangers who murdered his family long ago would win.

"Losing each other will always be a possibility." Faith gripped his hand. "We always stand to have our hearts broken, our lives ripped apart, but what is the alternative?"

He looked at her curiously. "What do you mean?"

"I mean if we never love, we never have to feel, but loneliness itself is a feeling. Once you love someone—"

"Choosing not to be with them out of fear only fulfills what you're scared of happening."

"Exactly." She leaned into the fingers softly stroking her cheek. "Whether we're destined to die together of old age or be pulled apart tomorrow, I'd rather spend that time with you, loving you, even with my own heart telling me to fear."

A disbelieving breath puffed from his lips. "What do you have to fear? I've fallen hopelessly."

Faith's gaze dropped to the floor, a heavy burden on her chest. How could she voice the secret places in her heart when saying those words could destroy her? "My mother died when I was young." She took an unsteady breath. "She was everything to me—and then one day she was gone." She blinked back the warm tears swelling in her eyes and met his gaze. "Now I can hardly remember what she looked like."

Faith bit her lip. "My father and I became very close in the years after she died. He spoiled me, tried to make up for her loss any way he could. He had me convinced our love could do anything as long as we had each other."

Gideon's fingertips traced her jaw. "And then he let you down."

She nodded, swallowing. "I found out after all those years of loving and trusting him that it was a lie. His promises and care for me at the core were just an illusion. His love was self-serving, not actual affection or concern for me. Empty and meaningless." She tried to say more, but the words caught on a sob that barely escaped her throat.

"Oh, Faith." His hand cupped her cheek. "That has nothing to do with you. It concerns only him. He's a fool if he chose to blunder his relationship with someone like you."

Her hands scrunched her dress. "I know he's a vile, evil man, but he's also my father. I love him despite everything he's done." Her chest rose with fervency. "I think it hurts more *because* I love him, and because I trusted he had that same level of care for me—that it would always be there."

Tears squeezed from the corners of Faith's eyes, and she laid her head on the sofa next to Gideon's body. "I knew him my whole life, and still he managed to fool me. How naive was I to believe everything he said without question?"

Outside, the wind howled, rattling the shutters. Droplets of rain peppered the windows. Faith shivered at the sight of it, even with the fire in Abeline's hearth dispelling the chill.

Gideon's fingers gently brushed through her hair. "You were not naive to trust your father. A father is somebody you're supposed to rely on. The fault lies with him."

Gazing into the curving lines of her palms, Faith exhaled. "Yes, but I was fooled just the same. Who will fool me next—the apparent easy target in a deceiver's game?"

His hand stilled on her head, the seconds ticking by as her heart swelled with fear, her every insecurity on display for him to see. At last his fingers softly curled around the loose tendrils of her hair.

"Look at me. Faith, look at me."

Her head languidly revolved to the side, her eyes downcast before daring to make the slow climb to his. The intensity in his stare filtered through her, so raw and vulnerable, it stole her breath.

"I will never, ever deceive you." His thick eyelashes batted. "I realize now that probably doesn't sound like much coming from someone who cheats his way through life, but"—his gaze anchored on her again—"it's true. I promise I'll never lie to you."

Despite the doubts still clinging to her from her father's atrocities, she smiled against his hand. "I don't believe you will, Gideon Valdez. I feel at home with you—so much more at home than I've ever been."

The sheen of tears filled his eyes, his smile faltering with emotion. "You *are* home."

Rising on her knees, Faith came close and pressed a kiss to his lips. Their salty tears mingled, the promise of a thousand future embraces and a life ahead devoid of the hollow loneliness she'd endured this year. Faith kissed him with the hope of a soul finding rest in the knowledge that it had found its true companion.

Twenty Six

FIRELIGHT DANCED OVER THE walls of Abeline Baxter's sitting room as Gideon rested atop her sofa with Faith's head cradled on his chest. His fingers moved through her abundant hair, its smooth texture like silk beneath his fingertips. She smelled like heaven—rose petal perfume with the hint of rain.

How profound the idea that she loved him too and wanted to share a life that included him. Gideon breathed in the aroma of cedar burning in the fireplace and relaxed. The raging sting in his shoulder had subsided to a dull ache as he lay atop Abeline's cushions contemplating their future. What a beautiful picture it could make if only they stuck together. How different his life would look with her in it.

The urge to gamble and cheat fell away as they cuddled together in companionable silence. He would have to find a new way to earn money—one worthy of a respectable woman like the one in his arms.

She sat up, a sly look on her full lips. "Are you hungry yet? I can't imagine what Abeline must have cooked up in all this time."

His stomach groaned in response. "I wouldn't mind food—as long as she doesn't care about me eating on her sofa."

"Abeline doesn't mind." Faith climbed to her feet and stretched, her slender form silhouetted by firelight. "She's more concerned about you healing. I'm surprised she hasn't come in here to pamper you yet."

One side of Gideon's mouth lifted. "Maybe she wanted to give us a few minutes alone."

"That is like her."

Faith turned toward the hallway and froze, her back rigid and fingers locked in a spread position. A sharp gasp sucked through her lips, her stare fixed to the window.

Gideon lifted his head, craning his neck to see whatever had her attention. "What is it?"

Her gaze remained locked on the blustery scene outside a moment longer before she blinked and looked his way. "Did you see that?"

Gideon frowned. "See what? I can't see much of anything from my spot on the sofa."

"I thought I saw a shadow move across the yard, like a person." She hugged herself as she moved toward the window. "I don't see it anymore."

"The sheriff said he was coming back with my things, didn't he? Maybe it's him."

Faith glanced at the clock on the wall. "Has it been that long already?" She pressed a hand to the glass. "I don't see his horse in the drive or any sign of him."

"It could have been the wind blowing one of the trees around."

She glanced back, her look serious. "I suppose so. It could have been my imagination." She attempted a cheerful expression. "At least we know it isn't Adam Graves again coming to finish us off."

Her footsteps shuffled down the hall as she retreated into the kitchen. Gideon lay still a few minutes before boredom and curiosity had the best of him. Wincing, he slowly hung his legs over the edge of the sofa and forced his body into a sitting position. Pain raged from his shoulder down his arm, spearing into his chest. He breathed against it, determined to peer out the glass Faith had just stood by. Only the black silhouettes of pines swishing against one another met his eye. Abeline Baxter's home in the woods was likely the safest place they could be.

Moments later, Faith returned with a small tray laden with sliced bread and a hard wedge of cheese. "What are you doing sitting up?" She laid her collection on the tea table. "You need to rest in order to recover."

"I can rest and recover just fine sitting up." Gideon tossed her a wink. "Though I do appreciate the concern."

Faith simpered, sliding into the seat next to him. "I just want to see you get better as quickly as you can." Leaning forward, she plucked a slice of bread from the tray and handed it to him. "Here, this is all I can find for now—a loaf of bread and some cheese she keeps in the icebox."

He laughed, taking the bread from her. "It's quite all right with me, but I'm a little surprised. Doesn't she normally have all sorts of baked goods lying around?"

Faith reached out to slice off a bit of cheese. "She does. I was surprised to find the kitchen empty. She told me she was going in there to prepare food, but I couldn't find her anywhere."

He accepted the piece of cheese she handed to him and laid it over the top of his bread. "Perhaps she went out to the chicken coop to retrieve more eggs."

Faith sighed listlessly. "I surely hope not. The poor woman. With the state we found her in the other night, she's liable to be anywhere this time of night, doing God knows what. She shouldn't be out here all alone."

Chewing the savory blend of yeast and cheddar, Gideon mulled her words over. "Perhaps we can do something about that once I recover—help her make the kind of arrangements she needs at her age."

Faith's mouth lifted sadly. "I'd like that. She deserves someone caring about her." Pushing off the sofa, she rose to pace the room. "She's such a kind lady. I don't understand how she doesn't have more support."

"Didn't she have any children?"

"I thought she had a son, but I'm not sure. I suppose I was so caught up in my own endeavors, I never bothered to ask her." She glanced around before she found a photograph framed on the wall. Faith wandered to it, fondness in her eyes. "My father had this picture in his study. It's of the town at the church's groundbreaking. He was just a boy here."

Rising on her toes, she pulled the photograph off the wall and handed it to Gideon. "There's Abeline and her husband Colton." She tapped the glass to indicate a young woman with blonde hair and a smartly dressed man beside her. "They were so young then. She was so beautiful."

Eyes scanning the crowd of pleasant smiles and Sunday dresses, Gideon landed on an image of a boy in short pants and knee-high socks standing near the Baxters. "Could this be their son?"

Faith leaned over the picture, squinting. "It might be. He's standing closer to them than anyone else. And look." She indicated the space between the boy and Abeline's skirt. "Is he holding her hand?"

"I believe so. The dress is just blocking it."

Lifting the frame closer, Faith examined the photograph carefully. "In all my years of seeing this picture, I never noticed that before. So Abeline and Colton at least had one child. I wonder if he survived." Her gaze drifted off before falling on a bookcase nestled in the corner. "Look, she has albums over there. Perhaps we can find out."

Bustling to the small bookcase, Faith hunkered down and began sorting through the collection. "Is it rude of me to go through them without asking?"

Gideon's brow arched. "Will it stop you if I say yes?"

She tossed him a sardonic smirk, straightening with a large volume already secured in her arms. "I'm choosing to believe Abeline would welcome interest in her cherished memories. What mother doesn't want to talk about her son?"

Plopping down beside him, she opened the album over both their laps. The first page contained an old daguerreotype, water-stained and faded around the edges. In it, a young Abeline Baxter, garbed in a lace wedding gown, beamed back at them. Beside her, Colton appeared equally joyous in a tailored suit and stylishly combed hair.

Gideon paused a moment on those youthful eyes staring back. How weighty a lesson to learn, to understand that even an innocent beginning like that could turn vicious.

The next pages displayed portraits of an early Gold Strike—crude structures erected against a wooded backdrop, the farmhouse in which they now sat, new and fresh as a summer daisy. Faith flipped to the next page and gasped with delight. Another seated portrait shone beneath the lamplight—Colton and Abeline, perhaps a few years older, with a curly-haired baby seated in Abeline's lap.

"He was so cute." Faith plastered a hand to her cheek, overcome by the dimpled image of the young boy. "I bet Abeline got nothing done that year but hours of cuddling him."

After that, page after page revealed more family photographs, the boy in them growing from a chubby, towheaded baby to a strapping young man. Faith leaned over the final image, entranced by the picture of him standing next to the farmhouse, arm in arm with his mother.

"The two of them looked so happy here." Her head shook. "I wonder where he went."

"She never told you about him?" Gideon narrowed in again on the lean young man, familiar in a way, yet unlike anyone he could remember meeting. "It appears they had a close relationship."

She clicked her tongue. "Not that I remember, but that could be my own shortcoming. I will have to ask Abeline about him. That's if—" Her words died in the quiet space, fading beneath the crackle of the fire in the hearth.

"If something didn't happen to him." He had already guessed the substance of the concern in her eyes.

"Yes, I certainly don't want to bring it up if he's no longer with us. That could only hurt her worse." She came to life with a jolt. "Where is Abeline, anyway? She's not in the kitchen, and I don't hear her upstairs. I feel like I should check on her. Look for her outside, maybe."

The idea put Gideon on alert. "If you're going outside, I'm coming with you."

"Nonsense. You're not well enough to go walking around the farm with me." She patted his arm in reassurance. "Anyway, I'll be fine. Jeremiah Anderson is dead, and Adam Graves is at the Gold Strike jail. There's no one left to ambush us."

"If I've learned anything from gambling as a profession, it's that there is always someone left to ambush you." Gideon said it with a chuckle in his voice, but his fingers instinctively curled around her wrist. "Please don't go out there. We can wait for Sheriff McCraw or go together."

Her mouth crimped wryly. "You think I'm helpless, don't you?"

"Not helpless, but the thought of you in danger again—" His fingers constricted against her pulsing wrist. "It's just not something I'm willing to face again so soon." He couldn't help the chill that splintered through him to remember crouching beneath a table with bullets flying just outside the door.

"Fine. We'll wait." Faith's gaze drifted to the window. "I just can't help worrying about Abeline. If she did go out, she could be freezing by now. What if she became disoriented and can't remember how to get back?"

"On her own farm? I think that's unlikely." Yet despite his unaffected words, doubt wiggled its way into his gut. He could only stall for so long. Gideon knew as well as Faith they couldn't leave an old woman to fend for herself if she didn't return. His gaze darted to the front door. If only she'd reemerge on her own.

Gideon froze as something twitched at the corner of his vision. His eyes swung up to the window, where a long, distant shadow moved swiftly past the glass. He waited, but nothing stirred again save the shivering branches of pines.

"Did you see it this time?" Faith's voice lifted weakly, her fingertips pressing into his palm.

"I did." His stare remained fixed to the window, every nerve in his body preparing for someone to jump unexpectedly into his field of vision.

Letting go of his hand, Faith stood and crept to the glass, staying off to one side. She pulled the curtain back with one trembling hand, peering past it like a child gazing into an imagined world. "I don't see anything. It certainly isn't Ellis." She let out a clipped sigh. "This is ridiculous. Clearly Abeline is out there wandering around and needs our help."

Determination seized her frame as Faith pointed herself toward the coat stand by the door and reached for her shawl. In one quick tug, she yanked it off the others and draped it over her shoulders. She would venture off this time with his blessing or not.

Gideon sat up, instant pain burning through his muscles like fire eating through the fibers of a rope. He held back a wince behind clenched teeth. "I'm coming with you." Setting one hand on the couch cushions, he fought the dizzy sensation already tilting his world on its axis.

Faith's shoes clicked across the floor until she stood over him, a solid hand on his healthy shoulder. "You're mad if you think you're going outside in your condition."

Battling the fog, Gideon braced himself on the sofa and tried again. Extreme pain lanced through him when he attempted to push off the cushions. White light streaked his vision. Only the reassuring hand clutching his shoulder grounded him in reality.

"Gideon, my love, please don't strain yourself." Her breath warmed his cheek as she bent over him. "It's only Abeline. I'm perfectly fine handling this on my own. I won't have you injured worse when I can easily go outside and get her myself."

His eyes squeezed shut, blocking the tears of pain and frustration frothing beneath them. If he could fight her, he would. He would struggle through every ounce of pain to keep her safe. His body, pierced with that coward's bullet, had other plans. He would have to let her go out there alone, vulnerable to a world that had only sought to harm her.

"I promise you I'm fine." Her tender voice touched him deep within. "I'll only be a minute. Once Abeline is back home safe, we'll sit up all night by the fire and talk about our future. How does that sound?"

Gideon's eyes languidly drifted open to find her face, silhouetted by sparkling firelight, so near to his. "Come back quickly. We have other things to accomplish." Expending the energy to lean in, he pressed his lips to hers and enjoyed the honey taste of her.

Faith smiled against him, letting the kiss linger several more seconds before she pulled away. "There will be plenty of that too." Standing, she tucked her shawl in tighter around her. "I will get her and come right back. You have nothing to concern yourself over."

In the wake of her parting, Gideon could do nothing but stare after the door she'd shut behind her. Curse this bullet wound and its incapacitating effects. The night he'd rescued her in the alley flashed through his mind, clear and jarring as if he lived it this very moment. If only he could prove as strong and present tonight. He could do nothing but wait, powerless as Faith wandered around in the dark alone.

His gaze meandered over the neat room, the well-kept furniture and floral paintings. With Faith outside and his mind unable to rest, what would he possibly do with his time? Already every tick of the Swiss clock on the wall drove harder at his nerves. If he could do nothing but sit here helplessly, he needed something to occupy his mind.

The bookcase from which Faith had taken the album sat too far away to retrieve any reading material. The fireplace flamed with orange light and popped as the logs tumbled over one another. He could only stare at it so long, imagining Faith getting lost in the woods while he sat here eating cheese. He sighed, reaching for another bite. Faith knew these forests far better than he did. She was not a helpless woman.

The photograph album she'd found sat on the cushion she'd vacated. Gideon thumbed through it again, poring over the sepia-toned images of a family growing year by year. He paused at the final photograph, studying it. The young, clean-shaven man next to Abeline bore a familiar countenance, but he couldn't pinpoint why.

Strange that he posed alone with his mother while his father still lived. A photographer would have been commissioned to the house. Colton hadn't taken the time to stand with them for one rare image?

Gideon flipped to the next page, finding it blank. The next bore nothing, and the next. He'd almost decided to close the album when notes from the final page showed through. Turning to the back cover, he discovered a full paper tacked into the album, covered in writing. Names were jotted across the page in a sectioned pattern.

"A family tree." Gideon's finger traced from the top of the page down, noting the generations and children that sprouted off them. The years began in the 1600s or 1700s, depending on the line, and ended with several branches flourishing outward with at least a dozen children. Curious if they'd lost the only son in their photographs, he scanned the names until he found Colton and Abeline.

Gideon stilled, his blood chilling, as his eyes fixed on the final name beneath theirs: *Adam Graves Baxter.* His fingers curled around the page as his mind went off kilter. Adam Graves Baxter? Could it be?

He turned back to the final photograph of the man and squinted. Yes, he knew that face. Even under the grime and untamed whiskers, that was the man who'd shot him at the Hammond house, the one who'd wrestled him to the ground in the barn. No wonder he'd been snooping around Abeline's farm—the place he'd grown up, where his mother lived.

His hand raked shakily through his hair. Did she know he'd come to see her? Did she have contact with him at all? He thought back to the bone-chilling conversation in the upstairs room of the Hammond house. Graves wanted to take care of his mother. He wanted to make sure she was safe.

Her reaction to finding out he'd been arrested replayed in his mind. No wonder her skin had whitened, why she'd found the news so troubling. Her only son sat in a Gold Strike jail cell, destined to face a lifetime behind bars for what he'd done. Did she know about her son beforehand? Was she a part of the scheme to steal the gold? How could she be?

Gideon sat up from the couch, grimacing as shattering pain sliced through him. He couldn't sit here a moment longer, his questions unanswered, his anxiety building every second. Growling through his pain, he shoved himself off the couch and stood on trembling legs. The entire right side of his body begged him to collapse back on the sofa. His vision fuzzed. Yet Gideon kept on, staggering to the door.

With a grunt, he ripped it open, his dark hair flying back on the wind. The temperatures had dipped since they rode in, nipping at his skin and driving a chill up his spine. Gideon stomped over the rickety porch floor, pausing a moment to rest against the railing before stumbling down the steps and into the drive.

Within the stream of moonlight showering the cobblestone, two images stopped him dead in his tracks—Faith, crying and shaking, and the old woman behind her, clutching a handful of her dress and jabbing a rifle into her back.

Twenty Seven

Faith did her best to still the jitters coursing through her, yet her body trembled in wave after uncontrollable wave. Her eyes found Gideon in the dark, tears blurring her vision, her lips wet with salty moisture. She'd led them both into a trap.

Moments before, she had searched the yard with her shawl wrapped tightly around her, calling Abeline's name through the baying wind. She'd scanned the yard again, tucking strands of loose hair behind her ears, shielding her face until she made out Abeline's hunched form near the cellar doors. Thank God she'd found her before Abeline could wander too far from the house.

"Abeline!" she shouted, pushing her way through the blustery fog and scattered leaves whirling about the air. "Abeline, it's Faith. You must come with me."

Abeline had stiffened upon her approach, something long and solid in her hand. As Faith fought her way toward her, the object materialized, a rifle gleaming beneath the thin strands of moonlight. Why did Abeline need a rifle? Was she that scared of being out here all alone? She couldn't let this continue. The poor woman needed help.

Abeline silently assessed her, her fingers curling protectively around the gun. Her hair, normally pinned up neatly, fell in wisps about her face. She had a smudge of dirt on her cheek and forehead, her skirts muddied.

"Oh, Abeline, did you fall?" She examined the rest of the woman's frail body, searching for injuries. When Abeline said nothing, she laid a hand on her shoulder. "You poor thing. You must be so confused. Let's get you inside."

Instead of following her lead, Abeline surveyed the darkened property once more, as if in search of something. Her gaze flitted between the cellar and the house, then across the dancing trees.

"There's nothing out there. It's just us." Faith squeezed her shoulder reassuringly. "I know this probably doesn't make sense right now, but I need you to come with me. It's warmer inside. We can get you something hot to drink, maybe something to eat."

Abeline blinked, though when her eyes met Faith's, they bore not a hint of confusion—only dead certainty. An impatient sigh pressed from her. "There's no use in pretenses anymore, Faith. I have nothing left to lose."

"Pretenses?" Faith's head shook as she sought the woman's arm. "You don't understand. We just need to go inside."

"No, *you* don't understand." Abeline's look turned compassionate, though tinged with annoyance. "How could you, with your pure and trusting ways? You can't even comprehend the deception in me when I'm out here hunting someone down with a rifle."

Faith stumbled backward, the breath snatched from her. Hunting someone down? She focused on the rifle in Abeline's firm grip. "Have you taken complete leave of your senses? There's no one here but Gideon and I."

Abeline's eyes rolled up. "You really see me as nothing but a helpless old woman, don't you? I suppose that's my fault for playing the role so well."

As her words settled over Faith, tingles of apprehension flecked her skin. The elderly woman before her gradually morphed from the sweet widow who'd taken her in to something far more threatening. How much of the kind person she'd come to love was merely a lie?

"Don't look at me like that. I didn't mean for this to happen." Abeline peered toward the trees once more. "If only Adam had listened to me to begin with. She was too much of a risk, too much for the two of us to handle—especially at my age."

Faith frowned in confusion. "Who was?"

"Sylvia Hammond, of course." Abeline's eyes, uncharacteristically stern and unfeeling, met hers. "Who else do you think I'm looking for out here?"

Sylvia Hammond? The woman who'd been kidnapped on her way to Billings? What did she have to do with any of this? A cold, nauseating feeling took root inside of Faith.

Abeline swiped silver strands of hair from her face. "Now here I am, alone, looking for a fugitive at my age, when all I want to do is mourn the loss of my son."

Faith's lips parted as pieces began to click together in her mind. *Adam dragged me into this.* The pictures in her album of a baby growing into a child, then a young man. It all made sense now. Adam Graves was her son. He'd taken Sylvia Hammond against her will, and now Abeline was left to pick up the shattered pieces of his plan.

Footsteps crunched the ground behind them. Before Faith could make sense of the sounds, a hand yanked her back and hard metal pressed into her side. She could do nothing but freeze up like an icicle as Abeline thrust her rifle into Faith's ribs.

"Don't come any closer." She still bore that sweet, inviting lilt that had often calmed Faith's raging nerves, but something darker and graver had slipped into her tone. She had no interest in playing games with Gideon.

He stood fixed in place, his hands in the air. "I won't cause any trouble for you. I just want to make sure she's safe."

Abeline huffed derisively. "Do you think I want to hurt this sweet girl? Of course not. Throw down that pistol on your belt and I'll lower my gun."

He did as told without question, his gun flopping into the dirt. His solemn look bore into Faith—through her skin, beneath her flesh and into her core. His soul met hers in that wild, churning air.

"If I may ask," he said, his gaze shifting to Abeline, "what do you plan to do? We know about your son now, and about Sylvia. How do you plan to get out of this situation without hurting people?"

Abeline's breath rasped behind Faith's head. "I don't know. I never intended to do this without Adam. He was supposed to find a way to free Sylvia on the promise that she wouldn't reveal what she knew."

Gideon studied her carefully. "Is that why you kept her? She had too much information about your son?"

"No." Her grip tightened on Faith's gown. "I kept her because she has too much information about *me*. And now so do you."

"Now that she's broken free, she could bring the authorities to your door at a moment's notice."

Abeline's voice rose again, its uncompromising quality laced with the hint of vulnerability. "I can only deal with one problem at a time." The tip of her rifle jammed into Faith's ribs, eliciting a cry of surprise. "Now walk forward. Both of you get in the cellar."

Faith twisted weakly her way. "He can't take those stairs. He's injured."

Even as she coerced Faith with the threat of death, Abeline's wrinkled eyes shone soft in the moonlight. "He must, Faith. I can't have the two of you out in the open when the sheriff comes back here."

"And when Sylvia finds him and tells him you locked her in your cellar?" Gideon asked. "What then? It's going to be the first place he looks."

Silence, rife with wind and a few chilling sprinkles, fell over them. Abeline's grip on Faith slackened before she gently prodded her forward. "Like I said, one problem at a time. I'll figure it out as we go. I always do."

A short walk brought them to the open cellar doors positioned near the house amid the weed-speckled ground. Gideon went first, his every labored movement bespeaking his pain. Faith cringed when his shoulder bumped the wall and he held in a whimper. What would this venture beneath the earth do to his injury?

A slow climb down a sloping wooden ladder brought them to a wide room dug into the earth. Faith eased down the last of the creaking rungs and took the cellar in through wide, fearful eyes. On one side stood what one would expect in any root cellar—dusty shelves of preserves, canned goods with peeling labels, a collection of freshly picked vegetables.

Her gaze drifted across the dirt floor to a mattress laid in the corner topped in a tangled sheet and blanket. A jug of water sat beside it, along with a bucket—presumably for relieving oneself. A shiver coursed through her. What corner of hell had she crawled into?

"Both of you sit down on that mattress," Abeline ordered, indicating the uninviting bed on the floor.

Obedient to her command, Faith sank to her knees on the mattress and helped Gideon nestle in next to her. Not a word of complaint left his lips, though they whitened with the effort. Sweat seeped from his pores, dampening his dark hair.

Abeline watched them with a mournful look in her eye, the rifle still firm in her grip but pointed toward the floor. She smoothed her hand across her brow. "This wasn't supposed to happen. I had the perfect plan. The Hammond woman ruined it."

Faith blinked through the muddled light. "What do you mean she ruined it? She was running away when you took her, was she not? You had no need to kidnap her. She only wanted to escape."

Abeline stared back, her aged eyes glassy, her disheveled hair now loose and tumbling over her thin shoulders. "I told Adam the same thing, but he wouldn't listen to me. He saw her at the train depot, waited until it stopped in the next city, and ambushed her. She's been here ever since."

"Months," Faith breathed. "She's been down here for months." The idea of her wasting away in this dank, mildewy room chilled her through.

"Yes. Keeping a grown woman locked up for all that time would challenge anybody, but an old woman like me—" Her head shook ruefully. "I never should have listened to him when he told me it would only last a short time."

Gideon shifted beside Faith. "What was it she knew that scared your son so much? Why risk your life to keep her here?"

Abeline's gaze found him, her normally kind eyes void of emotion. "I suppose it won't hurt to tell you. You already know enough about me to put me behind bars for the rest of my life—whatever short time I have, anyway."

She collapsed into a chair nearby, her joints crackling with the effort. Her head rested in her open palm, her face half-covered. "Sylvia Hammond knows just about everything from all the chatter that comes through her shop, and having children with Red Fox only makes her more dangerous. What she knew about my son would have made him a prime target for the criminals in this town. Had she divulged it, he wouldn't have lasted the day."

Faith leaned in, her palms supporting her on the pliant mattress. "What does she know about your son? You can tell us, Abeline. We'll try to help, I promise."

The old woman lifted her head just enough to smile sadly at Faith. "I do believe you would, my dear, but it's too late now, and Adam's story is far too complicated to tell in one conversation."

Abeline's chest heaved, her gaze drifting to the far wall. "A long time ago, we were all a happy family—Colton and I, then Adam. We had many good years together before everything changed."

Faith swallowed. "Before Adam went down the wrong path, you mean?"

"No, before Colton became cruel and selfish. Before he ripped our family apart."

Memories flooded Faith's mind of Adam Graves lying on the floor in the Hammond house, cursing the father he claimed ruined his life. "He was an abusive man. He hurt your son."

Abeline's stony eyes swung to hers. "Yes, in more ways than one. Colton inflicted scars upon Adam's heart long before he ever touched him physically. From a very young age, he told him he was worthless, that he would never amount to anything unless he became serious about business and finance like his father. He convinced him he was stupid."

She covered her face in spread fingers. "Then the beatings started, and I didn't know what to do." Her breath hitched around the sob at the base of her throat.

"Oh, Abeline." With the anguish splashed across Abeline's face, Faith could almost forget the woman held her in a terrifying root cellar at the point of a rifle.

Abeline's shoulders shook as her tears silently fell. When they finally ceased, she sniffed and ran a palm over her cheek. "The rest of the world sees Colton as a hero, but I've known who he was for a very long time, and there was nothing heroic about him. He destroyed our son's life."

"He kept him from marrying the woman he loved, didn't he?" Gideon asked. At the question in Abeline's eyes, he shrugged. "He told us that himself at the old Hammond place just before he shot me."

Her gaze tumbled to her lap, her lips pinching together. "Yes, my son had his sights set on a beautiful girl, Angelica Foster. I believe she would have agreed to marry him if Colton hadn't interfered.

He convinced Adam that he didn't measure up, that she would outright refuse him, and he'd be humiliated. So Adam did as his father wished, and he went away to school to better himself, with the intention of coming back home to claim her."

She closed her eyes against the bitter memory. "Meanwhile, Jude Hammond weaseled his way into her affections and ran off with her to live in squalor. When my son found out, he was heartbroken. He quit school. He wandered the country for a time, aimlessly drifting about like a tumbleweed tossed by the wind."

"But he came back." Faith scrunched the blanket beside her, invested in the tragic tale.

"He did. He came back with long hair and a full beard, a new identity." Abeline smiled mournfully. "He was determined to make something of himself and to force his father to watch. So he used the money he'd earned on the road to purchase the dilapidated mill and turn it back into a successful business. He dropped the name of Baxter, and people didn't recognize him. He just became a new person, as if born that very day. Only his father and I knew."

Faith tucked her knees in tight against her chest, perching her chin atop them. "You never crossed paths? Nobody ever saw you together?"

"Adam and I met in secret, but the two of them never spoke again. They lived side by side in town in silent competition, nobody ever suspecting a thing—until Sylvia Hammond figured out who he was."

"She recognized him?" Gideon asked.

Abeline nodded. "She had spent enough time around him in youth. She tried to hide it, but we both took notice. She knew exactly who my son was."

Faith's lashes batted. "I don't understand. Why did it matter if she recognized him? So what if she knew Adam was your son?"

Laying the rifle across her lap, Abeline absently slid her fingers down the barrel. "Because by then the two of us had hatched a plan—my son and I. We'd already set it in motion, and after Colton died, we couldn't afford our secret getting out."

Gideon's hand inched toward Faith's arm, a gentle warning she chose not to heed. "You, Mrs. Baxter? You had something to do with your husband's death?"

Solemn, weighty quiet answered back before Abeline fixed her with a solid expression. "I would never plot to kill my husband, but that doesn't mean I couldn't see the natural trajectory of his decisions. The town only saw what he wanted them to, his donations and charity work. The face he put on when he greeted them. The reality of living with him was far more sinister."

Her fingers curled around the barrel of her gun. "My husband was planning to take over this entire valley, to steal money that didn't belong to him and use it to create a monopoly on every business he could, including my son's. How else could he show him he was right all along, that Adam was not fit for running a business without him, that he'd won?"

She sighed heavily. "Unfortunately for him, another man had the exact same plan, and there wasn't room for two. I saw the writing on the wall long before my husband took Mr. Pierce's bullet and died in the dirt. I read his plans to steal the gold, correspondences between him and Sheriff Jones and Jeremiah Anderson. I put the pieces together. Then he came home shot through the hand, and the next day's papers told of a break-in at Edward Carter's house. Colton was playing with fire, and he deserved the consequences his decisions brought upon him."

Faith laid a hand over her heart, her blood pumping furiously beneath. "Did you know Edward Carter planned to kill him?"

"I knew it was likely after what Colton had done. I knew it had to happen if Adam and I ever wanted to be free, to live life without him, to be a family once again."

Exchanging a look of concern with Gideon, Faith reached out to take his hand. "What about my father? He could have killed your husband, taken off with the gold. You would have been left with nothing."

Abeline's mirthless laughter bounded off the walls. "You have no idea how good that scenario sounds—to have only this house without Colton in it, to finally be at peace." Her head wagged. "I knew Carter would get what he deserved, too. The new sheriff just needed a little coaxing."

"Coaxing?" Faith's mind raced back to that day in the church before a bullet had severed her ties with her father forever. Abeline had presented Ellis with something—an item that had caused him to run from the building with Cora at his side. "The cigar."

"It was a bit heavy-handed, I admit, but it worked." Abeline settled against the chair. "They didn't find that on Colton's body. I knew the type of cigar your father smoked, and I presented it to the sheriff as a clue. One look into his records was all it would take to put him in prison. Then Colton and your father both would be taken care of for good."

Stunned silence enveloped the room for several moments. Faith had always known Abeline Baxter was a smart, capable woman, but this, she would never have imagined. Colton Baxter got far more than he bargained for when they'd wed those many years ago.

Abeline's eyes rested thoughtfully upon her as the wind swished madly above and echoed into the underground cellar. "Without my interference, perhaps your father wouldn't have been caught so swiftly. Your life might look very different now. I stole a great deal from you that day. I acknowledge it."

She told the truth, and yet, when Faith really dared to ponder it, she couldn't imagine another path for her life to take. Her father was supposed to be caught, and she to forge an avenue away from him. Abeline had only helped the process along.

Faith's fingers tensed around Gideon's, an unexpected quandary eating at her. "So did you take me in because you really wanted to help me, or because you wanted to keep an eye on me?" *Was the relationship I thought we had a lie, or was I merely a means to an end?*

"Oh, child." Abeline's head tilted in sympathy. "I wanted to take you in even before you learned of your father's treachery. You deserved better than him." Her chest swelled. "My son was unhappy about it. He said it would be too risky to have you around, but I wouldn't hear his arguments. I wanted you here.

"I convinced myself he would find a way to quietly free Sylvia someplace where no one knew us. Then he found the code to the bank vault in his father's things. He came home with news of stealing the gold and a plan to run away, and I knew." Her eyes closed and fluttered open again. "I knew he'd already become like his father, and no amount of money or power would ever satisfy his craving for more. Again, I was alone in the world." She blinked back her tears, her haunted gaze settling in the shadowed corner.

The wind beat down harder, buffeting over the ground above. The open cellar doors squealed and bashed against one another. Across the quiet space flickering with lamplight, Faith's heart stretched. If only she could wrap her arms around Abeline now, mend the broken heart her husband had shattered over so many years of cruelty.

Somewhere in the distance, a horse neighed. Faith sat up, Gideon close behind, as the sound neared. Abeline grasped her weapon, standing abruptly. All eyes swung to the open passageway through which the drum of hoofbeats approached.

"I've wasted too much time." Abeline marched to a set of shelves built into the wall and seized a length of rope. "My son is in jail, Sylvia's on the run, and I'm here with two innocent captives." She frantically paced the floor, disturbing the dirt.

"You can stop this, Abeline." Faith scooted to the edge of the mattress. "You don't have to build upon your husband and son's mistakes. Let us free, and we'll explain everything to Ellis. He'll understand."

Yet already the old woman had advanced toward them, her stern look accepting no arguments. "It's too late for that now. I've already made my bed. Now turn around, the both of you. Don't make this harder than it has to be."

Twenty Eight

THE BITTER AIR INSIDE Abeline Baxter's root cellar cut to the bone. Gideon scooted closer to Faith's quivering frame, snuggling her against him as best he could. The wind above them raged, scattering leaves and branches across the door Abeline had secured shut, its spectral echo over the yard warning anyone riding up of the secrets buried beneath the earth. Gideon's eyes shifted across the room—barely a room at all, just four crude walls hewn from the dirt and rough shelves laden with jars of preserved fruits and vegetables.

"What do you think she's telling him?" Faith asked, her voice a mere murmur in the forgotten space. "She'll have to think of an excuse as to why we're not in her house."

He bristled. What tales could a woman as deceitful as that old bat weave to suit her purposes? Faith could find a way to forgive her and have sympathy for her tragic life, but as Gideon surveyed the barbaric circumstances in which this Hammond woman had lived for so long, he could find no such clemency in his heart.

"She could easily make up a story, say I was well enough to go upstairs and we are both asleep now. The sheriff is bound to believe it, of course. Everyone believes a poor widowed old woman."

Faith shifted beside him, readjusting the hands bound behind her back. "I know she told us she'd shoot Ellis if we made a sound or tried to escape, but I just don't believe she actually would. Not the Abeline I know."

Gideon's brow hooked. "Do you care to go outside and test that theory?"

"No." She gave a defeated sigh. "I just think Abeline is doing this all out of desperation—shock over what happened with her son. She won't make good on her threats to harm anyone."

"Are you so sure about that? What about Sylvia Hammond?"

The quiet built thick and high between them before she finally spoke. "I suppose even a woman like Abeline Baxter would do just about anything to protect her son."

He turned toward her. The ropes twisted around his wrists, chafing his skin. "Like hurt Ellis McCraw? Like hurt you?"

Poignant sadness peered out through her eyes. "Abeline wouldn't hurt me." She swallowed. "At least I don't think so. She's been such a comfort and support since my father's incarceration. I owe her everything."

Gideon's jaw worked as heat surged up his body. What did this Baxter woman have to do before Faith could see her treachery? No wonder her father had been able to commit crimes beneath her nose for so long. Gideon hung his head. He regretted the thought as soon as it materialized.

Faith sighed. "I just can't help picturing her as that poor woman with a son being abused, with an unfaithful husband, stuck in a prison of being the only one who knew the monster lurking beneath his shell. I'd likely have done the same in her position—let everyone else kill each other just to be rid of them."

Gideon shot her a disbelieving look. "No, you wouldn't have. I know you, Faith. Had you been in Abeline's shoes, you would have believed the best in Colton, but when he started to show his colors, you would have stood up. You would have defended that boy." He leaned closer, leveling his gaze with hers. "You shot your own father to protect the innocent. You are so much stronger than Abeline Baxter could ever hope to be."

Faith blinked, her lashes batting back the moisture brightening her eyes. "And here I thought that action made me a traitor."

"Not a traitor. No. A woman with a strong head on her shoulders. If you were Abeline, you would have loved your son enough to stand up and tell him no when he tried to capture a woman and bring her to your home. You would never have put her down here and deluded yourself into hoping for a peaceful resolution."

Her eyes searched his a moment before her gaze plummeted to her lap. "I suppose we're all a hodgepodge of different characteristics, good and bad—with the propensity for evil, even if we must talk ourselves into it." Her gaze flitted around the cellar. "You're right; I could never have done what she did, but I don't know what I would have done in her place. None of us do, really. Living with Colton Baxter for a husband must have been traumatizing."

"Maybe I would have fallen prey to such temptations, but you, Faith"—his gaze meandered up her bound arm, over her graceful neck and into her eyes. "You are so much more than you realize. I should have rushed her when I had the chance instead of sitting here like a coward."

"Gideon, no." Her head shook vehemently. "You've been shot. Your health matters too. You could have been hurt worse, ripped open your wound—"

"It wouldn't have mattered. As long as you're safe, I would give my life a hundred times over." The truth of that fact multiplied again and again as he stared into the depths of her eyes. Suddenly he was that child again. Hopeless. Helpless. Beholden to the whims of people who killed as if hunting for sport. A stronger man would have pulled Faith out of this a long time ago.

"We're in this together now." Her tender voice touched his thoughts as she laid her head atop his shoulder. "Whatever happens, we look out for one another."

With a kiss to the top of her head, he nodded. "I won't leave you, Faith, wherever this night leads us. You have my solemn vow that you won't face it alone."

The night beyond the dank cellar wailed with spinning wind, clattering the doors against one another. Gideon could barely discern when they squealed back on their hinges and bashed against the ground overhead. The ladder groaned as Abeline's shoes appeared, each rung carrying her closer. When she stood in the dirt before them, dust besmirching her skirts and rifle still in hand, she looked them over with the eyes of a seasoned hawk.

Faith's breath hastened. "What happened?"

Setting her rifle against the wall, Abeline motioned for Faith to turn. "Sheriff McCraw dropped off Mr. Valdez's possessions. He couldn't stay long." Her fingers began loosening the knots around Faith's wrists.

"Did he ask why we weren't there?" Faith asked, shooting a look of concern toward Gideon. Her look mirrored the fear in his heart. If the sheriff had already come and gone, their best chance for escape had ridden away with him.

"If he had concerns, he didn't voice them." Abeline kept on fussing with the ropes until her handiwork unraveled. "He didn't even come in. Gave me everything on the front porch and went on his way." She turned and snatched up her gun again. "Doesn't seem like much of a lawman. I heard he was a distractible sort. Couldn't keep his mind off the goings-on in town, I reckon—not to notice someone like me."

Someone like her. The truth in her words nauseated Gideon. A person could manage a whole host of evil with an innocent front like Abeline Baxter's.

Abeline seized one of Faith's arms. "Come along."

Despite Abeline's pull on her, Faith stayed rooted to the floor. "Where are we going?"

"Out there." Her glistening white head indicated the ladder. "I have a wagon all hitched up."

Faith frowned uneasily. "A wagon?" Her gaze darted between Abeline and Gideon. "Why do we need a wagon?"

"Because I need to get into town and I can't ride like I once did." Abeline tugged on her arm. "Come along, dear. Let's get this over and done."

"I'm not going anywhere until you tell me what's going on." Faith's chin jutted up defiantly. "You owe me that much after what you've done, Abeline. You know you do."

With a weary sigh, Abeline brushed the wayward strands of white hair out of her eyes, leaving behind a dirty smear on her face. "All that's left of my world is in that jail cell in Gold Strike. I can't watch him vanish from my life forever, and I only have one card left to play."

Icy realization trickled from Gideon's head down his shoulders and spine. "You're going to hold her hostage to get him back."

Her sad, wrinkled gaze met his. "I don't have a choice. They'll take my son away if I don't, especially after they find out what happened to Sylvia Hammond."

Gideon's teeth clenched together. "So you're willing to put Faith's life at risk so that you and your son don't have to face the consequences of your poor choices?"

"Calm yourself." She tossed him a look of pure exhaustion. "I won't hurt her. The whole town knows her. They care about her well-being, especially Ellis McCraw. They'll take one look at her and let us go, I promise."

Hot air blew out his nostrils. "And if they don't?"

"If they don't, I'll find a way to keep her safe."

"Not at the expense of your son, you won't."

Abeline's eyes hardened, but she said nothing, only curled her wrinkled fingers more tightly around Faith's arm.

"What about him?" Faith swiped a stray tear from her cheek. "He's injured. He can't stay down here forever."

"You can come back here and free him when I leave this place with my son. Once we're far enough away, you may do whatever you like."

Faith dug in her heels. "That's not good enough. Gideon needs a proper place to rest. He could freeze down here."

"And you will not use her as a pawn in your games," he said, his muscles straining against the ropes tethering his wrists together.

With a firm grip on her rifle, Abeline yanked Faith hard enough to make her stumble forward. "This is not an ideal situation for me either, believe me—but we are going to see this through." She took in a tremulous breath. *"I am going to see this through, even if it kills me."* The normally buoyant light in her eye had converted to fire—a mother's instinct to protect her child. Gideon understood in that moment she would do anything to free her son, no matter how corrupt. The kindly old woman had been usurped by someone far more feral.

"Don't go with her, Faith." *Wrestle the gun out of her hands. Take control.* His body ached to spring up, fight back this time rather than sit by idly while she trampled everything he loved underfoot.

Deliberation battled in Faith's eyes as Abeline led her to the ladder. She turned back, her gaze latching with his, unsure.

Gideon glanced at the gun. *Do it. Take it.*

Her eyes widened, landing on the weapon in question before swinging back to him. Surely she knew she could overpower the woman if she just tried. She shook her head, the barely perceptible wag sinking through Gideon like a stone plummeting through water. She still believed in the woman's goodness. She still had hope. Facing the ladder, she gripped it on either side and took a step up.

"No, Faith!"

But she ignored him, her determination stronger than her doubt. After everything she'd gone through, she still believed in people. Gideon swallowed back his raging panic. Her trust could undo her, and still he loved her for it.

He gritted his teeth, straining to climb to his knees, but by the time he reached the floor, the pair had already disappeared up the ladder. Chest heaving, he could do nothing but watch helplessly as the woman he loved marched into the unknown, ready to battle a world far too corrupt for her pure heart.

Faith kept her head high and her shoulders back as she tromped through the wind-swept night. Abeline's hand, still fixed to her arm, had slackened, barely hanging on as their feet carried them toward the once-charming farmhouse. She had no need to coerce or threaten Faith. She came willingly, summoning every ounce of courage she possessed.

Gideon had been reared on disappointment, scarred by wounds so deep they would forever mar his belief in humanity. But Faith could still hang on to hope. She could still believe that Abeline was capable of more than her basest instincts, that if she only obeyed, she and Gideon might both walk out of this horrible night together unharmed.

In her youth at her father's farm, Faith had raised horses—tended to their needs, trained them into mounts safe and dependable to ride. Many of them had come to her frightened, abused, wild. Faith had suffered injuries and many frustrations attempting to make the animals understand if they only listened, her instructions would keep them safe and teach them a better way.

Those years of work echoed through her now. She would not be a wild horse, bent on her own way, flailing and kicking at anything she could. She would approach this with a calm and sober mind.

"I hitched up the wagon yonder." Abeline pointed toward the wooden contraption sitting lonely near the corral.

Faith's heart dipped at the sight of Starlight still penned in. If Abeline had used her for the wagon, Faith might have found a way to unhitch her and break free. She glanced back at the cellar doors slapping against one another in the wind. That notion probably wouldn't have worked anyway, with Gideon stuck in the cellar and Abeline the one with the rifle.

She glanced at it as Abeline led her up to the wagon. Gideon had clearly wanted her to grab it from Abeline's hold, but every time she pictured herself lunging at the old woman and potentially hurting her, she couldn't force her limbs to move. Besides, if it went wrong, one of them could have been inadvertently shot.

"Climb on up," Abeline said, letting Faith's arm go. "I'd like to get this done before I lose my nerve."

Faith complied, lifting her skirt to find the wheel hub with her boot, and propelled herself upward. She landed with a soft thud on the seat, her eyes roaming to the horses' leads. Would one of these two cooperate with her if she needed to escape quickly?

A flurry of neighing and stomping hooked her attention, sweeping her gaze to the corral. Beyond the fence, Starlight voiced her displeasure, pounding her hooves on the hard soil and scattering potent dust in the air.

No, Starlight. Faith was sitting perfectly still, as calm as could be. How did this doll of a horse understand the imminent danger? She jerked her head through the air, her nostrils blowing out white puffs.

The wagon shook as Abeline climbed into the seat beside Faith. With a grunt of exertion, she set the rifle on her other side, propped against the seat, and took up the reins. Icy fear scampered over Faith as she searched the quivering trees and aromatic forest. In seconds they would be on their way, off this farm and on the trail to Gold Strike, where anything might happen. The idea of leaving

Gideon behind wrenched at her stomach until she could barely breathe.

"Abeline?" Her gentle question prompted the woman's eyes to hers. "I just want to tell you that I don't think ill of you—not really. I knew you before all this happened, and you've always been the kindest, most gracious woman to me."

She paused, her eyes scouring the ridges and furrows of Abeline's face, the lines her husband and son must have deepened. "I understand what you did, and I'm so sorry for what you've had to endure."

Abeline blinked, her eyes wide with emotion, before she ironed out her skirt with one hand. "I appreciate that, dear. I've felt alone for a very long time, especially when it was just me and Colton in that big house, and I thought it would last forever."

Faith reached for her hand, soaking up its warmth despite its rigid form. "You deserved better than that. When did you know that Colton wasn't the person you thought you'd married?" Her shoulders lifted. "I'm nowhere near that monumental step, but I'd like to know, to be aware of what to look for. People say I'm too trusting."

A sad smile slipped up Abeline's mouth. "That's not always a negative thing. We need people in this world with open hearts—to keep us honest, if nothing else."

She sighed, her gaze roving the farmhouse, where light still streamed from the windows. "The truth is, I knew not long after I married him that he wouldn't uphold our sacred vows. He was running around with that woman from the bank. He didn't think I knew, but I always did. The way she looked at him, it—" She shook her head. "It rankled me. I almost left him, but I found out about Adam, and I knew we couldn't survive on our own."

Her nostrils flared, the weight of remembering sagging her shoulders. "So I kept up the charade for years, pretending I couldn't see what was right under my nose, acting like the perfect doting wife while I watched our marriage crumble around us." She squeezed Faith's fingers reassuringly. "I hope for much better for you once this ordeal is all over. I hope you can do better than I did—in all aspects of your life. Make something more of the time you have. Every moment is precious."

The smallest of hopes lifted inside Faith. If Abeline understood she would work with her, why keep up this reckless trajectory that could get them both killed? She angled closer, her fingers gripping the old woman's. "I hope to do just that. If you'll allow me to help you, we can figure this out together. You don't have to walk this road alone."

The compassion fell from Abeline's eyes, replaced with something colder, harder—a burdened sorrow that invited no company. Her hand released Faith as she lifted the reins and sat forward. "I can't do that, Faith. Adam is all that matters now. I *must* go to him. There is nothing left for me of this life." Her wrinkled chin jutted out in practiced determination as she reached for the brake.

No recourse remained but to go along and hope for the best—or attempt to overtake the old woman as Gideon wanted her to. Faith's gaze coasted over the rifle as Abeline prepared to command the horses forward. If she lunged for it, she could risk pushing Abeline out of the wagon and onto the ground. The thought twisted her middle.

Abeline clicked her tongue, flicking the reins over the horses. "Drive on."

The wagon trundled to life, bumping across the moonlit ground. Faith gripped the side in whitened knuckles. She could jump out before they got too far, run into the woods. Yet what might happen to Gideon if she attempted a feat so careless? Better to stay grounded and think of a superior plan.

The road stretched before them—a quiet path nesting between the blustering trees, untouched beneath the soft white strands of moonlight. Faith blinked when a shadowed figure stumbled across it, form crooked and arms outstretched. The horses whinnied in response, stomping ferociously but halting their forward motion.

Heart pumping, Faith leaned forward and squinted through the muddled light. Long, dark hair hung around thin shoulders, matted and barely concealing a pair of glimmering, almost crazed eyes. A tattered dress hung off the weak frame of a woman.

She breathed unsteadily, her wide eyes fixing on Abeline as she stumbled toward the wagon. "You've kept me in bondage these many months. I did not break free to watch you carry this innocent girl off and ruin her life too."

The aged hands gripping the reins trembled, but a fire lit in Abeline's eyes. As the women stared each other down amid the tempestuous winds, Faith steeled herself for a showdown like she'd never faced before.

Twenty Nine

Time stood still as the crazed-looking woman in the tattered dress marched forward, her finger spearing the chilly night air. "Abeline Baxter," her voice rasped, "you come down from that wagon before I pull you out with my bare hands."

Faith took a tremulous breath, her hand bunching her skirts. She squinted through the scant moonlight at the approaching figure. "Is—is that—"

"Sylvia Hammond." Abeline's voice sounded deeper, lacking its usual joviality.

Blinking, Faith turned her gaze to the old woman, who still clutched the reins in her wrinkled hands. "*That's* Sylvia Hammond? You really kept her here all this time? You—" No, it couldn't be true. The kind woman she knew would never enslave and neglect someone.

But cold resolution had overshadowed Abeline's face as she stared down her nose at the woman. "I did what I had to. She was too observant from that little shop of hers. She understood the relationship between Adam and I when no one else put the pieces together. She was going to take that information to the authorities, to implicate my son in his father's murder. I couldn't let that happen."

A gust of wind blew back Faith's hair, dousing her in a dreadful cold. "Then you lied to me. You told me you had no part in the plot to kill your husband—that you only watched it unfold."

Abeline stared for a prolonged moment at her skirts as they beat against her legs. When her eyes finally lifted to Faith, all pretenses of the kindly old widow had fled. "Had you been married to a monster like that, you would have killed him too, one way or another."

"Abeline!" Sylvia's voice screeched again, ripping through the tense air. "I'm giving you one last warning. Climb down—*now*."

Jerking to life, Abeline reached for the rifle nested beside her.

Sharp panic shot through Faith as she bolted up in her seat. "Abeline, no. You can't."

Ignoring her, Abeline hoisted the rifle butt on her shoulder and peered with one eye through the sights. Before Faith could stop her, the blast of a gunshot volleyed across the night. Quick as a flash, Sylvia ducked beneath the horses, narrowly missing the bullet that whizzed through the air.

Abeline stood, cocking the gun again and training it on the ground between the horses.

Jetting to her feet, Faith reached for her. "Abeline, no! You can't do this! I won't let you!" Her fingers clamped around Abeline's frail shoulders just as a second shot boomed.

Yanking her backward, Faith sputtered on the acrid gunpowder clouding the air. Her ears rang. Her heart hammered. Abeline grunted and twisted within her hold, struggling as Sylvia's form materialized from between the animals and began clattering up the front of the wagon. She had murder in her eyes, pure vengeance. How could she not after the torture she must have endured?

Abeline struggled to position her gun, but Faith held firm. Sylvia was upon them now, her eyes wild and fingers reaching like the sinister branches of a dead tree. With astonishing force, Abeline threw back her elbow, its pointed tip ramming into Faith's skull. She yelped as pain exploded through her head and her body tumbled backward.

Faith's vision blurred, a dizzying display of white light as her body fell back and back until it collided with solid earth. Blackness overtook her consciousness. The world spun. She tried to push off the cold ground but failed, her awareness fading in and out until she felt as if settling into the bottom of a deep pit far from the world around her.

The vague murmur of voices edged her mind, barely touching its deepest recesses. Faith moaned through her pain, focusing on the sound. The clamor rose louder, more distinctive. Faith's eyes fluttered open, peering through the haze, blinking back the fog.

Several feet away, the horses stomped and whinnied. Beyond that, a tangled mass rolled back and forth, two bodies locked in combat on the ground, desperate to gain an advantage. With a wince, Faith propped herself on her elbows and tried to steady her swaying vision. Pain swelled down her arm and across her shoulders. She pushed up until her hands were splayed over the dewy grass, holding her body up.

Moonlight revealed the two struggling women—Abeline in her old age, and Sylvia, weak from captivity. They fought with all the tenacity they could muster, yet neither appeared to possess the strength to overcome the other. Faith watched in horror as Sylvia finally won out, pinning Abeline to the ground and clamping a hand over her throat.

Every instinct inside Faith came screaming to life. Despite her pain, she shoved off the ground and crawled across the dewy grass. Her muscles stung, her head throbbing, her heartbeat rising in her ears as she reached for Abeline's gun, discarded by the horses' hooves.

The old woman's breath rose in noisy rasps now as Sylvia's hands pressed harder, draining the life out of her. Sylvia's eyes bulged, white in the moonlight, brimming with rage.

"Sylvia," Faith panted, her fingers coiling around the rifle barrel and drawing it to herself. "Sylvia, stop!" Stumbling to her feet, Faith lifted the rifle to her shoulder and cocked it, fixing it on the pair of struggling women. "Sylvia Hammond, climb off her now. I don't want to shoot you, but I will." Anything to put an end to this horrific show of unhampered violence.

Sylvia's head swung her way, her dark, unwashed hair slinging in the night. Her eyes narrowed on the gun pointed her way, her hands slackening on Abeline's throat. Then her laugh filled the air—deep, hollow, disturbingly inhuman. "You want to shoot me, honey? You might as well. There's not much of me left."

Faith shifted on her feet, her rifle steady in place. "I don't want to shoot you. You tried to rescue me. But I can't watch you kill an old woman." Her voice hitched. "I just can't."

A mournful glint entered Sylvia's eyes as they drifted back to Abeline, still lying at her mercy. "I'd like to hear your thoughts on the matter had this woman kept you underground for months, chained you, left you a bucket to relieve yourself in, fed you at her convenience."

Her bitter stare slid over Abeline. "I had months of my life stolen away—months in which I fantasized about nothing else than putting an end to her."

Faith's heart swelled. How dreadful a spot to sit in—so horrible, she doubted she could comprehend it. "What she did was unconscionable. I don't blame you for wanting her dead, but Sylvia, this isn't you. I know you. The kind woman at the dress shop would never have hurt anybody."

Sylvia clenched her teeth, her eyes briefly closing. "She had never seen what I have. She didn't know loss like I do." Her shoulders began to shake, the glitter of tears peppering her cheeks.

Faith blinked back her own tears. "Let that loss be your last. I beg you not to add to it this night. You have a family, sons who need you, a life to live beyond this wretched place."

The wind whipped through her hair as Sylvia hung her head. "A lifetime behind bars would be worth seeing this woman get what she deserves."

"Perhaps, but it would also carry the burden of her death. That will weigh on you for the rest of your days. I know it will."

A laden moment passed, heavy and solemn, where only the whine of the wind in the trees could compete with the rush of blood in Faith's ears. Sylvia stared into Abeline's eyes several agonizing moments before she released her and sat up, swiping the wetness from her face. "You're not worth another second of my time—not even a stray thought." Hardening her jaw, she rose from her knees, her tattered form a ghastly silhouette before the luminescent sky.

Wordlessly, Faith shifted the rifle toward Abeline. "Get up."

She pressed her lips together but made no argument, rolling to her side and pushing up with a grunt of effort. The process took longer for her, bones fragile and joints weak. She reached for the wagon wheel to steady herself and pull her haggard frame to standing.

Faith could almost breathe again when the slightest of movements caught her eye. Abeline had been using the wagon bed to pull herself up, but she paused in mid-motion, her hand to her lower back, seemingly overwhelmed by the strain. Then, rather than straighten all the way, she bent in one swift movement and reached beneath the wagon bed.

Faith stiffened, her finger hooking the trigger, her gun pivoting on Abeline. Yet already, that aged hand pointed her way, a pistol in its grip.

Abeline's eyes narrowed, her look purposeful. "Drop the gun, Faith. There's nothing left for you to do for me."

For her? Faith's hand slicked on the rifle. "What's to stop me from shooting you? I've already proven myself with my father. You know I will."

"Because there aren't any bullets in that gun. I expended them all."

A cold weight dropped in Faith's stomach as she uncocked her gun and checked the chamber. *Nothing.* Her eyes swung back to Abeline, who remained steady and calm despite everything that had just transpired. Had she unwittingly helped Abeline realize this maniacal plan of hers?

She looked from the gun aimed her way into Abeline's face, her body beginning to tremble. She had waited all that time for Faith to save her, just so she could turn the tables. Was there no end to her treachery?

Abeline glanced away from Faith's penetrating gaze. "I will do anything for my son. You know that. *Anything.*" Her hand flicked toward the wagon. "Now get back up there. I won't have any more of this foolishness."

Faith glanced at Sylvia. "What about her?"

"Forget about her. Climb up in the wagon."

Sweat emerged on Faith's brow, an eerie sensation crawling up her spine. *Forget about her.* As the world had these many months as she dwelt beneath the earth. Faith saw the true picture so clearly now. Abeline couldn't hope to fight against two significantly younger women. She would have to exterminate one of them.

Drawing in a breath of pine and earth, she stood taller. "I will not, nor will I ever do anything you say again, Abeline."

Abeline's irritated glance slid her way, her gun leveling with Faith. "Do it now, Faith. If it's a choice between you and my son, I will pick him every time, I promise you."

Despite her galloping heart and skin peppered in gooseflesh, Faith set her teeth and stared down the barrel of Abeline's pistol. "Do as you must, but from this moment, I stand with Sylvia Hammond. Just as she, I will not cower to your threats."

The gun cocked, Abeline's finger steadying on the trigger. Faith forced herself to stand, transfixed on the cold steel readying to end her life, knowing this final stand would be her last.

Gideon stared up at the closed cellar doors slapping in the violent wind. Moments ago, gunshots had blasted through the tranquil night, echoing down into this burrow beneath the earth. He'd expended every bit of strength he possessed just crawling to his feet.

Breath ragged, his focus narrowed on the outside. He waited, every second torturous, his hard breath clogging his lungs, until the sound of shouting carried on the breeze. "I can't do this." No, he couldn't stand by and watch as another person he loved met a gruesome fate. He *wouldn't* stand by and do nothing again.

Clenching his teeth, Gideon twisted his arms until he thought his wrists would bleed. The ropes binding him only cut into his skin, every rough fiber biting like steel. His fingers grappled with the knots holding him in place, but they could barely brush the frayed strands of rope.

He took another enormous breath, thick with must and dirt. There had to be a way out. *There had to be.* If he didn't make it to Faith in time, he might never see her again. The thought drenched his entire body in panic. Gideon squeezed his eyes closed, wrenching his wrists around until blood emerged. Sweat foamed from every pore, leaking into his eyes and salting his lips. This couldn't be the way this ended. It couldn't. He would do anything to protect her. He would die for her.

His eyes flew open, his gaze flitting about the room before landing on a shelf stacked with preserves. With a determined gait, Gideon marched across the cellar and lifted his arm just enough to sweep away the jars with his elbow. The room erupted in the smash of broken glass. He bent over the mess on the floor, inspecting the pieces. If he could extract a shard from among the slop, he could use it to cut through his ropes. But how, with his hands tethered behind his back?

Leaning back against the shelf, he tried to slow his breathing. How heavy the hand of defeat rested upon him as he imagined Faith at Abeline's mercy—a trusting innocent, betrayed by yet another one she loved. A guttural growl ripped up his body, born of a frustration so deep he could hardly stomach it. Turning his good shoulder against the shelf, he slammed into it, immediately regretting the action when pain shot up his body.

As he rested against the wood, it rattled beneath him. Gideon frowned, surveying the shelf at a closer angle. He'd nearly knocked one board completely off the wall. It hung by a single nail now, barely clinging with the last of its threads to the other.

Gideon's heart picked up speed. He rammed his shoulder into the shelf again, triumphant when it swung down with a loud squeal. The exposed nail remained—old and rusted, the first promising thing Gideon had seen all day.

Whirling around, he inched himself backward until his body lined up with the jagged nail protruding from the broken shelf. Climbing to his toes, he managed to lift his hands over the nail, up and down, back and forth, a continuous motion that made his arms ache and his back cry out in anguish. Biting his lip, he focused every bit of effort he could channel into working the rope across that nail until one fiber broke, and then another—until enough fell away to free himself.

Letting the last of the ropes fall to the ground, Gideon lifted quaking, bloody hands before his eyes. Trails of crimson ran from his wrists down his palms. His skin had nearly purpled to black where the ropes had rubbed against it, but he was free—free to find *her.*

The sounds above had faded, replaced by the rush of wind. Gideon stomped toward the ladder, the only way out of this prison cell. The first step up nearly buckled him, intense pain surging through his body. His shoulder blared when he reached for the ladder and gripped hard. Gideon bore every step with teeth gritted, fighting against his agony. The inescapable truth prodded him forward. He loved her too much to allow this cruel world to take her.

The ferocious wind aided him as he thrust back one of the cellar doors. It slammed to the ground, thrown back with unearthly force. Gideon held tight to the mouth of the cellar, his knuckles white, summoning his last bit of strength to pull himself into the open air. He breathed heavily, seated in the dirt, his legs dangling into the hollow space below.

Everywhere he looked, trees danced, leaves flying and spindly branches whipping in the wind. Bracing himself against the ground, he rose with a roar of exertion. The wind nearly toppled him, knocking him off balance and causing him to stumble.

When Gideon regained his footing, he frantically searched the yard. The house appeared peaceful as ever, yellow lamplight glowing in the windows and the scent of Abeline's pansies wafting his way. A mingling of voices caught his attention, directing it to a huddle of moving shadows not far from the barn. Gideon set off toward it, straining to see better, his pulse thumping wildly. Whatever he saw in the shadows of that barn, he knew one thing—they did not want to face *him*.

Details emerged one at a time—the silhouette of horses hooked to a wagon, barely visible beneath the soft glow of moonlight. Then a woman, if one could call her that. A skeletal form with wild, matted hair stood near the pair of horses. The final sight stabbed him square in the gut. Faith stood tall, her chin lifted, her face defiant, staring down the barrel of a pistol aimed between her eyes.

His limbs went cold, his fingers like ice. His stomach lurched at the sight of her, so brave and determined, facing death without batting an eyelash. Abeline's finger hooked the trigger, preparing to fire. *No. No!* He would die before he let that happen.

"Rah!" Without thought, he barreled toward her, the animal living within him springing to life.

Abeline's eyes rounded. She allowed him only a second to gain ground before her pistol pointed his way, unleashing a bullet that narrowly whizzed past his ear.

"No!" Faith's sweet voice wrenched his gut. "Abeline, no! Stop!" She lunged toward the old woman, but Abeline released a bullet and then another, shooting mercilessly at Gideon's approaching form.

He ducked and swerved, managing to evade yet another shot. His feet carried him powerfully forward, refusing to bow to her intimidation. He would take a hundred more bullets if it meant saving Faith's life. He couldn't live in a world where she wasn't—not anymore.

Gunpowder clouded his vision, funneling down his throat and stinging his eyes. Somehow amid the barrage of shooting, Faith and the woman beside her descended on Abeline, attempting to wrestle her to the ground. Gideon hollered, barreling toward her like a runaway steam engine. He thought of nothing—*nothing* but putting an end to the evil threatening to bring harm on the woman he loved. A pair of horrified eyes met his approach as her pistol flew into the air.

Abeline crossed her arms in front of her face and grimaced. "Stop it! Stop it, I surrender." She stumbled back, panting from exertion. "There is nothing left of me anyway." The sad wilt of her body told a story far more elaborate than her words.

Gideon bent to retrieve her pistol from the ground. "There *should* be nothing left after what you did to Faith."

She glared in return. "If I'd had anything more reliable than a pistol on hand, I'd have hit you."

"Perhaps, but you didn't." He returned the disgusted look she gave him.

"Gideon!" Faith jumped up, rushing to him.

The feel of her arms wound tightly around him had never before brought so much peace, so much reassurance that no matter what happened from this day, she still lived and breathed. They could survive anything that came their way. He held her until her shivers subsided and she melted against him, until they stood as one inseparable being, bound together by love.

She pulled back, her worried gaze wandering to his shoulder. "How are you still on your feet? We have to get you rest, a visit from a real doctor."

Gideon's head shook swiftly. "I don't even feel it. I don't." He cupped her smooth cheeks, swimming in the depths of her soft brown eyes.

Her mouth dimpled, a bit of humor easing her concern. "That's because you're in shock, my love."

His thumb brushed over the cleft in her chin, his enamored stare drinking in every inch of her. "Shock or no, I'm so in love with you, Faith Carter—and that will never change." His lips captured hers, the fervent promise of a man brought to the brink of death and saved by a force so much bigger than he could comprehend. As he held her close, he knew he would never let her go again.

Thirty

"Just like that. Good. Now balance it like so." Faith hoisted her tray on her hip and demonstrated how to carry glasses as she walked.

"That doesn't seem so difficult." Allison copied her movements, strutting across the little kitchen in a few easy strides before losing her balance and dropping her practice cups across the floor. "Good thing they're made of wood." Sinking to her knees, she set to reassembling her tray.

A good-natured laugh bubbled up Faith's throat. "Well, don't worry. It took me a while to perfect it. Just keep practicing. You're sure to be my star waitress in no time."

Allison shot her a thoroughly sardonic look from the floor. "We'll just see about that. Perhaps I'll hop on the train out of here and find a place where my skills are truly appreciated."

Faith sighed. "Do as you feel you must, but know you will always have a place here." Allison didn't realize it yet, but a lifetime of waiting tables would surpass prostitution in every way. She would soon know the joy of an honest day's work, and after experiencing it for herself, Faith doubted she would ever go back.

As Allison returned to her frustrated attempts at serving, Faith pushed through the kitchen door and into the saloon of the Wild Rose. She smiled to herself. Every table gleamed, the floors mopped clean of the blood and gunpowder dragged in from the gruesome fight in the street. The shattered glass was gone, clean goblets and tumblers lined up behind a freshly lacquered bar. The room smelled of lemons and lye soap after days of scrubbing it out with Cora. They had replaced the broken piano strings, repainted the walls. It looked nothing like it had only months ago, yet still retained the nostalgic charm of the place Old Joe had lovingly fostered through so many years of turmoil in Gold Strike.

Old Joe. Her heart squeezed to remember him plunking down the stairs at noon after drinking all night with his clientele, faithfully guarding his establishment with the watchful eyes of a loving father. She would never forget his kindness to her when the rest of the town turned its back, nor the path forward he'd given her, even in death.

Her eyes misted as they landed on his cherished rifle, now proudly displayed on the wall. "Thank you." The words barely escaped her, thick with emotion. If only he hadn't met such a tragic end at the point of Anderson's rifle. The rest of the Anderson Gang had scattered after the gunfight in town, and, true to his word, Red Fox had retreated elsewhere to live a quiet life with Sylvia and their son. Gold Strike had finally found the peace it had so long craved.

Faith sighed, reliving it all. How desperately she wished she could have seen evil for what it was long before it threatened the lives of those she loved most. She had never seen Abeline coming. Now her son rotted along with Faith's father in a prison cell, found guilty of burglary, kidnapping, and attempted murder. The court had looked on Abeline with clemency in her old age, but her deeds had ostracized her from Gold Strike forever. Faith didn't wish to imagine where she would spend the rest of her life, regretting the day she had begun to weave a tapestry of deception so elaborate, she'd trapped herself with it.

The broad form behind the bar caught her gaze. Gideon stood along the back wall, hammering a freshly developed photograph in a wooden frame into an exposed beam. The muscles in his back shifted as he hammered in the last of his nails and stood back to admire his work. Her heart still picked up speed every time she looked at him.

Time had healed his injured shoulder, though a scar remained where Adam Graves's bullet had pierced his flesh. At the time, the act had felt devastating. Now it was merely a memory, a bump in an otherwise perfect road that had led them to each other.

He swiveled sideways, catching her staring with a sly grin. "May I help you, ma'am? Perhaps pour you a drink?" His fingers splayed before the assortment of liquor bottles lined up beside the glasses.

"Now, Mr. Valdez, I've told you I don't drink." Faith sidled up to the bar and leaned her elbows on the glossy wood.

Gideon studied her with the playful look in his dark eyes she'd come to adore. "My mistake. You have to forgive me. I don't often meet proprietors of saloons who don't imbibe themselves."

Her brow lifted. "Well, you've met one now. This is about business, not about enjoying myself."

Gideon propped his palms against the bar on either side of her, leaning close enough to dot her skin in glorious flecks of warmth. "It is a *little* fun, isn't it?" His fathomless gaze settled into hers. "Buying the saloon with me, finding out what we can make of ourselves."

Her face scrunched in playful thought. "Perhaps a little. I do get to enjoy watching the barkeep go about his day. I must admit he has struck my fancy."

His mouth lifted in an impossibly handsome, lopsided grin. "Is that so?"

Faith shrugged. "Perhaps. I mean, he's one of many. There are so many options in this place."

Her casual joke sparked mischief in his eyes. Before Faith could scamper away, he'd already passed through the bar gate and caught her around the waist. Faith giggled as he pinned her against him, mercilessly tickling her sides.

When she finally managed a breath, she leaned against his sturdy frame. "All right, fine. You're the only man who strikes my fancy." Her eyes found his, growing solemn. "You're the only man who ever could."

"Yes, well"—Gideon lifted the fingers she'd rested on his solid chest—"I think I secured that spot in your life when I put this ring on your finger, Mrs. Valdez."

Her heart leapt to remember that day, when she'd let go of the painful bonds tying her to a dishonest father and chose to trust Gideon enough to give him her heart. "Indeed you did, Mr. Valdez."

With a contented sigh, she glanced around the room—at their freshly hung wedding photo, at the empty tables and repainted walls, the new light fixtures dangling from the ceiling. They had only been able to secure this place with the remainder of Gideon's savings and a hefty loan from a very appreciative bank. She might never see a dime of her father's money, and somehow that fact didn't lose her a moment's sleep. The life they could build here together outshone the one of her past in every conceivable way.

Her fingers gripped his soft cotton shirt as the scent of his musky cologne tickled her nose. "What about you?"

He pushed back a wisp of her hair. "Hmm?"

Faith dared to meet his gaze. "You gave up so much for me—the life you'd built over the years, the skills you'd acquired. I can't help wondering if you'll regret stashing away your cards, giving up poker to run this place with me."

He stared at her a quiet moment, his gaze lingering on her every feature before he held her tighter against him. "I was merely running, Faith—running with no direction and no end in sight. I was running without a purpose, except to forget the unbearable pain of my past."

His warm hand swept her cheekbone to her jaw and anchored there. "When I found you, there was nowhere left to run. Every ambition I'd ever held flew off on the wind the moment I saw you."

Gideon's fingertips wove with her loose strands of blonde hair, twisting around its ends. "Poker was a means of escape, forgetting what I'd lost, but now"—his head shook slightly, his adoring gaze taking her in—"now I have everything. Besides"—he glanced out at the scattered tables— "when I get the itch to play, I'm in the perfect place."

Faith smiled against his hand. "We really did it, didn't we? Let go of the past. We found a future together." When she stopped to think about it, the idea took her breath away.

"Yes, my dear, we did." Gideon settled his forehead on hers, closing his eyes in unshakable joy. "We have the world before us and we'll never look back."

Faith wound her arms around her husband's waist and tucked her head against his chest, secure in the knowledge that she was finally safe—to love and to dream as she always should have.

Thanks

Thank you all for completing another series with me. With all the excitement, danger, and romance of the Old West, this one has been so much fun to write. I will miss my time in Gold Strike, but I look forward to the adventures to come!

Special thanks to ARC readers and book bloggers for your wonderful reviews, friends and family for your support, and anyone who has brought encouragement to my writing journey. I continue to write because I love it, and sharing these stories with you keeps me motivated.

I am so excited for the next chapter. Please stay tuned!

Books by Laurie Sanford

The Memory Chase

The Guardians' Plot
The Moon King's Bounty
Traitor Isle
To Capture a Unicorn

The Gold Strike Chronicles

The Fox and the Nightingale
The Cat and the Crow
The Eagle and the Fawn

Stand-Alones

The Glass Dancer

For exclusive scenes you can't get anywhere else, head to
www.lauriesanfordbooks.com.

About the Author

Laurie Sanford is a writer of historical romance, adventure, and fantasy. Her novels take readers on vivid journeys through the past, sweeping landscapes of imaginary kingdoms, and rips in time. Every story promises excitement, sweet romance, and happy endings.

Laurie attended Pacific Union College in Napa Valley, where she earned her Bachelor's Degree. She studied to become a teacher, but wound up as a dispatcher, a job she loves and finds fulfillment doing. Laurie is happily married with three children who have given her more joy than she could have ever imagined.

When she's not at work or wrangling little ones, Laurie enjoys writing (her first love that now comes fifth in line), reading or watching anything historical, traveling (33 states and 7 countries so far), exploring nature, cooking, playing guitar, and studying genealogy. Having a family is the greatest blessing she has ever been bestowed, and everything she has she owes to Jesus Christ.